The Soul of Lilith

The Soul of Lilith
Marie Corelli

MINT EDITIONS

The Soul of Lilith was first published in 1892.

ISBN 9781513290485 | E-ISBN 9781513293332

Published by Mint Editions®

 MINT
EDITIONS

minteditionbooks.com

Publishing Director: Jennifer Newens
Design & Production: Rachel Lopez Metzger
Project Manager: Micaela Clark
Typesetting: Westchester Publishing Services

Contents

THE SOUL OF LILITH, VOLUME 3

Introductory Note

The following story does not assume to be what is generally understood by a "novel." It is simply the account of a strange and daring experiment once actually attempted, and is offered to those who are interested in the unseen "possibilities" of the Hereafter, merely for what it is,—a single episode in the life of a man who voluntarily sacrificed his whole worldly career in a supreme effort to prove the apparently Unprovable.

THE SOUL OF LILITH
VOLUME 1

I

THE theatre was full,—crowded from floor to ceiling; the lights were turned low to give the stage full prominence,—and a large audience packed close in pit and gallery as well as in balcony and stalls, listened with or without interest, whichever way best suited their different temperaments and manner of breeding, to the well-worn famous soliloquy in "Hamlet"—"To be or not to be." It was the first night of a new rendering of Shakespeare's ever puzzling play,—the chief actor was a great actor, albeit not admitted as such by the petty cliques,—he had thought out the strange and complex character of the psychological Dane for himself, with the result that even the listless, languid, generally impassive occupants of the stalls, many of whom had no doubt heard a hundred Hamlets, were roused for once out of their chronic state of boredom into something like attention, as the familiar lines fell on their ears with a slow and meditative richness of accent not commonly heard on the modern stage. This new Hamlet chose his attitudes well,—instead of walking or rather strutting about as he uttered the soliloquy, he seated himself and for a moment seemed lost in silent thought;—then, without changing his position he began, his voice gathering deeper earnestness as the beauty and solemnity of the immortal lines became more pronounced and concentrated.

> *"To die—to sleep;—*
> *To sleep!—perchance to dream; ay, there's the rub.*
> *For in that sleep of death what dreams may come*
> *When we have shuffled off this mortal coil*
> *Must give us pause. . ."*

Here there was a brief and impressive silence. In that short interval, and before the actor could resume his speech, a man entered the theatre with noiseless step and seated himself in a vacant stall of the second row. A few heads were instinctively turned to look at him, but in the semi-gloom of the auditorium, his features could scarcely be discerned, and Hamlet's sad rich voice again compelled attention.

> *"Who would fardels bear.*
> *To grunt and sweat under a weary life.*

> *But that the dread of something after death.*
> *The undiscovered country from whose bourne*
> *No traveller returns, puzzles the will*
> *And makes us rather bear those ills we have*
> *Than fly to others that we know not of?*
> *Thus conscience does make cowards of us all;*
> *And thus the native hue of resolution*
> *Is sicklied o'er with the pale cast of thought;*
> *And enterprises of great pith and moment.*
> *With this regard, their currents turn awry*
> *And lose the name of action."*

The scene went on to the despairing interview with Ophelia, which was throughout performed with such splendid force and feeling as to awaken a perfect hurricane of applause;—then the curtain went down, the lights went up, the orchestra recommenced, and again inquisitive eyes were turned towards the latest new-comer in the stalls who had made his quiet entrance in the very midst of the great philosophical Soliloquy. He was immediately discovered to be a person well worth observing; and observed he was accordingly, though he seemed quite unaware of the attention he was attracting. Yet he was singular-looking enough to excite a little curiosity even among modern fashionable Londoners, who are accustomed to see all sorts of eccentric beings, both male and female, æsthetic and common-place, and he was so distinctively separated from ordinary folk by his features and bearing, that the rather loud whisper of an irrepressible young American woman—"I'd give worlds to know who that man is!" was almost pardonable under the circumstances. His skin was dark as a mulatto's,—yet smooth, and healthily coloured by the warm blood flushing through the olive tint,—his eyes seemed black, but could scarcely be seen on account of the extreme length and thickness of their dark lashes,—the fine, rather scornful curve of his short upper lip was partially hidden by a black moustache; and with all this blackness and darkness about his face, his hair, of which he seemed to have an extraordinary profusion, was perfectly white. Not merely a silvery white, but a white as pronounced as that of a bit of washed fleece or newly-fallen snow. In looking at him it was impossible to decide whether he was old or young,—because, though he carried no wrinkles or other defacing marks of Time's power to destroy, his features wore an impress of such stern and deeply resolved thought as is seldom or never the heritage of those to whom youth still belongs. Nevertheless, he seemed a long way off from being old,—so that, altogether, he was a puzzle to his neighbours in the stalls, as well as to certain fair women in the boxes, who levelled their opera-glasses at him with a pertinacity which might have made him uncomfortably self-conscious had he looked up. Only he did not look up; he leaned back in his seat with a slightly listless air, studied his programme intently, and appeared half asleep, owing to the way in which his eyelids drooped, and the drowsy sweep of his lashes. The irrepressible American girl almost forgot "Hamlet," so absorbed was she in staring at him, in spite of the sotto-voce remonstrances of her decorous mother, who sat beside her,—and presently, as if aware of, or annoyed by, her scrutiny, he lifted his eyes, and looked full at her. With an instinctive movement she recoiled,—and her own eyes fell. Never in all her giddy, thoughtless little life had she seen such fiery, brilliant, night-black orbs,—they made her feel uncomfortable,—gave her the "creeps," as she afterwards declared;—she shivered, drawing her satin opera-wrap more closely about her, and stared at the stranger no more. He soon removed his piercing gaze from her to the stage, for now the great "Play scene" of "Hamlet" was in progress, and was from first to last a triumph for the actor chiefly concerned. At the next fall of the curtain, a fair, dissipated-looking young fellow leaned over from the third row of stalls, and touched the white-haired individual lightly on the shoulder.

"My dear El-Râmi! You here? At a theatre? Why, I should never have thought you capable of indulging in such frivolity!"

"Do you consider 'Hamlet' frivolous?" queried the other, rising from his seat to shake hands, and showing himself to be a man of medium height, though having such peculiar dignity of carriage as made him appear taller than he really was.

"Well, no!"—and the young man yawned rather effusively. "To tell you the truth, I find him insufferably dull."

"You do?" and the person addressed as El-Râmi smiled slightly. "Well,—naturally you go with the opinions of your age. You would no doubt prefer a burlesque?"

"Frankly speaking, I should! And now I begin to think of it, I don't know really why I came here. I had intended to look in at the Empire—there's a new ballet going on there—but a fellow at the club gave me this stall, said it was a 'first-night,' and all the rest of it—and so—"

"And so Fate decided for you," finished El-Râmi sedately. "And instead of admiring the pretty ladies without proper clothing at the Empire, you find yourself here, wondering why the deuce Hamlet the Dane could not find anything better to do than bother himself about his father's ghost! Exactly! But, being here, you are here for a purpose, my friend;" and he lowered his voice to a confidential whisper. "Look!—Over there—observe her well!—sits your future wife;"—and he indicated, by the slightest possible nod, the American girl before alluded to. "Yes,—the pretty creature in pink, with dark hair. You don't know her? No, of course you don't—but you will. She will be introduced to you tonight before you leave this theatre. Don't look so startled— there's nothing miraculous about her, I assure you! She is merely Miss Chester, only daughter of Jabez Chester, the latest New York millionaire. A charmingly shallow, delightfully useless, but enormously wealthy little person!—you will propose to her within a month, and you will be accepted. A very good match for you, Vaughan—all your debts paid, and everything set straight with certain Jews. Nothing could be better, really—and, remember,—I am the first to congratulate you!"

He spoke rapidly, with a smiling, easy air of conviction; his friend meanwhile stared at him in profound amazement and something of fear.

"By Jove, El-Râmi!"—he began nervously—"you know, this is a little too much of a good thing. It's all very well to play prophet sometimes, but it can be overdone."

"Pardon!" and El-Râmi turned to resume his seat. "The play begins again. Insufferably dull as 'Hamlet' may be, we are bound to give him some slight measure of attention."

Vaughan forced a careless smile in response, and threw himself indolently back in his own stall, but he looked annoyed and puzzled. His eyes wandered from the back of El-Râmi's white head to the half-seen profile of the American heiress who had just been so coolly and convincingly pointed out to him as his future wife.

"I don't know the girl from Adam,"—he thought irritably, "and I don't want to know her. In fact, I won't know her. And if I won't, why, I shan't know her. Will is everything, even according to El-Râmi. The fellow's always so confoundedly positive of his prophecies. I should like to confute him for once and prove him wrong."

Thus he mused, scarcely heeding the progress of Shakespeare's great tragedy, till, at the close of the scene of Ophelia's burial, he saw El-Râmi rise and prepare to leave the auditorium. He at once rose himself.

"Are you going?" he asked.

"Yes;—I do not care for 'Hamlet's' end, or for anybody's end in this particular play. I don't like the hasty and wholesale slaughter that concludes the piece. It is inartistic."

"Shakespeare inartistic?" queried Vaughan, smiling.

"Why yes, sometimes. He was a man, not a god;—and no man's work can be absolutely perfect. Shakespeare had his faults like everybody else,—and with his great genius he would have been the first to own them. It is only your little mediocrities who are never wrong. Are you going also?"

"Yes; I mean to damage your reputation as a prophet, and avoid the chance of an introduction to Miss Chester—for this evening, at any rate."

He laughed as he spoke, but El-Râmi said nothing. The two passed out of the stalls together into the lobby, where they had to wait a few minutes to get their hats and overcoats, the man in charge of the cloakroom having gone to cool his chronic thirst at the convenient "bar." Vaughan made use of the enforced delay to light his cigar.

"Did you think it a good 'Hamlet'?" he asked his companion carelessly while thus occupied.

"Excellent," replied El-Râmi. "The leading actor has immense talent, and thoroughly appreciates the subtlety of the part he has to play;—but his supporters are all sticks,—hence the scenes drag where he himself is not in them. That is the worst of the 'star' system,—a system which is perfectly ruinous to histrionic art. Still—no matter how it is performed, 'Hamlet' is always interesting. Curiously inconsistent, too, but impressive."

"Inconsistent? how?" asked Vaughan, beginning to puff rings of smoke into the air, and to wonder impatiently how much longer the keeper of the cloak-room meant to stay absent from his post.

"Oh, in many ways. Perhaps the most glaring inconsistency of the whole conception comes out in the great soliloquy, 'To be or not to be.'"

"Really?" and Vaughan became interested.—"I thought that was considered one of the finest bits in the play."

"So it is. I am not speaking of the lines themselves, which are magnificent, but of their connection with 'Hamlet's' own character. Why does he talk of a 'bourne from whence no traveller returns,' when he has, or thinks he has, proof positive of the return of his own father in spiritual form;—and it is just concerning that return that he makes all the pother? Don't you see inconsistency there?"

"Of course,—but I never thought of it," said Vaughan, staring. "I don't believe anyone but yourself has ever thought of it. It is quite unaccountable. He certainly does say 'no traveller returns,'—and he says it after he has seen the ghost too."

"Yes," went on El-Râmi, warming with his subject. "And he talks of the 'dread of something after death,' as if it were only a 'dread,' and not a Fact;—whereas if he is to believe the spirit of his own father, which he declares is 'an honest ghost,' there is no possibility of doubt on the matter. Does not the mournful phantom say—"

> *"But that I am forbid*
> *To tell the secrets of my prison-house*
> *I could a tale unfold, whose lightest word*
> *Would harrow up thy soul; freeze thy young blood;*
> *Make thy two eyes like stars start from their spheres;*
> *Thy knotted and combinèd locks to part.*
> *And each particular hair to stand on end. . . ?"*

"By Jove! I say, El-Râmi; don't look at me like that!" exclaimed Vaughan uneasily, backing away from a too close proximity to the brilliant flashing eyes and absorbed face of his companion, who had recited the lines with extraordinary passion and solemnity.

El-Râmi laughed.

"Did I scare you? Was I too much in earnest? I beg your pardon! True enough,—'this eternal blazon must not be, to ears of flesh and blood!' But, the 'something after death' was a peculiarly aggravating reality to that poor ghost, and Hamlet knew that it was so when he spoke of it as a mere 'dread.' Thus, as I say, he was inconsistent, or, rather, Shakespeare did not argue the case logically."

"You would make a capital actor,"—said Vaughan, still gazing at him in astonishment. "Why, you went on just now as if,—well, as if you meant it, you know."

"So I did mean it," replied El-Râmi lightly—"for the moment! I always find 'Hamlet' a rather absorbing study; so will you, perhaps, when you are my age."

"Your age?" and Vaughan shrugged his shoulders. "I wish I knew it! Why, nobody knows it. You may be thirty or a hundred—who can tell?"

"Or two hundred—or even three hundred?" queried El-Râmi, with a touch of satire in his tone;—"why stint the measure of limitless time? But here comes our recalcitrant knave"—this, as the keeper of the cloakroom made his appearance from a side-door with a perfectly easy and unembarrassed air, as though he had done rather a fine thing than otherwise in keeping two gentlemen waiting his pleasure. "Let us get our coats, and be well away before the decree of Fate can be accomplished in making you the winner of the desirable Chester prize. It is delightful to conquer Fate—if one can!"

His black eyes flashed curiously, and Vaughan paused in the act of throwing on his overcoat to look at him again in something of doubt and dread.

At that moment a gay voice exclaimed:

"Why, here's Vaughan!—Freddie Vaughan—how lucky!" and a big handsome man of about two or three and thirty sauntered into the lobby from the theatre, followed by two ladies. "Look here, Vaughan, you're just the fellow I wanted to see. We've left Hamlet in the thick of his fight, because we're going on to the Somers's ball,—will you come with us? And I say, Vaughan, allow me to introduce to you my friends— Mrs. Jabez Chester, Miss Idina Chester—Sir Frederick Vaughan."

For one instant Vaughan stood inert and stupefied; the next he remembered himself, and bowed mechanically. His presentation to the Chesters was thus suddenly effected by his cousin, Lord Melthorpe, to whom he was indebted for many favours, and whom he could not afford to offend by any show of brusquerie. As soon as the necessary salutations were exchanged, however, he looked round vaguely, and in a sort of superstitious terror, for the man who had so surely prophesied this introduction. But El-Râmi was gone. Silently and without adieu he had departed, having seen his word fulfilled.

II

"Who is the gentleman that just left you?" asked Miss Chester, smiling prettily up into Vaughan's eyes, as she accepted his proffered arm to lead her to her carriage,—"Such a distinguished-looking dreadful person!"

Vaughan smiled at this description.

"He is certainly rather singular in personal appearance," he began, when his cousin, Lord Melthorpe, interrupted him.

"You mean El-Râmi? It was El-Râmi, wasn't it? Ah, I thought so. Why did he give us the slip, I wonder? I wish he had waited a minute—he is a most interesting fellow."

"But who is he?" persisted Miss Chester. She was now comfortably ensconced in her luxurious brougham, her mother beside her, and two men of "title" opposite to her—a position which exactly suited the aspirations of her soul. "How very tiresome you both are! You don't explain him a bit; you only say he is 'interesting,' and of course one can see that; people with such white hair and such black eyes are always interesting, don't you think so?"

"Well, I don't see why they should be," said Lord Melthorpe dubiously. "Now, just think what horrible chaps Albinos are, and they have white hair and pink eyes—"

"Oh, don't drift off on the subject of Albinos, please!" pleaded Miss Chester, with a soft laugh. "If you do, I shall never know anything about this particular person—El-Râmi, did you say? Isn't it a very odd name? Eastern, of course?"

"Oh yes! he is a pure Oriental thoroughbred," replied Lord Melthorpe, who took the burden of the conversation upon himself, while he inwardly wondered why his cousin Vaughan was in such an evidently taciturn mood. "That is, I mean, he is an Oriental of the very old stock, not one of the modern Indian mixtures of vice and knavery. But when he came from the East, and why he came from the East, I don't suppose anyone could tell you. I have only met him two or three times in society, and on those occasions he managed to perplex and fascinate a good many people. My wife, for instance, thinks him quite a marvellous man; she always asks him to her parties, but he hardly ever comes. His name in full is El-Râmi-Zarânos, though I believe he is best known as El-Râmi simply."

"And what is he?" asked Miss Chester. "An artist?—a literary celebrity?"

"Neither, that I am aware of. Indeed, I don't know what he is, or how he lives. I have always looked upon him as a sort of magician—a kind of private conjurer, you know."

"Dear me!" said fat Mrs. Chester, waking up from a semi-doze, and trying to get interested in the subject. "Does he do drawing-room tricks?"

"Oh no, he doesn't do tricks;" and Lord Melthorpe looked a little amused. "He isn't that sort of man at all; I'm afraid I explain myself badly. I mean that he can tell you extraordinary things about your past and future—"

"Oh, by your hand—I know!" and the pretty Idina nodded her head sagaciously. "There really is something awfully clever in palmistry. I can tell fortunes that way!"

"Can you?" Lord Melthorpe smiled indulgently, and went on,—"But it so happens that El-Râmi does not tell anything by the hand,—he judges by the face, figure, and movement. He doesn't make a profession of it; but, really, he does foretell events in rather a curious way now and then."

"He certainly does!" agreed Vaughan, rousing himself from a reverie into which he had fallen, and fixing his eyes on the small piquante features of the girl opposite him. "Some of his prophecies are quite remarkable."

"Really! How very delightful!" said Miss Chester, who was fully aware of Sir Frederick's intent, almost searching, gaze, but pretended to be absorbed in buttoning one of her gloves. "I must ask him to tell me what sort of fate is in store for me—something awful, I'm positive! Don't you think he has horrid eyes?—splendid, but horrid? He looked at me in the theatre—"

"My dear, you looked at him first," murmured Mrs. Chester.

"Yes; but I'm sure I didn't make him shiver. Now, when he looked at me, I felt as if someone were pouring cold water very slowly down my back. It was such a creepy sensation! Do fasten this, mother—will you?" and she extended the hand with the refractory glove upon it to Mrs. Chester, but Vaughan promptly interposed:

"Allow me!"

"Oh, well! if you know how to fix a button that is almost off!" she said laughingly, with a blush that well became her transparent skin.

"I can make an attempt"—said Vaughan, with due humility. "If I succeed, will you give me one or two dances presently?"

"With pleasure!"

"Oh! you are coming in to the Somers's, then!" said Lord Melthorpe, in a pleased tone. "That's right. You know, Fred, you're so absent-minded tonight, that you never said 'Yes' or 'No' when I asked you to accompany us."

"Didn't I? I'm awfully sorry!" and, having fastened the glove with careful daintiness, he smiled. "Please set down my rudeness and distraction to the uncanny influence of El-Râmi; I can't imagine any other reason."

They all laughed carelessly, as people in an idle humour laugh at trifles, and the carriage bore them on to their destination—a great house in Queen's Gate, where a magnificent entertainment was being held in honour of some Serene and Exalted foreign potentate who had taken it into his head to see how London amused itself during a "season." The foreign potentate had heard that the splendid English capital was full of gloom and misery—that its women were unapproachable, and its men difficult to make friends with; and all these erroneous notions had to be dispersed in his serene and exalted brain, no matter what his education cost the "Upper Ten" who undertook to enlighten his barbarian ignorance.

Meanwhile, the subject of Lord Mel—thorpe's conversation—El-Râmi, or El-Râmi-Zarânos, as he was called by those of his own race—was walking quietly homewards with that firm, swift, yet apparently unhasting pace which so often distinguishes the desert-born savage, and so seldom gives grace to the deportment of the cultured citizen. It was a mild night in May; the weather was unusually fine and warm; the skies were undarkened by any mist or cloud, and the stars shone forth with as much brilliancy as though the city lying under their immediate ken had been the smiling fairy, Florence, instead of the brooding giant, London. Now and again El-Râmi raised his eyes to the sparkling belt of Orion, which glittered aloft with a lustre that is seldom seen in the hazy English air;—he was thinking his own thoughts, and the fact that there were many passers to and fro in the streets besides himself did not appear to disturb him in the least, for he strode through their ranks, without any hurry or jostling, as if he alone existed, and they were but shadows.

"What fools are the majority of men!" he mused. "How easy to gull them, and how willing they are to be gulled! How that silly young Vaughan marvelled at my prophecy of his marriage!—as if it were not as easy to foretell as that two and two inevitably make four! Given the characters of people in the same way that you give figures, and you are certain to arrive at a sum-total of them in time. How simple the process of calculation as to Vaughan's matrimonial prospects! Here are the set of numerals I employed: Two nights ago I heard Lord Melthorpe say he meant to marry his cousin Fred to Miss Chester, daughter of Jabez Chester, of New York,—Miss Chester herself entered the room a few minutes later on, and I saw the sort of young woman she was. Tonight at the theatre I see her again;—in an opposite box, well back in shadow, I perceive Lord Melthorpe. Young Vaughan, whose character I know to be of such weakness that it can be moulded whichever way a stronger will turns it, sits close behind me; and I proceed to make the little sum-total. Given Lord Melthorpe, with a determination that resembles the obstinacy of a pig rather than of a man; Frederick Vaughan, with no determination at all; and the little Chester girl, with her heart set on an English title, even though it only be that of a baronet, and the marriage is certain. What was un certain was the possibility of their all meeting tonight; but they were all there, and I counted that possibility as the fraction over,—there is always a fraction over in character-sums; it stands as Providence or Fate, and must always be allowed for. I chanced it,—and won. I always do win in these things,—these ridiculous trifles of calculation, which are actually accepted as prophetic utterances by people who never will think out anything for themselves. Good heavens! what a monster-burden of crass ignorance and wilful stupidity this poor planet has groaned under ever since it was hurled into space! Immense!— incalculable! And for what purpose? For what progress? For what end?"

He stopped a moment; he had walked from the Strand up through Piccadilly, and was now close to Hyde Park. Taking out his watch, he glanced at the time—it was close upon midnight. All at once he was struck fiercely from behind, and the watch he held was snatched from his hand by a man who had no sooner committed the theft than he uttered a loud cry, and remained inert and motionless. El-Râmi turned quietly round, and surveyed him.

"Well, my friend?" he inquired blandly—"What did you do that for?"

The fellow stared about him vaguely, but seemed unable to answer,— his arm was stiffly outstretched, and the watch was clutched fast within his palm.

"You had better give that little piece of property back to me," went on El-Râmi, coldly smiling,—and, stepping close up to his assailant, he undid the closed fingers one by one, and, removing the watch, restored it to his own pocket. The thief's arm at the same moment fell limply at his side; but he remained where he was, trembling violently as though seized with a sudden ague-fit.

"You would find it an inconvenient thing to have about you, I assure you. Stolen goods are always more or less of a bore, I believe. You seem rather discomposed? Ah! you have had a little shock,—that's all. You've heard of torpedos, I dare say? Well, in this scientific age of ours, there are human torpedos going about; and I am one of them. It is necessary to be careful whom you touch nowadays,—it really is, you know! You will be better presently—take time!"

He spoke banteringly, observing the thief meanwhile with the most curious air, as though he were some peculiar specimen of beetle or frog. The wretched man's features worked convulsively, and he made a gesture of appeal:

"Yer won't 'ave me took up!" he muttered hoarsely. "I'm starvin'!"

"No, no!" said El-Râmi persuasively—"you are nothing of the sort. Do not tell lies, my friend; that is a great mistake—as great a mistake as thieving. Both things, as you practise them, will put you to no end of trouble,—and to avoid trouble is the chief aim of modern life. You are not starving—you are as plump as a rabbit,"—and, with a dexterous touch, he threw up the man's loose shirt-sleeve, and displayed the full, firm flesh of the strong and sinewy arm beneath. "You have had more meat in you today than I can manage in a week; you will do very well. You are a professional thief,—a sort of—lawyer, shall we say? Only, instead of protesting the right you have to live, politely by means of documents and red-tape, you assert it roughly by stealing a watch. It's very frank conduct,—but it is not civil; and, in the present state of ethics, it doesn't pay—it really doesn't. I'm afraid I'm boring you! You feel better? Then—good-evening!"

He was about to resume his walk, when the now-recovered rough took a hasty step towards him.

"I wanted to knock yer down!" he began.

"I know you did,"—returned El-Râmi composedly. "Well—would you like to try again?"

The man stared at him, half in amazement, half in fear.

"Yer see," he went on, "yer pulled out yer watch, and it was all jools and sparkles—"

"And it was a glittering temptation"—finished El-Râmi. "I see. I had no business to pull it out; I grant it; but, being pulled out, you had no business to want it. We were both wrong; let us both endeavour to be wiser in future. Good-night!"

"Well, I'm blowed if ye're not a rum un, and an orful un!" exclaimed the man, who had certainly received a fright, and was still nervous from the effects of it. "Blowed if he ain't the rummest card!"

But the "rummest card" heard none of these observations. He crossed the road, and went on his way serenely, taking up the thread of his interrupted musings as though nothing had occurred.

"Fools—fools all!" he murmured. "Thieves steal, murderers slay, labourers toil, and all men and women lust and live and die—to what purpose? For what progress? For what end? Destruction or new life? Heaven or hell? Wisdom or caprice? Kindness or cruelty? God or the Devil? Which? If I knew that I should be wise,—but till I know, I am but a fool also,—a fool among fools, fooled by a Fate whose secret I mean to discover and conquer—and defy!"

He paused,—and, drawing a long, deep breath, raised his eyes to the stars once more. His lips moved as though he repeated inwardly some vow or prayer, then he proceeded at a quicker pace, and stopped no more till he reached his destination, which was a small, quiet and unfashionable square off Sloane Street. Here he made his way to an unpretentious-looking little house, semi-detached, and one of a row of similar buildings; the only particularly distinctive mark about it being a heavy and massively-carved ancient oaken door, which opened easily at the turn of his latch-key, and closed after him without the slightest sound as he entered.

III

A dim red light burned in the narrow hall, just sufficient to enable him to see the wooden peg on which he was accustomed to hang his hat and overcoat,—and as soon as he had divested himself of his outdoor garb, he extinguished even that faint glimmer of radiance. Opening a side-door, he entered his own room—a picturesque apartment running from east to west, the full length of the house. From its appearance it had evidently once served as drawing-room and dining-room, with folding-doors between; but the folding-doors had been dispensed with, and the place they had occupied was now draped with heavy amber silk. This silk seemed to be of some peculiar and costly make, for it sparkled with iridescent gleams of silver like diamond-dust when El-Râmi turned on the electric burner, which, in the form of a large flower, depended from the ceiling by quaintly-worked silver chains, and was connected by a fine wire with a shaded reading-lamp on the table. There was not much of either beauty or value in the room,—yet without being at all luxurious, it suggested luxury. The few chairs were of the most ordinary make, all save one, which was of finely carved ebony, and was piled with silk cushions of amber and red,—the table was of plain painted deal, covered with a dark woollen cloth worked in and out with threads of gold,—there were a few geometrical instruments about,—a large pair of globes,—a rack on the wall stocked with weapons for the art of fence,—and one large book-case full of books. An ebony-cased pianette occupied one corner,—and on a small side-table stood a heavily-made oaken chest, brass-bound and double-locked. The furniture was completed by a plain camp-bedstead such as soldiers use, which at the present moment was partly folded up and almost hidden from view by a rough bearskin thrown carelessly across it.

El-Râmi sat down in the big ebony chair and looked at a pile of letters lying on his writing-table. They were from all sorts of persons,—princes, statesmen, diplomats, financiers, and artists in all the professions,—he recognised the handwriting on some of the envelopes, and his brows contracted in a frown as he tossed them aside still unopened.

"They must wait," he said half aloud. "Curious that it is impossible for a man to be original without attracting around him a set of unoriginal minds, as though he were a honey-pot and they the flies!

Who would believe that I, poor in worldly goods, and living in more or less obscurity, should, without any wish of my own, be in touch with kings?—should know the last new policy of governments before it is made ripe for public declaration?—should hold the secrets of 'my lord' and 'my lady' apart from each other's cognisance, and be able to amuse myself with their little ridiculous matrimonial differences, as though they were puppets playing their parts for use at a marionette show! I do not ask these people to confide in me,—I do not want them to seek me out,—and yet the cry is, 'still they come!'—and the attributes of my own nature are such, that like a magnet, I attract, and so am never left in peace. Yet perhaps it is well it should be thus,—I need the external distraction,—otherwise my mind would be too much like a bent bow,—fixed on the one centre,—the Great Secret,—and its powers might fail me at the last. But no!—failure is impossible now. Steeled against love,—hate,—and all the merely earthly passions of mankind as I am,—I must succeed—and I will!"

He leaned his head on one hand, and seemed to suddenly concentrate his thoughts on one particular subject,—his eyes dilated and grew luridly brilliant as though sparks of fire burnt behind them. He had not sat thus for more than a couple of minutes, when the door opened gently, and a beautiful youth clad in a loose white tunic and vest of Eastern fashion, made his appearance, and standing silently on the threshold seemed to wait for some command.

"So, Féraz! you heard my summons?" said El-Râmi gently.

"I heard my brother speak,"—responded Féraz in a low melodious voice that had a singularly dreamy far-away tone within it—"Through a wall of cloud and silence his beloved accents fell like music on my ears;—he called me and I came."

And sighing lightly, he folded his arms cross-wise on his breast and stood erect and immovable, looking like some fine statue just endowed by magic with the flush of life. He resembled El-Râmi in features, but was fairer-skinned,—his eyes were softer and more femininely lovely,—his hair, black as night, clustered in thick curls over his brow, and his figure, straight as a young palm-tree, was a perfect model of strength united with grace. But just now he had a strangely absorbed air,—his eyes, though they were intently fixed on El-Râmi's face, looked like the eyes of a sleep-walker, so dreamy were they while wide-open,—and as he spoke he smiled vaguely as one who hears delicious singing afar off.

El-Râmi studied him intently for a minute or two,—then, removing his gaze, pressed a small silver hand-bell at his side. It rang sharply out on the silence.

"Féraz!"

Féraz started,—rubbed his eyes,—glanced about him, and then sprang towards his brother with quite a new expression,—one of grace, eagerness and animation, that intensified his beauty and made him still more worthy the admiration of a painter or a sculptor.

"El-Râmi! at last! How late you are! I waited for you long— and then I slept. I am sorry! But you called me in the usual way, I suppose?—and I did not fail you? Ah no! I should come to you if I were dead!"

He dropped on one knee, and raised El-Râmi's hand caressingly to his lips.

"Where have you been all the evening?" he went on. "I have missed you greatly—the house is so silent."

El-Râmi touched his clustering curls tenderly.

"You could have made music in it with your lute and voice, Féraz, had you chosen," he said. "As for me, I went to see 'Hamlet.'"

"Oh, why did you go?" demanded Féraz impetuously. "I would not see it—no! not for worlds! Such poetry must needs be spoilt by men's mouthing of it,—it is better to read it, to think it, to feel it,—and so one actually sees it,—best."

"You talk like a poet,"—said El-Râmi indulgently. "You are not much more than a boy, and you think the thoughts of youth. Have you any supper ready for me?"

Féraz smiled and sprang up, left the room, and returned in a few minutes with a daintily arranged tray of refreshments, which he set before his brother with all the respect and humility of a well-trained domestic in attendance on his master.

"You have supped?" El-Râmi asked, as he poured out wine from the delicately shaped Italian flask beside him.

Féraz nodded.

"Yes. Zaroba supped with me. But she was cross tonight—she had nothing to say."

El-Râmi smiled. "That is unusual!"

Féraz went on. "There have been many people here,—they all wanted to see you. They have left their cards. Some of them asked me my name and who I was. I said I was your servant—but they would not believe me.

There were great folks among them—they came in big carriages with prancing horses. Have you seen their names?"

"Not I."

"Ah, you are so indifferent," said Féraz gaily,—he had now quite lost his dreamy and abstracted look, and talked on in an eager boyish way that suited his years,—he was barely twenty. "You are so bent on great thoughts that you cannot see little things. But these dukes and earls who come to visit you do not consider themselves little,—not they!"

"Yet many of them are the least among little men," said El-Râmi with a touch of scorn in his mellow accents. "Dowered with great historic names which they almost despise, they do their best to drag the memory of their ancient lineage into dishonour by vulgar passions, low tastes, and a scorn as well as lack of true intelligence. Let us not talk of them. The English aristocracy was once a magnificent tree, but its broad boughs are fallen,—lopped off and turned into saleable timber,—and there is but a decaying stump of it left. And so Zaroba said nothing to you tonight?"

"Scarce a word. She was very sullen. She bade me tell you all was well,—that is her usual formula. I do not understand it;—what is it that should be well or ill? You never explain your mystery!"

He smiled, but there was a vivid curiosity in his fine eyes,—he looked as if he would have asked more had he dared to do so.

El-Râmi evaded his questioning glance. "Speak of yourself," he said. "Did you wander at all into your Dreamland today?"

"I was there when you called me," replied Féraz quickly. "I saw my home,—its trees and flowers,—I listened to the ripple of its fountains and streams. It is harvest-time there, do you know? I heard the reapers singing as they carried home the sheaves."

His brother surveyed him with a fixed and wondering scrutiny.

"How absolute you are in your faith!" he said half enviously. "You think it is your home,—but it is only an idea after all,—an idea, born of a vision."

"Does a mere visionary idea engender love and longing?" exclaimed Féraz impetuously. "Oh no, El-Râmi,—it cannot do so! I know the land I see so often in what you call a 'dream,'—its mountains are familiar to me,—its people are my people; yes!—I am remembered there, and so are you,—we dwelt there once,—we shall dwell there again. It is your home as well as mine,—that bright and far-off star where there is no death but only sleep,—why were we exiled from our happiness, El-Râmi? Can your wisdom tell?"

"I know nothing of what you say," returned El-Râmi brusquely. "As I told you, you talk like a poet,—harsher men than I, would add, like a madman. You imagine you were born or came into being in a different planet to this,—that you lived there,—that you were exiled from thence by some mysterious doom, and were condemned to pass into human existence here;—well, I repeat, Féraz—this is your own fancy,—the result of the strange double life you lead, which is not by my will or teaching. I believe only in what can be proved—and this that you tell me is beyond all proof."

"And yet," said Féraz meditatively,—"though I cannot reason it out, I am sure of what I feel. My 'dream' is more life-like than life itself,—and as for my beloved people yonder, I tell you I have heard them singing the harvest-home."

And with a quick soft step, he went to the piano, opened it and began to play. El-Râmi leaned back in his chair mute and absorbed,—did ever common keyed instrument give forth such enchanting sounds? Was ever written music known that could, when performed, utter such divine and dulcet eloquence? There was nothing earthly in the tune,—it seemed to glide from under the player's fingers like a caress upon the air,—and an involuntary sigh broke from El-Râmi's lips as he listened. Féraz heard that sigh, and turned round smiling.

"Is there not something familiar in the strain?" he asked. "Do you not see them all, so fair and light and lithe of limb, coming over the fields homewards as the red Ring burns low in the western sky? Surely—surely you remember?"

A slight shudder shook El-Râmi's frame,—he pressed his hands over his eyes, and seemed to collect himself by a strong effort,—then walking over to the piano, he took his young brother's hands from the keys and held them for a moment against his breast.

"Keep your illusions"—he said in a low voice that trembled slightly. "Keep them,—and your faith,—together. It is for you to dream, and for me to prove. Mine is the hardest lot. There may be truth in your dreams,—there may be deception in my proofs—Heaven only knows! Were you not of my own blood, and dearer to me than most human things, I should, like every scientist worthy of the name, strive to break off your spiritual pinions and make of you a mere earth-grub even as most of us are made,—but I cannot do it,—I have not the heart to do it,—and if I had the heart"—he paused a moment,—then went on slowly—"I have not the power. Good-night!"

He left the room abruptly without another word or look,—and the beautiful young Féraz gazed after his retreating figure doubtfully and with something of wondering regret. Was it worth while, he thought, to be so wise, if wisdom made one at times so sad?—was it well to sacrifice Faith for Fact, when Faith was so warm and Fact so cold? Was it better to be a dreamer of things possible, or a worker-out of things positive? And how much was positive after all? and how much possible? He balanced the question lightly with himself,—it was like a discord in the music of his mind, and disturbed his peace. He soon dismissed the jarring thought, however, and closing the piano, glanced round the room to make sure that nothing more was required for his brother's service or comfort that night, and then he went away to resume his interrupted slumbers,—perchance to take up the chorus of his "people" singing in what he deemed his native star.

IV

El-Râmi meanwhile slowly ascended the stairs to the first floor, and there on the narrow landing paused, listening. There was not a sound in the house,—the delicious music of the strange "harvest-song" had ceased, though to El-Râmi's ears there still seemed to be a throb of its melody in the air, like perfume left from the carrying by of flowers. And with this vague impression upon him he listened,—listened as it were to the deep silence; and as he stood in this attentive attitude, his eyes rested on a closed door opposite to him,—a door which might, if taken off its hinges and exhibited at some museum, have carried away the palm for perfection in panel-painting. It was so designed as to resemble a fine trellis-work, hung with pale clambering roses and purple passion-flowers,—on the upper half among the blossoms sat a meditative cupid, pressing a bud against his pouting lips, while below him, stretched in full-length desolation on a bent bough, his twin brother wept childishly over the piteous fate of a butterfly that lay dead in his curled pink palm. El-Râmi stared so long and persistently at the pretty picture that it might have been imagined he was looking at it for the first time and was absorbed in admiration, but truth to tell he scarcely saw it. His thoughts were penetrating beyond all painted semblances of beauty,—and,—as in the case of his young brother Féraz,—those thoughts were speedily answered. A key turned in the lock,—the door opened, and a tall old woman, bronze-skinned, black-eyed, withered, uncomely yet imposing of aspect, stood in the aperture.

"Enter, El-Râmi!" she said in a low yet harsh voice—"The hour is late,—but when did ever the lateness of hours change or deter your sovereign will! Yet truly as God liveth, it is hard that I should seldom be permitted to pass a night in peace!"

El-Râmi smiled indifferently, but made no reply, as it was useless to answer Zaroba. She was stone deaf, and therefore not in a condition to be argued with. She preceded him into a small ante-room, provided with no other furniture than a table and chair;—one entire side of the wall however was hung with a magnificent curtain of purple velvet bordered in gold. On the table were a slate and pencil, and these implements El-Râmi at once drew towards him.

"Has there been any change today?" he wrote.

Zaroba read the words.

"None," she replied.

"She has not moved?"

"Not a finger."

He paused, pencil in hand,—then he wrote—

"You are ill-tempered. You have your dark humour upon you."

Zaroba's eyes flashed, and she threw up her skinny hands with a wrathful gesture.

"Dark humour!" she cried in accents that were almost shrill—"Ay!—and if it be so, El-Râmi, what is my humour to you? Am I anything more to you than a cipher,—a mere slave? What have the thoughts of a foolish woman, bent with years and close to the dark gateways of the tomb, to do with one who deems himself all wisdom? What are the feelings of a wretched perishable piece of flesh and blood to a self-centred god and opponent of Nature like El-Râmi-Zarânos!" She laughed bitterly. "Pay no heed to me, great Master of the Fates invisible!—superb controller of the thoughts of men!—pay no heed to Zaroba's 'dark humours' as you call them. Zaroba has no wings to soar with—she is old and feeble, and aches at the heart with a burden of unshed tears,—she would fain have been content with this low earth whereon to tread in safety,—she would fain have been happy with common joys,—but these are debarred her, and her lot is like that of many a better woman,—to sit solitary among the ashes of dead days and know herself desolate!"

She dropped her arms as suddenly as she had raised them. El-Râmi surveyed her with a touch of derision, and wrote again on the slate.

"I thought you loved your charge?"

Zaroba read, and drew herself up proudly, looking almost as dignified as El-Râmi himself.

"Does one love a statue?" she demanded. "Shall I caress a picture? Shall I rain tears or kisses over the mere semblance of a life that does not live,—shall I fondle hands that never return my clasp? Love! Love is in my heart—yes! like a shut-up fire in a tomb,—but you hold the key, El-Râmi, and the flame dies for want of air."

He shrugged his shoulders, and putting the pencil aside, wrote no more. Moving towards the velvet curtain that draped the one side of the room he made an imperious sign. Zaroba, obeying the gesture mechanically and at once, drew a small pulley, by means of which the rich soft folds of stuff parted noiselessly asunder, displaying such a wonderful interior of luxury and loveliness as seemed for the moment almost unreal. The apartment opened to view was lofty and perfectly circular in shape, and was hung from top to bottom with silken hangings of royal purple embroidered all over with curious arabesque patterns in gold. The same rich material was caught up from the edges of the ceiling to the centre, like the drapery of a pavilion or tent, and was there festooned with golden fringes and tassels. From out the midst of this warm mass of glistening colour, swung a gold lamp which shed its light through amber-hued crystal,—while the floor below was carpeted with the thickest velvet pile, the design being pale purple pansies on a darker ground of the same almost neutral tint. A specimen of everything beautiful, rare and costly seemed to have found its way into this one room, from the exquisitely wrought ivory figure of a Psyche on her pedestal, to the tall vase of Venetian crystal which held lightly up to view, dozens of magnificent roses that seemed born of full midsummer, though as yet in the capricious English climate, it was scarcely spring. And all the beauty, all the grace, all the evidences of perfect taste, art, care and forethought, were gathered together round one centre,—one unseeing, unresponsive centre,—the figure of a sleeping girl. Pillowed on a raised couch such as might have served a queen for costliness, she lay fast bound in slumber,—a matchless piece of loveliness,—stirless as marble,—wondrous as the ideal of a poet's dream. Her delicate form was draped loosely in a robe of purest white, arranged so as to suggest rather than conceal its exquisite outline,—a silk coverlet was thrown lightly across her feet, and her head rested on cushions of the softest, snowiest satin. Her exceedingly small white hands were crossed upon her breast over a curious jewel,—a sort of giant ruby cut in the shape of a star, which scintillated with a thousand sparkles in the light, and coloured the under-tips of her fingers with a hue like wine, and her hair, which was of extraordinary length and beauty, almost clothed her body down to the knee, as with a mantle of shimmering gold. To say merely that she was lovely would scarcely describe her,—for the loveliness that is generally understood as such, was here so entirely surpassed and intensified that it would be difficult if not impossible to express its charm. Her face had the usual attributes of what might be deemed perfection,—that is, the lines were purely oval,—the features delicate, the skin most transparently fair, the lips a dewy red, and the fringes of the closed eyes were long, dark and delicately upcurled;—but this was not all. There was something else,—something quite undefinable, that gave a singular glow and radiance to the whole countenance, and suggested the burning of a light through alabaster,—a creeping of some subtle fire through the veins which made the fair body seem the mere reflection of some greater fairness within. If those eyes were to open, one thought, how wonderful their lustre must needs be!—if that perfect figure rose up and moved, what a harmony would walk the world in maiden shape!—and yet,—watching that hushed repose, that scarcely perceptible breathing, it seemed more than certain that she would never rise,—never tread earthly soil in common with earth's creatures,—never be more than what she seemed,—a human flower, gathered and set apart—for whom? For God's love? or Man's pleasure? Either, neither, or both?

El-Râmi entered the rich apartment followed by Zaroba, and stood by the couch for some minutes in silence. Whatever his thoughts were, his face gave no clue to them,—his features being as impassive as though cast in bronze. Zaroba watched him curiously, her wrinkled visage expressive of some strongly-suppressed passion. The sleeping girl stirred and smiled in her sleep,—a smile that brightened her countenance as much as if a sudden glory had circled it with a halo.

"Ay, she lives for you!" said Zaroba. "And she grows fairer every day. She is the sun, and you the snow. But the snow is bound to melt in due season,—and even you, El-Râmi-Zarânos, will hardly baffle the laws of Nature!"

El-Râmi turned upon her with a fierce mute gesture that had something of the terrible in it,—she shrank from the cold glance of his intense eyes, and in obedience to an imperative wave of his hand moved away to a further corner of the room, where, crouching down upon the floor, she took up a quaint implement of work, a carved triangular frame of ebony, with which she busied herself, drawing glittering threads in and out of it with marvellous speed and dexterity. She made a weird picture there, squatted on the ground in her yellow cotton draperies, her rough gray hair gleaming like spun silk in the light, and the shining threadwork in her withered hands. El-Râmi looked at her sitting thus, and was suddenly moved with compassion—she was old and sad,— poor Zaroba! He went up to her where she crouched, and stood above her, his ardent fiery eyes seeming to gather all their wonderful lustre into one long, earnest and pitiful regard. Her work fell from her hands, and as she met that burning gaze, a vague smile parted her lips,—her frowning features smoothed themselves into an expression of mingled placidity and peace.

"Desolate Zaroba!" said El-Râmi slowly lifting his hands. "Widowed and solitary soul! Deaf to the outer noises of the world, let the ears of thy spirit be open to my voice—and hear thou all the music of the past! Lo, the bygone years return to thee and picture themselves afresh upon thy tired brain!—again thou dost listen to the voices of thy children at play,—the wild Arabian desert spreads out before thee in the sun like a sea of gold,—the tall palms lift themselves against the burning sky—the tent is pitched by the cool spring of fresh water,—and thy savage mate, wearied out with long travel, sleeps, pillowed on thy breast. Thou art young again, Zaroba!—young, fair and beloved!—be happy so! Dream and rest!"

As he spoke he took the aged woman's unresisting hands and laid her gently, gently, by gradual degrees down in a recumbent posture, and placing a cushion under her head watched her for a few seconds.

"By Heaven!" he muttered, as he heard her regular breathing and noted the perfectly composed expression of her face. "Are dreams after all the only certain joys of life? A poet's fancies,—a painter's visions—the cloud-castles of a boy's imaginings—all dreams!—and only such dreamers can be called happy. Neither Fate nor Fortune can destroy their pleasure,—they make sport of kings and hold great nations as the merest toys of thought—oh sublime audacity of Vision! Would I could dream so!—or rather, would I could prove my dreams not dreams at all, but the reflections of the absolute Real! 'Hamlet' again!

"To die—to sleep—To sleep, perchance to dream—ay! there's the rub!"

Imagine it!—to die and dream of Heaven—or Hell,—and all the while if there should be no reality in either!"

With one more glance at the now soundly slumbering Zaroba, he went back to the couch, and gazed long and earnestly at the exquisite maiden there reclined,—then bending over her, he took her small fair left hand in his own, pressing his fingers hard round the delicate wrist.

"Lilith!—Lilith!" he said in low, yet commanding accents. "Lilith!—Speak to me! I am here!"

V

Deep silence followed his invocation,—a silence he seemed to expect and be prepared for. Looking at a silver timepiece on a bracket above the couch, he mentally counted slowly a hundred beats,—then pressing the fragile wrist he held still more firmly between his fingers, he touched with his other hand the girl's brow, just above her closed eyes. A faint quiver ran through the delicate body,—he quickly drew back and spoke again.

"Lilith! Where are you?"

The sweet lips parted, and a voice soft as whispered music responded—

"I am here!"

"Is all well with you?"

"All is well!"

And a smile irradiated the fair face with such a light as to suggest that the eyes must have opened,—but no!—they were fast shut.

El-Râmi resumed his strange interrogation.

"Lilith! What do you see?"

There was a moment's pause,—then came the slow response—

"Many things,—things beautiful and wonderful. But you are not among them. I hear your voice and I obey it, but I cannot see you—I have never seen you."

El-Râmi sighed, and pressed more closely the soft small hand within his own.

"Where have you been?"

"Where my pleasure led me"—came the answer in a sleepy yet joyous tone—"My pleasure and—your will."

El-Râmi started, but immediately controlled himself, for Lilith stirred and threw her other arm indolently behind her head, leaving the great ruby on her breast flashingly exposed to view.

"Away, away, far, far away!" she said, and her accents sounded like subdued singing—"Beyond,—in those regions whither I was sent—beyond—" her voice stopped and trailed off into drowsy murmurings—"beyond—Sirius—I saw—"

She ceased, and smiled—some happy thought seemed to have rendered her mute.

El-Râmi waited a moment, then took up her broken speech.

"Far beyond Sirius you saw—what?"

Moving, she pillowed her cheek upon her hand, and turned more fully round towards him.

"I saw a bright new world"—she said, now speaking quite clearly and connectedly—"A royal world of worlds; an undiscovered Star. There were giant oceans in it,—the noise of many waters was heard throughout the land,—and there were great cities marvellously built upon the sea. I saw their pinnacles of white and gold-spires of coral, and gates that were studded with pearl,—flags waved and music sounded, and two great Suns gave double light from heaven. I saw many thousands of people—they were beautiful and happy—they sang and danced and gave thanks in the everlasting sunshine, and knelt in crowds upon their wide and fruitful fields to thank the Giver of life immortal."

"Life immortal!" repeated El-Râmi,—"Do not these people die, even as we?"

A pained look, as of wonder or regret, knitted the girl's fair brows.

"There is no death—neither here nor there"—she said steadily—"I have told you this so often, yet you will not believe. Always you bid me seek for death,—I have looked, but cannot find it."

She sighed, and El-Râmi echoed the sigh.

"I wish"—and her accents sounded plaintively—"I wish that I could see you! There is some cloud between us. I hear your voice and I obey it, but I cannot see who it is that calls me."

El-Râmi paid no heed to these dove-like murmurings,—moreover, he seemed to have no eyes for the wondrous beauty of the creature who lay thus tranced and in his power,—set on his one object, the attainment of a supernatural knowledge, he looked as pitiless and impervious to all charm as any Grand Inquisitor of old Spain.

"Speak of yourself and not of me"—he said authoritatively,—"How can you say there is no death?"

"I speak truth. There is none."

"Not even here?"

"Not anywhere."

"O daughter of vision, where are the eyes of your spirit!" demanded El-Râmi angrily—"Search again and see! Why should all Nature arm itself against Death if there be no death?"

"You are harsh,"—said Lilith sorrowfully—"Should I tell you what is not true? If I would, I cannot. There is no death—there is only change. Beyond Sirius, they sleep."

El-Râmi waited; but she had paused again.

"Go on"—he said—"They sleep—why and when?"

"When they are weary"—responded Lilith. "When all is done that they can do, and when they need rest, they sleep, and in their sleep they change;—the change is—"

She ceased.

"The change is death,"—said El-Râmi positively,—"for death is everywhere."

"Not so!" replied Lilith quickly, and in a ringing tone of clarion-like sweetness. "The change is life,—for Life is everywhere!"

There ensued a silence. The girl turned away, and bringing her hand slowly down from behind her head, laid it again upon her breast over the burning ruby gem. El-Râmi bent above her closely.

"You are dreaming, Lilith,"—he said as though he would force her to own something against her will. "You speak unwisely and at random."

Still silence.

"Lilith!—Lilith!" he called.

No answer;—only the lovely tints of her complexion, the smile on her lips and the tranquil heaving of her rounded bosom indicated that she lived.

"Gone!" and El-Râmi's brow clouded; he laid back the little hand he held in its former position and looked at the girl long and steadily— "And so firm in her assertion!—as foolish an assertion as any of the fancies of Féraz. No death?—Nay—as well say no life. She has not fathomed the secret of our passing hence; no, not though her flight has outreached the realm of Sirius."

> "But that the dread of something after death.
> The undiscovered country from whose bourne
> No traveller returns, puzzles the will."

"Ay, puzzles the will and confounds it! But must I be baffled then?— or is it my own fault that I cannot believe? Is it truly her spirit that speaks to me?—or is it my own brain acting upon hers in a state of trance? If it be the latter, why should she declare things that I never dream of, and which my reason does not accept as possible? And if it is indeed her Soul, or the ethereal Essence of her that thus soars at periodic intervals of liberty into the Unseen, how is it that she never comprehends Death or Pain? Is her vision limited only to behold harmonious systems moving to a sound of joy?"

And seized by a sudden resolution, he caught both the hands of the tranced girl and held them in his own, the while he fixed his eyes upon her quiet face with a glance that seemed to shoot forth flame.

"Lilith! Lilith! By the force of my will and mastery over thy life, I bid thee return to me! O flitting spirit, ever bent on errands of pleasure, reveal to me the secrets of pain! Come back, Lilith! I call thee—come!"

A violent shudder shook the beautiful reposeful figure,—the smile faded from her lips, and she heaved a profound sigh.

"I am here!"

"Listen to my bidding!" said El-Râmi, in measured accents that sounded almost cruel. "As you have soared to heights ineffable, even so descend to lowest depths of desolation! Understand and seek out sorrow,—pierce to the root of suffering,-explain the cause of unavailing agony! These things exist. Here in this planet of which you know nothing save my voice,—here, if nowhere else in the wide Universe, we gain our bread with bitterness and drink our wine with tears. Solve me the mystery of Pain,—of Injustice,—of an innocent child's anguish on its death-bed,—ay! though you tell me there is no death!—of a good man's ruin,—of an evil woman's triumph,—of despair—of self-slaughter,—of all the horrors upon horrors piled, which make up this world's present life. Listen, O too ecstatic and believing Spirit!—we have a legend here that a God lives,—a wise all-loving God,—and He, this wise and loving one, has out of His great bounty invented for the torture of his creatures,—HELL! Find out this Hell, Lilith!—Prove it!—bring the plan of its existence back to me. Go,—bring me news of devils,—and suffer, if spirits can suffer, in the unmitigated sufferings of others! Take my command and go hence,—find out God's Hell!—so shall we afterwards know the worth of Heaven!"

He spoke rapidly,—impetuously,—passionately;—and now he allowed the girl's hands to fall suddenly from his clasp. She moaned a little,—and instead of folding them one over the other as before, raised them palm to palm in an attitude of prayer. The colour faded entirely from her face,—but an expression of the calmest, grandest wisdom, serenity and compassion came over her features as of a saint prepared for martyrdom. Her breathing grew fainter and fainter till it was scarcely perceptible,—and her lips parted in a short sobbing sigh,—then they moved and whispered something. El-Râmi stooped over her more closely.

"What is it?" he asked eagerly—"what did you say?"

"Nothing. . . only. . . farewell!" and the faint tone stirred the silence like the last sad echo of a song—"And yet. . . once more. . . farewell!"

He drew back, and observed her intently. She now looked like a recumbent statue, with those upraised hands of hers so white and small and delicate,—and El-Râmi remembered that he must keep the machine of the Body living, if he desired to receive through its medium the messages of the Spirit. Taking a small phial from his breast, together with the necessary surgeon's instrument used for such purposes, he pricked the rounded arm nearest to him, and carefully injected into the veins a small quantity of a strange sparkling fluid which gave out a curiously sweet and pungent odour;—as he did this, the lifted hands fell gently into their original position, crossed over the ruby star. The breathing grew steadier and lighter,—the lips took fresh colour,—and El-Râmi watched the effect with absorbed interest and attention.

"One might surely preserve her body so for ever," he mused half aloud. "The tissues renewed,—the blood re-organized,—the whole system completely nourished with absolute purity; and not a morsel of what is considered food, which contains so much organic mischief, allowed to enter that exquisitely beautiful mechanism, which exhales all waste upon the air through the pores of the skin as naturally as a flower exhales perfume through its leaves. A wonderful discovery!—if all men knew it, would not they deem themselves truly immortal, even here? But the trial is not over yet,—the experiment is not perfect. Six years has she lived thus, but who can say whether indeed Death has no power over her? In those six years she has changed,—she has grown from childhood to womanhood,—does not change imply age?—and age suggest death, in spite of all science? O inexorable Death!—I will pluck its secret out if I die in the effort!"

He turned away from the couch,—then seemed struck by a new idea.

"If I die, did I say? But can I die? Is her Spirit right? Is my reasoning wrong? Is there no pause anywhere?—no cessation of thought?—no end to the insatiability of ambition? Must we plan and work and live— For Ever?"

A shudder ran through him,—the notion of his own perpetuity appalled him. Passing a long mirror framed in antique silver, he caught sight of himself in it,—his dark handsome face, rendered darker by the contrasting whiteness of his hair,—his full black eyes,-his fine but disdainful mouth,—all looked back at him with the scornful reflex of his own scornful regard.

He laughed a little bitterly.

"There you are, El-Râmi Zarânos!" he murmured half aloud. "Scoffer and scientist,—master of a few common magnetic secrets such as the priests of ancient Egypt made sport of, though in these modern days of 'culture,' they are sufficient to make most men your tools! What now? Is there no rest for the inner calculations of your mind? Plan and work and live for ever? Well, why not? Could I fathom the secrets of a thousand universes, would that suffice me? No! I should seek for the solving of a thousand more!"

He gave a parting glance round the room,—at the fair tranced form on the couch, at the placid Zaroba slumbering in a corner, at the whole effect of the sumptuous apartment, with its purple and gold, its roses, its crystal and ivory adornments,—then he passed out, drawing to the velvet curtains noiselessly behind him. In the small anteroom, he took up the slate and wrote upon it—

> I shall not return hither for forty-eight hours. During this interval admit as much full daylight as possible. Observe the strictest silence, and do not touch her.
>
> El-Râmi

Having thus set down his instructions he descended the stairs to his own room, where, extinguishing the electric light, he threw himself on his hard camp-bedstead and was soon sound asleep.

VI

I do not believe in a future state. I am very much distressed about it."

The speaker was a stoutish, able-bodied individual in clerical dress, with rather a handsome face and an easy agreeable manner. He addressed himself to El-Râmi, who, seated at his writing-table, observed him with something of a satirical air.

"You wrote me this letter?" queried El-Râmi, selecting one from a heap beside him. The clergyman bent forward to look, and recognising his own handwriting, smiled a bland assent.

"You are the Rev. Francis Anstruther, Vicar of Laneck,—a great favourite with the Bishop of your diocese, I understand?"

The gentleman bowed blandly again,—then assumed a meek and chastened expression.

"That is, I was a favourite of the Bishop's at one time"—he murmured regretfully—"and I suppose I am now, only I fear that this matter of conscience—"

"Oh, it is a matter of conscience?" said El-Râmi slowly—"You are sure of that?"

"Quite sure of that!" and the Reverend Francis Anstruther sighed profoundly.

"'Thus conscience does make cowards of us all—'"

"I beg your pardon?" and the clergyman opened his eyes a little.

"Nay, I beg yours!—I was quoting 'Hamlet.'"

"Oh!"

There was a silence. El-Râmi bent his dark flashing eyes on his visitor, who seemed a little confused by the close scrutiny. It was the morning after the circumstances narrated in the previous chapter,— the clock marked ten minutes to noon,—the weather was brilliant and sunshiny, and the temperature warm for the uncertain English month of May. El-Râmi rose suddenly and threw open the window nearest him, as if he found the air oppressive.

"Why did you seek me out?" he demanded, turning towards the reverend gentleman once more.

"Well, it was really the merest accident—"

"It always is!" said El-Râmi with a slight dubious smile.

"I was at Lady Melthorpe's the other day, and I told her my difficulty. She spoke of you, and said she felt certain you would be able to clear up my doubts—"

"Not at all. I am too busy clearing up my own," said El-Râmi brusquely.

The clergyman looked surprised.

"Dear me!—I thought, from what her ladyship said, that you were scientifically certain of—"

"Of what?" interrupted El-Râmi—"Of myself? Nothing more uncertain in the world than my own humour, I assure you! Of others? I am not a student of human caprice. Of life?—of death? Neither. I am simply trying to prove the existence of a 'something after death'—but I am certain of nothing, and I believe in nothing, unless proved."

"But," said Mr. Anstruther anxiously—"you will, I hope, allow me to explain that you leave a very different impression on the minds of those to whom you speak, than the one you now suggest. Lady Melthorpe, for instance—"

"Lady Melthorpe believes what it pleases her to believe,"—said El-Râmi quietly—"All pretty, sensitive, imaginative women do. That accounts for the immense success of Roman Catholicism with women. It is a graceful, pleasing, comforting religion,—moreover it is really becoming to a woman,—she looks charming with a rosary in her hand, or a quaint old missal,—and she knows it. Lady Melthorpe is a believer in ideals,—well, there is no harm in ideals,—long may she be able to indulge in them."

"But Lady Melthorpe declares that you are able to tell the past and the future," persisted the clergyman—"And that you can also read the present;—if that is so, you must surely possess visionary power?"

El-Râmi looked at him stedfastly.

"I can tell you the past;"—he said—"And I can read your present;— and from the two portions of your life I can calculate the last addition, the Future,—but my calculation may be wrong. I mean wrong as regards coming events;—past and present I can never be mistaken in, because there exists a natural law, by which you are bound to reveal yourself to me."

The Reverend Francis Anstruther moved uneasily in his chair, but managed to convey into his countenance the proper expression of politely incredulous astonishment.

"This natural law," went on El-Râmi, laying one hand on the

celestial globe as he spoke, "has been in existence ever since man's formation, but we are only just now beginning to discover it, or rather re-discover it, since it was tolerably well-known to the priests of ancient Egypt. You see this sphere;"—and he moved the celestial globe round slowly—"It represents the pattern of the heavens according to our solar system. Now a Persian poet of old time, declared in at few wild verses, that solar systems taken in a mass, could be considered the brain of heaven, the stars being the thinking, moving molecules of that brain. A sweeping idea,—what your line-and-pattern critics would call 'far-fetched'—but it will serve me just now for an illustration of my meaning. Taking this 'brain of heaven' by way of simile then, it is evident we—we human pigmies,—are, notwithstanding our ridiculous littleness and inferiority, able to penetrate correctly enough into some of the mysteries of that star-teeming intelligence,—we can even take patterns of its shifting molecules"—and again he touched the globe beside him,—"we can watch its modes of thought—and calculate when certain planets will rise and set,—and when we cannot see its action, we can get its vibrations of light, to the marvellous extent of being able to photograph the moon of Neptune, which remains invisible to the eye even with the assistance of a telescope. You wonder what all this tends to?—well,—I speak of vibrations of light from the brain of heaven,— vibrations which we know are existent; and which we prove by means of photography; and because we see the results in black and white, we believe in them. But there are other vibrations in the Universe, which cannot be photographed,—the vibrations of the human brain, which like those emanating from the 'brain of heaven' are full of light and fire, and convey distinct impressions or patterns of thought. People speak of 'thought-transference' from one subject to another as if it were a remarkable coincidence,—whereas you cannot put a stop to the transference of thought,—it is in the very air, like the germs of disease or health,—and nothing can do away with it."

"I do not exactly understand"—murmured the clergyman with some bewilderment.

"Ah, you want a practical demonstration of what seems a merely abstract theory? Nothing easier!"—and moving again to the table he sat down, fixing his dark eyes keenly on his visitor—"As the stars pattern heaven in various shapes, like the constellation Lyra, or Orion, so you have patterned your brain with pictures or photographs of your past and your present. All your past, every scene of it, is impressed in the curious little brain-particles that lie in their various cells,—you have forgotten some incidents, but they would all come back to you if you were drowning or being hung;—because suffocation or strangulation would force up every infinitesimal atom of brain-matter into extraordinary prominence for the moment. Naturally your present existence is the most vivid picture with you, therefore perhaps you would like me to begin with that?"

"Begin?—how?" asked Mr. Anstruther, still in amazement.

"Why,—let me take the impression of your brain upon my own. It is quite simple, and quite scientific. Consider yourself the photographic negative, and me the sensitive paper to receive the impression! I may offer you a blurred picture, but I do not think it likely. Only if you wish to hide anything from me I would advise you not to try the experiment."

"Really, sir,—this is very extraordinary!—I am at a loss to comprehend—"

"Oh, I will make it quite plain to you—" said El-Râmi with a slight smile—"There is no witchcraft in it—no trickery,—nothing but the commonest A B C science. Will you try?—or would you prefer to leave the matter alone? My demonstration will not convince you of a 'future state,' which was the subject you first spoke to me about,—it will only prove to you the physiological phenomena surrounding your present constitution and condition."

The Reverend Francis Anstruther hesitated. He was a little startled by the cold and convincing manner with which El-Râmi spoke,—at the same time he did not believe in his words, and his own incredulity inclined him to see the "experiment," whatever it was. It would be all hocus-pocus, of course,—this Oriental fellow could know nothing about him,—he had never seen him before, and must therefore be totally ignorant of his private life and affairs. Considering this for a moment, he looked up and smiled.

"I shall be most interested and delighted,"—he said—"to make the trial you suggest. I am really curious. As for the present picture or photograph on my brain, I think it will only show you my perplexity as to my position with the Bishop in my wavering state of mind—"

"Or conscience—" suggested El-Râmi—"You said it was a matter of conscience."

"Quite so—quite so! And conscience is the most powerful motor of a man's actions Mr.—Mr. El-Râmi! It is indeed the voice of God!"

"That depends on what it says, and how we hear it—" said El-Râmi rather dryly—"Now if we are to make this 'demonstration,' will you put your left hand here, in my left hand? So,—your left palm must press closely upon my left palm,—yes—that will do. Observe the position, please;—you see that my left fingers rest on your left wrist, and are therefore directly touching the nerves and arteries running through your heart from your brain. By this, you are, to use my former simile, pressing me, the sensitive paper, to your photographic negative—and I make no doubt we shall get a fair impression. But to prevent any interruption to the brainwave rushing from you to me, we will add this little trifle," and he dexterously slipped a steel band over his hand and that of his visitor as they rested thus together on the table, and snapt it to,—"a sort of handcuff, as you perceive. It has nothing in the world to do with our experiment. It is simply placed there to prevent your moving your hand away from mine, which would be your natural impulse if I should happen to say anything disagreeably true. And to do so, would of course cut the ethereal thread of contact between us. Now, are you ready?"

The clergyman grew a shade paler. El-Râmi seemed so very sure of the result of this singular trial, that it was a little bit disagreeable. But having consented to the experiment, he felt he was compelled to go through with it, so he bowed a nervous assent. Whereupon El-Râmi closed his brilliant eyes, and sat for one or two minutes silent and immovable. A curious fidgetiness began to trouble the Reverend Francis Anstruther,—he tried to think of something ridiculous, something altogether apart from himself, but in vain,—his own personality, his own life, his own secret aims seemed all to weigh upon him like a sudden incubus. Presently tingling sensations pricked his arm as with burning needles,—the hand that was fettered to that of El-Râmi felt as hot as though it were being held to a fire. All at once El-Râmi spoke in a low tone, without opening his eyes—

"The shadow-impression of a woman. Brown-haired, dark-eyed,— of a full, luscious beauty, and a violent, unbridled, ill-balanced will. Mindless, but physically attractive. She dominates your thought."

A quiver ran through the clergyman's frame,—if he could only have snatched away his hand he would have done it then.

"She is not your wife—" went on El-Râmi—"she is the wife of your wealthiest neighbour. You have a wife,—an invalid,—you have also eight children,—but these are not prominent in the picture at present. The woman with the dark eyes and hair is the chief figure. Your plans are made for her—"

He paused, and again the wretched Mr. Anstruther shuddered.

"Wait—wait!" exclaimed El-Râmi suddenly in a tone of animation—"Now it comes clearly. You have decided to leave the Church, not because you do not believe in a future state,—for this you never have believed at any time—but because you wish to rid yourself of all moral and religious responsibility. Your scheme is perfectly distinct. You will make out a 'case of conscience' to your authorities, and resign your living,—you will then desert your wife and children,—you will leave your country in the company of the woman whose secret lover you are—"

"Stop!" cried the Reverend Mr. Anstruther, savagely endeavouring to wrench away his hand from the binding fetter which held it remorselessly to the hand of El-Râmi—"Stop! You are telling me a pack of lies!"

El-Râmi opened his great flashing orbs and surveyed him first in surprise, then with a deep unutterable contempt. Unclasping the steel band that bound their two hands together, he flung it by, and rose to his feet.

"Lies?" he echoed indignantly. "Your whole life is a lie, and both Nature and Science are bound to give the reflex of it. What! would you play a double part with the Eternal Forces and think to succeed in such desperate fooling? Do you imagine you can deceive supreme Omniscience, which holds every star and every infinitesimal atom of life in a network of such instant vibrating consciousness and contact, that in terrible truth there are and can be 'no secrets hid'? You may if you like act out the wretched comedy of feigning to deceive your God—the God of the Churches,—but beware of trifling with the real God,—the absolute Ego Sum of the Universe."

His voice rang out passionately upon the stillness,—the clergyman had also risen from his chair, and stood, nervously fumbling with his gloves, not venturing to raise his eyes.

"I have told you the truth of yourself,"—continued El-Râmi more quietly—"You know I have. Why then do you accuse me of telling you lies? Why did you seek me out at all if you wished to conceal yourself and your intentions from me? Can you deny the testimony of your own brain reflected on mine? Come, confess! be honest for once,—do you deny it?"

"I deny everything;"—replied the clergyman,—but his accents were husky and indistinct.

"So be it!"—and El-Râmi gave a short laugh of scorn. "Your 'case of conscience' is evidently very pressing! Go to your Bishop—and tell him you cannot believe in a future state,—I certainly cannot help you to prove that mystery. Besides, you would rather there were no future state,—a 'something after death' must needs be an unpleasant point of meditation for such as you. Oh yes!—you will get your freedom;—you will get all you are scheming for, and you will be quite a notorious person for awhile on account of the delicacy of your sense of honour and the rectitude of your principles. Exactly!—and then your final coup,—your running away with your neighbour's wife will make you notorious again—in quite another sort of fashion. Ah!—every man is bound to weave the threads of his own destiny, and you are weaving yours;—do not be surprised if you find you have made of them a net wherein to become hopelessly caught, tied and strangled. It is no doubt unpleasant for you to hear these things,—what a pity you came to me!"

The Reverend Francis Anstruther buttoned his glove carefully.

"Oh, I do not regret it," he said. "Any other man might perhaps feel himself insulted, but—"

"But you are too much of a 'Christian' to take offence—yes, I dare say!" interposed El-Râmi satirically,—"I thank you for your amiable forbearance! Allow me to close this interview"—and he was about to ring the bell, when his visitor said hastily and with an effort at appearing unconcerned—

"I suppose I may rely on your secrecy respecting what has passed?"

"Secrecy?" and El-Râmi raised his black eyebrows disdainfully— "What you call secrecy I know not. But if you mean that I shall speak of you and your affairs,—why, make yourself quite easy on that score. I shall not even think of you after you have left this room. Do not attach too much importance to yourself, reverend sir,—true, your name will soon be mentioned in the newspapers, but this should not excite you to an undue vanity. As for me, I have other things to occupy me, and clerical 'cases of conscience' such as yours, fail to attract either my wonder or admiration!" Here he touched the bell.—"Féraz!" this, as his young brother instantly appeared—"The door!"

The Reverend Francis Anstruther took up his hat, looked into it, glanced nervously round at the picturesque form of the silent Féraz, then with a sudden access of courage, looked at El-Râmi. That handsome Oriental's fiery eyes were fixed upon him,—the superb head, the dignified figure, the stately manner, all combined to make him feel uncomfortable and awkward; but he forced a faint smile—it was evident he must say something.

"You are a very remarkable man, Mr. . . El-Râmi"—he stammered. . . "It has been a most interesting. . . and. . . instructive morning!"

El-Râmi made no response other than a slight frigid bow.

The clergyman again peered into the depths of his hat.

"I will not go so far as to say you were correct in anything you said"— he went on—"but there was a little truth in some of your allusions,— they really applied, or might be made to apply to past events,—by-gone circumstances. . . you understand?"

El-Râmi took one step towards him.

"No more lies in Heaven's name!" he said in a stern whisper. "The air is poisoned enough for today. Go!"

Such a terrible earnestness marked his face and voice that the Reverend Francis retreated abruptly in alarm, and stumbling out of the room hastily, soon found himself in the open street with the great oaken door of El-Râmi's house shut upon him. He paused a moment, glanced at the sky, then at the pavement, shook his head, drew a long breath, and seemed on the verge of hesitation; then he looked at his watch,—smiled a bland smile, and hailing a cab, was driven to lunch at the Criterion, where a handsome woman with dark hair and eyes, met him with mingled flattery and upbraiding, and gave herself pouting and capricious airs of offence, because he had kept her ten minutes waiting.

VII

That afternoon El-Râmi prepared to go out as was his usual custom, immediately after the mid-day meal, which was served to him by Féraz, who stood behind his chair like a slave all the time he ate and drank, attending to his needs with the utmost devotion and assiduity. Féraz indeed was his brother's only domestic,—Zaroba's duties being entirely confined to the mysterious apartments upstairs and their still more mysterious occupant. El-Râmi was in a taciturn mood,—the visit of the Reverend Francis Anstruther seemed to have put him out, and he scarcely spoke, save in monosyllables. Before leaving the house, however, his humour suddenly softened, and noting the wistful and timorous gaze with which Féraz regarded him, he laughed outright.

"You are very patient with me, Féraz!" he said—"And I know I am as sullen as a bear."

"You think too much;"—replied Féraz gently—"And you work too hard."

"Both thought and labour are necessary," said El-Râmi—"You would not have me live a life of merely bovine repose?"

Féraz gave a deprecating gesture.

"Nay—but surely rest is needful. To be happy, God Himself must sometimes sleep."

"You think so?" and El-Râmi smiled—"Then it must be during His hours of repose and oblivion that the business of life goes wrong, and Darkness and the Spirit of Confusion walk abroad. The Creator should never sleep."

"Why not, if He has dreams?" asked Féraz—"For if Eternal Thought becomes Substance, so a God's Dream may become Life."

"Poetic as usual, my Féraz"—replied his brother—"and yet perhaps you are not so far wrong in your ideas. That Thought becomes substance, even with man's limited powers, is true enough;—the thought of a perfect, form grows up embodied in the weight and Substance of marble, with the sculptor,—the vague fancies of a poet, being set in ink on paper, become Substance in book-shape, solid enough to pass from one hand to the other;—even so may a God's mere Thought of a world create a Planet. It is my own impression that thoughts, like atoms, are imperishable, and that even dreams, being forms of thought, never die. But I must not stay here talking,—adieu! Do not sit up for me tonight—I shall not return,—I am going down to the coast."

"To Ilfracombe?" questioned Féraz—"So long a journey, and all to see that poor mad soul?"

El-Râmi looked at him stedfastly.

"No more 'mad,' Féraz, than you are with your notions about your native star! Why should a scientist who amuses himself with the reflections on a Disc of magnetic crystal be deemed 'mad'? Fifty years ago the electric inventions of Edison would have been called 'impossible,'—and he, the in—ventor, considered hopelessly insane. But now we know these seeming 'miracles' are facts, we cease to wonder at them. And my poor friend with his Disc is a harmless creature;—his 'craze,' if it be a craze, is as innocent as yours."

"But I have no craze"—said Féraz composedly,—"all that I know and see, lives in my brain like music,—and though I remember it perfectly, I trouble no one with the story of my past."

"And he troubles no one with what he deems may be the story of the future"—said El-Râmi—"Call no one 'mad' because he happens to have a new idea—for time may prove such 'madness' a merely perfected method of reason. I must hasten, or I shall lose my train."

"If it is the 2.40 from Waterloo, you have time," said Féraz—"It is not yet two o'clock. Do you leave any message for Zaroba?"

"None. She has my orders."

Féraz looked full at his brother, and a warm flush coloured his handsome face.

"Shall I never be worthy of your con—fidence?" he asked in a low voice—"Can you never trust me with your great secret, as well as Zaroba?"

El-Râmi frowned darkly.

"Again, this vulgar vice of curiosity? I thought you were exempt from it by this time."

"Nay, but hear me, El-Râmi"—said Féraz eagerly, distressed at the anger in his brother's eyes—"It is not curiosity,—it is something else,—something that I can hardly explain, except. . . Oh, you will only laugh at me if I tell you. . . but yet—"

"But what?" demanded El-Râmi sternly.

"It is as if a voice called me,"—answered Féraz dreamily—"a voice from those upper chambers, which you keep closed, and of which only Zaroba has the care—a voice that asks for freedom and for peace. It is such a sorrowful voice,—but sweet,—more sweet than any singing. True, I hear it but seldom,—only when I do, it haunts me for hours and hours. I know you are at some great work up there,—but can you make such voices ring from a merely scientific laboratory? Now you are angered!"

His large soft brilliant eyes rested appealingly upon his brother, whose features had grown pale and rigid.

"Angered!" he echoed, speaking as it seemed with some effort,—"Am I ever angered at your—your fancies? For fancies they are, Féraz,—the voice you hear is like the imagined home in that distant star you speak of,—an image and an echo on your brain—no more. My 'great work,' as you call it, would have no interest for you;—it is nothing but a test-experiment, which, if it fails, then I fail with it, and am no more El-Râmi-Zarânos, but the merest fool that ever clamoured for the moon." He said this more to himself than to his brother, and seemed for the moment to have forgotten where he was,—till suddenly rousing himself with a start, he forced a smile.

"Farewell for the present, gentle visionary!" he said kindly,—"You are happier with your dreams than I with my facts,—do not seek out sorrow for yourself by rash and idle questioning."

With a parting nod he went out, and Féraz, closing the door after him, remained in the hall for a few moments in a sort of vague reverie. How silent the house seemed, he thought with a half-sigh. The very atmosphere of it was depressing, and even his favourite occupation, music, had just now no attraction for him. He turned listlessly into his brother's study,—he determined to read for an hour or so, and looked about in search of some entertaining volume. On the table he found a book open,—a manuscript, written on vellum in Arabic, with curious uncanny figures and allegorical designs on the headings and margins. El-Râmi had left it there by mistake,—it was a particularly valuable treasure which he generally kept under lock and key. Féraz sat down in front of it, and resting his head on his two hands, began to read at the page where it lay open. Arabic was his native tongue,—yet he had some difficulty in making out this especial specimen of the language, because the writing was anything but distinct, and some of the letters had a very odd way of vanishing before his eyes, just as he had fixed them on at word. This was puzzling as well as irritating,—he must have something the matter with his sight or his brain, he concluded, as these vanishing letters always came into position again after a little. Worried by the phenomenon, he seized the book and carried it to the full light of the open window, and there succeeded in making out the meaning of one passage which was quite sufficient to set him thinking. It ran as follows:

*"Wherefore, touching illusions and impressions, as also strong emotions of love, hatred, jealousy or revenge, these nerve and brain sensations are easily conveyed from one human subject to another by Suggestion. The first process is to numb the optic nerve. This is done in two ways—I. By causing the subject to fix his eyes steadily on a round shining case containing a magnet, while you shall count two hundred beats of time. II. By wilfully making your own eyes the magnet, and fixing your subject thereto. Either of these operations will temporarily paralyze the optic nerves, and arrest the motion of the blood in the vessels pertaining. Thus the brain becomes insensible to external impressions, and is only awake to internal suggestions, which you may make as many and as devious as you please. Your subject will see exactly what you choose him to see, hear what you wish him to hear, do what you bid him do, so long as you hold him by your power, which if you understand the laws of light, sound, and air-vibrations, you may be able to retain for an indefinite period. The same force applies to the magnetising of a multitude as of a single individual."

Féraz read this over and over again,—then returning to the table, laid the book upon it with a deeply engrossed air. It had given him unpleasant matter for reflection.

"A dreamer—a visionary, he calls me—" he mused, his thoughts reverting to his absent brother—"Full of fancies poetic and musical,—now can it be that I owe my very dreams to his dominance? Does he make me subservient to him, as I am, or is my submission to his will, my own desire? Is my 'madness' or 'craze,' or whatever he calls it, of his working? and should I be more like other men if I were separated from him? And yet what has he ever done to me, save make me happy? Has he placed me under the influence of any magnet such as this book describes? Certainly not that I am aware of. He has made my inward spirit clearer of comprehension, so that I hear him call me even by a thought,—I see and know beautiful things of which grosser souls have no perception,—and am I not content?—Yes, surely I am!—surely I should be,—though at times there seems a something missing,—a something to which I cannot give a name."

---

* From "The Natural Law of Miracles," written in Arabic 400 B.C.

MARIE CORELLI

He sighed,—and again buried his head between his hands,—he was conscious of a dreary sensation, unusual to his bright and fervid nature,—the very sunshine streaming through the window seemed to lack true brilliancy. Suddenly a hand was laid upon his shoulder,—he started and rose to his feet with a bewildered air,—then smiled, as he saw that the intruder was only Zaroba.

VIII

Only Zaroba,—gaunt, grim, fierce-eyed Zaroba, old and unlovely, yet possessing withal an air of savage dignity, as she stood erect, her amber-coloured robe bound about her with a scarlet girdle, and her gray hair gathered closely under a small coif of the same vivid hue. Her wrinkled visage had more animation in it than on the previous night, and her harsh voice grew soft as she looked at the picturesque glowing beauty of the young man beside her, and addressed him.

"El-Râmi has gone?" she asked.

Féraz nodded. He generally made her understand him either by signs, or the use of the finger-alphabet, at which he was very dexterous.

"On what quest?" she demanded.

Féraz explained rapidly and mutely that he had gone to visit a friend residing at a distance from town.

"Then he will not return tonight;"—muttered Zaroba thoughtfully—"He will not return tonight."

She sat down, and clasping her hands across her knees, rocked herself to and fro for some minutes in silence. Then she spoke, more to herself than to her listener.

"He is an angel or a fiend," she said in low meditative accents. "Or maybe he is both in one. He saved me from death once—I shall never forget that. And by his power he sent me back to my native land last night—I bound my black tresses with pearl and gold, and laughed and sang,—I was young again!"—and with a sudden cry she raised her hands above her head and clapped them fiercely together, so that the silver bangles on her arms jangled like bells;—"As God liveth, I was young! You know what it is to be young"—and she turned her dark orbs half enviously upon Féraz, who, leaning against his brother's writing-table, regarded her with interest and something of awe—"or you should know it! To feel the blood leap in the veins, while the happy heart keeps time like the beat of a joyous cymbal,—to catch the breath and tremble with ecstasy as the eyes one loves best in the world flash lightning-passion into your own,—to make companions of the roses, and feel the pulses quicken at the songs of birds,—to tread the ground so lightly as to scarcely know whether it is earth or air—this is to be young!—young!—and I was young last night. My love was with me,—my love, my more than lover—'Zaroba, beautiful Zaroba!' he said, and his kisses were as honey on my lips—'Zaroba, pearl of passion! fountain of sweetness in a desert land!—thine eyes are fire in which I burn my soul,—thy round arms the prison in which I lock my heart! Zaroba, beautiful Zaroba!'— Beautiful! Ay!—through the power of El-Râmi I was fair to see—last night! . . . only last night!"

Her voice sank down into a feeble wailing, and Féraz gazed at her compassionately and in a little wonder,—he was accustomed to see her in various strange and incomprehensible moods, but she was seldom so excited as now.

"Why do you not laugh?" she asked suddenly and with a touch of defiance—"Why do you not laugh at me?—at me, the wretched Zaroba,—old and unsightly—bent and wrinkled!—that I should dare to say I was once beautiful!—It is a thing to make sport of—an old forsaken woman's dream of her dead youth."

With an impulsive movement that was as graceful as it was becoming, Féraz, for sole reply, dropped on one knee beside her, and taking her wrinkled hand, touched it lightly but reverently with his lips. She trembled, and great tears rose in her eyes.

"Poor boy!" she muttered—"Poor child!—a child to me, and yet a man! As God liveth, a man!" She looked at him with a curious stedfastness. "Good Féraz, forgive me—I did you wrong—I know you would not mock the aged, or make wanton sport of their incurable woes,—you are too gentle. I would in truth you were less mild of spirit—less womanish of heart!"

"Womanish!" and Féraz leaped up, stung by the word, he knew not why. His heart beat strangely—his blood tingled,—it seemed to him that if he had possessed a weapon, his instinct would have been to draw it then. Never had he looked so handsome; and Zaroba, watching his expression, clapped her withered hands in a sort of witch-like triumph.

"Ha!"—she cried—"The man's mettle speaks! There is something more than the dreamer in you then—something that will help you to explain the mystery of your existence—something that says—'Féraz, you are the slave of destiny—up! be its master! Féraz, you sleep— awake!'" and Zaroba stood up tall and imposing, with the air of an inspired sorceress delivering a prophecy—"Féraz, you have manhood— prove it! Féraz, you have missed the one joy of life—Love!—Win it!"

Féraz stared at her amazed. Her words were such as she had never addressed to him before, and yet they moved him with a singular uneasiness. Love? Surely he knew the meaning of love? It was an ideal passion, like the lifting-up of life in prayer. Had not his brother told him that perfect love was unattainable on this planet?—and was it not a word the very suggestions of which could only be expressed in music? These thoughts ran through his mind while he stood inert and wondering,—then rousing himself a little from the effects of Zaroba's outburst, he sat down at the table, and taking up a pencil, wrote as follows—

"You talk wildly, Zaroba—you cannot be well. Let me hear no more—you disturb my peace. I know what love is—I know what life is. But the best part of my life and love is not here,—but elsewhere."

Zaroba took the paper from his hand, read it, and tore it to bits in a rage.

"O foolish youth!" she exclaimed—"Your love is the love of a Dream,—your life is the life of a Dream! You see with another's eyes— you think through another's brain. You are a mere machine, played upon by another's will! But not forever shall you be deceived—not forever,—" here she gave a slight start and looked around her nervously as though she expected someone to enter the room suddenly—"Listen! Come to me to—night,—tonight when all is dark and silent,—when every sound in the outside street is stilled,—come to me—and I will show you a marvel of the world!—one who, like you, is the victim of a Dream!" She broke off abruptly and glanced from right to left in evident alarm,—then with a fresh impetus of courage, she bent towards her companion again and whispered in his ear—"Come!"

"But where?" asked Féraz in the language of signs.

"Up yonder!" said Zaroba firmly, regardless of the utter amazement with which Féraz greeted this answer—"Up, where El-Râmi hides his great secret. Yes—I know he has forbidden you to venture there,—even so has he forbidden me to speak of what he cherishes so closely,—but are we slaves, you and I? Do you purpose always to obey him? So be it, an you will! But if I were you,—a man—I would defy both gods and fiends if they opposed my liberty of action. Do as it pleases you,—I, Zaroba, have given, you the choice,—stay and dream of life—or come and live it! Till tonight—farewell!"

She had reached the door and vanished through it, before Féraz could demand more of her meaning,—and he was left alone, a prey to the most torturing emotions. "The vulgar vice of curiosity!" That was the phrase his brother had used to him scarcely an hour agone,—and yet, here he was, yielding to a fresh fit of the intolerable desire that had possessed him for years to know El-Râmi's great secret. He dropped wearily into a chair and thought all the circumstances over. They were as follows,—

In the first place he had never known any other protector or friend than his brother, who, being several years older than himself, had taken sole charge of him after the almost simultaneous death of their father and mother, an event which he knew had occurred somewhere in the East, but how or when, he could not exactly remember, nor had he ever been told much about it. He had always been very happy in El-Râmi's companionship, and had travelled with him nearly all over the world,— and though they had never been rich, they had always had sufficient wherewith to live comfortably, though how even this small competence was gained, Féraz never knew. There had been no particular mystery about his brother's life, however, till on one occasion, when they were travelling together across the Syrian desert, where they had come upon a caravan of half-starved Arab wanderers in dire distress from want and sickness. Among them was an elderly woman at the extreme point of death, and an orphan child named Lilith, who was also dying. El-Râmi had suddenly, for no special reason, save kindness of heart and compassion, offered his services as physician to the stricken little party, and had restored the elderly woman, a widow, almost miraculously to health and strength in a day or two. This woman was no other than Zaroba. The sick child however, a girl of about twelve years old, died. And here began the puzzle. On the day of this girl's death, El-Râmi, with sudden and inexplicable haste, had sent his young brother on to Alexandria, bidding him there take ship immediately for the Island of Cyprus, and carry to a certain monastery some miles from Famagousta, a packet of documents, which he stated were of the most extraordinary value and importance. Féraz had obeyed, and according to further instructions, had remained as a visitor in that Cyprian religious retreat, among monks unlike any other monks he had ever seen or heard of, till he was sent for, whereupon, according to command, he rejoined El-Râmi in London. He found him, somewhat to his surprise, installed in the small house where they now were,—with the woman Zaroba, whose presence was another cause of blank astonishment, especially as she seemed to have nothing to do but keep certain rooms upstairs in order. But all the questions Féraz poured out respecting her, and everything that had happened since their parting in the Syrian desert, were met by equivocal replies or absolute silence on his brother's part, and by-and-bye the young man grew accustomed to his position. Day by day he became more and more subservient to El-Râmi's will, though he could never quite comprehend why he was so willingly submissive. Of course he knew that his brother was gifted with certain powers of physical magnetism,—because he had allowed himself to be practised upon, and he took a certain interest in the scientific development of those powers, this being, as he quite comprehended, one of the branches of study on which El-Râmi was engaged. He knew that his brother could compel response to thought from a distance,—but, as there were others of his race who could do the same thing, and as that sort of mild hypnotism was largely practised in the East, where he was born, he attached no special importance to it. Endowed with various gifts of genius such as music and poetry, and a quick perception of everything beautiful and artistic, Féraz lived in a tranquil little Eden of his own,—and the only serpent in it that now and then lifted its head to hiss doubt and perplexity was the inexplicable mystery of those upstair rooms over which Zaroba had guardianship. The merest allusion to the subject excited El-Râmi's displeasure; and during the whole time they had lived together in that house, now nearly six years, he had not dared to speak of it more than a very few times, while Zaroba, on her part, had faithfully preserved the utmost secrecy. Now, she seemed disposed to break the long-kept rules,—and Féraz knew not what to think of it.

"Is everything destiny, as El-Râmi says?" he mused—"Or shall I follow my own desires in the face of destiny? Shall I yield to temptation—or shall I overcome it? Shall I break his command,—lose his affection and be a free man,—or shall I obey him still, and be his slave? And what should I do with my liberty if I had it, I wonder? Womanish! What a word! Am I womanish?" He paced up and down the room in sudden irritation and haughtiness;—the piano stood open, but its ivory keys failed to attract him,—his brain was full of other suggestions than the making of sweet harmony.

"Do not seek out sorrow for yourself by rash and idle questioning."

So his brother had said at parting. And the words rang in his ears as he walked to and fro restlessly, thinking, wondering, and worrying his mind with vague wishes and foreboding anxieties, till the shining afternoon wore away and darkness fell.

MARIE CORELLI

IX

A Rough night at sea,—but the skies were clear, and the great worlds of God which we call stars, throbbed in the heavens like lustrous lamps, all the more brilliantly for there being no moon to eclipse their glory. A high gale was blowing, and the waves dashed up on the coast of Ilfracombe with an organ-like thud and roar as they broke in high jets of spray, and then ran swiftly back again with a soft swish and ripple suggestive of the downward chromatic scale played rapidly on well-attuned strings. There was freshness and life in the dancing wind;—the world seemed well in motion;—and, standing aloft among the rocks, and looking down at the tossing sea, one could realize completely the continuous whirl of the globe beneath one's feet, and the perpetual movement of the planet-studded heavens. High above the shore, on a bare jutting promontory, a solitary house faced seaward;—it was squarely built and surmounted with a tower, wherein one light burned fitfully, its pale sparkle seeming to quiver with fear as the wild wind fled past joyously, with a swirl and cry like some huge sea-bird on the wing. It looked a dismal residence at its best, even when the sun was shining,—but at night its aspect was infinitely more dreary. It was an old house, and it enjoyed the reputation of being haunted,—a circumstance which had enabled its present owner to purchase the lease of it for a very moderate sum. He it was who had built the tower, and whether because of this piece of extravagance or for other unexplained reasons, he had won for himself personally, almost as uncanny a reputation as the house had possessed before he occupied it. A man who lived the life of a recluse,—who seemed to have no relations with the outside world at all,—who had only one servant, (a young German whom the shrewder gossips declared was his "keeper")—who lived on such simple fare as certainly would never have contented a modern Hodge earning twelve shillings a week, and who seemed to purchase nothing but strange astronomical and geometrical instruments,—surely such a queer personage must either be mad, or in league with some evil "secret society,"—the more especially that he had had that tower erected, into which, after it was finished, no one but himself ever entered so far as the people of the neighbourhood could tell. Under all these suspicious circumstances, it was natural he should be avoided; and avoided he was by the good folk of Ilfracombe, in that pleasantly diverting fashion which causes provincial respectability to shudder away from the merest suggestion of superior intelligence.

And yet poor old Dr. Kremlin was a being not altogether to be despised. His appearance was perhaps against him, inasmuch as his clothes were shabby, and his eyes rather wild,—but the expression of his meagre face was kind and gentle, and a perpetual compassion for everything and everybody, seemed to vibrate in his voice and reflect itself in his melancholy smile. He was deeply occupied—so he told a few friends in Russia, where he was born,—in serious scientific investigations,—but the "friends," deeming him mad, held aloof till those investigations should become results. If the results proved disappointing, there would be no need to notice him any more,—if successful, why then, by a mystic process known only to themselves, the "friends" would so increase and multiply that he would be quite inconveniently surrounded by them. In the meantime, nobody wrote to him, or came to see him, except El-Râmi; and it was El-Râmi now, who, towards ten o'clock in the evening, knocked at the door of his lonely habitation and was at once admitted with every sign of deference and pleasure by the servant Karl.

"I'm glad you've come, sir,"—said this individual cheerfully,—"The Herr Doctor has not been out all day, and he eats less than ever. It will do him good to see you."

"He is in the tower as usual, at work?" enquired El-Râmi, throwing off his coat.

Karl assented, with rather a doleful look,—and opening the door of a small dining-room, showed the supper-table laid for two.

El-Râmi smiled.

"It's no good, Karl!" he said kindly—"It's very well meant on your part, but it's no good at all. You will never persuade your master to eat at this time of night, or me either. Clear all these things away,—and make your mind easy,—go to bed and sleep. Tomorrow morning prepare as excellent a breakfast as you please—I promise you we'll do justice to it! Don't look so discontented—don't you know that over-feeding kills the working capacity?"

"And over-starving kills the man,—working-capacity and all"—responded Karl lugubriously—"However, I suppose you know best, sir!"

"In this case I do"—replied El-Râmi—"Your master expects me?"

Karl nodded,—and El-Râmi, with a brief "good-night," ascended the staircase rapidly and soon disappeared. A door banged aloft—then all was still. Karl sighed profoundly, and slowly cleared away the useless supper.

"Well! How wise men can bear to starve themselves just for the sake of teaching fools, is more than I shall ever understand!" he said half aloud—"But then I shall never be wise—I am an ass and always was. A good dinner and a glass of good wine have always seemed to me better than all the science going,—there's a shameful confession of ignorance and brutality together, if you like. 'Where do you think you will go to when you die, Karl?' says the poor old Herr Doctor. And what do I say? I say—'I don't know, mein Herr—and I don't care. This world is good enough for me so long as I live in it.' 'But afterwards Karl,—afterwards!' he says, with his gray head shaking. And what do I say? Why, I say—'I can't tell, mein Herr! but whoever sent me Here will surely have sense enough to look after me There!' And he laughs, and his head shakes worse than ever. Ah! Nothing can ever make me clever, and I'm very glad of it!"

He whistled a lively tune softly, as he went to bed in his little side-room off the passage, and wondered again, as he had wondered hundreds of times before, what caused that solemn low humming noise that throbbed so incessantly through the house, and seemed so loud when everything else was still. It was a grave sound,—suggestive of a long-sustained organ-note held by the pedal-bass;—the murmuring of seas and rivers seemed in it, as well as the rush of the wind. Karl had grown accustomed to it, though he did not know what it meant,—and he listened to it, till drowsiness made him fancy it was the hum of his mother's spinning wheel, at home in his native German village among the pine-forests, and so he fell happily asleep.

Meanwhile El-Râmi, ascending to the tower, knocked sharply at a small nail-studded door in the wall. The mysterious murmuring noise was now louder than ever,—and the knock had to be repeated three or four times before it was attended to. Then the door was cautiously opened, and the "Herr Doctor" himself looked out, his wizened, aged, meditative face illumined like a Rembrandt picture by the small hand-lamp he held in his hand.

"Ah!—El-Râmi!" he said in slow yet pleased tones—"I thought it might be you. And like 'Bernardo'—you 'come most carefully upon your hour.'"

He smiled, as one well satisfied to have made an apt quotation, and opened the door more widely to admit his visitor.

"Come in quickly,"—he said—"The great window is open to the skies, and the wind is high,—I fear some damage from the draught,—come in—come in!"

His voice became suddenly testy and querulous,—and El-Râmi stepped in at once without reply. Dr. Kremlin shut to the door carefully and bolted it—then he turned the light of the lamp he carried, full on the dark handsome face and dignified figure of his companion.

"You are looking well—well,"—he muttered—"Not a shade older—always sound and strong! Just Heavens!—if I had your physique, I think with Archimedes, that I could lift the world! But I am getting very old,—the life in me is ebbing fast,—and I have not done my work— . . . God! . . . God! I have not done my work!"

He clenched his hands, and his voice quavered down into a sound that was almost a groan. El-Râmi's black beaming eyes rested on him compassionately.

"You are worn out, my dear Kremlin,"—he said gently—"worn out and exhausted with long toil. You shall sleep tonight. I have come according to my promise, and I will do what I can for you. Trust me—you shall not lose the reward of your life's work by want of time. You shall have time,—even leisure to complete your labours,—I will give you 'length of days'!"

The elder man sank into a chair trembling, and rested his head wearily on one hand.

"You cannot;"—he said faintly—"you cannot stop the advance of death, my friend! You are a very clever man—you have a far-reaching subtlety of brain,—but your learning and wisdom must pause there—there at the boundary-line of the grave. You cannot overstep it or penetrate beyond it—you cannot slacken the pace of the on-rushing years;—no, no! I shall be forced to depart with half my discovery uncompleted."

El-Râmi smiled,—a slightly derisive smile.

"You, who have faith in so much that cannot be proved, are singularly incredulous of a fact that can be proved;"—he said—"Anyway, whatever you choose to think, here I am in answer to your rather sudden summons—and here is your saving remedy;—" and he placed a gold-stoppered flask on the table near which they sat—"It is, or might be called, a veritable distilled essence of time,—for it will do what they say God cannot do, make the days spin backward!"

Dr. Kremlin took up the flask curiously.

"You are so positive of its action?"

"Positive. I have kept one human creature alive and in perfect health for six years on that vital fluid alone."

"Wonderful!—wonderful!"—and the old scientist held it close to the light, where it seemed to flash like a diamond,—then he smiled dubiously—"Am I the new Faust, and you Mephisto?"

"Bah!" and El-Râmi shrugged his shoulders carelessly—"An old nurse's tale!—yet, like all old nurses' tales and legends of every sort under the sun, it is not without its grain of truth. As I have often told you, there is really nothing imagined by

the human brain that is not possible of realization, either here or hereafter. It would be a false note and a useless calculation to allow thought to dwell on what cannot be,—hence our airiest visions are bound to become facts in time. All the same, I am not of such superhuman ability that I can make you change your skin like a serpent, and blossom into youth and the common vulgar lusts of life, which to the thinker must be valueless. No. What you hold there, will simply renew the tissues, and gradually enrich the blood with fresh globules—nothing more,—but that is all you need. Plainly and practically speaking, as long as the tissues and the blood continue to renew themselves, you cannot die except by violence."

"Cannot die!" echoed Kremlin, in stupefied wonder—"Cannot die?"

"Except by violence—" repeated El-Râmi with emphasis—"Well!—and what now? There is nothing really astonishing in the statement. Death by violence is the only death possible to anyone familiar with the secrets of Nature, and there is more than one lesson to be learned from the old story of Cain and Abel. The first death in the world, according to that legend, was death by violence. Without violence, life should be immortal, or at least renewable at pleasure."

"Immortal!" muttered Dr. Kremlin—"Immortal! Renewable at pleasure! My God!—then I have time before me—plenty of time!"

"You have, if you care for it—" said El-Râmi with a tinge of melancholy in his accents—"and if you continue to care for it. Few do, nowadays."

But his companion scarcely heard him. He was balancing the little flask in his hand in wonderment and awe.

"Death by violence?"—he repeated slowly. "But, my friend, may not God Himself use violence towards us? May He not snatch the unwilling soul from its earthly tenement at an unexpected moment,—and so, all the scheming and labour and patient calculation of years be ended in one flash of time?"

"God—if there be a God, which some are fain to believe there is,— uses no violence—" replied El-Râmi—"Deaths by violence are due to the ignorance, or brutality, or long-inherited fool-hardiness and interference of man alone."

"What of shipwreck?—storm?—lightning?"—queried Dr. Kremlin, still playing with the flask he held.

"You are not going to sea, are you?" asked El-Râmi, smiling—"And surely you, of all men, should know that even shipwrecks are clue to a lack of mathematical balance in ship-building. One little trifle of exactitude, which is always missing, unfortunately,—one little delicate scientific adjustment, and the fiercest storm and wind could not prevail against the properly poised vessel. As for lightning—of course people are killed by it if they persist in maintaining an erect position like a lightning-rod or conductor, while the electrical currents are in full play. If they were to lie flat down, as savages do, they could not attract the descending force. But who, among arrogant stupid men, cares to adopt such simple precautions? Any way, I do not see that you need fear any of these disasters."

"No no,"—said the old man meditatively, "I need not fear,—no, no! I have nothing to fear."

His voice sank into silence. He and El-Râmi were sitting in a small square chamber of the tower,—very narrow, with only space enough for the one tiny table and two chairs which furnished it,—the walls were covered with very curious maps, composed of lines and curves and zig-zag patterns, meaningless to all except Kremlin himself, whose dreamy gaze wandered to them between-whiles with an ardent yearning and anxiety. And ever that strange deep, monotonous humming noise surged through the tower as of a mighty wheel at work, the vibration of the sound seeming almost to shake the solid masonry, while mingling with it now and again came the wild sea-bird cry of the wind. El-Râmi listened.

"And still it moves?" he queried softly, using almost the words of Galileo,—"e pur, si muove."

Dr. Kremlin looked up, his pale eyes full of a sudden fire and animation.

"Ay!—still it moves!" he responded with a touch of eager triumph in his tone—"Still it moves—and still it sounds! The music of the Earth, my friend!—the dominant note of all Nature's melody! Hear it!—round, full, grand and perfect!—one tone in the ascending scale of the planets,—the song of one Star,—our Star—as it rolls on its predestined way! Come!—come with me!" and he sprang up excitedly—"It is a night for work;—the heavens are clear as a mirror,—come and see my Dial of the Fates,—you have seen it before, I know, but there are new reflexes upon it now,—new lines of light and colour,—ah, my good El-Râmi, if you could solve my Problem, you would be soon wiser than you are! Your gift of long life would be almost valueless compared to my proof of what is beyond life—"

"Yes—if the proof could be obtained—" interposed El-Râmi.

"It shall be obtained!" cried Kremlin wildly—"It shall! I will not die till the secret is won. I will wrench it out from the Holy of Holies—I will pluck it from the very thoughts of God!"

He trembled with the violence of his own emotions,—then passing his hand across his forehead, he relapsed into sudden calm, and smiling gently, said again—

"Come!"

El-Râmi rose at once in obedience to this request,—and the old man preceded him to a high narrow door which looked like a slit in the wall, and which he unbarred and opened with an almost jealous care. A brisk puff of wind blew in their faces through the aperture, but this subsided into mere cool freshness of air, as they entered and stood together within the great central chamber of the tower,—a lofty apartment, where the strange work of Kremlin's life was displayed in all its marvellous complexity,—a work such as no human being had ever attempted before, or would be likely to attempt again.

X

The singular object that at once caught and fixed the eye in fascinated amazement and something of terror, was a huge Disc, suspended between ceiling and floor by an apparently inextricable mesh and tangle of wires. It was made of some smooth glittering substance like crystal, and seemed from its great height and circumference to occupy nearly the whole of the lofty tower-room. It appeared to be lightly poised and balanced on a long steel rod,—a sort of gigantic needle which hung from the very top of the tower. The entire surface of the Disc was a subdued blaze of light,—light which fluctuated in waves and lines, and zig-zag patterns like a kaleidoscope, as the enormous thing circled round and round, as it did, with a sort of measured motion, and a sustained solemn buzzing sound. Here was the explanation of the mysterious noise that vibrated throughout the house,—it was simply the movement of this round shield-like mass among its wonderful network of rods and wires. Dr. Kremlin called it his "crystal" Disc,—but it was utterly unlike ordinary crystal, for it not only shone with a transparent watery clearness, but possessed the scintillating lustre of a fine diamond cut into numerous prisms, so that El-Râmi shaded his eyes from the flash of it as he stood contemplating it in silence. It swirled round and round steadily; facing it, a large casement window, about the size of half the wall, was thrown open to the night, and through this could be seen a myriad sparkling stars. The wind blew in, but not fiercely now, for part of the wrath of the gale was past,—and the wash of the sea on the beach below had exactly the same tone in it as the monotonous hum of the Disc as it moved. At one side of the open window a fine telescope mounted on a high stand, pointed out towards the heavens,—there were numerous other scientific implements in the room, but it was impossible to take much notice of anything but the Disc itself, with its majestic motion and the solemn sound to which it swung. Dr. Kremlin seemed to have almost forgotten El-Râmi's presence,—going up to the window, he sat down on a low bench in the corner, and folding his arms across his breast gazed at his strange invention with a fixed, wondering, and appealing stare.

"How to unravel the meaning—how to decipher the message!" he muttered—"Sphinx of my brain, tell me, is there No answer? Shall the actual offspring of my thought refuse to clear up the riddle I propound?

Nay, is it possible the creature should baffle the creator? See! the lines change again—the vibrations are altered,—the circle is ever the circle, but the reflexes differ,—how can one separate or classify them—how?"

Thus far his half-whispered words were audible,—when El-Râmi came and stood beside him. Then he seemed to suddenly recollect himself, and looking up, he rose to his feet and spoke in a perfectly calm and collected manner.

"You see"—he said, pointing to the Disc with the air of a lecturer illustrating his discourse—"To begin with, there is the fine hair's-breadth balance of matter which gives perpetual motion. Nothing can stop that movement save the destruction of the whole piece of mechanism. By some such subtly delicate balance as that, the Universe moves,—and nothing can stop it save the destruction of the Universe. Is not that fairly reasoned?"

"Perfectly," replied El-Râmi, who was listening with profound attention.

"Surely that of itself,—the secret of perpetual motion,—is a great discovery, is it not?" questioned Kremlin eagerly.

El-Râmi hesitated.

"It is," he said at last. "Forgive me if I paused a moment before replying,—the reason of my doing so was this. You cannot claim to yourself any actual discovery of perpetual motion, because that is Nature's own particular mystery. Perhaps I do not explain myself with sufficient clearness,—well, what I mean to imply is this—namely, that your wonderful dial there would not revolve as it does, if the Earth on which we stand were not also revolving. If we could imagine our planet stopping suddenly in its course, your Disc would stop also,—is not that correct?"

"Why, naturally!" assented Kremlin impatiently. "Its movement is mathematically calculated to follow, in a slower degree, but with rhythmical exactitude, the Earth's own movement, and is so balanced as to be absolutely accurate to the very half-quarter of a hair's-breadth."

"Yes,—and there is the chief wonder of your invention," said El-Râmi quietly. "It is that peculiarly precise calculation of yours that is so marvellous, in that it enables you to follow the course of perpetual motion. With perpetual motion itself you have nothing to do,—you cannot find its why or its when or its how,—it is eternal as Eternity. Things must move,—and we all move with them—your Disc included."

"But the moving things are balanced—so!" said Kremlin, pointing triumphantly to his work—"On one point—one pivot!"

"And that point—?" queried El-Râmi dubiously.

"Is a Central Universe"—responded Kremlin—"where God abides."

El-Râmi looked at him with dark, dilating, burning eyes.

"Suppose," he said suddenly—"suppose—for the sake of argument—that this Central Universe you imagine exists, were but the outer covering or shell of another Central Universe, and so on through innumerable Central Universes for ever and ever and ever, and no point or pivot reachable!"

Kremlin uttered a cry, and clasped his hands with a gesture of terror.

"Stop—stop!" he gasped—"Such an idea is frightful!—horrible! Would you drive me mad?—mad, I tell you? No human brain could steadily contemplate the thought of such pitiless infinity!"

He sank back on the seat and rocked himself to and fro like a person in physical pain, the while he stared at El-Râmi's majestic figure and dark meditative face as though he saw some demon in a dream. El-Râmi met his gaze with a compassionate glance in his own eyes.

"You are narrow, my friend,"—he observed—"as narrow of outward and onward conception as most scientists are. I grant you the human brain has limits; but the human Soul has none! There is no 'pitiless infinity' to the Soul's aspirations,—it is never contented,—but eternally ambitious, eternally enquiring, eternally young, it is ready to scale heights and depths without end, unconscious of fatigue or satiety. What of a million million Universes? I—even I—can contemplate them without dismay,—the brain may totter and reel at the multiplicity of them,—but the Soul would absorb them all and yet seek space for more!"

His rich, deep tranquil voice had the effect of calming Kremlin's excited nerves. He paused in his uneasy rocking to and fro, and listened as though he heard music.

"You are a bold man, El-Râmi," he said slowly—"I have always said it,—bold even to rashness. Yet with all your large ideas I find you inconsistent; for example, you talk of the Soul now, as if you believed in it,—but there are times when you declare yourself doubtful of its existence."

"It is necessary to split hairs of argument with you, I see"—returned El-Râmi with a slight smile,—"Can you not understand that I may believe in the Soul without being sure of it? It is the natural instinct of every man to credit himself with immortality, because this life is so short and unsatisfactory,—the notion may be a fault of heritage perhaps, still it is implanted in us all the same. And I do believe in the Soul,—but I require certainty to make my mere belief an undeniable Fact. And the whole business of my life is to establish that fact provably, and beyond any sort of doubt whatever,—what inconsistency do you find there?"

"None—none—" said Kremlin hastily—"But you will not succeed,—yours is too daring an attempt,—too arrogant and audacious a demand upon the Unknown Forces."

"And what of the daring and arrogance displayed here?" asked El-Râmi, with a wave of his hand towards the glittering Disc in front of them.

Kremlin jumped up excitedly.

"No, no!—you cannot call the mere scien—tific investigation of natural objects arrogant," he said—"Besides, the whole thing is so very simple after all. It is well known that every star in the heavens sends forth perpetual radiations of light; which radiations in a given number of minutes, days, months or years, reach our Earth. It depends of course on the distance between the particular star and our planet, as to how long these light-vibrations take to arrive here. One ray from some stars will occupy thousands of years in its course,—in fact, the original planet from which it fell, may be swept out of existence before it has time to penetrate our atmosphere. All this is in the lesson-books of children, and is familiar to every beginner in the rudiments of astronomy. But apart from time and distance, there is no cessation to these light-beats or vibrations; they keep on arriving for ever, without an instant's pause. Now, my great idea, was, as you know, to catch these reflexes on a mirror or dial of magnetic spar,—and you see for yourself that this thing, which seemed impossible, is to a certain extent done. Magnetic spar is not a new substance to you, any more than it was to the Egyptian priests of old—and the quality it has, of attracting light in its exact lines wherever light falls, is no surprise to you, though it might seem a marvel to the ignorant. Every little zigzag or circular flash on that Disc, is a vibration of light from some star,—but what puzzles and confounds my skill is this;—That there is a Meaning in those lines—a distinct Meaning which asks to be interpreted,—a picture which is ever on the point of declaring itself, and is never declared. Mine is the torture of a Tantalus watching night after night that mystic Dial!"

He went close up to the Disc, and pointed out one particular spot on its surface where at that moment there was a glittering tangle of little prismatic tints.

"Observe this with me—" he said, and El-Râmi approached him— "Here is a perfect cluster of light-vibrations,—in two minutes by my watch they will be here no longer,—and a year or more may pass before they appear again. From what stars they fall, and why they have deeper colours than most of the reflexes, I cannot tell. There—see!" and he looked round with an air of melancholy triumph mingled with wonder, as the little spot of brilliant colour suddenly disappeared like the moisture of breath from a mirror—"They are gone! I have seen them four times only since the Disc was balanced twelve years ago,—and I have tried in every way to trace their origin—in vain—all, all in vain! If I could only decipher the Meaning!—for as sure as God lives there is a Meaning there."

El-Râmi was silent, and Dr. Kremlin went on.

"The air is a conveyer of Sound—" he said meditatively—"The light is a conveyer of Scenes. Mark that well. The light may be said to create landscape and generate Colour. Reflexes of light make pictures,—witness the instantaneous flash, which with the aid of chemistry, will give you a photograph in a second. I firmly believe that all reflexes of light are so many letters of a marvellous alphabet, which if we could only read it, would enable us to grasp the highest secrets of creation. The seven tones of music, for example, are in Nature;—in any ordinary storm, where there is wind and rain and the rustle of leaves, you can hear the complete scale on which every atom of musical composition has ever been written. Yet what ages it took us to reduce that scale to a visible tangible form,—and even now we have not mastered the quarter-tones heard in the songs of birds. And just as the whole realm of music is in seven tones of natural Sound, so the whole realm of light is in a pictured Language of Design, Colour, and Method, with an intention and a message, which we—we human beings—are intended to discover. Yet with all these great mysteries waiting to be solved, the most of us are content to eat and drink and sleep and breed and die, like the lowest cattle, in brutish ignorance of more than half our intellectual privileges. I tell you, El-Râmi, if I could only find out and place correctly one of those light-vibrations, the rest might be easy."

He heaved a profound sigh,—and the great Disc, circling steadily with its grave monotonous hum, might have passed for the wheel of Fate which he, poor mortal, was powerless to stop though it should grind him to atoms.

El-Râmi watched him with interest and something of compassion for a minute or two,—then he touched his arm gently.

"Kremlin, is it not time for you to rest?" he asked kindly—"You have not slept well for many nights,—you are tired out,—why not sleep now, and gather strength for future labours?"

The old man started, and a slight shiver ran through him.

"You mean—?" he began.

"I mean to do for you what I promised—" replied El-Râmi—"You asked me for this—" and he held up the gold-stoppered flask he had brought in with him from the next room—"It is all ready prepared for you—drink it, and tomorrow you will find yourself a new man."

Dr. Kremlin looked at him suspiciously—and then began to laugh with a sort of hysterical nervousness.

"I believe—" he murmured indistinctly and with affected jocularity—"I believe that you want to poison me! Yes—yes!—to poison me and take all my discoveries for yourself! You want to solve the great Star-problem and take all the glory and rob me—yes, rob me of my hard-earned fame!—yes—it is poison—poison!"

And he chuckled feebly, and hid his face between his hands.

El-Râmi heard him with an expression of pain and pity in his fine eyes.

"My poor old friend—" he said gently—"You are wearied to death—so I pardon you your sudden distrust of me. As for poison—see!" and he lifted the flask he held to his lips and drank a few drops—"Have no fear! Your Star-problem is your own,—and I desire that you should live long enough to read its great mystery. As for me, I have other labours;—to me stars, solar systems, aye! whole Universes are nothing,—my business is with the Spirit that dominates Matter—not with Matter itself. Enough; will you live or will you die? It rests with yourself to choose—for you are ill, Kremlin—very ill,—your brain is fagged and weak—you cannot go on much longer like this. Why did you send for me if you do not believe in me?"

The old Doctor tottered to the window—bench and sat down,—then looking up, he forced a smile.

"Don't you see for yourself what a coward I have become?" he said—"I tell you I am afraid of everything;—of you—of myself—and worst of all, of that—" and he pointed to the Disc—"which lately seems to have grown stronger than I am." He paused a moment—then went on with an effort—"I had a strange idea the other night,—I thought, suppose

God, in the beginning, created the Universe simply to divert Himself— just as I created my Dial there;—and suppose it had happened that instead of being His servant as He originally intended, it had become His master?—that He actually had no more power over it? Suppose He were dead? We see that the works of men live ages after their death,— why not the works of God? Horrible—horrible! Death is horrible! I do not want to die, El-Râmi!" and his faint voice rose to a querulous wail—"Not yet—not yet! I cannot!—I must finish my work—I must know—I must live—"

"You shall live," interrupted El-Râmi. "Trust me—there is no death in this!"

He held up the mysterious flask again. Kremlin stared at it, shaking all over with nervousness—then on a sudden impulse clutched it.

"Am I to drink it all?" he asked faintly.

El-Râmi bent his head in assent.

Kremlin hesitated a moment longer—then with the air of one who takes a sudden desperate resolve, he gave one eager yearning look at the huge revolving Disc, and putting the flask to his lips, drained its contents. He had scarcely swallowed the last drop, when he sprang to his feet, uttered a smothered cry, staggered, and fell on the floor motionless. El-Râmi caught him up at once, and lifted him easily in his strong arms on to the window-seat, where he laid him down gently, placing coverings over him and a pillow under his head. The old man's face was white and rigid as the face of a corpse, but he breathed easily and quietly, and El-Râmi, knowing the action of the draught he had administered, saw there was no cause for anxiety in his condition. He himself leaned on the sill of the great open window and looked out at the starlit sky for some minutes, and listened to the sonorous plashing of the waves on the shore below. Now and then he glanced back over his shoulder at the great Dial and its shining star-patterns.

"Only Lilith could decipher the meaning of it all," he mused. "Perhaps,—some day—it might be possible to ask her. But then, do I in truth believe what she tells me?-would he believe? The transcendentally uplifted soul of a woman!—ought we to credit the message obtained through so ethereal a means? I doubt it. We men are composed of such stuff that we must convince ourselves of a fact by every known test before we finally accept it,—like St. Thomas, unless we put our rough hand into the wounded side of Christ, and thrust our fingers into the nail-prints, we will not believe. And I shall never resolve myself as to which is the wisest course,—to accept everything with the faith of a child, or dispute everything with the arguments of a controversialist. The child is happiest; but then the question arises—Were we meant to be happy? I think not,—since there is nothing that can make us so for long."

His brow clouded and he stood absorbed, looking at the stars, yet scarcely conscious of beholding them. Happiness! It had a sweet sound,— an exquisite suggestion; and his thoughts clung round it persistently as bees round honey. Happiness!—What could engender it? The answer came unbidden to his brain—"Love!" He gave an involuntary gesture of irritation, as though someone had spoken the word in his ear.

"Love!" he exclaimed half aloud. "There is no such thing—not on earth. There is Desire,—the animal attraction of one body for another, which ends in disgust and satiety. Love should have no touch of coarseness in it,—and can anything be coarser than the marriage-tie?— the bond which compels a man and woman to live together in daily partnership of bed and board, and reproduce their kind like pigs, or other common cattle. To call that love is a sacrilege to the very name,— for Love is a divine emotion, and demands divinest comprehension."

He went up to where Kremlin lay reclined,—the old man slept profoundly and peacefully,—his face had gained colour and seemed less pinched and meagre in outline. El-Râmi felt his pulse,—it beat regularly and calmly. Satisfied with his examination, he wheeled away the great telescope into a corner, and shut the window against the night air,—then he lay down himself on the floor, with his coat rolled under him for a pillow, and composed himself to sleep till morning.

XI

The next day dawned in brilliant sunshine; the sea was as smooth as a lake, and the air pleasantly warm and still. Dr. Kremlin's servant Karl got up in a very excellent humour,—he had slept well, and he awoke with the comfortable certainty of finding his eccentric master in better health and spirits, as this was always the case after one of El-Râmi's rare visits. And Karl, though he did not much appreciate learning, especially when the pursuit of it induced people, as he said, to starve themselves for the sake of acquiring wisdom, did feel in his own heart that there was something about El-Râmi that was not precisely like other men, and he had accordingly for him not only a great attraction, but a profound respect.

"If anybody can do the Herr Doctor good, he can—" he thought, as he laid the breakfast-table in the little dining-room whose French windows opened out to a tiny green lawn fronting the sea,—"Certainly one can never cure old age,—that is an ailment for which there is no remedy; but however old we are bound to get, I don't see why we should not be merry over it and enjoy our meals to the last. Now let me see—what have I to get ready—" and he enumerated on his fingers—"Coffee—toast—rolls,—butter—eggs—fish,—I think that will do;—and if I just put these few roses in the middle of the table to tempt the eye a bit,"—and he suited the action to the word—"There now!—if the Herr Doctor can be pleased at all—"

"Breakfast, Karl! breakfast!" interrupted a clear cheerful voice, the sound of which made Karl start with nervous astonishment. "Make haste, my good fellow! My friend here has to catch an early train."

Karl turned round, stared, and stood motionless, open-mouthed, and struck dumb with sheer surprise. Could it be the old Doctor who spoke? Was it his master at all,—this hale, upright, fresh-faced individual who stood before him, smiling pleasantly and giving his orders with such a brisk air of authority? Bewildered and half afraid, he cast a desperate glance at El-Râmi, who had also entered the room, and who, seeing his confusion, made him a quick secret sign.

"Yes—be as quick as you can, Karl," he said. "Your master has had a good night, and is much better, as you see. We shall be glad of our breakfast; I told you we should, last night. Don't keep us waiting!"

"Yes, sir—no, sir!" stammered Karl, trying to collect his scattered senses and staring again at Dr. Kremlin,—then, scarcely knowing whether he was on his head or his heels, he scrambled out of the room into the passage, where he stood for a minute stupefied and inert.

"It must be devil's work!" he exclaimed amazedly. "Who but the devil could make a man look twenty years younger in a single night? Yes—twenty years younger,—he looks that, if he looks a day. God have mercy on us!—what will happen next—what sort of a service have I got into?—Oh, my poor mother!"

This last was Karl's supremest adjuration,—when he could find nothing else to say, the phrase "Oh, my poor mother!" came as naturally to his lips as the familiar "D—n it!" from the mouth of an old swaggerer in the army or navy. He meant nothing by it, except perhaps a vague allusion to the innocent days of his childhood, when he was ignorant of the wicked ways of the wicked world, and when "Oh, my poor mother!" had not the most distant idea as to what was going to become of her hopeful first-born.

Meantime, while he went down into the kitchen and bustled about there, getting the coffee, frying the fish, boiling the eggs, and cogitating with his own surprised and half-terrified self, Dr. Kremlin and his guest had stepped out into the little garden together, and they now stood there on the grass-plot surveying the glittering wide expanse of ocean before them. They spoke not a word for some minutes,—then, all at once, Kremlin turned round and caught both El-Râmi's hands in his own and pressed them fervently—there were tears in his eyes.

"What can I say to you?" he murmured in a voice broken by strong emotion—"How can I thank you? You have been as a god to me;—I live again,—I breathe again,—this morning the world seems new to my eyes,—as new as though I had never seen it before. I have left a whole cycle of years, with all their suffering and bitterness, behind me, and I am ready now to commence life afresh."

"That is well!" said El-Râmi gently, cordially returning the pressure of his hands. "That is as it should be. To see your strength and vitality thus renewed, is more than enough reward for me."

"And do I really look younger?—am I actually changed in appearance?" asked Kremlin eagerly.

El-Râmi smiled. "Well, you saw poor Karl's amazement"—he replied. "He was afraid of you, I think—and also of me. Yes, you are changed, though not miraculously so. Your hair is as gray as ever,—the same furrows of thought are on your face;—all that has occurred is the simple renewal of the tissues, and revivifying of the blood,—and this gives you the look of vigour and heartiness you have this morning."

"But will it last?—will it last?" queried Kremlin anxiously.

"If you follow my instructions, of course it will—" returned El-Râmi—"I will see to that. I have left with you a certain quantity of the vital fluid,—all you have to do is to take ten drops every third night, or inject it into your veins if you prefer that method;—then,—as I told you,—you cannot die, except by violence."

"And no violence comes here"—said Kremlin with a smile, glancing round at the barren yet picturesque scene—"I am as lonely as an unmated eagle on a rock,—and the greater my solitude the happier I am. The world is very beautiful—that I grant,—but the beings that inhabit it spoil it for me, albeit I am one of them. And so I cannot die, except by violence? Almost I touch immortality! Marvellous El-Râmi! You should be a king of nations!"

"Too low a destiny!" replied El-Râmi—"I had rather be a ruler of planets."

"Ah, there is your stumbling-block!" said Kremlin, with sudden seriousness,—"You soar too high—you are never contented."

"Content is impossible to the Soul," returned El-Râmi,—"Nothing is too high or too low for its investigation. And whatever can be done, should be done, in order that the whole gamut of life may be properly understood by those who are forced to live it."

"And do not you understand it?"

"In part—yes. But not wholly. It is not sufficient to have traced the ripple of a brain-wave through the air and followed its action and result with exactitude,—nor is it entirely satisfactory to have all the secrets of physical and mental magnetism, and attraction between bodies and minds, made clear and easy without knowing the reason of these things. It is like the light-vibrations on your Disc,—they come—and go; but one needs to know why and whence they come and go. I know much—but I would fain know more."

"But is not the pursuit of knowledge infinite?"

"It may be—if infinity exists. Infinity is possible—and I believe in it,—all the same I must prove it."

"You will need a thousand life-times to fulfil such works as you attempt!" exclaimed Kremlin.

"And I will live them all;"—responded El-Râmi composedly—"I have sworn to let nothing baffle me, and nothing shall!"

Dr. Kremlin looked at him in vague awe,—the dark haughty handsome face spoke more resolvedly than words.

"Pardon me, El-Râmi"—he said with a little diffidence—"It seems a very personal question to put, and possibly you may resent it, still I have often thought of asking it. You are a very handsome and very fascinating man—you would be a fool if you were not perfectly aware of your own attractiveness,—well, now tell me—have you never loved anybody?—any woman?"

The sleepy brilliancy of El-Râmi's fine eyes lightened with sudden laughter.

"Loved a woman?—I?" he exclaimed—"The Fates forbid! What should I do with the gazelles and kittens and toys of life, such as women are? Of all animals on earth, they have the least attraction for me. I would rather stroke a bird's wings than a woman's hair, and the fragrance of a rose pressed against my lips is sweeter and more sincere than any woman's kisses. As the females of the race, women are useful in their way, but not interesting at any time—at least, not to me."

"Do you not believe in love then?" asked Kremlin.

"No. Do you?"

"Yes,"—and Kremlin's voice was very tender and impressive—"I believe it is the only thing of God in an almost godless world."

El-Râmi shrugged his shoulders.

"You talk like a poet. I, who am not poetical, cannot so idealize the physical attraction between male and female, which is nothing but a law of nature, and is shared by us in common with the beasts of the field."

"I think your wisdom is in error there"—said Kremlin slowly— "Physical attraction there is, no doubt—but there is something else— something more subtle and delicate, which escapes the analysis of both philosopher and scientist. Moreover it is an imperative spiritual sense, as well as a material craving,—the soul can no more be satisfied without love than the body."

"That is your opinion—" and El-Râmi smiled again,—"But you see a contradiction of it in me. I am satisfied to be without love,—and certainly I never look upon the ordinary woman of the day, without the disagreeable consciousness that I am beholding the living essence of sensualism and folly."

"You are very bitter," said Kremlin wonderingly—"Of course no 'ordinary' woman could impress you,—but there are remarkable women,—women of power and genius and lofty ambition."

"Les femmes incomprises—oh yes, I know!" laughed El-Râmi—"Troublesome creatures all, both to themselves and others. Why do you talk on these subjects, my dear Kremlin?—Is it the effect of your rejuvenated condition? I am sure there are many more interesting matters worthy of discussion. I shall never love—not in this planet; in some other state of existence I may experience the 'divine' emotion. But the meannesses, vanities, contemptible jealousies, and low spites of women such as inhabit this earth fill me with disgust and repulsion,—besides, women are treacherous,—and I loathe treachery."

At that moment Karl appeared at the dining-room window as a sign that breakfast was served, and they turned to go indoors.

"All the same, El-Râmi—" persisted Kremlin, laying one hand on his friend's arm—"Do not count on being able to escape the fate to which all humanity must succumb—"

"Death?" interposed El-Râmi lightly—"I have almost conquered that!"

"Aye, but you cannot conquer Love!" said Kremlin impressively—"Love is stronger than Death."

El-Râmi made no answer,—and they went in to breakfast. They did full justice to the meal, much to Karl's satisfaction, though he could not help stealing covert glances at his master's changed countenance, which had become so much fresher and younger since the previous day. How such a change had been effected he could not imagine, but on the whole he was disposed to be content with the evident improvement.

"Even if he is the devil himself—" he considered, his thoughts reverting to El-Râmi—"I am bound to say that the devil is a kind-hearted fellow. There's no doubt about that. I suppose I am an abandoned sinner only fit for the burning—but if God insists on making us old and sick and miserable, and the devil is able to make us young and strong and jolly, why let us be friends with the devil, say I! Oh my poor mother!"

With such curious emotions as these in his mind, it was rather difficult to maintain a composed face, and wait upon the two gentlemen with that grave deportment which it is the duty of every well-trained attendant to assume,—however, he managed fairly well, and got accustomed at last to hand his master a cup of coffee without staring at him till his eyes almost projected out of his head.

El-Râmi took his departure soon after breakfast, with a few recommendations to his friend not to work too hard on the problems suggested by the Disc.

"Ah, but I have now found a new clue;" said Kremlin triumphantly—"I found it in sleep. I shall work it out in the course of a few weeks, I dare say—and I will let you know if the result is successful. You see, thanks to you, my friend, I have time now,—there is no need to toil with feverish haste and anxiety—death that seemed so near, is thrust back in the distance—"

"Even so!" said El-Râmi with a strange smile—"In the far, far distance,—baffled and kept at bay. Oddly enough, there are some who say there is no death—"

"But there is—there must be!—" exclaimed Kremlin quickly.

El-Râmi raised his hand with a slight commanding gesture.

"It is not a certainty—" he said—"inasmuch as there is No certainty. And there is no 'Must-Be,'—there is only the Soul's 'Shall-Be'!"

And with these somewhat enigmatical words, he bade his friend farewell, and went his way.

XII

It was yet early in the afternoon when he arrived back in London. He went straight home to his own house, letting himself in as usual with his latch-key. In the hall he paused, listening. He half expected to hear Féraz playing one of his delicious dreamy improvisations,—but there was not a sound anywhere, and the deep silence touched him with an odd sense of disappointment and vague foreboding. His study door stood slightly ajar,—he pushed it wider open very noiselessly and looked in. His young brother was there, seated in a chair near the window, reading. El-Râmi gazed at him dubiously, with a slowly dawning sense that there was some alteration in his appearance which he could not all at once comprehend. Presently he realized that Féraz had evidently yielded to some overwhelming suggestion of personal vanity, which had induced him to put on more brilliant attire. He had changed his plain white linen garb for one of richer material, composed in the same Eastern fashion,—he wore a finely-chased gold belt, from which a gold-sheathed dagger depended,—and a few gold ornaments gleamed here and there among the drawn silken folds of his upper vest. He looked handsome enough for a new Agathon as he sat there apparently absorbed in study,—the big volume he perused resting partly on his knee,—but El-Râmi's brow contracted with sudden anger as he observed him from the half-open doorway where he stood, himself unseen,—and his dark face grew very pale. He threw the door back on its hinges with a clattering sound and entered the room.

"Féraz!"

Féraz looked up, lifting his eyelids indifferently and smiling coldly.

"What, El-Râmi! Back so early? I did not expect you till nightfall."

"Did you not?" said his brother, advancing slowly—"Pray how was that? You know I generally return after a night's absence early in the next day. Where is your usual word of welcome? What ails you? You seem in a very odd humour!"

"Do I?"—and Féraz stretched himself a little,—rose, yawning, and laid down the volume he held on the table—"I am not aware of it myself, I assure you. How did you find your old madman? And did you tell him you were nearly as mad as he?"

El-Râmi's eyes flashed indignant amazement and wrath.

"Féraz!—What do you mean?"

With a fierce impulsive movement Féraz turned and fully faced him,—all his forced and feigned calmness gone to the winds,—a glowing picture of youth and beauty and rage commingled.

"What do I mean?" he cried—"I mean this! That I am tired of being your slave-your 'subject' for conjurer's tricks of mesmerism,—that from henceforth I resist your power,—that I will not serve you—will not obey you—will not yield—no!—not an inch of my liberty—to your influence,—that I am a free man, as you are, and that I will have the full rights of both my freedom and manhood. You shall play no more with me; I refuse to be your dupe as I have been. This is what I mean!—and as I will have no deception or subterfuge between us,—for I scorn a lie,—hear the truth from me at once;—I know your secret—I have seen Her!"

El-Râmi stood erect,—immovable;—he was very pale; his breath came and went quickly—once his hand clenched, but he said nothing.

"I have seen Her!" cried Féraz again, flinging up his arms with an ecstatic wild gesture—"A creature fairer than any vision!—and you—you have the heart to bind her fast in darkness and in nothingness,—you it is who have shut her sight to the world,—you have made for her, through your horrible skill, a living death in which she knows nothing, feels nothing, sees nothing, loves nothing! I tell you it is a cursed deed you are doing,—a deed worse than murder—I would not have believed it of you! I thought your experiments were all for good,—I never would have deemed you capable of cruelty to a helpless woman! But I will release her from your spells,—she is too beautiful to be made her own living monument,—Zaroba is right—she needs life—joy—love!—she shall have them all;—through me!"

He paused, out of breath with the heat and violence of his own emotions;—El-Râmi stood, still immovably regarding him.

"You may be as angered as you please"—went on Féraz with sullen passion—"I care nothing now. It was Zaroba who bade me go up yonder and see her where she slept; . . . it was Zaroba—"

"'The woman tempted me and I did eat—'" quoted El-Râmi coldly,—"Of course it was Zaroba. No other than a woman could thus break a sworn word. Naturally it was Zaroba,—the paid and kept slave of my service, who owes to me her very existence,—who persuaded my brother to dishonour."

"Dishonour!" and Féraz laid his hand with a quick, almost savage gesture on the hilt of the dagger at his belt. El-Râmi's dark eyes blazed upon him scornfully.

"So soon a braggart of the knife?" he said. "What theatrical show is this? You—you—the poet, the dreamer, the musician—the gentle lad whose life was one of peaceful and innocent reverie—are you so soon changed to the mere swaggering puppy of manhood who pranks himself out in gaudy clothing, and thinks by vulgar threatening to overawe his betters? If so, 'tis a pity—but I shall not waste time in deploring it. Hear me, Féraz—I said 'dishonour,'—swallow the word as best you may, it is the only one that fits the act of prying into secrets not your own. But I am not angered,—the mischief wrought is not beyond remedy, and if it were there would be still less use in bewailing it. What is done cannot be undone. Now tell me,—you say you have seen Her. Whom have you seen?"

Féraz regarded him amazedly.

"Whom have I seen?" he echoed—"Whom should I see, if not the girl you keep locked in those upper rooms,—a beautiful maiden, sleeping her life away, in cruel darkness and ignorance of all things true and fair!"

"An enchanted princess, to your fancy—" said El-Râmi derisively. "Well, if you thought so, and if you believed yourself to be a new sort of Prince Charming, why, if she were only sleeping, did you not wake her?"

"Wake her?" exclaimed Féraz excitedly,—"Oh, I would have given my life to see those fringed lids uplift and show the wonders of the eyes beneath! I called her by every endearing name—I took her hands and warmed them in my own—I would have kissed her lips—"

"You dared not!" cried El-Râmi, fired beyond his own control, and making a fierce bound towards him—"You dared not pollute her by your touch!"

Féraz recoiled,—a sudden chill ran through his blood. His brother was transformed with the passion that surged through him,—his eyes flashed—his lips quivered—his very form seemed to tower up and tremble and dilate with rage.

"El-Râmi!" he stammered nervously, feeling all his newly-born defiance and bravado oozing away under the terrible magnetism of this man, whose fury was nearly as electric as that of a sudden thunderstorm,—"El-Râmi, I did no harm,—Zaroba was there beside me—"

"Zaroba!" echoed El-Râmi furiously—"Zaroba would stand by and see an angel violated, and think it the greatest happiness that could befall her sanctity! To be of common clay, with household joys and kitchen griefs, is Zaroba's idea of noble living. Oh rash unhappy Féraz! you say you know my secret—you do not know it—you cannot guess it! Foolish, ignorant boy!—did you think yourself a new Christ with power to raise the Dead?"

"The dead?" muttered Féraz, with white lips—"The dead? She—the girl I saw—lives and breathes. . ."

"By my will alone!" said El-Râmi—"By my force—by my knowledge—by my constant watchful care,—by my control over the subtle threads that connect Spirit with Matter. Otherwise, according to all the laws of ordinary nature, that girl is dead—she died in the Syrian desert six years ago!"

XIII

At these words, pronounced slowly and with emphatic distinctness, Féraz staggered back dizzily and sank into a chair,—drops of perspiration bedewed his forehead, and a sick faint feeling overcame him. He said nothing,—he could find no words in which to express his mingled horror and amazement. El-Râmi watched him keenly,—and presently Féraz, looking up, caught the calm, full and fiery regard of his brother's eyes. With a smothered cry, he raised his hands as though to shield himself from a blow.

"I will not have it;"—he muttered faintly—"You shall not force my thoughts,—I will believe nothing against my own will. You shall no longer delude my eyes and ears—I have read—I know,—I know how such trickery is done!"

El-Râmi uttered an impatient exclamation, and paced once or twice up and down the room.

"See here, Féraz;"—he said, suddenly stopping before the chair in which his brother sat,—"I swear to you that I am not exercising one iota of my influence upon you. When I do, I will tell you, that you may be prepared to resist me if you choose. I am using no power of any kind upon you—be satisfied of that. But, as you have forced your way into the difficult labyrinth of my life's work, it is as well that you should have an explanation of what seems to you full of mysterious evil and black magic. You accuse me of wickedness,—you tell me I am guilty of a deed worse than murder. Now this is mere rant and nonsense,—you speak in such utter ignorance of the facts, that I forgive you, as one is bound to forgive all faults committed through sheer want of instruction. I do not think I am a wicked man"—he paused, with an earnest, almost pathetic expression on his face—"at least I strive not to be. I am ambitious and sceptical—and I am not altogether convinced of there being any real intention of ultimate good in the arrangements of this world as they at present exist,—but I work without any malicious intention; and without undue boasting I believe I am as honest and conscientious as the best of my kind. But that is neither here nor there,—as I said before, you have broken into a secret not intended for your knowledge—and that you may not misunderstand me yet more thoroughly than you seem to do, I will tell you what I never wished to bother your brains with. For you have been very happy till now, Féraz—happy in the beautiful simplicity of the life you led—the life of a poet and dreamer,—the happiest life in the world!"

He broke off, with a short sigh of mingled vexation and regret— then he seated himself immediately opposite his brother and went on—

"You were too young to understand the loss it was to us both when our parents died,—or to know the immense reputation our father Nadir Zarânos had won throughout the East for his marvellous skill in natural science and medicine. He died in the prime of his life,—our mother followed him within a month,—and you were left to my charge,—you a child then, and I almost a man. Our father's small but rare library came into my possession, together with his own manuscripts treating of the scientific and spiritual organization of Nature in all its branches,—and these opened such extraordinary vistas of possibility to me as to what might be done if such and such theories could be practically carried out and acted upon, that I became fired with the ardour of discovery. The more I studied, the more convinced and eager I became in the pursuit of such knowledge as is generally deemed supernatural, and beyond the reach of all human inquiry. One or two delicate experiments in chemistry of a rare and subtle nature were entirely successful,—and by-and-bye I began to look about for a subject on whom I could practise the power I had attained. There was no one whom I could personally watch and surround with my hourly influence except yourself,—therefore I made my first great trial upon you."

Féraz moved uneasily in his chair,—his face wore a doubtful, half-sullen expression, but he listened to El-Râmi's every word with vivid and almost painful interest.

"At that time you were a mere boy—" pursued El-Râmi—"but strong and vigorous, and full of the mischievous pranks and sports customary to healthy boyhood. I began by slow degrees to educate you—not with the aid of schools or tutors—but simply by my Will. You had a singularly unretentive brain,—you were never fond of music—you would never read,—you had no taste for study. Your delight was to ride—to swim like a fish,—to handle a gun—to race, to leap,—to play practical jokes on other boys of your own age and fight them if they resented it;—all very amusing performances no doubt, but totally devoid of intelligence. Judging you dispassionately, I found that you were a very charming gamesome animal,—physically perfect—with a Mind somewhere if one could only discover it, and a Soul or Spirit behind the Mind—if one could only discover that also. I set myself the task of finding out both these hidden portions of your composition—and of not only finding them, but moulding and influencing them according to my desire and plan."

A faint tremor shook the younger man's frame—but he said nothing.

"You are attending to me closely, I hope?" said El-Râmi pointedly—"because you must distinctly understand that this conversation is the first and last we shall have on the matter. After today, the subject must drop between us forever, and I shall refuse to answer any more questions. You hear?"

Féraz bent his head.

"I hear—" he answered with an effort—"And what I hear seems strange and terrible!"

"Strange and terrible?" echoed El-Râmi. "How so? What is there strange or terrible in the pursuit of Wisdom? Yet—perhaps you are right, and the blank ignorance of a young child is best,—for there is something appalling in the infinitude of knowledge—an infinitude which must remain infinite, if it be true that there is a God who is forever thinking, and whose thoughts become realities."

He paused, with a rapt look,—then resumed in the same even tone,—

"When I had made up my mind to experimentalize upon you, I lost no time in commencing my work. One of my chief desires was to avoid the least risk of endangering your health—your physical condition was admirable, and I resolved to keep it so. In this I succeeded. I made life a joy to you—the mere act of breathing a pleasure—you grew up before my eyes like the vigorous sapling of an oak that rejoices in the mere expansion of its leaves to the fresh air. The other and more subtle task was harder,—it needed all my patience—all my skill,-but I was at last rewarded. Through my concentrated influence, which surrounded you as with an atmosphere in which you moved, and slept, and woke again, and which forced every fibre of your brain to respond to mine, the animal faculties which were strongest in you, became subdued and tamed,—and the mental slowly asserted themselves. I resolved you should be a poet and musician—you became both;—you developed an ardent love of study, and every few months that passed gave richer promise of your ripening intelligence. Moreover, you were happy,—happy in everything—happiest perhaps in your music, which became your leading passion. Having thus, unconsciously to yourself, fostered your mind by the silent workings of my own, and trained it to grow up like a flower to the light, I thought I might make my next attempt, which was to probe for that subtle essence we call the Soul—the large wings that are hidden in the moth's chrysalis;—and influence that too;—but there—there by some inexplicable opposition of forces, I was baffled."

Féraz raised himself half out of his chair, his lips parted in breathless eagerness—his eyes dilated and sparkling.

"Baffled?" he repeated hurriedly—"How do you mean?—in what way?"

"Oh, in various ways—" replied El-Râmi, looking at him with a somewhat melancholy expression—"Ways that I myself am not able to comprehend. I found I could influence your Inner Self to obey me,—but only to a very limited extent, and in mere trifles,—for example, as you yourself know, I could compel you to come to me from a certain distance in response to my thought,—but in higher things you escaped me. You became subject to long trances,—this I was prepared for, as it was partially my work,—and during these times of physical unconsciousness, it was evident that your Soul enjoyed a life and liberty superior to anything these earth-regions can offer. But you could never remember all you saw in these absences,—indeed, the only suggestions you seem to have brought away from that other state of existence are the strange melodies you play sometimes, and that idea you have about your native Star."

A curious expression flitted across Féraz's face as he heard—and his lips parted in a slight smile, but he said nothing.

"Therefore,"—pursued his brother meditatively—"as I could get no clear exposition of other worlds from you, as I had hoped to do, I knew I had failed to command you in a spiritual sense. But my dominance over your Mind continued; it continues still,—nay, my good Féraz!"—this, as Féraz seemed about to utter some impetuous word—"Pray that you may never be able to shake off my force entirely,—for if you do, you will lose what the people of a grander and poetic day called Genius—and what the miserable Dry-as-Dusts of our modern era call Madness—the only gift of the gods that has ever served to enlighten and purify the world. But your genius, Féraz, belongs to me;—I gave it to you, and I can take it back again if I so choose;—and leave you as you originally were—a handsome animal with no more true conception of art or beauty than my Lord Melthorpe, or his spendthrift young cousin Vaughan."

Féraz had listened thus far in silence,—but now he sprang out of his chair with a reckless gesture.

"I cannot bear it!" he said—"I cannot bear it! El-Râmi, I cannot—I will not!"

"Cannot bear what?" inquired his brother with a touch of satire in his tone—"Pray be calm!—there is no necessity for such melodramatic excitement. Cannot bear what?"

"I will not owe everything to you!" went on Féraz, passionately—"How can I endure to know that my very thoughts are not my own, but emanate from you?—that my music has been instilled into me by you?—that you possess me by your power, body and brain,—great Heaven! it is awful—intolerable—impossible!"

El-Râmi rose and laid one hand gently on his shoulder—he recoiled shudderingly—and the elder man sighed heavily.

"You tremble at my touch,—" he said sadly—"the touch of a hand that has never wilfully wrought you harm, but has always striven to make life beautiful to you? Well!—be it so!—you have only to say the word, Féraz, and you shall owe me nothing. I will undo all I have done,—and you shall reassume the existence for which Nature originally made you—an idle voluptuous wasting of time in sensualism and folly. And even that form of life you must owe to Someone,—even that you must account for—to God!"

The young man's head drooped,—a faint sense of shame stirred in him, but he was still resentful and sullen.

"What have I done to you," went on El-Râmi, "that you should turn from me thus, all because you have seen a dead woman's face for an hour? I have made your thoughts harmonious—I have given you pleasure such as the world's ways cannot give—your mind has been as a clear mirror in which only the fairest visions of life were reflected. You would alter this?—then do so, if you decide thereon,—but weigh the matter well and long, before you shake off my touch, my tenderness, my care."

His voice faltered a little—but he quickly controlled his emotion, and continued—

"I must ask you to sit down again and hear me out patiently to the end of my story. At present I have only told you what concerns yourself—and how the failure of my experiment upon the spiritual part of your nature, obliged me to seek for another subject on whom to continue my investigations. As far as you are personally concerned, no failure is

MARIE CORELLI

apparent—for your spirit is allowed frequent intervals of supernatural freedom, in which you have experiences that give you peculiar pleasure, though you are unable to impart them to me with positive lucidity. You visit a Star—so you say—with which you really seem to have some home connection—but you never get beyond this, so that it would appear that any higher insight is denied you. Now what I needed to obtain, was not only a higher insight, but the highest knowledge that could possibly be procured through a mingled combination of material and spiritual essences, and it was many a long and weary day before I found what I sought. At last my hour came—as it comes to all who have the patience and fortitude to wait for it."

He paused a moment—then went on more quickly—

"You remember of course that occasion of which we chanced upon a party of Arab wanderers who were journeying across the Syrian desert?—all poor and ailing, and almost destitute of food or water?"

"I remember it perfectly!" and Féraz, seating himself opposite his brother again, listened with renewed interest and attention.

"They had two dying persons with them," continued El-Râmi—"An elderly woman—a widow, known as Zaroba,—the other an orphan girl of about twelve years of age named Lilith. Both were perishing of fever and famine. I came to the rescue. I saved Zaroba,—and she, with the passionate im—pulsiveness of her race, threw herself in gratitude at my feet, and swore by all her most sacred beliefs that she would be my slave from henceforth as long as she lived. All her people were dead, she told me—she was alone in the world—she prayed me to let her be my faithful servant. And truly, her fidelity has never failed—till now. But of that hereafter. The child Lilith, more fragile of frame and weakened to the last extremity of exhaustion—in spite of my unremitting care—died. Do you thoroughly understand me—she died."

"She died!" repeated Féraz slowly—"Well—what then?"

"I was supporting her in my arms"—said El-Râmi, the ardour of his description growing upon him, and his black eyes dilating and burning like great jewels under the darkness of his brows—"when she drew her last breath and sank back—a corpse. But before her flesh had time to stiffen,—before the warmth had gone out of her blood,—an idea, wild and daring, flashed across my mind. 'If this child has a Soul,' I said to myself—'I will stay it in its flight from hence! It shall become the new Ariel of my wish and will—and not till it has performed my bidding to the utmost extent will I, like another Prospero, give it its true liberty.

And I will preserve the body, its mortal shell, by artificial means, that through its medium I may receive the messages of the Spirit in mortal language such as I am able to understand.' No sooner had I conceived my bold project than I proceeded to carry it into execution. I injected into the still warm veins of the dead girl a certain fluid whose properties I alone know the working of—and then I sought and readily obtained permission from the Arabs to bury her in the desert, while they went on their way. They were in haste to continue their journey, and were grateful to me for taking this office off their hands. That very day—the day the girl died—I sent you from me, as you know, bidding you make all possible speed, on an errand which I easily invented, to the Brethren of the Cross in the Island of Cyprus,—you went obediently enough,—surprised perhaps, but suspecting nothing. That same evening when the heats abated and the moon rose, the caravan re—sumed its pilgrimage, leaving Lilith's dead body with me, and also the woman Zaroba, who volunteered to remain and serve me in my tent, an offer which I accepted, seeing that it was her own desire, and that she would be useful to me. She, poor silly soul, took me then for a sort of god, because she was unable to understand the miracle of her own recovery from imminent death, and I felt certain I could rely upon her fidelity. Part of my plan I told her,—she heard with mingled fear and reverence,—the magic of the East was in her blood, however, and she had a superstitious belief that a truly 'wise man' could do anything. So, for several days we stayed encamped in the desert—I passing all my hours beside the dead Lilith,—dead, but to a certain extent living through artificial means. As soon as I received proof positive that my experiment was likely to be successful, I procured means to continue my journey on to Alexandria, and thence to England. To all enquirers I said the girl was a patient of mine who was suffering from epileptic trances, and the presence of Zaroba, who filled her post admirably as nurse and attendant, was sufficient to stop the mouths of would-be scandal-mongers. I chose my residence in London, because it is the largest city in the world, and the one most suited to pursue a course of study in, without one's motives becoming generally known. One can be more alone in London than in a desert if one chooses. Now, you know all. You have seen the dead Lilith,—the human chrysalis of the moth,—but there is a living Lilith too—the Soul of Lilith, which is partly free and partly captive, but in both conditions is always the servant of my Will!"

Féraz looked at him in mingled awe and fear.

"El-Râmi,"—he said tremulously—"What you tell me is wonderful—terrible—almost beyond belief,—but, I know something of your power and I must believe you. Only—surely you are in error when you say that Lilith is dead? How can she be dead, if you have given her life?"

"Can you call that life which sleeps perpetually and will not wake?" demanded El-Râmi.

"Would you have her wake?" asked Féraz, his heart beating quickly.

El-Râmi bent his burning gaze upon him.

"Not so,—for if she wakes, in the usual sense of waking—she dies a second death from which there can be no recall. There is the terror of the thing. Zaroba's foolish teaching, and your misguided yielding to her temptation, might have resulted in the fatal end to my life's best and grandest work. But—I forgive you;—you did not know,—and she—she did not wake."

"She did not wake," echoed Féraz softly. "No—but—she smiled!"

El-Râmi still kept his eyes fixed upon him,—there was an odd sense of irritation in his usually calm and coldly balanced organization—a feeling he strove in vain to subdue. She smiled!—the exquisite Lilith—the life-in-death Lilith smiled, because Féraz had called her by some endearing name! Surely it could not be!—and smothering his annoyance, he turned towards the writing-table and feigned to arrange some books and papers there.

"El-Râmi—" murmured Féraz again, but timidly—"If she was a child when she died as you say—how is it she has grown to womanhood?"

"By artificial vitality,"—said El-Râmi—"As a flower is forced under a hot-house,—and with no more trouble, and less consciousness of effort than a rose under a glass dome."

"Then she lives,—" declared Féraz impetuously. "She lives,—artificial or natural, she has vitality. Through your power she exists, and if you chose, oh, if you chose, El-Râmi, you could wake her to the fullest life—to perfect consciousness,—to joy—to love!—Oh, she is in a blessed trance—you cannot call her dead!"

El-Râmi turned upon him abruptly.

"Be silent!" he said sternly—"I read your thoughts,—control them, if you are wise! You echo Zaroba's prating—Zaroba's teaching. Lilith is dead, I tell you,—dead to you,—and, in the sense you mean—dead to me."

XIV

After this, a long silence fell between them. Féraz sat moodily in his chair, conscious of a certain faint sense of shame. He was sorry that he had wilfully trespassed upon his brother's great secret,—and yet there was an angry pride in him,—a vague resentment at having been kept so long in ignorance of this wonderful story of Lilith,—which made him reluctant to acknowledge himself in the wrong. Moreover, his mind was possessed and haunted by Lilith's face,—the radiant face that looked like that of an angel sleeping,—and perplexedly thinking over all he had heard, he wondered if he would ever again have the opportunity of beholding what had seemed to him the incarnation of ideal loveliness. Surely yes!—Zaroba would be his friend,—Zaroba would let him gaze his fill on that exquisite form—would let him touch that little, ethereally delicate hand, as soft as velvet and as white as snow! Absorbed in these reflections, he scarcely noticed that El-Râmi had moved away from him to the writing-table, and that he now sat there in his ebony chair, turning over the leaves of the curious Arabic volume which Féraz had had such trouble in deciphering on the previous day. The silence in the room continued; outside there was the perpetual sullen roar of raging restless London,—now and again the sharp chirruping of contentious sparrows, arguing over a crumb of food as parliamentary agitators chatter over a crumb of difference, stirred the quiet air. Féraz stretched himself and yawned,—he was getting sleepy, and as he realized this fact, he nervously attributed it to his brother's influence, and sprang up abruptly, rubbing his eyes and pushing his thick hair from his brows. At his hasty movement, El-Râmi turned slowly towards him with a grave yet kindly smile.

"Well, Féraz"—he said—"Do you still think me 'wicked' now you know all? Speak frankly—do not be afraid."

Féraz paused, irresolute.

"I do not know what to think—" he answered hesitatingly,—"Your experiment is of course wonderful,—but—as I said before—to me, it seems terrible."

"Life is terrible—" said El-Râmi—"Death is terrible,—Love is terrible,—God is terrible. All Nature's pulses beat to the note of Terror,—terror of the Unknown that May Be,—terror of the Known that Is!"

His deep voice rang with impressive solemnity through the room,—

his eyes were full of that strange lurid gleam which gave them the appearance of having a flame behind them.

"Come here, Féraz," he continued—"Why do you stand at so cautious a distance from me? With that brave show-dagger at your belt, are you a coward? Silly lad!—I swear to you my influence shall not touch you unless I warn you of it beforehand. Come!"

Féraz obeyed, but slowly and with an uncertain step. His brother looked at him attentively as he came,—then, with a gesture indicating the volume before him, he said—"You found this book on my table yesterday and tried to read it,—is it not so?"

"I did."

"Well, and have you learnt anything from it?" pursued El-Râmi with a strange smile.

"Yes. I learnt how the senses may be deceived by trickery—" retorted Féraz with some heat and quickness—"and how a clever magnetizer—like yourself—may fool the eye and delude the ear with sights and sounds that have no existence."

"Precisely. Listen to this passage;"—and El-Râmi read aloud—"The King when he had any affair, assembled the Priests without the City Memphis, and the People met together in the streets of the said City. Then they (the Priests) made their entrance one after another in order, the drum beating before them to bring the people together; and every-one made some miraculous discovery of his Magick and Wisdom. One had, to their thinking who looked on him, his face surrounded with a light like that of the Sun, so that none could look earnestly upon him. Another seemed clad with a Robe beset with precious stones of divers colours, green, red, or yellow, or wrought with gold. Another came mounted on a Lion compassed with Serpents like Girdles. Another came in covered with a canopy or pavilion of Light. Another appeared surrounded with Fire turning about him, so as that nobody durst come near him. Another was seen with dreadful birds perching about his head and shaking their wings like black eagles and vultures. In fine, everyone did what was taught him;—yet all was but Apparition and Illusion without any reality, insomuch that when they came up to the King they spake thus to him:—You imagined that it was so-and-so,—but the truth is that it was such or such a thing.'* The A B C of

---

* This remarkable passage on the admitted effects of hypnotism as practised by the priests of ancient Egypt, will be found in an old history of the building of the Pyramids

magnetism is contained in the last words—" continued El-Râmi lifting his eyes from the book,—"The merest tyro in the science knows that; and also realizes that the Imagination is the centre of both physical and bodily health or disease. And did you learn nothing more?"

Féraz made a half-angry gesture in the negative.

"What a pity!"—and his brother surveyed him with good-humoured compassion—"To know how a 'miracle' is done is one thing—but to do it is quite another matter. Now let me recall to your mind what I previously told you—that from this day henceforth, I forbid you to make any allusion to the subject of my work. I forbid you to mention the name of Lilith,—and I forbid you to approach or to enter the room where her body lies. You understand me?—I forbid you!"

Féraz's eyes flashed angry opposition, and he drew himself up with a haughty self-assertiveness.

"You forbid me!" he echoed proudly—"What right have you to forbid me anything? And how if I refuse to obey?"

El-Râmi rose and confronted him, one hand resting on the big Arabic volume.

"You will not refuse—" he said—"because I will take no refusal. You will obey, because I exact your obedience. Moreover, you will swear by the Most Holy Name of God, that you will never, either to me, or to any other living soul, speak a syllable concerning my life's greatest experiment,—you will swear that the name of Lilith shall never pass your lips—"

But here Féraz interrupted him.

"El-Râmi, I will not swear!" he cried desperately—"The name of Lilith is sweet to me!—why should I not utter it,—why should I not sing of it—why should I not even remember it in my prayers?"

A terrible look darkened El-Râmi's countenance; his brows contracted darkly, and his lips drew together in a close resolute line.

"There are a thousand reasons why—" he said in low fierce accents,— "One is, that the soul of Lilith and the body of Lilith are mine, and that you have no share in their possession. She does not need your songs— still less has she need of your prayers. Rash fool!—you shall forget the name of Lilith—and you shall swear, as I command you. Resist my will if you can,—now!—I warn you in time!"

---

entitled—"The Egyptian Account of the Pyramids"—Written in the Arabic by Murtadi the son of Gaphiphus—date about 1400.

He seemed to grow in height as he spoke,—his eyes blazed ominously, and Féraz, meeting that lightning-like glance, knew how hopeless it would be for him to attempt to oppose such an intense force as was contained in this man's mysterious organization. He tried his best,—but in vain,—with every second he felt his strength oozing out of him—his power of resistance growing less and less.

"Swear!" said El-Râmi imperatively—"Swear in God's Name to keep my secret—swear by Christ's Death!—swear on this!"

And he held out a small golden crucifix.

Mechanically, but still devoutly, Féraz instantly dropped on one knee, and kissed the holy emblem.

"I swear!" he said—but as he spoke, the rising tears were in his throat, and he murmured—"Forget the name of Lilith!—never!"

"In God's Name!" said El-Râmi.

"In God's Name!"

"By Christ's Death!"

Féraz trembled. In the particular form of religion professed by himself and his brother, this was the most solemn and binding vow that could be taken. And his voice was faint and unsteady as he repeated it—

"By Christ's Death!"

El-Râmi put aside the crucifix.

"That is well;—" he said, in mild accents which contrasted agreeably with his previous angry tone—"Such oaths are chronicled in heaven, remember,—and whoever breaks his sworn word is accursed of the gods. But you,—you will keep your vow, Féraz,—and. . . you will also forget the name of Lilith,—if I choose!"

Féraz stood mute and motionless,—he would have said something, but somehow words failed him to express what was in his mind. He was angry, he said to himself,—he had sworn a foolish oath against his will, and he had every right to be angry—very angry, but with whom? Surely not with his brother—his friend,—his protector for so many years? As he thought of this, shame and penitence and old affection grew stronger and welled up in his heart, and he moved slowly towards El-Râmi, with hands outstretched.

"Forgive me;"—he said humbly. "I have offended you—I am sorry. I will show my repentance in whatever way you please,—but do not, El-Râmi—do not ask me, do not force me to forget the name of Lilith,—it is like a note in music, and it cannot do you harm that I should think of it sometimes. For the rest I will obey you faithfully,—and for what is past, I ask your pardon."

El-Râmi took his hands and pressed them affectionately in his own.

"No sooner asked than granted—" he said—"You are young, Féraz,—and I am not so harsh as you perhaps imagine. The impulsiveness of youth should always be quickly pardoned—seeing how gracious a thing youth is, and how short a time it lasts. Keep your poetic dreams and fancies—take the sweetness of thought without its bitterness,—and if you are content to have it so, let me still help to guide your fate. If not, why, nothing is easier than to part company, part as good friends and brethren always,—you on your chosen road and I on mine,—who knows but that after all you might not be happier so?"

Féraz lifted his dark eyes, heavy with unshed tears.

"Would you send me from you?" he asked falteringly.

"Not I! I would not send you,—but you might wish to go."

"Never!" said Féraz resolutely—"I feel that I must stay with you—till the end."

He uttered the last words with a sigh, and El-Râmi looked at him curiously.

"Till the end?"—he repeated—"What end?"

"Oh, the end of life or death or anything;" replied Féraz with forced lightness—"There must surely be an end somewhere, as there was a beginning."

"That is rather a doubtful problem!" said El-Râmi—"The great question is, was there ever a Beginning? and will there ever be an End?"

Féraz gave a languid gesture.

"You inquire too far,"—he said wearily—"I always think you inquire too far. I cannot follow you—I am tired. Do you want anything?—can I do anything? or may I go to my room? I want to be alone for a little while, just to consider quietly what my life is, and what I can make of it."

"A truly wise and philosophical subject of meditation!" observed El-Râmi, and he smiled kindly and held out his hand. Féraz laid his own slender fingers somewhat listlessly in that firm warm palm;—then—with a sudden start, looked eagerly around him. The air seemed to have grown denser,—there was a delicious scent of roses in the room, and hush! . . . What entrancing voices were those that sang in the distance? He listened absorbed;—the harmonies were very sweet and perfect—almost he thought he could distinguish words. Loosening his hand from his brother's clasp, the melody seemed to grow fainter and fainter,—recognising this, he roused himself with a quick movement, his eyes flashing with a sudden gleam of defiance.

"More magic music!" he said—"I hear the sound of singing, and you know that I hear it! I understand!—it is imagined music—your work, El-Râmi,—your skill. It is wonderful, beautiful,—and you are the most marvellous man on earth!—you should have been a priest of old Egypt! Yes—I am tired—I will rest;—I will accept the dreams you offer me for what they are worth,—but I must remember that there are realities as well as dreams,—and I shall not forget the name of—Lilith!"

He smiled audaciously, looking as graceful as a pictured Adonis in the careless yet proud attitude he had unconsciously assumed,—then with a playful yet affectionate salutation he moved to the doorway.

"Call me if you want me," he said.

"I shall not want you;"—replied his brother, regarding him steadily.

The door opened and closed again,—Féraz was gone.

Shutting up the great volume in front of him, El-Râmi rested his arms upon it, and stared into vacancy with darkly-knitted brows.

"What premonition of evil is there in the air?" he muttered—"What restless emotion is at work within me? Are the Fates turning against me?—and am I after all nothing but the merest composition of vulgar matter—a weak human wretch capable of being swayed by changeful passions? What is it? What am I that I should vex my spirit thus—all because Lilith smiled at the sound of a voice that was not mine!"

XV

Just then there came a light tap at his door. He opened it,—and Zaroba stood before him. No repentance for her fault of disobedience and betrayal of trust, clouded that withered old face of hers,—her deep-set dark eyes glittered with triumph, and her whole aspect was one of commanding, and almost imperious dignity. In fact, she made such an ostentatious show of her own self-importance in her look and manner that El-Râmi stared at her for a moment in haughty amazement at what he considered her effrontery in thus boldly facing him after her direct violation of his commands. He eyed her up and down—she returned him glance for glance unquailingly.

"Let me come in—" she said in her strong harsh voice—"I make no doubt but that the poor lad Féraz has told you his story—now, as God liveth, you must hear mine."

El-Râmi turned upon his heel with a contemptuous movement, and went back to his own chair by the writing-table. Zaroba, paying no heed to the wrath conveyed by this mute action, stalked in also, and shutting the door after her, came and stood close beside him.

"Write down what you think of me—" she said, pointing with her yellow forefinger at the pens and paper—"Write the worst. I have betrayed my trust. That is true. I have disobeyed your commands after keeping them for six long years. True again. What else?"

El-Râmi fixed his eyes upon her, a world of indignation and reproach in their brilliant depths, and snatching up a pencil he wrote on a slip of paper rapidly—

"Nothing else—nothing more than treachery! You are unworthy of your sacred task you are false to your sworn fidelity."

Zaroba read the lines as quickly as he wrote them, but when she came to the last words she made a swift gesture of denial and drew herself up haughtily.

"No—not false!" she said passionately—"Not false to you, El-Râmi, I swear! I would slay myself rather than do you wrong. You saved my life, though my life was not worth saving, and for that gentle deed I would pour out every drop of my blood to requite you. No, no! Zaroba is not false—she is true!"

She tossed up her arms wildly,—then suddenly folding them tight across her chest, she dropped her voice to a gentler and more appealing tone.

"Hear me, El-Râmi!—Hear me, wise man and Master of the magic of the East!—I have done well for you;—well! I have disobeyed you for your own sake,—I have betrayed my trust that you may discover how and where you may find your best reward. I have sinned with the resolved intent to make you happy,—as God liveth, I speak truth from my heart and soul!"

El-Râmi turned towards her, his face expressing curiosity in spite of himself. He was very pale, and outwardly he was calm enough—but his nerves were on the rack of suspense—he wondered what sudden frenzied idea had possessed this woman that she should comport herself as though she held some strange secret of which the very utterance might move heaven and earth to wonderment. Controlling his feelings with an effort, he wrote again—

"There exists no reason for disloyalty. Your excuses avail nothing—let me hear no more of them. Tell me of Lilith—what news?"

"News!" repeated Zaroba scornfully—"What news should there be? She breathes and sleeps as she has breathed and slept always—she has not stirred. There is no harm done by my bidding Féraz look on her,—no change is wrought except in you, El-Râmi!—except in you!"

Half springing from his chair he confronted her—then recollecting her deafness, he bit his lips angrily and sank back again with an assumed air of indifference.

"You have heard Féraz—" pursued Zaroba, with that indescribable triumph of hers lighting up her strong old face—"You must now hear me. I thank the gods that my ears are closed to the sound of human voices, and that neither reproach nor curse can move me to dismay. And I am ignorant of your magic, El-Râmi,—the magic that chills the blood and sends the spirit flitting through the land of dreams,—the only magic I know is the magic of the heart—of the passions,—a natural witchcraft that conquers the world!"

She waved her arms to and fro—then crossing them on her bosom, she made a profound half-mocking salutation.

"Wise El-Râmi Zarânos!" she said. "Proud ruler of the arts and sciences that govern Nature,—have you ever, with all your learning, taken the measure of your own passions, and slain them so utterly that they shall never rise up again? They sleep at times, like the serpents of the desert, coiled up in many a secret place,—but at the touch of some unwary heel, some casual falling pebble, they unwind their lengths-they raise their glittering heads, and sting! I, Zaroba, have felt them here"—and she pressed her hands more closely on her breast—"I have felt their poison in my blood—sweet poison, sweeter than life!—their stings have given me all the joy my days have ever known. But it is not of myself that I should speak—it is of you—of you, whose life is lonely, and for whom the coming years hold forth no prospect of delight. When I lay dying in the desert and you restored me to strength again, I swore to serve you with fidelity. As God liveth, El-Râmi, I have kept my vow,—and in return for the life you gave me I bid you take what is yours to claim—the love of Lilith!"

El-Râmi rose out of his chair, white to the lips, and his hand shook. If he could have concentrated his inward forces at that moment, he would have struck Zaroba dumb by one effort of his will, and so put an end to her undesired eloquence,—but something, he knew not what, disturbed the centre of his self-control, and his thoughts were in a whirl. He despised himself for the unusual emotion which seized him—inwardly he was furious with the garrulous old woman,—but outwardly he could only make her an angry imperative sign to be silent.

"Nay, I will not cease from speaking—" said Zaroba imperturbably—"for all has to be said now, or never. The love of Lilith! imagine it, El-Râmi!—the clinging of her young white arms—the kisses of her sweet red mouth,—the open glances of her innocent eyes—all this is yours, if you but say the word. Listen! For six and more long years I have watched her—and I have watched you. She has slept the sleep of death-in-life, for you have willed it so,—and in that sleep, she has imperceptibly passed from childhood to womanhood. You—cold as a man of bronze or marble,—have made of her nothing but a 'subject' for your science,—and never a breath of love or longing on your part, or even admiration for her beauty, has stirred the virgin-trance in which she lies. And I have marvelled at it—I have thought—and I have prayed;—the gods have answered me, and now I know!"

She clapped her hands ecstatically, and then went on.

"The child Lilith died,—but you, El-Râmi, you caused her to live again. And she lives still—yes, though it may suit your fancy to declare her dead. She is a woman—you are a man;—you dare not keep her longer in that living death—you dare not doom her to perpetual darkness!—the gods would curse you for such cruelty, and who may abide their curse? I, Zaroba, have sworn it—Lilith shall know the joys of love!—and you, El-Râmi Zarânos, shall be her lover!—and for this holy end I have employed the talisman which alone sets fire to the sleeping passions. . ." and she craned her neck forward and almost hissed the word in his ear—'Jealousy!'"

El-Râmi smiled—a cold derisive smile, which implied the most utter contempt for the whole of Zaroba's wild harangue. She, however, went on undismayed, and with increasing excitement—

"Jealousy!" she cried—"The little asp is in your soul already, proud El-Râmi Zarânos, and why? Because another's eyes have looked on Lilith! This was my work! It was I who led Féraz into her chamber,—it was I who bade him kneel beside her as she slept,—it was I who let him touch her hand,—and though I could not hear his voice I know he called upon her to awaken. In vain!—he might as well have called the dead—I knew she would not stir for him—her very breath belongs to you. But I—I let him gaze upon her beauty and worship it,—all his young soul was in his eyes—he looked and looked again and loved what he beheld! And mark me yet further, El-Râmi,—I saw her smile when Féraz took her hand,—so, though she did not move, she felt; she felt a touch that was not yours,—not yours, El-Râmi!—as God liveth, she is not quite so much your own as once she was!"

As she said this and laughed in that triumphant way, El-Râmi advanced one step towards her with a fierce movement as though he would have thrust her from the room,—checking himself, however, he seized the pencil again and wrote—

"I have listened to you with more patience than you deserve. You are an ignorant woman and foolish—your fancies have no foundation whatever in fact. Your disobedience might have ruined my life's work,—as it is, I dare say some mischief has been done. Return to your duties, and take heed how you trespass against my command in future. If you dare to speak to me on this subject again I will have you shipped back to your own land and left there, as friendless and as unprovided for as you were when I saved you from death by famine. Go—and let me hear no more foolishness."

Zaroba read, and her face darkened and grew weary—but the pride and obstinacy of her own convictions remained written on every line of her features. She bowed her head resignedly, however, and said in slow even tones—

"El-Râmi Zarânos is wise,—El-Râmi Zarânos is master. But let him remember the words of Zaroba. Zaroba is also skilled in the ways and the arts of the East,—and the voice of Fate speaks sometimes to the lowest as well as to the highest. There are the laws of Life and the laws of Death—but there are also the laws of Love. Without the laws of Love, the Universe would cease to be,—it is for El-Râmi Zarânos to prove himself stronger than the Universe,—if he can!"

She made the usual obsequious "salaam" common to Eastern races, and then with a swift, silent movement left the room, closing the door noiselessly behind her. El-Râmi stood where she had left him, idly tearing up the scraps of paper on which he had written his part of the conversation,—he was hardly conscious of thought, so great were his emotions of surprise and self-contempt.

"'O what a rogue and peasant-slave am I!'" he muttered, quoting his favourite "Hamlet"—"Why did I not paralyze her tongue before she spoke? Where had fled my force,—what became of my skill? Surely I could have struck her down before me with the speed of a lightning-flash—only-she is a woman—and old. Strange how these feminine animals always harp on the subject of love, as though it were the Be-all and End-all of everything. The love of Lilith! Oh fool! The love of a corpse kept breathing by artificial means! And what of the Soul of Lilith? Can It love? Can It hate? Can It even feel? Surely not. It is an ethereal transparency,—a delicate film which takes upon itself the reflex of all existing things without experiencing personal emotion. Such is the Soul, as I believe in it—an immortal Essence, in itself formless, yet capable of taking all forms,—ignorant of the joys or pains of feeling, yet reflecting all shades of sensation as a crystal reflects all colours in the prism. This, and no more."

He paced up and down the room—and a deep involuntary sigh escaped him.

"No—" he murmured, as though answering some inward query— "No, I will not go to her now—not till the appointed time. I resolved on an absence of forty-eight hours, and forty-eight hours it shall be. Then I will go,—and she will tell me all—I shall know the full extent of the mischief done. And so Féraz 'looked and looked again, and loved what he beheld!' Love! The very word seems like a desecrating blot on the virgin soul of Lilith!"

XVI

Féraz meanwhile was fast asleep in his own room. He had sought to be alone for the purpose of thinking quietly and connectedly over all he had heard,—but no sooner had he obtained the desired solitude than a sudden and heavy drowsiness overcame him, such as he was unable to resist, and throwing himself on his bed, he dropped into a profound slumber, which deepened as the minutes crept on. The afternoon wore slowly away,—sunset came and passed,—the coming shadows lengthened, and just as the first faint star peeped out in the darkening skies he awoke, startled to find it so late. He sprang from his couch, bewildered and vexed with himself,—it was time for supper, he thought, and El-Râmi must be waiting. He hastened to the study, and there he found his brother conversing with a gentleman,—no other than Lord Melthorpe, who was talking in a loud cheerful voice, which contrasted oddly with El-Râmi's slow musical accents, that ever had a note of sadness in them. When Féraz made his hurried entrance, his eyes humid with sleep, yet dewily brilliant,—his thick dark hair tangled in rough curls above his brows, Lord Melthorpe stared at him in honestly undisguised admiration, and then glanced at El-Râmi inquiringly.

"My brother, Féraz Zarânos—" said El-Râmi, readily performing the ceremony of introduction—"Féraz, this is Lord Melthorpe,—you have heard me speak of him."

Féraz bowed with his usual perfect grace, and Lord Melthorpe shook hands with him.

"Upon my word!", he said good-humouredly, "this young gentleman reminds one of the 'Arabian Nights,' El-Râmi! He looks like one of those amazing fellows who always had remarkable adventures; Prince Ahmed, or the son of a king, or something—don't you know?"

El-Râmi smiled gravely.

"The Eastern dress is responsible for that idea in your mind, no doubt—" he replied—"Féraz wears it in the house, because he moves more easily and is more comfortable in it than in the regulation British attire, which really is the most hideous mode of garb in the world. Englishmen are among the finest types of the human race, but their dress does them scant justice."

"You are right—we're all on the same tailor's pattern—and a frightful pattern it is!" and his lordship put up his eyeglass to survey Féraz once more, the while he thought—"Devilish handsome fellow!—would make quite a sensation in the room—new sort of craze for my lady." Aloud he said—"Pray bring your brother with you on Tuesday evening—my wife will be charmed."

"Féraz never goes into society—" replied El-Râmi—"But of course, if you insist—"

"Oh, I never insist—" declared Lord Melthorpe, laughing—"You are the man for insisting, not I. But I shall take it as a favour if he will accompany you."

"You hear, Féraz—" and El-Râmi looked at his brother inquiringly— "Lord Melthorpe invites you to a great reception next Tuesday evening. Would you like to go?"

Féraz glanced from one to the other half smilingly, half doubtfully.

"Yes, I should like it," he said at last.

"Then we shall expect you,—" and Lord Melthorpe rose to take his leave,—"It's a sort of diplomatic and official affair—fellows will look in either before or after the Foreign Office crush, which is on the same evening, and orders and decorations will be in full force, I believe. Oh, by the way, Lady Melthorpe begged me to ask you most particularly to wear Oriental dress."

"I shall obey her ladyship;"—and El-Râmi smiled a little satirically— the character of the lady in question was one that always vaguely amused him.

"And your brother will do the same, I hope?"

"Assuredly!" and El-Râmi shook hands with his visitor, bidding Féraz escort him to the door. When he had gone, Féraz sprang into the study again with all the eager impetuosity of a boy.

"What is it like—a reception in England?" he asked—"And why does Lord Melthorpe ask me?"

"I cannot imagine!" returned his brother dryly—"Why do you want to go?"

"I should like to see life;"—said Féraz.

"See life!" echoed El-Râmi somewhat disdainfully—"What do you mean? Don't you 'see life' as it is?"

"No!" answered Féraz quickly—"I see men and women—but I don't know how they live, and I don't know what they do."

"They live in a perpetual effort to outreach and injure one another"— said El-Râmi, "and all their forces are concentrated on bringing themselves into notice. That is how they live,—that is what they do. It is not a dignified or noble way of living, but it is all they care about. You will see illustrations of this at Lord Melthorpe's reception. You will find the woman with the most diamonds giving herself peacock-like airs over the woman who has fewest,—you will see the snob-millionaire treated with greater consideration by everyone than the born gentleman who happens to have little of this world's wealth. You will find that no one thinks of putting himself out to give personal pleasure to another,—you will hear the same commonplace observations from every mouth,—you will discover a lack of wit, a dearth of kindness, a scarcity of cheerfulness, and a most desperate want of tact in every member of the whole fashionable assemblage. And so you shall 'see life'—if you think you can discern it there. Sufficient for the day is the evil thereof!—meanwhile let us have supper,—time flies, and I have work to do tonight that must be done."

Féraz busied himself nimbly about his usual duties—the frugal meal was soon prepared and soon dispensed with, and at its close, the brothers sat in silence, El-Râmi watching Féraz with a curious intentness, because he felt for the first time in his life that he was not quite master of the young man's thoughts. Did he still remember the name of Lilith? El-Râmi had willed that every trace of it should vanish from his memory during that long afternoon sleep in which the lad had indulged himself unresistingly,—but the question was now—Had that force of will gained the victory? He, El-Râmi, could not tell—not yet—but he turned the problem over and over in his mind with sombre irritation and restlessness. Presently Féraz broke the silence. Drawing from his vest-pocket a small manuscript book, and raising his eyes, he said—

"Do you mind hearing something I wrote last night? I don't quite know how it came to me—I think I must have been dreaming—"

"Read on;"—said El-Râmi—"If it be poesy, then its origin cannot be explained. Were you able to explain it, it would become prose."

"I dare say the lines are not very good,"—went on Féraz diffidently—"yet they are the true expression of a thought that is in me. And whether I owe it to you, or to my own temperament, I have visions now and then—visions not only of love, but of fame—strange glories that I almost realize, yet cannot grasp. And there is a sadness and futility in it all that grieves me... everything is so vague and swift and fleeting. Yet if love, as you say, be a mere chimera,—surely there is such a thing as Fame?"

"There is—" and El-Râmi's eyes flashed, then darkened again—"There is the applause of this world, which may mean the derision of the next. Read on!"

Féraz obeyed. "I call it for the present 'The Star of Destiny'"—he said; and then his mellifluous voice, rich and well modulated, gave flowing musical enunciation to the following lines:

> *The soft low plash of waves upon the shore.*
> *Mariners' voices singing out at sea.*
> *The sighing of the wind that evermore*
> *Chants to my spirit mystic melody,—*
> *These are the mingling sounds I vaguely hear*
> *As o'er the darkening misty main I gaze.*
> *Where one fair planet, warmly bright and clear*
> *Pours from its heart a rain of silver rays.*
> *O patient Star of Love! in yon pale sky*
> *What absolute serenity is thine!*
> *Beneath thy stedfast, half-reproachful eye*
> *Large Ocean chafes,—and white with bitter brine.*
> *Heaves restlessly, and ripples from the light*
> *To darker shadows,—ev'n as noble thought*
> *Recoils from human passion, to a night*
> *Of splendid gloom by its own mystery wrought.*

"What made you think of the sea?" interrupted El-Râmi.

Féraz looked up dreamily.

"I don't know,"—he said.

"Well!—go on!"

Féraz continued,—

> *O searching Star, I bring my grief to thee,—*
> *Regard it, Thou, as pitying angels may*
> *Regard a tortured saint,—and, down to me*
> *Send one bright glance, one heart-assuring ray*
> *From that high throne where thou in sheeny state*
> *Dost hang, thought-pensive, 'twixt the heaven and earth;*
> *Thou, sure, dost know the secret of my Fate.*
> *For thou did'st shine upon my hour of birth.*
> *O Star, from whom the clouds asunder roll.*

MARIE CORELLI

Tell this poor spirit pent in dying flesh.
This fighting, working, praying, prisoned soul.
Why it is trapped and strangled in the mesh
Of foolish Life and Time? Its wild young voice
Calls for release, unanswered and unstilled.
It sought not out this world,—it had no choice
Of other worlds where glory is fulfilled.
How hard to live at all, if living be
The thing it seems to us!—the few brief years
Made up of toil and sorrow, where we see
No joy without companionship of tears,—
What is the artist's fame?—the golden chords
Of rapt musician? or the poet's themes?
All incomplete!—the nailed down coffin boards
Are mocking sequels to the grandest dreams.

"That is not your creed,"—said El-Râmi with a searching look.

Féraz sighed. "No—it is not my actual creed—but it is my frequent thought."

"A thought unworthy of you,"—said his brother—"There is nothing left 'incomplete' in the whole Universe—and there is no sequel possible to Creation."

"Perhaps not,—but again perhaps there may be a sequel beyond all imagination or comprehension. And surely you must admit that some things are left distressingly incomplete. Shelley's 'Fragments' for instance, Keats's 'Hyperion'—Schubert's 'Unfinished' Symphony—"

"Incomplete here—yes—;" agreed El-Râmi—"But—finished elsewhere, as surely as day is day, and night is night. There is nothing lost,—no, not so much as the lightest flicker of a thought in a man's brain,—nothing wasted or forgotten,—not even so much as an idle word. We forget—but the forces of Nature are non-oblivious. All is chronicled and registered—all is scientifically set down in plain figures that no mistake may be made in the final reckoning."

"You really think that?—you really believe that?" asked Féraz, his eyes dilating eagerly.

"I do, most positively;"—said El-Râmi—"It is a Fact which Nature most potently sets forth, and insists upon. But is there no more of your verse?"

"Yes—" and Féraz read on—

O, we are sorrowful, my Soul and I:
We war together fondly—yet we pray
For separate roads,—the Body fain would die
And sleep i' the ground, low-hidden from the day—
The Soul erect, its large wings cramped for room.
Doth pantingly and passionately rebel.
Against this strange, uncomprehended doom
Called Life, where nothing is, or shall be well.

"Good!"—murmured El-Râmi softly—"Good—and true!"

Hear me, my Star!—star of my natal hour.
Thou calm unmoved one amid all clouds!
Give me my birth-right,—the imperial sway
Of Thought supreme above the common crowds,—
O let me feel thy swift compelling beam
Drawing me upwards to a goal divine;
Fulfil thy promise, O thou glittering Dream.
And let one crown of victory be mine;
Let me behold this world recede and pass
Like shifting mist upon a stormy coast
Or vision in a necromancer's glass;—
For I, 'mid perishable earth can boast
Of proven Immortality,—can reach
Glories ungrasped by minds of lower tone;—
Thus, in a silence vaster than all speech.
I follow thee, my Star of Love, alone!

He ceased. El-Râmi, who had listened attentively, resting his head on one hand, now lifted his eyes and looked at his young brother with an expression of mingled curiosity and compassion.

"The verses are good;"—he said at last—"good and perfectly rhythmical, but surely they have a touch of arrogance?—

'I 'mid perishable earth can boast
Of proven Immortality.'

What do you mean by 'proven' Immortality? Where are your proofs?"

"I have them in my inner consciousness;" replied Féraz slowly—"But to put them into the limited language spoken by mortals is impossible. There are existing emotions—existing facts, which can never be rendered into common speech. God is a Fact—but He cannot be explained or described."

El-Râmi was silent,—a slight frown contracted his dark even brows.

"You are beginning to think too much"—he observed, rising from his chair as he spoke—"Do not analyse yourself, Féraz, . . . self-analysis is the temper of the age, but it engenders distrust and sorrow. Your poem is excellent, but it breathes of sadness,—I prefer your 'star' songs which are so full of joy. To be wise is to be happy,—to be happy is to be wise—"

A loud rat-tat at the street-door interrupted him. Féraz sprang up to answer the imperative summons, and returned with a telegram. El-Râmi opened and read it with astonished eyes, his face growing suddenly pale.

"He will be here tomorrow night!" he exclaimed in a whisper—"Tomorrow night! He, the saint—the king—here tomorrow night! Why should he come?—What would he have with me?"

His expression was one of dazed bewilderment, and Féraz looked at him inquiringly.

"Any bad news?" he asked—"Who is it that is coming?"

El-Râmi recollected himself, and folding up the telegram, thrust it in his breast-pocket.

"A poor monk who is travelling hither on a secret mission solicits my hospitality for the night"—he replied hurriedly—"That is all. He will be here tomorrow."

Féraz stood silent, an incredulous smile in his fine eyes.

"Why should you stoop to deceive me, El-Râmi my brother?" he said gently at last—"Surely it is not one of your ways to perfection? Why try to disguise the truth from me?—I am not of a treacherous nature. If I guess rightly, this 'poor monk' is the Supreme Head of the Brethren of the Cross, from whose mystic band you were dismissed for a breach of discipline. What harm is there in my knowing of this?"

El-Râmi's hand clenched, and his eyes had that dark and terrible look in them that Féraz had learned to fear, but his voice was very calm.

"Who told you?" he asked.

"One of the monks at Cyprus long ago, when I went on your errand"—replied Féraz; "He spoke of your wisdom, your power, your brilliant faculties, in genuine regret that all for some slight matter in which you would not bend your pride, you had lost touch with their various centres of action in all parts of the globe. He said no more than this,—and no more than this I know."

"You know quite enough,"—said El-Râmi quietly—"If I have lost touch with their modes of work, I have gained insight beyond their reach. And,—I am sorry I did not at once say the truth to you—it is their chief leader who comes here tomorrow. No doubt,"—and he smiled with a sense of triumph—"no doubt he seeks for fresh knowledge, such as I alone can give him."

"I thought," said Féraz in a low half-awed tone—"that he was one of those who are wise with the wisdom of the angels?"

"If there are angels!" said El-Râmi with a touch of scorn—"He is wise in faith alone—he believes and he imagines,—and there is no question as to the strange power he has obtained through the simplest means,—but I—I have no faith!—I seek to prove—I work to know,—and my power is as great as his, though it is won in a different way."

Féraz said nothing, but sat down to the piano, allowing his hands to wander over the keys in a dreamy fashion that sounded like the far-off echo of a rippling mountain stream. El-Râmi waited a moment, listening,—then glanced at his watch—it was growing late.

"Good-night, Féraz;"—he said in gentle accents—"I shall want nothing more this evening. I am going to my work."

"Good-night,"—answered Féraz with equal gentleness, as he went on playing. His brother opened and closed the door softly;—he was gone.

As soon as he found himself alone, Féraz pressed the pedal of his instrument so that the music pealed through the room in rich salvos of sound—chord after chord rolled grandly forth, and sweet ringing notes came throbbing from under his agile finger-tips, the while he said aloud, with a mingling of triumph and tenderness—

"Forget! I shall never forget! Does one forget the flowers, the birds, the moonlight, the sound of a sweet song? Is the world so fair, that I should blot from my mind the fairest thing in it? Not so! My memory may fail me in a thousand things—but let me be tortured, harassed, perplexed with dreams, persuaded by fantasies, I shall never forget the name of—"

He stopped abruptly—a look of pain and terror and effort flashed into his eyes,—his hands fell on the keys of the piano with a discordant jangle,—he stared about him, wondering and afraid.

"The name—the name!" he muttered hoarsely—"A flower's name—

an angel's name—the sweetest name I ever heard! How is this?—Am I mad that my lips refuse to utter it? The name—the name of. . . My God! my God! I have forgotten it!"

And springing from his chair he stood for one instant in mute wrath, incredulity and bewilderment,—then throwing himself down again, he buried his face in his hands, his whole frame trembling with mingled terror and awe at the mystic power of El-Râmi's indomitable Will, which had, he knew, forced him to forget what most he desired to remember.

XVII

Within the chamber of Lilith all was very still. Zaroba sat there, crouched down in what seemed to be her favourite and accustomed corner, busy with the intricate threadwork which she wove with so much celerity;—the lamp burned brightly,—there were odours of frankincense and roses in the air,—and not so much as the sound of a suppressed sigh or soft breath stirred the deep and almost sacred quiet of the room. The tranced Lilith herself, pale but beautiful, lay calm and still as ever among the glistening satin cushions of her costly couch, and just above her, the purple draperies that covered the walls and ceiling were drawn aside to admit of the opening of a previously-concealed window, through which one or two stars could be seen dimly sparkling in the skies. A white moth, attracted by the light, had flown in by way of this aperture, and was now fluttering heedlessly and aimlessly round the lamp,—but by-and-bye it took a lower and less hazardous course, and finally settled on a shining corner of the cushion that supported Lilith's head. There the fragile insect rested,—now expanding its velvety white wings, now folding them close and extending its delicate feelers to touch and test the glittering fabric on which it found itself at ease,—but never moving from the spot it had evidently chosen for its night's repose. Suddenly, and without sound, El-Râmi entered. He advanced close up to the couch, and looked upon the sleeping girl with an eager, almost passionate intentness. His heart beat quickly;—a singular excitement possessed him, and for once he was unable to analyze his own sensations. Closer and closer he bent over Lilith's exquisite form,—doubtfully and with a certain scorn of himself, he took up a shining tress of her glorious hair and looked at it curiously as though it were something new, strange or unnatural. The little moth, disturbed, flew off the pillow and fluttered about his head in wild alarm, and El-Râmi watched its reckless flight as it made off towards the fatally-attractive lamp again, with meditative eyes, still mechanically stroking that soft lock of Lilith's hair which he held between his fingers.

"Into the light!" he murmured—"Into the very heart of the light!—into the very core of the Fire! That is the end of all ambition—to take wings and plunge so—into the glowing, burning molten Creative Centre—and die for our foolhardiness? Is that all?—or is there more behind? It is a question,—who may answer it?"

He sighed heavily, and leaned more closely over the couch, till the soft scarcely perceptible breath from Lilith's lips touched his cheek warmly like a caress. Observantly, as one might study the parts of a bird or a flower, he noted those lips, how delicately curved, how coral-red they were,—and what a soft rose-tint, like the flush of a pink sunrise on white flowers, was the hue which spread itself waveringly over her cheeks,—till there,—there where the long eyelashes curled up—wards, there were fine shadows,—shadows which suggested light,—such light as must be burning in those sweetly-closed eyes. Then there was the pure, smooth brow, over which little vine-like tendrils of hair caught and clung amorously,—and then—that wondrous wealth of the hair itself which like twin showers of gold, shed light on either side. It was all beautiful,—a wonderful gem of Nature's handiwork,—a masterpiece of form and colour which, but for him, El-Râmi, would long ere this have mouldered away to unsightly ash and bone, in a lonely grave dug hurriedly among the sands of the Syrian desert. He was almost, if not quite, the author of that warm if unnatural vitality that flowed through those azure veins and branching arteries,—he, like the Christ of Galilee, had raised the dead to life,—aye, if he chose, he could say as the Master said to the daughter of Jairus, "Maiden, arise!" and she would obey him—would rise and walk, and smile and speak, and look upon the world,—if he chose! The arrogance of Will burned in his brain;—the pride of power, the majesty of conscious strength made his pulses beat high with triumph beyond that of any king or emperor,—and he gazed down upon the tranced fair form, himself entranced, and all unconscious that Zaroba had come out of her corner, and that she now stood beside him, watching his face with passionate and inquisitive eagerness. Just as he reluctantly lifted himself up from his leaning position he saw her staring at him, and a frown darkened his brows. He made his usual imperative sign to her to leave the room,—a sign she was accustomed to understand and to obey—but this time she remained motionless, fixing her eyes steadily upon him.

"The conqueror shall be conquered, El-Râmi Zarânos—" she said slowly, pointing to the sleeping Lilith—"The victorious master over the forces unutterable, shall yet be overthrown! The work has begun,—the small seed has been sown—the great harvest shall be reaped. For in the history of Heaven itself, certain proud angels rose up and fought for the possession of supreme majesty and power—and they fell,—down-beaten to the darkness,—unforgiven; and are they not in darkness still? Even so must the haughty spirit fall that contends against God and the Universal Law."

She spoke impressively, and with a certain dignity of manner that gave an added force to her words,—but El-Râmi's impassive countenance showed no sign of having either heard or understood her. He merely repeated his gesture of dismissal, and this time Zaroba obeyed it. Wrapping her flowing robe closely about her, she withdrew, but with evident reluctance, letting the velvet portière fall only by slow degrees behind her, and to the last keeping her dark deep-set eyes fixed on El-Râmi's face. As soon as she had disappeared, he sprang to where the dividing-curtain hid a massive door between the one room and the antechamber,—this door he shut and locked,—then he returned to the couch, and proceeded according to his usual method, to will the wandering spirit of his "subject" into speech.

"Lilith! Lilith!"

As before, he had to wait ere any reply was vouchsafed to him. Impatiently he glanced at the clock, and counted slowly a hundred beats.

"Lilith!"

She turned round towards him, smiled, and murmured something— her lips moved, but whatever they uttered did not reach his ear.

"Lilith! Where are you?"

This time, her voice, though soft, was perfectly distinct.

"Here. Close to you, with your hand on mine."

El-Râmi was puzzled. True, he held her left hand in his own, but she had never described any actual sensation of human touch before.

"Then,—can you see me?" he asked somewhat anxiously.

The answer came sadly.

"No. Bright air surrounds me, and the colours of the air—nothing more."

"You are alone, Lilith?"

Oh, what a sigh came heaving from her breast!

"I am always alone!"

Half remorseful, he heard her. She had complained of solitude before,—and it was a thought he did not wish her to dwell upon. He made haste to speak again.

"Tell me,"—he said—"Where have you been Lilith, and what have you seen?"

There was silence for a minute or two, and she moved restlessly.

"You bade me seek out Hell for you"—she murmured at last—"I have searched but I cannot find it."

Another pause, and she went on.

"You spoke of a strange thing," she said—"A place of punishment, of torture, of darkness, of horror and despair,—there is no such dreary blot on all God's fair Creation. In all the golden spaces of the furthest stars I find no punishment, no pain, no darkness. I can discover nothing save beauty, light, and—Love!"

The last word was uttered softly, and sounded like a note of music, sweet but distant.

El-Râmi listened, bewildered, and in a manner disappointed.

"O Lilith, take heed what you say!" he exclaimed with some passion—"No pain?—no punishment? no darkness? Then this world is Hell and you know naught of it!"

As he said this, she moved uneasily among her pillows,—then, to his amazement, she suddenly sat up of her own accord, and went on speaking, enunciating her words with singular clearness and emphasis, always keeping her eyes closed and allowing her left hand to remain in his.

"I am bound to tell you what I know;"—she said—"But I am unable to tell you what is not true. In God's design I find no evil—no punishment, no death. If there are such things, they must be in your world alone,—they must be Man's work and Man's imaginng."

"Man's work—Man's imagining?" repeated El-Râmi—"And what is Man?"

"God's angel," replied Lilith quickly—"With God's own attribute of Free-Will. He, like his Maker, doth create,—he also doth destroy,—what he elects to do, God will not prevent. Therefore if Man makes Evil, Evil must exist till Man himself destroys it."

This was a deep and strange saying, and El-Râmi pondered over it without speaking.

"In the spaces where I roam," went on Lilith softly—"there is no evil. Those who are the Makers of Life in yonder fair regions, seek only what is pure. Why should pain exist, or sin be known? I do not understand."

"No"—said El-Râmi bitterly—"You do not understand, because you are yourself too happy,—happiness sees no fault in anything. Oh, you have wandered too far from earth and you forget! The tie that binds you to this planet is over-fragile,—you have lost touch with pain. I would that I could make you feel my thoughts!—for, Lilith, God is cruel, not kind, . . . upon God, and God alone, rests the weight of woe that burdens the universe, and for the eternal sorrow of things there is neither reason nor remedy."

Lilith sank back again in a recumbent posture, a smile upon her lips.

"O poor blind eyes!" she murmured—"Sad eyes that are so tired—too tired to bear the light!"

Her voice was so exquisitely pathetic that he was startled by its very gentleness,—his heart gave one fierce bound against his side, and then seemed almost to stand still.

"You pity me?" he asked tremulously.

She sighed. "I pity you"—she answered—"I pity myself."

Almost breathlessly he asked "Why?"

"Because I cannot see you—because you cannot see me. If I could see you—if you could see me as I am, you would know all—you would understand all."

"I do see you, Lilith" he said—"I hold your hand."

"No—not my real hand"—she said—"Only its shadow."

Instinctively he looked at the delicate fingers that lay in his palm—so rosy-tipped and warm. Only the "shadow" of a hand! Then where was its substance?

"It will pass away"—went on Lilith—"like all shadows—but I shall remain—not here, not here,—but elsewhere. When will you let me go?"

"Where do you wish to go?" he asked.

"To my friends," she answered swiftly and with eagerness—"They call me often—I hear their voices singing 'Lilith! Lilith!' and sometimes I see them beckoning me—but I cannot reach them. It is cruel, for they love me and you do not,—why will you keep me here unloved so long?"

He trembled and hesitated, fixing his dark eyes on the fair face, which, in spite of its beauty, was to him but as the image of a Sphinx that forever refused to give up its riddle.

"Is love your craving, Lilith?" he asked slowly—"And what is your thought—or dream—of love?"

"Love is no dream;"—she responded—"Love is reality—Love is Life. I am not fully living yet—I hover in the Realms Between, where spirits wait in silence and alone."

He sighed. "Then you are sad, Lilith?"

"No. I am never sad. There is light within my solitude, and the glory of God's beauty everywhere."

MARIE CORELLI

El-Râmi gazed down upon her, an expression very like despair shadowing his own features.

"Too far, too far she wends her flight;"—he muttered to himself wearily. "How can I argue on these vague and sublimated utterances! I cannot understand her joy—she cannot understand my pain. Evidently Heaven's language is incomprehensible to mortal ears. And yet;—Lilith!" he called again almost imperiously. "You talk of God as if you knew Him. But I—I know Him not—I have not proved Him,—tell me of His Shape, His Seeming,—if indeed you have the power."

She was silent. He studied her tranquil face intently,—the smile upon it was in very truth divine.

"No answer!" he said with some derision. "Of course,—what answer should there be! What Shape or Seeming should there be to a mere huge blind Force that creates without reason, and destroys without necessity!"

As he thus soliloquized, Lilith stirred, and flung her white arms upward as though in ecstasy, letting them fall slowly afterwards in a folded position behind her head.

"To the Seven declared tones of Music, add seventy million more,"—she said—"and let them ring their sweetest cadence, they shall make but a feeble echo of the music of God's voice. To all the shades of radiant colour, to all the lines of noblest form, add the splendour of eternal youth, eternal goodness, eternal joy, eternal power, and yet we shall not render into speech or song the beauty of our God! From His glance flows Light—from His presence rushes Harmony,—as He moves through Space great worlds are born; and at His bidding planets grow within the air like flowers. Oh to see Him passing 'mid the stars!—"

She broke off suddenly and drew a long deep breath, as of sheer delight,—but the shadow on El-Râmi's features darkened wearily.

"You teach me nothing, Lilith"—he said sadly and somewhat sternly—"You speak of what you see—or what you think you see—but you cannot convince me of its truth."

Her face grew paler,—the smile vanished from her lips, and all her delicate beauty seemed to freeze into a cold and grave rigidity.

"Love begets faith;"—she said—"Where we do not love, we doubt. Doubt breeds Evil, and Evil knows not God."

"Platitudes, upon my life!—mere plati—tudes!" exclaimed El-Râmi bitterly—"If this half-released spirit can do no more than prate of the same old laws and duties our preachers teach us, then indeed my service is vain. But she shall not baffle me thus;"—and bending over Lilith's figure, he unwound her arms from the indolent position in which they were folded, took her hands roughly in his own, and sitting on the edge of her couch, fixed his burning eyes upon her as though he sought to pierce her to the heart's core with their ardent, almost cruel lustre.

"Lilith!" he commanded—"Speak plainly, that I may fully understand your words. You say there is no hell?"

The answer came steadily.

"None."

"Then must evil go unpunished?"

"Evil wreaks punishment upon itself. Evil destroys itself. That is the Law."

"And the Prophets!" muttered El-Râmi scornfully—"Well! Go on, strange sprite! Why—for such things are known—why does goodness suffer for being good?"

"That never is. That is impossible."

"Impossible?" queried El-Râmi incredulously.

"Impossible,"—repeated the soft voice firmly. "Goodness seems to suffer, but it does not. Evil seems to prosper, but it does not."

"And God exists?"

"God exists."

"And what of Heaven?"

"Which heaven?" asked Lilith—"There are a million million heavens."

El-Râmi stopped—thinking,—then finally said—

"God's Heaven."

"You would say God's World;"—returned Lilith tranquilly—"Nay, you will not let me reach that centre. I see it; I feel it afar off—but your will binds me—you will not let me go."

"If I were to let you go what would you do?" asked El-Râmi—"Would you return to me?"

"Never! Those who enter the Perfect Glory, return no more to an imperfect light."

El-Râmi paused—he was arranging other questions to ask, when her next words startled him—

"Someone called me by my name,"—she said—"Tenderly and softly, as though it were a name beloved. I heard the voice—I could not answer—but I heard it—and I know that someone loves me. The sense of love is sweet, and makes your dreary world seem fair!"

El-Râmi's heart began to beat violently—the voice of Féraz had reached her in her trance then after all! And she remembered it!—more than this—it had carried a vague emotion of love to that vagrant and ethereal essence which he called her "soul" but which he had his doubts of all the while. For he was unable to convince himself positively of any such thing as "Soul;"—all emotions, even of the most divinely transcendent nature, he was disposed to set down to the action of brain merely. But he was scientist enough to know that the brain must gather its ideas from something,—something either external or internal,— even such a vague thing as an Idea cannot spring out of blank Chaos. And this was what especially puzzled him in his experiment with the girl Lilith—for, ever since he had placed her in the "life-in-death" condition she was, he had been careful to avoid impressing any of his own thoughts or ideas upon her. And, as a matter of fact, all she said about God, or about a present or a future state, was precisely the reverse of what he himself argued;—the question therefore remained—From Where and How did she get her knowledge? She had been a mere pretty, ignorant, half-barbaric Arab child, when she died (according to natural law), and, during the six years she had lived (by scientific law) in her strange trance, her brain had been absolutely unconscious of all external impressions, while of internal she could have none, beyond the memories of her childhood. Yet,—she had grown beautiful beyond the beauty of mortals, and she spoke of things beyond all mortal comprehension. The riddle of her physical and mental development seemed unanswerable,—it was the wonder, the puzzle, the difficulty, the delight of all El-Râmi's hours. But now there was mischief done. She spoke of love,—not divine impersonal love, as was her wont,—but love that touched her own existence with a vaguely pleasing emotion. A voice had reached her that never should have been allowed to penetrate her spiritual solitude, and realizing this, a sullen anger smouldered in El-Râmi's mind. He strove to consider Zaroba's fault and Féraz's folly with all the leniency, forbearance and forgiveness possible, and yet the strange restlessness within him gave him no peace. What should be done? What could be answered to those wistful words—"The sense of love is sweet, and makes your dreary world seem fair"?

He pondered on the matter, vaguely uneasy and dissatisfied. He, and he alone, was the master of Lilith,—he commanded and she obeyed,— but would it be always thus? The doubt turned his blood cold,—suppose she escaped him now, after all his studies and calculations! He resolved he would ask her no more questions that night, and very gently he released the little slender hands he held.

"Go, Lilith!" he said softly—"This world, as you say, is dreary—I will not keep you longer in its gloom—go hence and rest."

"Rest?" sighed Lilith inquiringly—"Where?"

He bent above her, and touched her loose gold locks almost caressingly.

"Where you choose!"

"Nay, that I may not!" murmured Lilith sadly. "I have no choice—I must obey the Master's will."

El-Râmi's heart beat high with triumph at these words.

"My will!" he said, more to himself than to her—"The force of it!—the marvel of it!-my will!"

Lilith heard,—a strange glory seemed to shine round her, like a halo round a pictured saint, and the voice that came from her lips rang out with singularly sweet clearness.

"Your will!" she echoed—"Your will—and also—God's will!"

He started, amazed and irresolute. The words were not what he expected, and he would have questioned their meaning, but that he saw on the girl's lovely features a certain pale composed look which he recognised as the look that meant silence.

"Lilith!" he whispered.

No answer. He stood looking down upon her, his face seeming sterner and darker than usual by reason of the intense, passionate anxiety in his burning eyes.

"God's will!" he echoed with some disdain—"God's will would have annihilated her very existence long ago out in the desert;—what should God do with her now that I have not done?"

His arrogance seemed to him perfectly justifiable; and yet he very well knew that, strictly speaking, there was no such thing as "annihilation" possible to any atom in the universe. Moreover, he did not choose to analyze the mystical reasons as to why he had been permitted by Fate or Chance to obtain such mastery over one human soul,—he preferred to attribute it all to his own discoveries in science,—his own patient and untiring skill,—his own studious comprehension of the forces of Nature,—and he was nearly, if not quite oblivious of the fact, that there is a Something behind natural forces, which knows and sees, controls and commands, and against which, if he places himself in opposition, Man is but the puniest, most wretched straw that was ever tossed or split by a whirlwind. As a rule, men of science work not for God so much as against Him, wherefore their most brilliant researches stop short of the goal. Great intellects are seldom devout,—for brilliant culture begets pride—and pride is incompatible with faith or worship. Perfect science, combined with perfect selflessness, would give us what we need,—a purified and reasoning Religion. But El-Râmi's chief characteristic was pride,—and he saw no mischief in it. Strong in his knowledge,—defiant of evil in the consciousness he possessed of his own extraordinary physical and mental endowments, he saw no reason why he should bow down in humiliated abasement before forces, either natural or spiritual, which he deemed himself able to control. And his brow cleared, as he once more bent over his tranced "subject" and with all the methodical precaution of a physician, felt her pulse, took note of her temperature and judged that for the present she needed no more of that strange Elixir which kept her veins aglow with such inexplicably beauteous vitality. Then—his ex—amination done—he left the room; and as he drew the velvet portière behind him, the little white moth that had flown in for a night's shelter, fluttered down from the golden lamp like a falling leaf, and dropped on the couch of Lilith, shrivelled and dead.

XVIII

The next day was very wet and stormy. From morning to night the rain fell in torrents, and a cold wind blew. El-Râmi stayed indoors, reading, writing, and answering a few of his more urgent correspondents, a great number of whom were total strangers to him, and who nevertheless wrote to him out of the sheer curiosity excited in them by the perusal of a certain book to which his name was appended as author. This book was a very original literary production,—the critics were angry with it, because it was so unlike anything else that ever was written. According to the theories set forth in its pages, Man the poor and finite, was proved to be a creature of superhuman and almost god-like attributes,—a "flattering unction" indeed, which when laid to the souls of commonplace egoists, had the effect of making them consider El-Râmi Zarânos a very wonderful person, and themselves more wonderful still. Only the truly great mind is humble enough to appreciate greatness, and of great minds there is a great scarcity. Most of El-Râmi's correspondents were of that lower order of intelligence which blandly accepts every fresh truth discovered as specially intended for themselves, and not at all for the world, as though indeed they were some particular and removed class of superior beings who alone were capable of understanding true wisdom. "Your work has appealed to me"—wrote one, "as it will not appeal to all, because I am able to enter into the divine spirit of things as the vulgar herd cannot do!" This, as if the "vulgar herd" were not also part of the "divine spirit of things"!

"I have delighted in your book"—wrote another, "because I am a poet, and the world, with its low aims and lower desires I abhor and despise!"

The absurdity of a man presuming to call himself a poet, and in the same breath declaring he "despises" the world,—the world which supports his life and provides him with all his needs,—never seems to occur to the minds of these poor boasters of a petty vanity. El-Râmi looked weary enough as he glanced quickly through a heap of such ill-judged and egotistical epistles, and threw them aside to be forever left unanswered. To him there was something truly horrible and discouraging in the contemplation of the hopeless, helpless, absolute stupidity of the majority of mankind. The teachings of Mother Nature being always straight and plain, it is remarkable what devious turnings and dark winding ways we prefer to stumble into rather than take the fair and open course. For example Nature says to us—"My children, Truth is simple,—and I am bound by all my forces to assist its manifestation. A Lie is difficult—I can have none of it—it needs other lies to keep it going,—its ways are full of complexity and puzzle,—why then, O foolish ones, will you choose the Lie and avoid the Truth? For, work as you may, the Truth must out, and not all the uproar of opposing multitudes can still its thunderous tongue." Thus Nature;—but we heed her not,—we go on lying stedfastly, in a strange delusion that thereby may deceive Eternal Justice. But Eternal Justice never is deceived,—never is obscured even, save for a moment, as a passing cloud obscures the sun.

"How easy after all to avoid mischief of any kind," mused El-Râmi now, as he put by his papers and drew two or three old reference volumes towards him—"How easy to live happily, free from care, free from sickness, free from every external or internal wretchedness, if we could but practise the one rule—Self-abnegation. It is all there,—and the ethereal Lilith may be right in her assurance as to the non-existence of Evil unless we ourselves create it. At least one half the trouble in the world might be avoided if we chose. Debt, for example,—that carking trouble always arises from living beyond one's means,—therefore why live beyond one's means? What for? Show? Vulgar ostentation? Luxury? Idleness? All these are things against which Heaven raises its eternal ban. Then take physical pain and sickness,—here Self is to blame again,—self-indulgence in the pleasures of the table,—sensual craving,—the marriage of weakly or ill-conditioned persons,—all simple causes from which spring incalculable evils. Avoid the causes and we escape the evils. The arrangements of Nature are all so clear and explicit, and yet we are forever going out of our way to find or invent difficulties. The farmer grumbles and writes letters to the newspapers if his turnip-fields are invaded by what he deems a 'destructive pest' in the way of moth or caterpillar, and utterly ignores the fact that these insects always appear for some wise reason or other, which he, absorbed in his own immediate petty interests, fails to appreciate. His turnips are eaten,—that is all he thinks or cares about,—but if he knew that those same turnips contain a particular microbe poisonous to human life, a germ of typhoid, cholera or the like, drawn up from the soil and ready to fructify in the blood of cattle or of men, and that these insects of which he complains are the scavengers sent by Nature to utterly destroy the Plague in embryo, he might pause in his grumbling to wonder at so much precaution taken by the elements for the preservation of his unworthy and ignorant being. Perplexing and at times maddening is this our curse of Ignorance,—but that the 'sins of the fathers are visited on the children' is a true saying is evident—for the faults of generations are still bred in our blood and bone."

He turned over the first volume before him listlessly,—his mind was not set upon study, and his attention wandered. He was thinking of Féraz, with whom he had scarcely exchanged a word all day. He had lacked nothing in the way of service, for swift and courteous obedience to his brother's wishes had characterized Féraz in every simple action, but there was a constraint between the two that had not previously existed. Féraz bore himself with a stately yet sad hauteur,—he had the air of a proud prince in chains who, being captive, performed his prison-work with exactitude and resignation as a matter of discipline and duty. It was curious that El-Râmi, who had steeled him—self as he imagined against every tender sentiment, should now feel the want of the impetuous confidence and grace of manner with which his young brother had formerly treated him.

"Everything changes—" he mused gloomily, "Everything must change, of course; and nothing is so fluctuating as the humour of a boy who is not yet a man, but is on the verge of manhood. And with Féraz my power has reached its limit,—I know exactly what I can do, and what I can not do with him,—it is a case of 'Thus far and no further.' Well,—he must choose his own way of life,—only let him not presume to set himself in my way, or interfere in my work! Ye gods!—there is nothing I would not do—"

He paused, ashamed; the blood flushed his face darkly and his hand clenched itself involuntarily. Conscious of the thought that had arisen within him, he felt a moment's shuddering horror of himself. He knew that in the very depths of his nature there was enough untamed savagery to make him capable of crushing his young brother's life out of him, should he dare to obstruct his path or oppose him in his labours. Realizing this, a cold dew broke out on his forehead and he trembled.

"O Soul of Lilith that cannot understand Evil!" he exclaimed—"Whence came this evil thought in me? Does the evil in myself engender it?—and does the same bitter gall that stirred the blood of Cain lurk in the depths of my being, till Opportunity strikes the wicked hour? Retro me, Sathanas! After all, there was something in the old beliefs—the pious horror of a devil,—for a devil there is that walks the world, and his name is Man!"

He rose and paced the room impatiently,—what a long day it seemed, and with what dreary persistence the rain washed against the windows! He looked out into the street,—there was not a passenger to be seen,—a wet dingy grayness pervaded the atmosphere and made everything ugly and cheerless. He went back to his books, and presently began to turn over the pages of the quaint Arabic volume into which Féraz had unwisely dipped, gathering therefrom a crumb of knowledge, which, like all scrappy information, had only led him to discontent.

"All these old experiments of the Egyptian priests were simple enough—" he murmured as he read,—"They had one substratum of science,—the art of bringing the countless atoms that fill the air into temporary shape. The trick is so easy and natural, that I fancy there must have been a certain condition of the atmosphere in earlier ages which of itself shaped the atoms,—hence the ideas of nymphs, dryads, fauns and watersprites; these temporary shapes which dazzled for some fleeting moments the astonished human eye and so gave rise to all the legends. To shape the atoms as a sculptor shapes clay, is but a phase of chemistry,—a pretty experiment—yet what a miracle it would always seem to the uninstructed multitude!"

He unlocked a drawer in his desk, and took from it a box full of red powder, and two small flasks, one containing minute globules of a glittering green colour like tiny emeralds,—the other full of a pale amber liquid. He smiled as he looked at these ingredients,—and then he gave a glance out through the window at the dark and rainy afternoon.

"To pass the time, why not?" he queried half aloud. "One needs a little diversion sometimes even in science."

Whereupon he placed some of the red powder in a small bronze vessel and set fire to it. A thick smoke arose at once and filled the room with cloud that emitted a pungent perfume, and in which his own figure was scarcely discernible. He cast five or six of the little green globules into this smoke; they dissolved in their course and melted within it,—and finally he threw aloft a few drops of the amber liquid. The effect was extraordinary, and would have seemed incredible to any onlooker, for through the cloud a roseate Shape made itself slowly visible,—a Shape that was surrounded with streaks of light and rainbow flame as with a garland. Vague at first, but soon growing more distinct, it gathered itself into seeming substance, and floated nearly to the ground,—then rising again, balanced itself lightly like a blown feather sideways upon the dense mist that filled the air. In form this "corruscation of atoms" as El-Râmi called it, resembled a maiden in the bloom of youth,—her flowing hair, her sparkling eyes, her smiling lips, were all plainly discernible;—but, that she was a mere phantasm and creature of the cloud was soon made plain, for scarcely had she declared herself in all her rounded laughing loveliness, than she melted away and passed into nothingness like a dream. The cloud of smoke grew thinner and thinner, till it vanished also so completely that there was no more left of it than a pale blue ring such as might have been puffed from a stray cigar. El-Râmi, leaning lazily back in his chair, had watched the whole development and finish of his "experiment" with indolent interest and amusement.

"How admirably the lines of beauty are always kept in these effects,"—he said to himself when it was over,—"and what a fortune I could make with that one example of the concentration of atoms if I chose to pass as a Miracle-maker. Moses was an adept at this kind of thing; so also was a certain Egyptian priest named Borsa of Memphis, who just for that same graceful piece of chemistry was judged by the people as divine,—made king,—and loaded with wealth and honour;—excellent and most cunning Borsa! But we—we do not judge anyone 'divine' in these days of ours, not even God,—for He is supposed to be simply the lump of leaven working through the loaf of matter,—though it will always remain a question as to why there is any leaven or any loaf at all existing."

He fell into a train of meditation, which caused him presently to take up his pen and write busily many pages of close manuscript. Féraz came in at the usual hour with supper,—and then only he ceased working, and shared the meal with his young brother, talking cheerfully, though saying little but commonplaces, and skilfully steering off any allusion to subjects which might tend to increase Féraz's evident melancholy. Once he asked him rather abruptly why he had not played any music that day.

"I do not know"—answered the young man coldly—"I seem to have forgotten music—with other things."

He spoke meaningly;—El-Râmi laughed; relieved and light at heart. Those "other things" meant the name of Lilith, which his will had succeeded in erasing from his brother's memory. His eyes sparkled, and his voice gathered new richness and warmth of feeling as he said kindly—

"I think not, Féraz,—I think you cannot have forgotten music.

Surely it is no extraneous thing, but part of you,—a lovely portion of your life which you would be loth to miss. Here is your little neglected friend,"—and, rising, he took out of its case an exquisitely shaped mandolin inlaid with pearl—"The dear old lute,—for lute it is, though modernized,—the same shaped instrument on which the rose and fuchsia-crowned youths of old Pompeii played the accompaniment to their love-songs; the same, the very same on which the long-haired, dusky-skinned maids of Thebes and Memphis thrummed their strange uncouth ditties to their black-browed warrior kings. I like it better than the violin—its form is far more pleasing—we can see Apollo with a lute, but it is difficult to fancy the Sun-god fitting his graceful arm to the contorted positions of a fiddle. Play something, Féraz"—and he smiled winningly as he gave the mandolin into his brother's hands—"Here,"—and he detached the plectrum from its place under the strings—"With this little piece of oval tortoiseshell, you can set the nerves of music quivering,—those silver wires will answer to your touch like the fibres of the human heart struck by the tremolo of passion."

He paused,—his eyes were full of an ardent light, and Féraz looked at him wonderingly. What a voice he had!—how eloquently he spoke!—how noble and thoughtful were his features!—and what an air of almost pathetic dignity was given to his face by that curiously snow-white hair of his, which so incongruously suggested age in youth! Poor Féraz!—his heart swelled within him; love and secret admiration for his brother contended with a sense of outraged pride in himself,—and yet—he felt his sullen amour-propre, his instinct of rebellion, and his distrustful reserve all oozing away under the spell of El-Râmi's persuasive tongue and fascinating manner,—and to escape from his own feelings, he bent over the mandolin and tried its chords with a trembling hand and downcast eyes.

"You speak of passion," he said in a low voice—"but you have never known it."

"Oh, have I not!" and El-Râmi laughed lightly as he resumed his seat—"Nay, if I had not I should be more than man. The lightning has flashed across my path, Féraz, I assure you, only it has not killed me; and I have been ready to shed my blood drop by drop, for so slight and imperfect a production of Nature as—a woman! A thing of white flesh and soft curves, and long hair and large eyes, and a laugh like the tinkle of a fountain in our Eastern courts,—a thing with less mind than a kitten, and less fidelity than a hound. Of course there are clever women and faithful women,—but then we men seldom choose these; we are fools, and we pay for our folly. And I also have been a fool in my time,—why should you imagine I have not? It is flattering to me, but why?"

Féraz looked at him again, and in spite of himself smiled, though reluctantly.

"You always seem to treat all earthly emotions with scorn—" he replied evasively, "And once you told me there was no such thing in the world as love."

"Nor is there—" said El-Râmi quickly—"Not ideal love—not everlasting love. Love in its highest, purest sense, belongs to other planets—in this its golden wings are clipped, and it becomes nothing more than a common and vulgar physical attraction."

Féraz thrummed his mandolin softly.

"I saw two lovers the other day—" he said—"They seemed divinely happy."

"Where did you see them?"

"Not here. In the land I know best—my Star."

El-Râmi looked at him curiously, but forbore to speak.

"They were beautiful—" went on Féraz. "They were resting together on a bank of flowers, in a little nook of that lovely forest where there are thousands of song-birds sweeter than nightingales. Music filled the air,—a rosy glory filled the sky,—their arms were twined around each other,—their lips met, and then—oh, then their joy smote me with fear, because,—because I was alone—and they were—together!"

His voice trembled. El-Râmi's smile had in it something of compassion.

"Love in your Star is a dream, Féraz—" he said gently—"But love here—here in this phase of things we call Reality,—means,—do you know what it means?"

Féraz shook his head.

"It means Money. It means lands, and houses and a big balance at the bank. Lovers do not subsist here on flowers and music,—they have rather more vulgar and substantial appetites. Love here is the disillusion of Love—there, in the region you speak of, it may perchance be perfect—"

A sudden rush of rain battering at the windows, accompanied by a gust of wind, interrupted him.

"What a storm!" exclaimed Féraz, looking up—"And you are expecting—"

A measured rat-tat-tat at the door came at that moment, and El-Râmi sprang to his feet. Féraz rose also, and set aside his mandolin. Another gust of wind whistled by, bringing with it a sweeping torrent of hail.

"Quick!" said El-Râmi, in a somewhat agitated voice—"It is—you know who it is. Give him reverent greeting, Féraz—and show him at once in here."

Féraz withdrew,—and when he had disappeared, El-Râmi looked about him vaguely with the bewildered air of a man who would fain escape from some difficult position, could he but discover an egress,—a slight shudder ran through his frame, and he heaved a deep sigh.

"Why has he come to me!" he muttered, "Why—after all these years of absolute silence and indifference to my work, does he seek me now?"

XIX

Standing in an attitude more of resignation than expectancy, he waited, listening. He heard the street-door open and shut again,—then came a brief pause, followed by the sound of a firm step in the outer hall,—and Féraz reappeared, ushering in with grave respect a man of stately height and majestic demeanour, cloaked in a heavy travelling ulster, the hood of which was pulled cowl-like over his head and almost concealed his features.

"Greeting to El-Râmi Zarânos—" said a rich mellow voice—"And so this is the weather provided by an English month of May! Well, it might be worse,—certes, also, it might be better. I should have disburdened myself of these 'lendings' in the hall, but that I knew not whether you were quite alone—" and, as he spoke, he threw off his cloak, which dripped with rain, and handed it to Féraz, disclosing himself in the dress of a Carthusian monk, all save the disfiguring tonsure. "I was not certain," he continued cheerfully—"whether you might be ready or willing to receive me."

"I am always ready for such a visitor—" said El-Râmi, advancing hesitatingly, and with a curious diffidence in his manner—"And more than willing. Your presence honours this poor house and brings with it a certain benediction."

"Gracefully said, El-Râmi!" exclaimed the monk with a keen flash of his deep-set blue eyes—"Where did you learn to make pretty speeches? I remember you of old time as brusque of tongue and obstinate of humour,—and even now humility sits ill upon you,—'tis not your favourite practised household virtue."

El-Râmi flushed, but made no reply. He seemed all at once to have become even to himself the merest foolish nobody before this his remarkable-looking visitor with the brow and eyes of an inspired evangelist, and the splendid lines of thought, aspiration and endeavour marking the already noble countenance with an expression seldom seen on features of mortal mould. Féraz now came forward to proffer wine and sundry other refreshments, all of which were courteously refused.

"This lad has grown, El-Râmi—" said the stranger, surveying Féraz with much interest and kindliness,—"since he stayed with us in Cyprus and studied our views of poesy and song. A promising youth he seems,—and still your slave?"

El-Râmi gave a gesture of deprecation.

"You mistake—" he replied curtly—"He is my brother and my friend,—as such he cannot be my slave. He is as free as air."

"Or as an eagle that ever flies back to its eyrie in the rocks out of sheer habit—" observed the monk with a smile—"In this case you are the eyrie, and the eagle is never absent long! Well—what now, pretty lad?" this, as Féraz, moved by a sudden instinct which he could not explain to himself, dropped reverently on one knee.

"Your blessing—" he murmured timidly. "I have heard it said that your touch brings peace,—and I—I am not at peace."

The monk looked at him benignly.

"We live in a world of storm, my boy—" he said gently—"where there is no peace but the peace of the inner spirit. That, with your youth and joyous nature, you should surely possess,—and if you have it not, may God grant it you! 'Tis the best blessing I can devise."

And he signed the Cross on the young man's forehead with a gentle lingering touch,—a touch under which Féraz trembled and sighed for pleasure, conscious of the delicious restfulness and ease that seemed suddenly to pervade his being.

"What a child he is still, this brother of yours!" then said the monk, turning abruptly towards El-Râmi—"He craves a blessing,—while you have progressed beyond all such need!"

El-Râmi raised his dark eyes,—eyes full of a burning pain and pride,—but made no answer. The monk looked at him steadily—and heaved a quick sigh.

"Vigilate et orate ut non intretis in tentationem!" he murmured,— "Truly, to forgive is easy—but to forget is difficult. I have much to say to you, El-Râmi,—for this is the last time I shall meet you 'before I go hence and be no more seen.'"

Féraz uttered an involuntary exclamation.

"You do not mean," he said almost breathlessly—"that you are going to die?"

"Assuredly not!" replied the monk with a smile—"I am going to live. Some people call it dying—but we know better,—we know we cannot die."

"We are not sure—" began El-Râmi.

"Speak for yourself, my friend!" said the monk cheerily—"I am sure,— and so are those who labour with me. I am not made of perishable composition any more than the dust is perishable. Every grain of dust contains a germ of life—I am co-equal with the dust, and I contain my germ also, of life that is capable of infinite reproduction."

El-Râmi looked at him dubiously yet wonderingly. He seemed the very embodiment of physical strength and vitality, yet he only compared himself to a grain of dust. And the very dust held the seeds of life!—true!—then, after all, was there anything in the universe, however small and slight, that could die utterly? And was Lilith right when she said there was no death? Wearily and impatiently El-Râmi pondered the question,—and he almost started with nervous irritation when the slight noise of the door shutting, told him that Féraz had retired, leaving him and his mysterious visitant alone together.

Some minutes passed in silence. The monk sat quietly in El-Râmi's own chair, and El-Râmi himself stood close by, waiting, as it seemed, for something; with an air of mingled defiance and appeal. Outside, the rain and wind continued their gusty altercation;—inside, the lamp burned brightly, shedding warmth and lustre on the student-like simplicity of the room. It was the monk himself who at last broke the spell of the absolute stillness.

"You wonder," he said slowly—"at the reason of my coming here,—to you, who are a recreant from the mystic tie of our brother—hood,—to you, who have employed the most sacred and venerable secrets of our Order, to wrest from Life and Nature the material for your own self-interested labours. You think I come for information—you think I wish to hear from your own lips the results of your scientific scheme of supernatural ambition,—alas, El-Râmi Zarânos!—how little you know me! Prayer has taught me more science than Science will ever grasp,—there is nothing in all the catalogue of your labours that I do not understand, and you can give me no new message from lands beyond the sun. I have come to you out of simple pity,—to warn you and if possible to save."

El-Râmi's dark eyes opened wide in astonishment.

"To warn me?" he echoed—"To save? From what?—Such a mission to me is incomprehensible."

"Incomprehensible to your stubborn spirit,—yes, no doubt it is—" said the monk, with a touch of stern reproach in his accents,—"For you will not see that the Veil of the Eternal, though it may lift itself for you a little from other men's lives, hangs dark across your own, and is impervious to your gaze. You will not grasp the fact that though it may be given to you to read other men's passions, you cannot read your own. You have begun at the wrong end of the mystery, El-Râmi,—you should have mastered yourself first before seeking to master others. And now there is danger ahead of you—be wise in time,—accept the truth before it is too late."

El-Râmi listened, impatient and incredulous.

"Accept what truth?" he asked somewhat bitterly—"Am I not searching for truth everywhere? and seeking to prove it? Give me any sort of truth to hold, and I will grasp it as a drowning sailor grasps the rope of rescue!"

The monk's eyes rested on him in mingled compassion and sorrow.

"After all these years—" he said—"are you still asking Pilate's question?"

"Yes—I am still asking Pilate's question!" retorted El-Râmi with sudden passion—"See you—I know who you are,—great and wise, a master of the arts and sciences, and with all your stores of learning, still a servant of Christ, which to me, is the wildest, maddest incongruity. I grant you that Christ was the holiest man that ever lived on earth,—and if I swear a thing in His name, I swear an oath that shall not be broken. But in His Divinity, I cannot, I may not, I dare not believe!—except in so far that there is divinity in all of us. One man, born of woman, destined to regenerate the world!—the idea is stupendous,—but impossible to reason!"

He paced the room impatiently.

"If I could believe it—I say 'if,'"—he continued, "I should still think it a clumsy scheme. For every human creature living should be a reformer and regenerator of his race."

"Like yourself?" queried the monk calmly. "What have you done, for example?"

El-Râmi stopped in his walk to and fro.

"What have I done?" he repeated—"Why—nothing! You deem me proud and ambitious,—but I am humble enough to know how little I know. And as to proofs,—well, it is the same story—I have proved nothing."

"So! Then are your labours wasted?"

"Nothing is wasted,—according to your theories even. Your theories—many of them—are beautiful and soul-satisfying, and this one of there being no waste in the economy of the universe is, I believe, true. But I cannot accept all you teach. I broke my connection with you because I could not bend my spirit to the level of the patience you enjoined. It was not rebellion,—no! for I loved and honoured you—and

I still revere you more than any man alive, but I cannot bow my neck to the yoke you consider so necessary. To begin all work by first admitting one's weakness!—no!—Power is gained by never-resting ambition, not by a merely laborious humility."

"Opinions differ on that point"—said the monk quietly—"I never sought to check your ambition—I simply said—Take God with you. Do not leave Him out. He Is. Therefore His existence must be included in everything, even in the scientific examination of a drop of dew. Without Him you grope in the dark—you lack the key to the mystery. As an example of this, you are yourself battering against a shut door, and fighting with a Force too strong for you."

"I must have proofs of God!" said El-Râmi very deliberately—"Nature proves her existence; let God prove His!"

"And does He not prove it?" inquired the monk with mingled passion and solemnity—"Have you to go further than the commonest flower to find Him?"

El-Râmi shrugged his shoulders with an air of light disdain.

"Nature is Nature,"—he said—"God—an there be a God—is God. If God works through Nature He arranges things very curiously on a system of mutual destruction. You talk of flowers,—they contain both poisonous and healing properties,—and the poor human race has to study and toil for years before finding out which is which. Is that just of Nature—or God? Children never know at all,—and the poor little wretches die often through eating poison-berries of whose deadly nature they were not aware. That is what I complain of—we are not aware of evil, and we are not made aware. We have to find it out for ourselves. And I maintain that it is wanton cruelty on the part of the Divine Element to punish us for ignorance which we cannot help. And so the plan of mutual destructiveness goes on, with the most admirable persistency; the eater is in turn eaten, and as far as I can make out, this seems to be the one Everlasting Law. Surely it is an odd and inconsequential arrangement? As for the business of creation, that is easy, if once we grant the existence of certain component parts of space. Look at this, for example"—and he took from a corner a thin steel rod about the size of an ordinary walking cane—"If I use this magnet, and these few crystals"—and he opened a box on the table, containing some sparkling powder like diamond dust, a pinch of which he threw up into the air—"and play with them thus, you see what happens!"

And with a dexterous steady motion, he waved the steel rod rapidly round and round in the apparently empty space where he had tossed aloft the pinch of powder, and gradually there grew into shape out of the seeming nothingness, a round large brilliant globe of prismatic tints, like an enormously magnified soap-bubble, which followed the movement of the steel magnet rapidly and accurately. The monk lifted himself a little in his chair and watched the operation with interest and curiosity—till presently El-Râmi dropped the steel rod from sheer fatigue of arm. But the globe went on revolving steadily by itself for a time, and El-Râmi pointed to it with a smile—

"If I had the skill to send that bubble-sphere out into space, solidify it, and keep it perpetually rolling," he said lightly, "it would in time exhale its own atmosphere and produce life, and I should be a very passable imitation of the Creator."

At that moment, the globe broke and vanished like a melting snowflake, leaving no trace of its existence but a little white dust which fell in a round circle on the carpet. After this display, El-Râmi waited for his guest to speak, but the monk said nothing.

"You see," continued El-Râmi—"it requires a great deal to satisfy me with proofs. I must have tangible Fact, not vague Imagining."

The monk raised his eyes,—what searching calm eyes they were!— and fixed them full on the speaker.

"Your Sphere was a Fact,"—he said quietly—"Visible to the eye, it glittered and whirled—but it was not tangible, and it had no life in it. It is a fair example of other Facts,—so-called. And you could not have created so much as that perishable bubble, had not God placed the materials in your hands. It is odd you seem to forget that. No one can work without the materials for working,—the question remains, from Whence came those materials?"

El-Râmi smiled with a touch of scorn.

"Rightly are you called Supreme Master!" he said—"for your faith is marvellous—your ideas of life both here and hereafter, beautiful. I wish I could accept them. But I cannot. Your way does not seem to me clear or reasonable,—and I have thought it out in every direction. Take the doctrine of original sin for example—what is original sin, and why should it exist?"

"It does not exist—" said the monk quickly—"except in so far that we have created it. It is we, therefore, who must destroy it."

El-Râmi paused, thinking. This was the same lesson Lilith had taught.

"If we created it—" he said at last, "and there is a God who is omnipotent, why were we allowed to create it?"

The monk turned round in his chair with ever so slight a gesture of impatience.

"How often have I told you, El-Râmi Zarânos," he said,—"of the gift and responsibility bestowed on every human unit—Free-Will. You, who seek for proofs of the Divine, should realize that this is the only proof we have in ourselves, of our close relation to 'the image of God.' God's Laws exist,—and it is our first business in life to know and understand these—afterwards, our fate is in our own hands,—if we transgress law, or if we fulfil law, we know, or ought to know, the results. If we choose to make evil, it exists till we destroy it—good we cannot make, because it is the very breath of the Universe, but we can choose to breathe in it and with it. I have so often gone over this ground with you, that it seems mere waste of words to go over it again,—and if you cannot, will not see that you are creating your own destiny and shaping it to your own will, apart from anything that human or divine experience can teach you, then you are blind indeed. But time wears on apace,—and I must speak of other things;—one message I have for you that will doubtless cause you pain." He waited a moment-then went on slowly and sadly—"Yes,—the pain will be bitter and the suffering long,—but the fiat has gone forth, and ere long, you will be called upon to render up the Soul of Lilith."

El-Râmi started violently,—flushed a deep red, and then grew deadly pale.

"You speak in enigmas—" he said huskily and with an effort—"What do you know—how have you heard—"

He broke off,—his voice failed him, and the monk looked at him compassionately.

"Judge not the power of God, El-Râmi Zarânos!" he said solemnly—"for it seems you cannot even measure the power of man. What!—did you think your secret experiment safely hid from all knowledge save your own?—nay! you mistake. I have watched your progress step by step—your proud march onward through such mysteries as never mortal mind dared penetrate before,—but even these wonders have their limits—and those limits are, for you, nearly reached. You must set your captive free!"

"Never!" exclaimed El-Râmi passionately. "Never, while I live! I defy the heavens to rob me of her!—by every law in nature, she is mine!"

"Peace!" said the monk sternly—"Nothing is yours,—except the fate you have made for yourself. That is yours; and that must and will be fulfilled. That, in its own appointed time, will deprive you of Lilith."

El-Râmi's eyes flashed wrath and pain.

"What have you to do with my fate?" he demanded—"How should you know what is in store for me? You are judged to have a marvellous insight into spiritual things, but it is not insight after all so much as imagination and instinct. These may lead you wrong,—you have gained them, as you yourself admit, through nothing but inward concentration and prayer—my discoveries are the result of scientific exploration,—there is no science in prayer!"

"Is there not?"—and the monk, rising from his chair, confronted El-Râmi with the reproachful majesty of a king who faces some recreant vassal—"Then with all your wisdom you are ignorant,—ignorant of the commonest laws of simple Sound. Do you not yet know—have you not yet learned that Sound vibrates in a million million tones through every nook and corner of the Universe? Not a whisper, not a cry from human lips is lost—not even the trill of a bird or the rustle of a leaf. All is heard,—all is kept,—all is reproduced at will forever and ever. What is the use of your modern toys, the phonograph and the telephone, if they do not teach you the fundamental and external law by which these adjuncts to civilization are governed? God—the great, patient loving God—hears the huge sounding-board of space re-echo again and yet again with rough curses on His Name,—with groans and wailings; shouts, tears and laughter send shuddering discord through His Everlasting Vastness, but amid it all there is a steady strain of music,—full, sweet and pure—the music of perpetual prayer. No science in prayer! Such science there is, that by its power the very ether parts asunder as by a lightning-stroke—the highest golden gateways are unbarred,—and the connecting-link 'twixt God and Man, stretches itself through Space, between and round all worlds, defying any force to break the current of its messages."

He spoke with fervour and passion,—El-Râmi listened silent and unconvinced.

"I waste my words, I know—" continued the monk—"For you, Yourself suffices. What your brain dares devise,—what your hand dares attempt, that you will do, unadvisedly, sure of your success without the help of God or man. Nevertheless—you may not keep the Soul of Lilith."

His voice was very solemn yet sweet; El-Râmi, lifting his head, looked full at him, wonderingly, earnestly, and as one in doubt. Then his mind seemed to grasp more completely his visitor's splendid presence,—the noble face, the soft commanding eyes,—and instinctively he bent his proud head with a sudden reverence.

"Truly you are a god-like man—" he said slowly—"God-like in strength, and pure-hearted as a child. I would trust you in many things, if not in all. Therefore,—as by some strange means you have possessed yourself of my secret,—come with me,—and I will show you the chiefest marvel of my science—the life I claim—the spirit I dominate. Your warning I cannot accept, because you warn me of what is impossible. Impossible—I say, impossible!—for the human Lilith, God's Lilith, died—according to God's will; my Lilith lives, according to My will. Come and see,—then perhaps you will understand how it is that I—I, and not God any longer,—claim and possess the Soul I saved!"

With these words, uttered in a thrilling tone of pride and passion, he opened the study door and with a mute inviting gesture, led the way out. In silence and with a pensive step, the monk slowly followed.

END OF VOLUME I

THE SOUL OF LILITH

VOLUME 2

I

Into the beautiful room, glowing with its regal hues of gold and purple, where the spell-bound Lilith lay, El-Râmi led his thoughtful and seemingly reluctant guest. Zaroba met them on the threshold and was about to speak,—but at an imperative sign from her master she refrained, and contented herself merely with a searching and inquisitive glance at the stately monk, the like of whom she had never seen before. She had good cause to be surprised,—for in all the time she had known him, El-Râmi had never permitted any visitor to enter the shrine of Lilith's rest. Now he had made a new departure,—and in the eagerness of her desire to know why this stranger was thus freely admitted into the usually forbidden precincts, she went her way downstairs to seek Féraz, and learn from him the explanation of what seemed so mysterious. But it was now past ten o'clock at night, and Féraz was asleep,—fast locked in such a slumber that though Zaroba shook him and called him several times, she could not rouse him from his deep and almost death-like torpor. Baffled in her attempt, she gave it up at last, and descended to the kitchen to prepare her own frugal supper,—resolving, however, that as soon as she heard Féraz stirring she would put him through such a catechism, that she would find out, in spite of El-Râmi's haughty reticence, the name of the unknown visitor and the nature of his errand.

Meanwhile, El-Râmi himself and his grave companion stood by the couch of Lilith, and looked upon her in all her peaceful beauty for some minutes in silence. Presently El-Râmi grew impatient at the absolute impassiveness of the monk's attitude and the strange look in his eyes—a look which expressed nothing but solemn compassion and reverence.

"Well!" he exclaimed almost brusquely—"Now you see Lilith, as she is."

"Not so!" said the monk quietly—"I do not see her as she is. But I have seen her,—whereas, . . . you have not!"

El-Râmi turned upon him somewhat angrily.

"Why will you always speak in riddles?" he said—"In plain language, what do you mean?"

"In plain language I mean what I say"—returned the monk composedly—"And I tell you I have seen Lilith. The Soul of Lilith is Lilith;—not this brittle casket made of earthy materials which we now look upon, and which is preserved from decomposition by an electric fluid. But—beautiful as it is—it is a corpse—and nothing more."

El-Râmi regarded him with an expression of haughty amazement.

"Can a corpse breathe?" he inquired—"Can a corpse have colour and movement? This Body was the body of a child when first I began my experiment,—now it is a woman's form full-grown and perfect—and you tell me it is a corpse!"

"I tell you no more than you told Féraz," said the monk coldly—"When the boy trespassed your command and yielded to the suggestion of your servant Zaroba, did you not assure him that Lilith was dead?"'

El-Râmi started;—these words certainly gave him a violent shock of amazement.

"God!" he exclaimed—"How can you know all this?—Where did you hear it? Does the very air convey messages to you from a distance?— Does the light copy scenes for you, or what is it that gives you such a superhuman faculty for knowing everything you choose to know?"

The monk smiled gravely.

"I have only one method of work, El-Râmi"—he said—"And that method you are perfectly aware of, though you would not adopt it when I would have led you into its mystery. 'No man cometh to the Father, but by Me.' You know that old well-worn text—read so often, heard so often, that its true meaning is utterly lost sight of and forgotten. 'Coming to the Father' means the attainment of a superhuman intuition—a superhuman knowledge,—but as you do not believe in these things, let them pass. But you were perfectly right when you told Féraz that this Lilith is dead;—of course she is dead,—dead as a plant that is dried but has its colour preserved, and is made to move its leaves by artificial means. This body's breath is artificial,—the liquid in its veins is not blood, but a careful compound of the electric fluid that generates all life,—and it might be possible to preserve it thus forever. Whether its growth would continue is a scientific question; it might and it might not,—probably it would cease if the Soul held no more communication with it. For its growth, which you consider so remarkable, is simply the result of a movement of the brain;—when you force back the Spirit to converse through its medium, the brain receives an impetus, which it communicates to the spine and nerves,—the growth and extension of the muscles is bound to follow. Nevertheless, it is really a chemically animated corpse; it is not Lilith. Lilith herself I know."

"Lilith herself you know!" echoed El-Râmi, stupefied—"You know. . . ! What is it that you would imply?"

"I know Lilith"—said the monk steadily, "as you have never known her. I have seen her as you have never seen her. She is a lonely creature,—a wandering angel, for ever waiting,—for ever hoping. Unloved, save by the Highest Love, she wends her flight from star to star, from world to world,—a spirit beautiful, but incomplete as a flower without its stem,—a bird without its mate. But her destiny is changing,—she will not be alone for long,—the hours ripen to their best fulfilment,—and Love, the crown and completion of her being, will unbind her chains and send her soaring to the Highest Joy in the glorious liberty of the free!"

While he spoke thus, softly, yet with eloquence and passion, a dark flush crept over El-Râmi's face,—his eyes glittered and his hand trembled—he seemed to be making some fierce inward resolve. He controlled himself, however, and asked with a studied indifference—

"Is this your prophecy?"

"It is not a prophecy; it is a truth;" replied the monk gently—"If you doubt me, why not ask Her? She is here."

"Here?" El-Râmi looked about vaguely, first at the speaker, then at the couch where the so-called "corpse" lay breathing tranquilly—"Here, did you say? Naturally,—of course she is here."

And his glance reverted again to Lilith's slumbering form.

"No—not here—" said the monk with a gesture towards the couch— "but—there!"

And he pointed to the centre of the room where the lamp shed a mellow golden lustre, on the pansy-embroidered carpet, and where from the tall crystal vase of Venice ware, a fresh, branching cluster of pale roses exhaled their delicious perfume. El-Râmi stared, but could see nothing,—nothing save the lamp-light and the nodding flowers.

"There?" he repeated bewildered—"Where?"

"Alas for you, that you cannot see her!" said the monk compassionately. "This blindness of your sight proves that for you the veil has not yet been withdrawn. Lilith is there, I tell you;—she stands close to those roses,— her white form radiates like lightning—her hair is like the glory of the sunshine on amber,—her eyes are bent upon the flowers, which are fully conscious of her shining presence. For flowers are aware of angels' visits, when men see nothing! Round her and above her are the trailing films of light caught from the farthest stars,—she is alone as usual,—her looks are wistful and appealing,—will you not speak to her?"

El-Râmi's surprise, vexation and fear were beyond all words as he heard this description,—then he became scornful and incredulous.

"Speak to her!" he repeated—"Nay—if you see her as plainly as you say—let her speak!"

"You will not understand her speech—" said the monk—"Not unless it be conveyed to you in earthly words through that earthly medium there—" and he pointed to the fair form on the couch—"But, otherwise you will not know what she is saying. Nevertheless—if you wish it,—she shall speak."

"I wish nothing—" said El-Râmi quickly and haughtily—"If you imagine you see her,—and if you can command this creature of your imagination to speak, why do so; but Lilith as I know her, speaks to none save me."

The monk lifted his hands with a solemn movement as of prayer—

"Soul of Lilith!" he said entreatingly—"Angel-wanderer in the spheres beloved of God—if, by the Master's grace I have seen the vision clearly—speak!"

Silence followed. El-Râmi fixed his eyes on Lilith's visible recumbent form,—no voice could make reply, he thought, save that which must issue from those lovely lips curved close in placid slumber,—but the monk's gaze was fastened in quite an opposite direction. All at once a strain of music, soft as a song played on the water by moonlight, rippled through the room. With mellow richness the cadence rose and fell,—it had a marvellous sweet sound, rhythmical and suggestive of words,—unimaginable words, fairies' language,—anything that was removed from mortal speech, but that was all the same capable of utterance. El-Râmi listened perplexed;—he had never heard anything so convincingly, almost painfully sweet,—till suddenly it ceased as it had begun, abruptly, and the monk looked round at him.

"You heard her?" he inquired—"Did you understand?"

"Understand what?" asked El-Râmi impatiently—"I heard music—nothing more."

The monk's eyes rested upon him in grave compassion.

"Your spiritual perception does not go far, El-Râmi Zarânos—" he said gently—"Lilith spoke;—her voice was the music."

El-Râmi trembled;—for once his strong nerves were somewhat shaken. The man beside him was one whom he knew to be absolutely truthful, unselfishly wise,—one who scorned "trickery" and who had no motive for deceiving him,—one also who was known to possess a strange and marvellous familiarity with "things unproved and unseen." In spite of his sceptical nature, all he dared assume against his guest, was that he was endowed with a perfervid imagination which persuaded him of the existence of what were really only the "airy nothings" of his brain. The irreproachable grandeur, purity and simplicity of the monk's life as known among his brethren, were of an ideal perfection never before attempted or attained by man,—and as he met the steady, piercing faithful look of his companion's eyes,—clear fine eyes such as, reverently speaking, one might have imagined the Christ to have had when in the guise of humanity He looked love on all the world,— El-Râmi was fairly at a loss for words. Presently he recovered himself sufficiently to speak, though his accents were hoarse and tremulous.

"I will not doubt you;—" he said slowly—"But if the Soul of Lilith is here present as you say,—and if it spoke, surely I may know the purport of its language!"

"Surely you may!" replied the monk—"Ask her in your own way to repeat what she said just now. There—" and he smiled gravely as he pointed to the couch—"there is your human phonograph!"

Perplexed, but willing to solve the mystery, El-Râmi bent above the slumbering girl, and taking her hands in his own, called her by name in his usual manner. The reply came soon—though somewhat faintly.

"I am here!"

"How long have you been here?" asked El-Râmi.

"Since my friend came."

"Who is that friend, Lilith?"

"One that is near you now—" was the response.

"Did you speak to this friend a while ago?"

"Yes!"

The answer was more like a sigh than an assent.

"Can you repeat what you said?"

Lilith stretched her fair arms out with a gesture of weariness.

"I said I was tired—" she murmured—"Tired of the search through Infinity for things that are not. A wayward Will bids me look for Evil—I search, but cannot find it;—for Hell, a place of pain and torment,— up and down, around and around the everlasting circles I wend my way, and can discover no such abode of misery. Then I bring back the messages of truth,—but they are rejected, and I am sorrowful. All the realms of God are bright with beauty save this one dark prison of Man's Fantastic Dream. Why am I bound here? I long to reach the light!—I am tired of the darkness!" She paused—then added—"This is what I said to one who is my friend."

Vaguely pained, and stricken with a sudden remorse, El-Râmi asked: "Am not I your friend, Lilith?"

A shudder ran through her delicate limbs. Then the answer came distinctly, yet reluctantly:

"No!"

El-Râmi dropped her hands as though he had been stung;—his face was very pale. The monk touched him on the shoulder.

"Why are you so moved?" he asked—"A spirit cannot lie;—an angel cannot flatter. How should she call you friend?—you, who detain her here solely for your own interested purposes?—To you she is a 'subject' merely,—no more than the butterfly dissected by the naturalist. The butterfly has hopes, ambitions, loves, delights, innocent wishes, nay even a religion,—what are all these to the grim spectacled scientist who breaks its delicate wings? The Soul of Lilith, like a climbing flower, strains instinctively upward,—but you—(for a certain time only) according to the natural magnetic laws which compel the stronger to subdue the weaker, have been able to keep this, her ethereal Essence, a partial captive under your tyrannical dominance. Yes—I say 'tyrannical,'—great wisdom should inspire love,—but in you it only inspires despotism. Yet with all your skill and calculation you have strangely overlooked one inevitable result of your great Experiment."

El-Râmi looked up inquiringly but said nothing.

"How it is that you have not foreseen this thing I cannot imagine"—continued the monk—"The body of Lilith has grown under your very eyes from the child to the woman by the merest material means,—the chemicals which Nature gives us, and the forces which Nature allows us to employ. How then should you deem it possible for the Soul to remain stationary? With every fresh experience its form expands—its desires increase,—its knowledge widens,—and the everlasting Necessity of Love compels its life to Love's primeval Source. The Soul of Lilith is awakening to its fullest immortal consciousness,—she realizes her connection with the great angelic worlds—her kindredship with those worlds' inhabitants, and as she gains this glorious knowledge more certainly, so she gains strength. And this is the result I warn you of—her force will soon baffle yours, and you will have no more influence over her than you have over the highest Archangel in the realms of the Supreme Creator."

"A woman's Soul!—only a woman's soul, remember that!" said El-Râmi dreamily—"How should it baffle mine? Of slighter character—of more sensitive balance—and always prone to yield,—how should it prove so strong? Though, of course, you will tell me that Souls, like Angels, are sexless."

"I will tell you nothing of the sort"—said the monk quietly. "Because it would not be true. All created things have Sex, even the Angels. 'Male and Female created He them'—recollect that,—when it is said God made Man in 'His Own Image.'"

El-Râmi's eyes opened wide in astonishment.

"What! Is it possible you would endow God Himself with the Feminine attributes as well as the Masculine?"

"There are Two Governing Forces of the Universe," replied the monk deliberately—"One, the masculine, is Love,—the other, feminine, is Beauty. These Two, reigning together, are GOD;—just as man and wife are One. From Love and Beauty proceed Law and Order. You cannot away with it—it is so. Love and Beauty produce and reproduce a million forms with more than a million variations—and when God made Man in His Own Image, it was as Male and Female. From the very first growths of life in all worlds,—from the small, almost imperceptible beginning of that marvellous Evolution which resulted in Humanity,—evolution which to us is calculated to have taken thousands of years, whereas in the Eternal countings it has occupied but a few moments, Sex was proclaimed in the lowliest sea-plants, of which the only remains we have are in the Silurian formations,—and was equally maintained in the humblest lingula inhabiting its simple bivalve shell. Sex is proclaimed throughout the Universe with an absolute and unswerving regularity through all grades of nature. Nay, there are even Male and Female Atmospheres which when combined produce forms of life."

"You go far,—I should say much too far in your supposed Law!" said El-Râmi wonderingly and a little derisively.

"And you, my good friend, stop short,—and oppose yourself against all Law, when it threatens to interfere with your work"—retorted the monk—"The proof is, that you are convinced you can keep the Soul of Lilith to wait upon your will at pleasure like another Ariel. Whereas the Law is, that at the destined moment she shall be free. Wise Shakespeare can teach you this,—Prospero had to give his 'fine spirit' liberty in the end. If you could shut Lilith up in her mortal frame again, to live a mortal life, the case might be different; but that you cannot do, since the mortal frame is too dead to be capable of retaining such a Fire-Essence as hers is now."

"You think that?" queried El-Râmi,—he spoke mechanically,—his thoughts were travelling elsewhere in a sudden new direction of their own.

The monk regarded him with friendly but always compassionate eyes.

"I not only think it—I know it!" he replied.

El-Râmi met his gaze fixedly.

"You would seem to know most things,"—he observed—"Now in this matter I consider that I am more humble-minded than yourself. For I cannot say I 'know' anything,—the whole solar system appears to me to be in a gradually changing condition,—and each day one set of facts is followed by another entirely new set which replace the first and render them useless—"

"There is nothing useless," interposed the monk—"not even a so-called 'fact' disproved. Error leads to the discovery of Truth. And Truth always discloses the one great unalterable Fact,—God."

"As I told you, I must have proofs of God"—said El-Râmi with a chill smile—"Proofs that satisfy me, personally speaking. At present I believe in Force only."

"And how is Force generated?" inquired the monk.

"That we shall discover in time. And not only the How, but also the Why. In the meantime we must prove and test all possibilities, both material and spiritual. And as far as such proving goes, I think you can scarcely deny that this experiment of mine on the girl Lilith is a wonderful one?"

"I cannot grant you that;"—returned the monk gravely—"Most Eastern magnetists can do what you have done, provided they have the necessary Will. To detach the Soul from the body, and yet keep the body alive, is an operation that has been performed by others and will be performed again,—but to keep Body and Soul struggling against each other in unnatural conflict, requires cruelty as well as Will. It is as I before observed, the vivisection of a butterfly. The scientist does not think himself barbarous—but his barbarity outweighs his science all the same."

"You mean to say there is nothing surprising in my work?"

"Why should there be?" said the monk curtly—"Barbarism is not wonderful! What is truly a matter for marvel is Yourself. You are the most astonishing example of self-inflicted blindness I have ever known!"

MARIE CORELLI

El-Râmi breathed quickly,—he was deeply angered, but he had self-possession enough not to betray it. As he stood, sullenly silent, his guest's hand fell gently on his shoulder—his guest's eyes looked earnest love and pity into his own.

"El-Râmi Zarânos," he said softly—"You know me. You know I would not lie to you. Hear then my words;—As I see a bird on the point of flight, or a flower just ready to break into bloom, even so I see the Soul of Lilith. She is on the verge of the Eternal Light—its rippling wave,—the great sweet wave that lifts us upward,—has already touched her delicate consciousness,—her aerial organism. You—with your brilliant brain, your astonishing grasp and power over material forces—you are on the verge of darkness,—such a gulf of it as cannot be measured—such a depth as cannot be sounded. Why will you fall? Why do you choose Darkness rather than Light?"

"Because my 'deeds are evil,' I suppose," retorted El-Râmi bitterly—"You should finish the text while you are about it. I think you misjudge me,—however, you have not heard all. You consider my labour as vain, and my experiment futile,—but I have some strange results yet to show you in writing. And what I have written I desire to place in your hands that you may take all to the monastery, and keep my discoveries,—if they are discoveries, among the archives. What may seem the wildest notions to the scientists of today may prove of practical utility hereafter."

He paused, and bending over Lilith, took her hand and called her by name. The reply came rather more quickly than usual.

"I am here!"

"Be here no longer, Lilith"—said El-Râmi, speaking with unusual gentleness,—"Go home to that fair garden you love, on the high hills of the bright world called Alcyone. There rest, and be happy till I summon you to earth again."

He released her hand,—it fell limply in its usual position on her breast,—and her face became white and rigid as sculptured marble. He watched her lying so for a minute or two, then turning to the monk, observed—

"She has left us at once, as you see. Surely you will own that I do not grudge her her liberty?"

"Her liberty is not complete"—said the monk quietly—"Her happiness therefore is only temporary."

El-Râmi shrugged his shoulders indifferently.

"What does that matter if, as you declare, her time of captivity is soon to end? According to your prognostications she will ere long set herself free."

The monk's fine eyes flashed forth a calm and holy triumph.

"Most assuredly she will!"

El-Râmi looked at him and seemed about to make some angry retort, but checking himself, he bowed with a kind of mingled submissiveness and irony, saying—

"I will not be so discourteous as to doubt your word! But—I would only remind you that nothing in this world is certain—"

"Except the Law of God!" interrupted the monk with passionate emphasis—"That is immutable,—and against that, El-Râmi Zarânos, you contend in vain! Opposed to that, your strength and power must come to naught,—and all they who wonder at your skill and wisdom shall by-and-by ask one another the old question—'What went ye out for to see?' And the answer shall describe your fate—'A reed shaken by the wind!'"

He turned away as he spoke and without another look at the beautiful Lilith, he left the room. El-Râmi stood irresolute for a moment, thinking deeply,—then, touching the bell which would summon Zaroba back to her usual duty of watching the tranced girl, he swiftly followed his mysterious guest.

II

He found him quietly seated in the study, close beside the window, which he had thrown open for air. The rain had ceased,—a few stars shone out in the misty sky, and there was a fresh smell of earth and grass and flowers, as though all were suddenly growing together by some new impetus.

"'The winter is past,—the rain is over and gone!—Arise, my love, my fair one, and come away!'" quoted the monk softly, half to himself and half to El-Râmi as he saw the latter enter the room—"Even in this great and densely peopled city of London, Nature sends her messengers of spring—see here!"

And he held out on his hand a delicate insect with shining iridescent wings that glistened like jewels.

"This creature flew in as I opened the window," he continued, surveying it tenderly. "What quaint and charming stories of Flower-land it could tell us if we could but understand its language! Of the poppy-palaces, and rose-leaf saloons coloured through by the kindly sun,—of the loves of the ladybirds and the political controversies of the bees! How dare we make a boast of wisdom!—this tiny denizen of air baffles us—it knows more than we do."

"With regard to the things of its own sphere it knows more, doubtless," said El-Râmi—"but concerning our part of creation, it knows less. These things are equally balanced. You seem to me to be more of a poet than either a devotee or a scientist."

"Perhaps I am!" and the monk smiled, as he carefully wafted the pretty insect out into the darkness of the night again—"Yet poets are often the best scientists, because they never know they are scientists. They arrive by a sudden intuition at the facts which it takes several Professors Dry-as—Dust years to discover. When once you feel you are a scientist, it is all over with you. You are a clever biped who has got hold of a crumb out of the Universal Loaf, and for all your days afterwards you are turning that crumb over and over under your analytical lens. But a poet takes up the whole Loaf unconsciously, and hands portions of it about at haphazard and with the abstracted behaviour of one in a dream,—a wild and extravagant process,—but then, what would you?—his nature could not do with a crumb. No—I dare not call myself 'poet'; if I gave myself any title at all, I would say, with all humbleness, that I am a sympathizer."

"You do not sympathize with me," observed El-Râmi gloomily.

"My friend, at the immediate moment, you do not need my sympathy. You are sufficient for yourself. But, should you ever make a claim upon me, be sure I shall not fail."

He spoke earnestly and cheerily, and smiled,—but El-Râmi did not return the smile. He was bending over a deep drawer in his writing-table, and after a little search he took out two bulky rolls of manuscript tied and sealed.

"Look there!" he said, indicating the titles with an air of triumph.

The monk obeyed and read aloud:

"'The Inhabitants of Sirius. Their Laws, Customs, and Progress.' Well?"

"Well!" echoed El-Râmi.—"Is such information, gained from Lilith in her wanderings, of no value?"

The monk made no direct reply, but read the title of the second Ms.

"'The World of Neptune. How it is composed of One Thousand Distinct Nations, united under one reigning Emperor, known at the present era as Ustalvian the Tenth.' And again I say—well? What of all this, except to hazard the remark that Ustalvian is a great creature, and supports his responsibilities admirably?"

El-Râmi gave a gesture of irritation and impatience.

"Surely it must interest you?" he said. "Surely you cannot have known these things positively—"

"Stop, stop, my friend!" interposed the monk.—"Do you know them positively? Do you accept any of Lilith's news as positive? Come,—you are honest—confess you do not! You cannot believe her, though you are puzzled to make out as to where she obtains information which has certainly nothing to do with this world, or any external impression. And that is why she is really a Sphinx to you still, in spite of your power over her. As for being interested, of course I am interested. It is impossible not to be interested in everything, even in the development of a grub. But you have not made any discovery that is specially new—to me. I have my own Messenger!" He raised his eyes one moment with a brief devout glance—then resumed quietly—"There are other 'detached' spirits, besides that of your Lilith, who have found their way to some of the planets, and have returned to tell the tale. In one of our monasteries we have a very exact description of Mars obtained in this same way—its landscapes, its cities, its people, its various nations—all very concisely given. These are but the beginnings of discoveries—the feeling for the Clue,—the Clue itself will be found one day."

"The Clue to what?" demanded El-Râmi. "To the stellar mysteries, or to Life's mystery?"

"To everything!" replied the monk firmly. "To everything that seems unclear and perplexing now. It will all be unravelled for us in such a simple way that we shall wonder why we did not discover it before. As I told you, my friend, I am, above all things, a sympathizer. I sympathize—God knows how deeply and passionately,—with what I may call the unexplained woe of the world. The other day I visited a poor fellow who had lost his only child. He told me he could believe in nothing,—he said that what people call the goodness of God was only cruelty. 'Why take this boy!' he cried, rocking the pretty little corpse to and fro on his breast—'Why rob me of the chief thing I had to live for? Oh, if I only knew—as positively as I know day is day, and night is night—that I should see my living child again, and possess his love in another world than this, should I repine as I do? No,—I should believe in God's wisdom,—and I should try to be a good man instead of a bad. But it is because I do not know, that I am broken-hearted. If there is a God, surely He might have given us some little certain clue by way of help and comfort!' Thus he wailed,—and my heart ached for him. Nevertheless the clue is to be had,—and I believe it will be found suddenly in some little, deeply-hidden unguessed Law,—we are on the track of it, and I fancy we shall soon find it."

"Ah!—and what of the millions of creatures who, in the bygone eras, having no clue, have passed away without any sort of comfort?" asked El-Râmi.

"Nature takes time to manifest her laws," replied the monk.—"And it must be remembered that what we call 'time' is not Nature's counting at all. The method Nature has of counting time may be faintly guessed by proven scientific fact,—as, for instance, take the Comet which appeared in 1744. Strict mathematicians calculated that this brilliant world (for it is a world) needs 122,683 years to perform one single circuit! And yet the circuit of a Comet is surely not so much time to allow for God and Nature to declare a Meaning!"

El-Râmi shuddered slightly.

"All the same, it is horrible to think of," he said.—"All those enormous periods,—those eternal vastnesses! For, during the 122,683 years we die, and pass into the Silence."

"Into the Silence or the Explanation?" queried the monk softly.— "For there is an Explanation,—and we are all bound to know it at some time or other, else Creation would be but a poor and bungling business."

"If we are bound to know," said El-Râmi, "then every living creature is bound to know, since every living creature suffers cruelly, in wretched ignorance of the cause of its suffering. To every atom, no matter how infinitely minute, must be given this 'explanation,'—to dogs and birds as well as men—nay, even to flowers must be declared the meaning of the mystery."

"Unless the flowers know already!" suggested the monk with a smile.—"Which is quite possible!"

"Oh, everything is 'possible' according to your way of thinking," said El-Râmi somewhat impatiently. "If one is a visionary, one would scarcely be surprised to see the legended 'Jacob's ladder' leaning against that dark midnight sky and the angels descending and ascending upon it. And so—" here he touched the two rolls of manuscript lying on the table—"you find no use in these?"

"I personally have no use for them," responded his guest,—"but as you desire it, I will take charge of them and place them in safe keeping at the monastery. Every little link helps to forge the chain of discovery, of course. By the way, while on this subject, I must not forget to speak to you about poor old Kremlin. I had a letter from him about two months ago. I very much fear that famous Disc of his will be his ruin."

"Such an intimation will console him vastly!" observed El-Râmi sarcastically.

"Consolation has nothing to do with the matter. If a man rushes wilfully into danger, danger will not move itself out of the way for him. I always told Kremlin that his proposed design was an unsafe one, even before he went out to Africa fifteen years ago in search of the magnetic spar—a crystalline formation whose extraordinary reflection-power he learned from me. However, it must be admitted that he has come marvellously close to the unravelling of the enigma at which he works. And when you see him next you may tell him from me, that if he can— mind, it is a very big 'if'—if he can follow the movements of the Third Ray on his Disc he will be following the signals from Mars. To make out the meaning of those signals is quite another matter—but he can safely classify them as the light-vibrations from that particular planet."

"How is he to tell which is the Third Ray that falls, among a fleeting thousand?" asked El-Râmi dubiously.

"It will be difficult of course, but he can try," returned the monk.— "Let him first cover the Disc with thick, dark drapery, and then when it is face to face with the stars in the zenith, uncover it quickly, keeping his eyes fixed on its surface. In one minute there will be three distinct flashes—the third is from Mars. Let him endeavour to follow that third ray in its course on the Disc, and probably he will arrive at something worth remark. This suggestion I offer by way of assisting him, for his patient labour is both wonderful and pathetic,—but,—it would be far better and wiser were he to resign his task altogether. Yet—who knows!—the ordained end may be the best!"

"And do you know this 'ordained end'?" questioned El-Râmi.

The monk met his incredulous gaze calmly.

"I know it as I know yours," he replied. "As I know my own, and the end (or beginning) of all those who are, or who have been, in any way connected with my life and labours."

"How can you know!" exclaimed El-Râmi brusquely.—"Who is there to tell you these things that are surely hidden in the future?"

"Even as a picture already hangs in an artist's brain before it is painted," said the monk,—"so does every scene of each human unit's life hang, embryo-like, in air and space, in light and colour. Explanations of these things are well-nigh impossible—it is not given to mortal speech to tell them. One must see,—and to see clearly, one must not become wilfully blind." he paused,—then added—"For instance, El-Râmi, I would that you could see this room as I see it."

El-Râmi looked about half carelessly, half wonderingly.

"And do I not?" he asked.

The monk stretched out his hand.

"Tell me first,—is there anything visible between this my extended arm and you?"

El-Râmi shook his head.

"Nothing."

Whereupon the monk raised his eyes, and in a low thrilling voice said solemnly—

"O God with whom Thought is Creation and Creation Thought, for one brief moment, be pleased to lift material darkness from the sight of this man Thy subject-creature, and by Thy sovereign-power permit him to behold with mortal eyes, in mortal life, Thy deathless Messenger!"

Scarcely had these words been pronounced than El-Râmi was conscious of a blinding flash of fire as though sudden lightning had struck the room from end to end. Confused and dazzled, he instinctively covered his eyes with his hand, then removing it, looked up, stupefied, speechless, and utterly overwhelmed at what he saw. Clear before him stood a wondrous Shape, seemingly human, yet unlike humanity,—a creature apparently composed of radiant colour, from whose transcendent form, great shafts of gold and rose and purple spread upward and around in glowing lines of glory. This marvellous Being stood, or rather was poised in a stedfast attitude, between him, El-Râmi, and the monk,—its luminous hands were stretched out on either side as though to keep those twain asunder—its starry eyes expressed an earnest watchfulness—its majestic patience never seemed to tire. A thing of royal stateliness and power, it stayed there immovable, parting with its radiant intangible Presence the two men who gazed upon it, one with fearless, reverent, yet accustomed eyes—the other with a dazzled and bewildered stare. Another moment and El-Râmi at all risks would have spoken,—but that the Shining Figure lifted its light-crowned head and gazed at him. The wondrous look appalled him,—unnerved him,—the straight, pure brilliancy and limpid lustre of those unearthly orbs sent shudders through him,—he gasped for breath—thrust out his hands, and fell on his knees in a blind, unconscious, swooning act of adoration, mingled with a sense of awe and something like despair,—when a dense chill darkness as of death closed over him, and he remembered nothing more.

III

When he came to himself, it was full daylight. His head was resting on someone's knee,—someone was sprinkling cold water on his face and talking to him in an incoherent mingling of Arabic and English,—who was that someone? Féraz? Yes!—surely it was Féraz! Opening his eyes languidly, he stared about him and attempted to rise.

"What is the matter?" he asked faintly. "What are you doing to me? I am quite well, am I not?"

"Yes, yes!" cried Féraz eagerly, delighted to hear him speak.—"You are well,—it was a swoon that seized you—nothing more! But I was anxious,—I found you here, insensible—"

With an effort El-Râmi rose to his feet, steadying himself on his brother's arm.

"Insensible!" he repeated vaguely.—"Insensible!—that is strange!—I must have been very weak and tired—and overpowered. But,—where is He—?"

"If you mean the Master," said Féraz, lowering his voice to an almost awe-stricken whisper—"He has gone, and left no trace,—save that sealed paper there upon your table."

El-Râmi shook himself free of his brother's hold and hurried forward to possess himself of the indicated missive,—seizing it, he tore it quickly open,—it contained but one line—"Beware the end! With Lilith's love comes Lilith's freedom."

That was all. He read it again and again—then deliberately striking a match, he set fire to it and burnt it to ashes. A rapid glance round showed him that the manuscripts concerning Neptune and Sirius were gone,—the mysterious monk had evidently taken them with him as desired. Then he turned again to his brother.

"When could he have gone?" he de—manded.—"Did you not hear the street-door open and shut?—no sound at all of his departure?"

Féraz shook his head.

"I slept heavily," he said apologetically. "But in my dreams it seemed as though a hand touched me, and I awoke. The sun was shining brilliantly—someone called 'Féraz! Féraz!'—I thought it was your voice, and I hurried into the room to find you, as I thought, dead,—oh! the horror of that moment of suspense!"

El-Râmi looked at him kindly, and smiled.

"Why feel horror, my dear boy?" he inquired.—"Death—or what we call death,—is the best possible fortune for everybody. Even if there were no Afterwards, it would still be an End—an end of trouble and tedium and infinite uncertainty. Could anything be happier?—I doubt it!"

And sighing, he threw himself into his chair with an air of exhaustion. Féraz stood a little apart, gazing at him somewhat wistfully—then he spoke—

"I too have thought that, El-Râmi," he said softly.—"As to whether this End, which the world and all men dread, might not be the best thing? And yet my own personal sensations tell me that life means something good for me if I only learn how best to live it."

"Youth, my dear fellow!" said El-Râmi lightly. "Delicious youth,—which you share in common with the scampering colt who imagines all the meadows of the world were made for him to race upon. This is the potent charm which persuades you that life is agreeable. But unfortunately it will pass,—this rosy morning-glory. And the older you grow the wiser and the sadder you will be,—I, your brother, am an excellent example of the truth of this platitude."

"You are not old," replied Féraz quickly. "But certainly you are often sad. You overwork your brain. For example, last night of course you did not sleep—will you sleep now?"

"No—I will breakfast," said El-Râmi, rousing himself to seem cheerful.—"A good cup of coffee is one of the boons of existence—and no one can make it as you do. It will put the finishing touch to my complete recovery."

Féraz took this hint, and hastened off to prepare the desired beverage,—while El-Râmi, left alone, sat for a few moments wrapped in a deep reverie. His thoughts reverted to and dwelt upon the strange and glorious Figure he had seen standing in that very room between him and the monk,—he wondered doubtfully if such a celestial visitant were anywhere near him now? Shaking off the fantastic impression, he got up and walked to and fro.

"What a fool I am!" he exclaimed half-aloud—"As if my eyes could not be as much deluded for once in a way, as the eyes of anyone else! It was a strange shape,—a marvellously divine-looking apparition;—but he evolved it—he is as great a master in the art of creating phantasma as Moses himself, and could, if he chose, make thunder echo at his will on another Mount Sinai. Upon my word, the things that men can do are as wonderful as the things that they would fain attempt; and the only miraculous part of this particular man's force is that he should have overpowered ME, seeing I am so strong. And then one other marvel,— (if it be true)—he could see the Soul of Lilith."

Here he came to a full stop in his walk, and with his eyes fixed on vacancy he repeated musingly—

"He could see the Soul of Lilith. If that is so—if that is possible, then I will see it too, if I die in the attempt. To see the Soul—to look upon it and know its form—to discern the manner of its organization, would surely be to prove it. Sight can be deceived, we know—we look upon a star (or think we look upon it), that may have disappeared some thirty thousand years ago, as it takes thirty thousand years for its reflex to reach us—all that is true—but there are ways of guarding against deception."

He had now struck upon a new line of thought,—ideas more daring than he had ever yet conceived began to flit through his brain,—and when Féraz came in with the breakfast he partook of that meal with avidity and relish, his excellent appetite entirely reassuring his brother with regard to his health.

"You are right, Féraz," he said, as he sipped his coffee.—"Life can be made enjoyable after a fashion, no doubt. But the best way to get enjoyment out of it is to be always at work—always putting a brick in to help the universal architecture."

Féraz was silent. El-Râmi looked at him inquisitively.

"Don't you agree with me?" he asked.

"No—not entirely"—and Féraz pushed the clustering hair off his brow with a slightly troubled gesture.—"Work may become as monotonous and wearisome as anything else if we have too much of it. If we are always working—that is, if we are always obtruding ourselves into affairs and thinking they cannot get on without us, we make an obstruction in the way, I think—we are not a help. Besides, we leave ourselves no time to absorb suggestions, and I fancy a great deal is learned by simply keeping the brain quiet and absorbing light."

"'Absorbing light?'" queried his brother perplexedly—"What do you mean?"

"Well, it is difficult to explain my meaning," said Féraz with hesitation—"but yet I feel there is truth in what I try to express. You see, everything absorbs something, and you will assuredly admit that the brain absorbs certain impressions?"

"Of course,—but impressions are not 'light'?"

"Are they not? Not even the effects of light? Then what is the art of photography? However, I do not speak of the impressions received from our merely external surroundings. If you can relieve the brain from conscious thought,—if you have the power to shake off outward suggestions and be willing to think of nothing personal, your brain will receive impressions which are to some extent new, and with which you actually have very little connection. It is strange,—but it is so;—you become obediently receptive, and perhaps wonder where your ideas come from. I say they are the result of light. Light can use up immense periods of time in travelling from a far distant star into our area of vision, and yet at last we see it,—shall not God's inspiration travel at a far swifter pace than star-beams, and reach the human brain as surely? This thought has often startled me,—it has filled me with an almost apprehensive awe,—the capabilities it opens up are so immense and wonderful. Even a man can suggest ideas to his fellow-man and cause them to germinate in the mind and blossom into action,—how can we deny to God the power to do the same? And so,—imagine it!—the first strain of the glorious 'Tannhauser' may have been played on the harps of Heaven, and rolling sweetly through infinite space may have touched in fine far echoes the brain of the musician who afterwards gave it form and utterance—ah yes!—I would love to think it were so!—I would love to think that nothing,—nothing is truly ours; but that all the marvels of poetry, of song, of art, of colour, of beauty, were only the echoes and distant impressions of that Eternal Grandeur which comes hereafter!"

His eyes flashed with all a poet's enthusiasm,—he rose from the table and paced the room excitedly, while his brother, sitting silent, watched him meditatively.

"El-Râmi, you have no idea," he continued—"of the wonders and delights of the land I call my Star! You think it is a dream—an unexplained portion of a splendid trance,—and I am now fully aware of what I owe to your magnetic influence,—your forceful spell that rests upon my life;—but see you!—when I am alone—quite, quite alone, when you are absent from me, when you are not influencing me, it is then I see the landscapes best,—it is then I hear my people sing! I let my brain rest;—as far as it is possible, I think of nothing,—then suddenly upon me falls the ravishment and ecstasy,—this world rolls up as it were in a whirling cloud and vanishes, and lo! I find myself at home. There is a stretch of forest-land in this Star of mine,—a place all dusky green with shadows, and musical with the fall of silvery waters,—that is my favourite haunt when I am there, for it leads me on and on through grasses and tangles of wild flowers to what I know and feel must be my own abode, where I should rest and sleep if sleep were needful; but this abode I never reach; I am debarred from entering in, and I do not know the reason why. The other day, when wandering there, I met two maidens bearing flowers,—they stopped, regarding me with pleased yet doubting eyes, and one said—'Look you, our lord is now returned!' And the other sighed and answered—'Nay! he is still an exile and may not stay with us.' Whereupon they bent their heads, and shrinking past me, disappeared. When I would have called them back I woke!—to find that this dull earth was once again my house of bondage."

El-Râmi heard him with patient interest.

"I do not deny, Féraz," he said slowly, "that your impressions are very strange—"

"Very strange? Yes!" cried Féraz. "But very true!"

He paused—then on a sudden impulse came close up to his brother, and laid a hand on his shoulder.

"And do you mean to tell me," he asked, "that you who have studied so much, and have mastered so much, yet receive no such impressions as those I speak of?"

A faint flush coloured El-Râmi's olive skin.

"Certain impressions come to me at times, of course," he answered slowly.—"And there have been certain seasons in my life when I have had visions of the impossible. But I have a coldly-tempered organization, Féraz,—I am able to reason these things away."

"Oh, you can reason the whole world away if you choose," said Féraz.—"For it is nothing after all but a pinch of star-dust."

"If you can reason a thing away it does not exist," observed El-Râmi dryly.—"Reduce the world, as you say, to a pinch of star-dust, still the pinch of star-dust is there—it Exists."

"Some people doubt even that!" said Féraz, smiling.

"Well, everything can be over-done," replied his brother,—"even the process of reasoning. We can, if we choose, 'reason' ourselves into madness. There is a boundary-line to every science which the human intellect dare not overstep."

"I wonder what and where is your boundary-line?" questioned Féraz lightly.—"Have you laid one down for yourself at all? Surely not!—for you are too ambitious."

El-Râmi made no answer to this observation, but betook himself to his books and papers. Féraz meanwhile set the room in order and cleared away the breakfast,—and these duties done, he quietly withdrew. Left to himself, El-Râmi took from the centre drawer of his writing-table a medium-sized manuscript book which was locked, and which he opened by means of a small key that was attached to his watch-chain, and bending over the title-page he critically examined it. Its heading ran thus—

"The title does not cover all the ground," he murmured as he read.—"And yet how am I to designate it? It is a vast subject, and presents different branches of treatment, and after all said and done, I may have wasted my time in planning it. Most likely I have,—but there is no scientist living who would refuse to accept it. The question is, shall I ever finish it?—shall I ever know positively that there Is without doubt, a Conscious, Personal Something or Someone after death who enters at once upon another existence? My new experiment will decide all—if I see the Soul of Lilith, all hesitation will be at an end—I shall be sure of everything which now seems uncertain. And then the triumph!—then the victory!"

His eyes sparkled, and dipping his pen in the ink he prepared to write, but ere he did so the message which the monk had left for him to read, recurred with a chill warning to his memory,—

"Beware the end! With Lilith's love comes Lilith's freedom."

He considered the words for a moment apprehensively,—and then a proud smile played round his mouth.

"For a Master who has attained to some degree of wisdom, his intuition is strangely erroneous this time," he muttered.—"For if there be any dream of love in Lilith, that dream, that love is Mine! And being mine, who shall dispute possession,—who shall take her from me? No one,—not even God,—for He does not break through the laws of Nature. And by those laws I have kept Lilith—and even so I will keep her still."

Satisfied with his own conclusions, he began to write, taking up the thread of his theory of religion where he had left it on the previous day. He had a brilliant and convincing style, and was soon deep in an elaborate and eloquent disquisition on the superior scientific reasoning contained in the ancient Eastern faiths, as compared with the modern scheme of Christianity, which limits God's power to this world only, and takes no consideration of the fate of other visible and far more splendid spheres.

IV

The few days immediately following the visit of the mysterious monk from Cyprus were quiet and uneventful enough. El-Râmi led the life of a student and recluse; Féraz, too, occupied himself with books and music, thinking much, but saying little. He had solemnly sworn never again to make allusion to the forbidden subject of his brother's great experiment, and he meant to keep his vow. For though he had in very truth absolutely forgotten the name "Lilith," he had not forgotten the face of her whose beauty had surprised his senses and dazzled his brain. She had become to him a nameless Wonder,— and from the sweet remembrance of her loveliness he gained a certain consolation and pleasure which he jealously and religiously kept to himself. He thought of her as a poet may think of an ideal goddess seen in a mystic dream,—but he never ventured to ask a question concerning her. And even if he had wished to do so,—even if he had indulged the idea of encouraging Zaroba to follow up the work she had begun by telling him all she could concerning the beautiful tranced girl, that course was now impossible. For Zaroba seemed stricken dumb as well as deaf,—what had chanced to her he could not tell,—but a mysterious silence possessed her; and though her large black eyes were sorrowfully eloquent, she never uttered a word. She came and went on various household errands, always silently and with bent head,—she looked older, feebler, wearier and sadder, but not so much as a gesture escaped her that could be construed into a complaint. Once Féraz made signs to her of inquiry after her health and well-being—she smiled mournfully, but gave no other response, and turning away, left him hurriedly. He mused long and deeply upon all this,—and though he felt sure that Zaroba's strange but resolute speechlessness was his brother's work, he dared not speculate too far or inquire too deeply. For he fully recognised El-Râmi's power,—a power so scientifically balanced, and used with such terrible and unerring precision, that there could be no opposition possible unless one were of equal strength and knowledge. Féraz knew he could no more compete with such a force than a mouse can wield a thunderbolt,—he therefore deemed it best to resign himself to his destiny and wait the course of events.

"For," he said within himself, "it is not likely one man should be permitted to use such strange authority over natural forces long,—it may be that God is trying him,—putting him to the proof, as it were, to find out how far he will dare to go,—and then—ah then!—what then? If his heart were dedicated to the service of God I should not fear—but—as it is,—I dread the end!"

His instinct was correct in this,—for in spite of his poetic and fanciful temperament, he had plenty of quick perception, and he saw plainly what El-Râmi himself was not very willing to recognise,— namely, that in all the labour of his life, so far as it had gone, he, El-Râmi, had rather opposed himself to the Unseen Divine, than striven to incorporate himself with it. He preferred to believe in Natural Force only; his inclination was to deny the possibility of anything behind That. He accepted the idea of Immortality to a certain extent, because Natural Force was forever giving him proofs of the perpetual regeneration of life—but that there was a Primal Source of this generating influence,— One, great and eternal, who would demand an account of all lives, and an accurate summing-up of all words and actions,—in this, though he might assume the virtue of faith, Féraz very well knew he had it not. Like the greater majority of scientists and natural philosophers generally, what Self could comprehend, he accepted,—but all that extended beyond Self,—all that made of Self but a grain of dust in a vast infinitude,—all that forced the Creature to prostrate himself humbly before the Creator and cry out "Lord, be merciful to me a sinner!" this he tacitly and proudly rejected. For which reasons the gentle, dreamy Féraz had good cause to fear,—and a foreboding voice forever whispered in his mind that man without God was as a world without light,—a black chaos of blank unfruitfulness.

With the ensuing week the grand "reception" to which El-Râmi and his brother had been invited by Lord Melthorpe came off with great éclat. Lady Melthorpe's "crushes" were among the most brilliant of the season, and this one was particularly so, as it was a special function held for the entertainment of the distinguished Crown Prince of a great nation. True, the distinguished Crown Prince was only "timed" to look in a little after midnight for about ten minutes, but the exceeding brevity of his stay was immaterial to the fashionable throng. All that was needed was just the piquant flavour,—the "passing" of a Royal Presence,—to make the gathering socially complete. The rooms were crowded—so much so indeed that it was difficult to take note of any one person in particular, yet in spite of this fact, there was a very general movement of interest and admiration when El-Râmi entered with his young and handsome brother beside him. Both had a look and manner too distinctly striking to escape observation:—their olive complexions, black melancholy eyes, and slim yet stately figures, were set off to perfection by the richness of the Oriental dresses they wore; and the grave composure and perfect dignity of their bearing offered a pleasing contrast to the excited pushing, waddling, and scrambling indulged in by the greater part of the aristocratic assemblage. Lady Melthorpe herself, a rather pretty woman attired in a very æsthetic gown, and wearing her brown hair all towzled and arranged "à la Grecque" in diamond bandeaux, caught sight of them at once, and was delighted. Such picturesque-looking creatures were really ornaments to a room, she thought with much interior satisfaction; and wreathing her face with smiles, she glided up to them.

"I am so charmed, my dear El-Râmi!" she said, holding out her jewelled hand.—"So charmed to see you—you so very seldom will come to me! And your brother! So glad! Why did you never tell me you had a brother? Naughty man! What is your brother's name? Féraz? Delightful!—it makes me think of Hafiz and Sadi and all those very charming Eastern people. I must find someone interesting to introduce to you. Will you wait here a minute—the crowd is so thick in the centre of the room that really I'm afraid you will not be able to get through it— do wait here, and I'll bring the Baroness to you—don't you know the Baroness? Oh, she's such a delightful creature—so clever at palmistry! Yes—just stay where you are,—I'll come back directly!"

And with sundry good-humoured nods her ladyship swept away, while Féraz glanced at his brother with an expression of amused inquiry.

"That is Lady Melthorpe?" he asked.

"That is Lady Melthorpe," returned El-Râmi—"our hostess, and Lord Melthorpe's wife; his, 'to have and to hold, for better for worse, for richer for poorer, in sickness and in health, to love, honour and cherish till death do them part,'" and he smiled somewhat satirically.— "It seems odd, doesn't it?—I mean, such solemn words sound out of place sometimes. Do you like her?"

Féraz made a slight sign in the negative.

"She does not speak sincerely," he said in a low tone.

El-Râmi laughed.

"My dear boy, you mustn't expect anyone to be 'sincere' in society. You said you wanted to 'see life'—very well, but it will never do to begin by viewing it in that way. An outburst of actual sincerity in this human mêlée"—and he glanced comprehensively over the brilliant throng—"would be like a match to a gunpowder magazine—the whole thing would blow up into fragments and be dispersed to the four winds of heaven, leaving nothing behind but an evil odour."

"Better so," said Féraz dreamily, "than that false hearts should be mistaken for true."

El-Râmi looked at him wistfully;—what a beautiful youth he really was, with all that glow of thought and feeling in his dark eyes! How different was his aspect to that of the jaded, cynical, vice-worn young men of fashion, some of whom were pushing their way past at that moment,—men in the twenties who had the air of being well on in the forties, and badly preserved at that—wretched, pallid, languid, exhausted creatures who had thrown away the splendid jewel of their youth in a couple of years' stupid dissipation and folly. At that moment Lord Melthorpe, smiling and cordial, came up to them and shook hands warmly, and then introduced with a few pleasant words a gentleman who had accompanied him as,—"Roy Ainsworth, the famous artist, you know!"

"Oh, not at all!" drawled the individual thus described, with a searching glance at the two brothers from under his drowsy eyelids.—"Not famous by any means—not yet. Only trying to be. You've got to paint something startling and shocking nowadays before you are considered 'famous';—and even then, when you've outraged all the proprieties, you must give a banquet, or take a big house and hold receptions, or have an electrically lit-up skeleton in your studio, or something of that sort, to keep the public attention fixed upon you. It's such a restless age."

El-Râmi smiled gravely.

"The feverish outburst of an unnatural vitality immediately preceding dissolution," he observed.

"Ah!—you think that? Well—it may be,—I'm sure I hope it is. I personally should be charmed to believe in the rapidly-approaching end of the world. We really need a change of planet as much as certain invalids require a change of air. Your brother, however"—and here he flashed a keen glance at Féraz—"seems already to belong to quite a different sphere."

Féraz looked up with a pleased yet startled expression.

"Yes,—but how did you know it?" he asked.

It was now the artist's turn to be embarrassed. He had used the words "different sphere" merely as a figure of speech, whereas this intelligent-looking young fellow evidently took the phrase in a literal sense. It was very odd!—and he hesitated what to answer, so El-Râmi came to the rescue.

"Mr. Ainsworth only means that you do not look quite like other people, Féraz, that's all. Poets and musicians often carry their own distinctive mark."

"Is he a poet?" inquired Lord Melthorpe with interest.—"And has he published anything?"

El-Râmi laughed good-humouredly.

"Not he! Why dear Lord Melthorpe, we are not all called upon to give the world our blood and brain and nerve and spirit. Some few reserve their strength for higher latitudes. To give greedy Humanity everything of one's self is rather too prodigal an expenditure."

"I agree with you," said a chill yet sweet voice close to them.—"It was Christ's way of work,—and quite too unwise an example for any of us to follow."

Lord Melthorpe and Mr. Ainsworth turned quickly to make way for the speaker,—a slight fair woman, with a delicate thoughtful face full of light, languor, and scorn, who, clad in snowy draperies adorned here and there with the cold sparkle of diamonds, drew near them at the moment. El-Râmi and his brother both noted her with interest,—she was so different from the other women present.

"I am delighted to see you!" said Lord Melthorpe as he held out his hand in greeting.—"It is so seldom we have the honour! Mr. Ainsworth you already know,—let me introduce my Oriental friends here,—El-Râmi Zarânos and his brother Féraz Zarânos,—Madame Irene Vassilius—you must have heard of her very often."

El-Râmi had indeed heard of her,—she was an authoress of high repute, noted for her brilliant satirical pen, her contempt of press-criticism, and her influence over, and utter indifference to, all men. Therefore he regarded her now with a certain pardonable curiosity as he made her his profoundest salutation, while she returned his look with equal interest.

"It is you who said that we must not give ourselves wholly away to the needs of Humanity, is it not?" she said, letting her calm eyes dwell upon him with a dreamy yet searching scrutiny.

"I certainly did say so, Madame," replied El-Râmi.—"It is a waste of life,—and Humanity is always ungrateful."

"You have proved it? But perhaps you have not tried to deserve its gratitude."

This was rather a home thrust, and El-Râmi was surprised and vaguely annoyed at its truth. Irene Vassilius still stood quietly observing him,—then she turned to Roy Ainsworth.

"There is the type you want for your picture," she said, indicating Féraz by a slight gesture.—"That boy, depicted in the clutches of your Phryne, would make angels weep."

"If I could make you weep I should have achieved something like success," replied the painter, his dreamy eyes dilating with a passion he could not wholly conceal.—"But icebergs neither smile nor shed tears,—and intellectual women are impervious to emotion."

"That is a mistaken idea,—one of the narrow notions common to men," she answered, waving her fan idly to and fro.—"You remind me of the querulous Edward Fitzgerald, who wrote that he was glad Mrs. Barrett-Browning was dead, because there would be no more 'Aurora Leighs.' He condescended to say she was a 'woman of Genius,' but what was the use of it? She and her Sex, he said, would be better minding the Kitchen and their Children. He and his Sex always consider the terrible possibilities to themselves of a badly cooked dinner and a baby's screams. His notion about the limitation of Woman's sphere, is Man's notion generally."

"It is not mine," said Lord Melthorpe.—"I think women are cleverer than men."

"Ah, you are not a reviewer!" laughed Madame Vassilius—"so you can afford to be generous. But as a rule men detest clever women, simply because they are jealous of them."

"They have cause to be jealous of you," said Roy Ainsworth.—"You succeed in everything you touch."

"Success is easy," she replied indifferently.—"Resolve upon it, and carry out that resolve—and the thing is done."

El-Râmi looked at her with new interest.

"Madame, you have a strong will!" he observed.—"But permit me to say that all your sex are not like yourself, beautiful, gifted, and resolute at one and the same time. The majority of women are deplorably unintelligent and uninteresting."

"That is precisely how I find the majority of men!" declared Irene Vassilius, with that little soft laugh of hers which was so sweet, yet so full of irony.—"You see, we view things from different standpoints.

Moreover, the deplorably unintelligent and uninteresting women are the very ones you men elect to marry, and make the mothers of the nation. It is the way of masculine wisdom,—so full of careful forethought and admirable calculation!" She laughed again, and continued—"Lord Melthorpe tells me you are a Seer,—an Eastern prophet arisen in these dull modern days—now will you solve me a riddle that I am unable to guess,—Myself?—and tell me if you can, who am I and what am I?"

"Madame," replied El-Râmi bowing profoundly, "I cannot in one moment unravel so complex an Enigma."

She smiled, not ill-pleased, and met his dark, fiery, penetrating glance unreservedly,—then, drawing off her long loose glove, she held out her small beautifully-shaped white hand.

"Try me," she said lightly, "for if there is any truth in 'brain-waves' or reflexes of the mind, the touch of my fingers ought to send electric meanings through you. I am generally judged as of a frivolous disposition because I am small in stature, slight in build, and have curly hair—all proofs positive, according to the majority, of latent foolishness. Colossal women, however, are always astonishingly stupid, and fat women lethargic—but a mountain of good flesh is always more attractive to man than any amount of intellectual perception. Oh, I am not posing as one of the 'misunderstood'; not at all—I simply wish you to look well at me first and take in my 'frivolous' appearance thoroughly, before being misled by the messages of my hand."

El-Râmi obeyed her in so far that he fixed his eyes upon her more searchingly than before,—a little knot of fashionable loungers had stopped to listen, and now watched her face with equal curiosity. No rush of embarrassed colour tinged the cool fairness of her cheeks—her expression was one of quiet, half-smiling indifference—her attitude full of perfect self-possession.

"No one who looks at your eyes can call you frivolous, Madame," said El-Râmi at last.—"And no one who observes the lines of your mouth and chin could suspect you of latent foolishness. Your physiognomy must have been judged by the merest surface-observers. As for stature, we are aware that goes for naught,—most of the heroes and heroines of history have been small and slight in build. I will now, if you permit me, take your hand."

She laid it at once in his extended palm,—and he slowly closed his own fingers tightly over it. In a couple of minutes, his face expressed nothing but astonishment.

"Is it possible!" he muttered—"can I believe—" he broke off hurriedly, interrupted by a chorus of voices exclaiming—"Oh, what is it?—do tell us!" and so forth.

"May I speak, Madame?" he inquired, bending towards Irene, with something of reverence.

She smiled assent.

"If I am surprised," he then said slowly, "it is scarcely to be wondered at, for it is the first time I have ever chanced across the path of a woman whose life was so perfectly ideal. Madame, to you I must address the words of Hamlet—'pure as ice, chaste as snow, thou shalt not escape calumny.' Such an existence as yours, stainless, lofty, active, hopeful, patient, and independent, is a reproach to men, and few will love you for being so superior. Those who do love you, will probably love in vain,—for the completion of your existence is not here—but Elsewhere."

Her soft eyes dilated wonderingly,—the people immediately around her stared vaguely at El-Râmi's dark impenetrable face.

"Then shall I be alone all my life as I am now?" she asked, as he released her hand.

"Are you sure you are alone?" he said with a grave smile.—"Are there not more companions in the poet's so-called solitude, than in the crowded haunts of men?"

She met his earnest glance, and her own face grew radiant with a certain sweet animation that made it very lovely.

"You are right," she replied simply—"I see you understand."

Then with a graceful salutation, she prepared to move away—Roy Ainsworth pressed up close to her.

"Are you satisfied with your fortune, Madame Vassilius?" he asked rather querulously.

"Indeed I am," she answered. "Why should I not be?"

"If loneliness is a part of it," he said audaciously, "I suppose you will never marry?"

"I suppose not," she said with a ripple of laughter in her voice.—"I fear I should never be able to acknowledge a man my superior!"

She left him then, and he stood for a moment looking after her with a vexed air,—then he turned anew towards El-Râmi, who was just exchanging greetings with Sir Frederick Vaughan. This latter young man appeared highly embarrassed and nervous, and seemed anxious to unburden himself of something which apparently was difficult to utter. He stared at Féraz, pulled the ends of his long moustache, and made scrappy remarks on nothing in particular, while El-Râmi observed him with amused intentness.

"I say, do you remember the night we saw the new Hamlet?" he blurted out at last.—"You know—I haven't seen you since—"

"I remember most perfectly," said El-Râmi composedly—"'To be or not to be' was the question then with you, as well as with Hamlet—but I suppose it is all happily decided now as 'to be.'"

"What is decided?" stammered Sir Frederick—"I mean, how do you know everything is decided, eh?"

"When is your marriage to take place?" asked El-Râmi.

Vaughan almost jumped.

"By Jove!—you are an uncanny fellow!" he exclaimed.—"However, as it happens, you are right. I'm engaged to Miss Chester."

"It is no surprise to me, but pray allow me to congratulate you!" and El-Râmi smiled.—"You have lost no time about it, I must say! It is only a fortnight since you first saw the lady at the theatre. Well!—confess me a true prophet!"

Sir Frederick looked uncomfortable, and was about to enter into an argument concerning the pros and cons of prophetic insight, when Lady Melthorpe suddenly emerged from the circling whirlpool of her fashionable guests and sailed towards them with a swan-like grace and languor.

"I cannot find the dear Baroness," she said plaintively. "She is so much in demand! Do you know, my dear El-Râmi, she is really almost as wonderful as you are! Not quite—oh, not quite, but nearly! She can tell you all your past and future by the lines of your hand, in the most astonishing manner! Can you do that also?"

El-Râmi laughed.

"It is a gipsy's trick," he said,—"and the bonâ-fide gipsies who practise it in country lanes for the satisfaction of servantgirls, get arrested by the police for 'fortune—telling.' The gipsies of the London drawing-rooms escape scot-free."

"Oh, you are severe!" said Lady Melthorpe, shaking her finger at him with an attempt at archness—"You are really very severe! You must not be hard on our little amusements,—you know in this age, we are all so very much interested in the supernatural!"

El-Râmi grew paler, and a slight shudder shook his frame. The Supernatural! How lightly people talked of that awful Something, that like a formless Shadow waits behind the portals of the grave!—that Something that evinced itself, suggested itself, nay, almost declared itself, in spite of his own doubts, in the momentary contact of a hand with his own, as in the case of Irene Vassilius. For in that contact he had received a faint, yet decided thrill through his nerves—a peculiar sensation which he recognised as a warning of something spiritually above himself,—and this had compelled him to speak of an "Elsewhere" for her, though for himself he persisted in nourishing the doubt that an "Elsewhere" existed. Roy Ainsworth, the artist, observing him closely, noted how stern and almost melancholy was the expression of his handsome dark face,—then glancing from him to his brother, was surprised at the marked difference between the two. The frank, open, beautiful features of Féraz seemed to invite confidence, and acting on the suggestion made to him by Madame Vassilius, he spoke abruptly.

"I wish you would sit to me," he said.

"Sit to you? For a picture, do you mean?" And Féraz looked delighted yet amazed.

"Yes. You have just the face I want. Are you in town?—can you spare the time?"

"I am always with my brother"—began Féraz hesitatingly.

El-Râmi heard him, and smiled rather sadly.

"Féraz is his own master," he said gently, "and his time is quite at his own disposal."

"Then come and let us talk it over," said Ainsworth, taking Féraz by the arm. "I'll pilot you through this crowd, and we'll make for some quiet corner where we can sit down. Come along!"

Out of old habit Féraz glanced at his brother for permission, but El-Râmi's head was turned away; he was talking to Lord Melthorpe. So, through the brilliant throng of fashionable men and women, many of whom turned to stare at him as he passed, Féraz went, half-eager, half-reluctant, his large fawn-like eyes flashing an innocent wonderment on the scene around him,—a scene different from everything to which he had been accustomed. He was uncomfortably conscious that there was something false and even deadly beneath all this glitter and show,—but his senses were dazzled for the moment, though the poet-soul of him instinctively recoiled from the noise and glare and restless movement of the crowd. It was his first entry into so-called "society";—and, though attracted and interested, he was also somewhat startled and abashed— for he felt instinctively that he was thrown upon his own resources,— that, for the present at any rate, his brother's will no longer influenced him, and with the sudden sense of liberty came the sudden sense of fear.

MARIE CORELLI

V

Towards midnight the expected Royal Personage came and went; fatigued but always amiable, he shed the sunshine of his stereotyped smile on Lady Melthorpe's "crush"—shook hands with his host and hostess, nodded blandly to a few stray acquaintances, and went through all the dreary, duties of social boredom heroically, though he was pining for his bed more wearily than any work-worn digger of the soil. He made his way out more quickly than he came in, and with his departure a great many of the more "snobbish" among the fashionable set disappeared also, leaving the rooms freer and cooler for their absence. People talked less loudly and assertively,—little groups began to gather in corners and exchange friendly chit-chat,—men who had been standing all the evening found space to sit down beside their favoured fair ones, and indulge themselves in talking a little pleasant nonsense,—even the hostess herself was at last permitted to occupy an arm-chair and take a few moments' rest. Some of the guests had wandered into the music-saloon, a quaintly decorated oak-panelled apartment which opened out from the largest drawing-room. A string band had played there till Royalty had come and gone, but now "sweet harmony" no longer "wagged her silver tongue," for the musicians were at supper. The grand piano was open, and Madame Vassilius stood near it, idly touching the ivory keys now and then with her small white, sensitive-looking fingers. Close beside her, comfortably ensconced in a round deep chair, sat a very stout old lady with a curiously large hairy face and a beaming expression of eye, who appeared to have got into her pink silk gown by some cruelly unnatural means, so tightly was she laced, and so much did she seem in danger of bursting. She perspired profusely and smiled perpetually, and frequently stroked the end of her very pronounced moustache with quite a mannish air. This was the individual for whom Lady Melthorpe had been searching,—the Baroness von Denkwald, noted for her skill in palmistry.

"Ach! it is warm!" she said in her strong German accent, giving an observant and approving glance at Irene's white-draped form.—"You are ze one womans zat is goot to look at. A peach mit ice-cream,—dot is yourself."

Irene smiled pensively, but made no answer.

The Baroness looked at her again, and fanned herself rapidly.

"It is sometings bad mit you?" she asked at last.—"You look sorrowful? Zat Eastern mans—he say tings disagreeable? You should pelieve me,—I have told you of your hand—ach! what a fortune!—splendid!—fame,—money, title,—a grand marriage—"

Irene lifted her little hand from the keyboard of the piano, and looked curiously at the lines in her pretty palm.

"Dear Baroness, there must be some mis—take," she said slowly.—"I was a lonely child,—and some people say that as you begin, so will you end. I shall never marry—I am a lonely woman, and it will always be so."

"Always, always—not at all!" and the Baroness shook her large head obstinately. "You will marry; and Gott in Himmel save you from a husband such as mine! He is dead—oh yes—a goot ting;—he is petter off—and so am I. Moch petter!"

And she laughed, the rise and fall of her ample neck causing quite a cracking sound in the silk of her bodice.

Madame Vassilius smiled again,—and then again grew serious. She was thinking of the "Elsewhere" that El-Râmi had spoken of,—she had noticed that all he said had seemed to be uttered involuntarily,—and that he had hesitated strangely before using the word "Elsewhere." She longed to ask him one or two more questions,—and scarcely had the wish formed itself in her mind, than she saw him advancing from the drawing-room, in company with Lord Melthorpe, Sir Frederick Vaughan, and the pretty frivolous Idina Chester, who, regardless of all that poets write concerning the unadorned simplicity of youth, had decked herself, American fashion, with diamonds enough for a dowager.

"It's too lovely!" the young lady was saying as she entered.—"I think, Mr. El-Râmi, you have made me out a most charming creature! Unemotional, harmless and innocently worldly '—that was it, wasn't it?' Well now, I think that's splendid! I had an idea you were going to find out something horrid about me;—I'm so glad I'm harmless! You're sure I'm harmless?"

"Quite sure!" said El-Râmi with a slight smile. "And there you possess a great superiority over most women."

And he stepped forward in obedience to Lady Melthorpe's signal, to be introduced to the 'dear' Baroness, whose shrewd little eyes dwelt upon him curiously.

"Do you believe in palmistry?" she asked him, after the ordinary greetings were exchanged.

"I'm afraid not," he answered politely—"though I am acquainted with the rules of the art as practised in the East, and I know that many odd coincidences do occur. But,—as an example—take my hand—I am sure you can make nothing of it."

He held out his open palm for her inspection—she bent over it, and uttered an exclamation of surprise. There were none of the usual innumerable little criss-cross lines upon it—nothing, in fact, but two deep dents from left to right, and one well-marked line running from the wrist to the centre.

"It is unnatural!" cried the Baroness in amazement.—"It is a malformation! There is no hand like it!"

"I believe not," answered El-Râmi composedly.—"As I told you, you can learn nothing from it—and yet my life has not been without its adventures. This hand of mine is my excuse for not accepting palmistry as an absolutely proved science."

"Must everything be 'proved' for you?" asked Irene Vassilius suddenly.

"Assuredly, Madame!"

"Then have you 'proved' the Elsewhere of which you spoke to me?"

El-Râmi flushed a little,—then paled again.

"Madame, the message of your inner spirit, as conveyed first through the electric medium of the brain, and then through the magnetism of your touch, told me of an 'Elsewhere.' I may not personally or positively know of any 'elsewhere,' than this present state of being,—but your interior Self expects an 'Elsewhere,'—apparently knows of it better than I do, and conveys that impression and knowledge to me, apart from any consideration as to whether I may be fitted to understand or receive it."

These words were heard with evident astonishment by the little group of people who stood by, listening.

"Dear me! How ve—ry curious!" murmured Lady Melthorpe.— "And we have always looked upon dear Madame Vassilius as quite a free-thinker,"—here she smiled apologetically, as Irene lifted her serious eyes and looked at her steadily—"I mean, as regards the next world and all those interesting subjects. In some of her books, for instance, she is terribly severe on the clergy."

"Not more so than many of them deserve, I am sure," said El-Râmi with sudden heat and asperity.—"It was not Christ's intention, I believe, that the preachers of His Gospel should drink and hunt, and make love to their neighbours' wives ad libitum, which is what a great many of them do. The lives of the clergy nowadays offer very few worthy examples to the laity."

Lady Melthorpe coughed delicately and warningly. She did not like plain speaking,—she had a "pet clergyman" of her own,—moreover, she had been bred up in the provinces among "county" folk, some of whom still believe that at one period of the world's history "God" was always wanting the blood of bulls and goats to smell "as a sweet savour in His nostrils." She herself preferred to believe in the possibility of the Deity's having "nostrils," rather than take the trouble to consider the effect of His majestic Thought as evinced in the supremely perfect order of the Planets and Solar Systems.

El-Râmi, however, went on regardlessly.

"Free-thinkers," he said, "are for the most part truth-seekers. If everybody gave way to the foolish credulity attained to by the believers in the 'Mahatmas' for instance, what an idiotic condition the world would be in! We want free-thinkers,—as many as we can get,—to help us to distinguish between the False and the True. We want to separate the Actual from the Seeming in our lives,—and there is so much Seeming and so little Actual that the process is difficult."

"Why, dat is nonsense!" said the Baroness von Denkenwald.—"Mit a Fact, zere is no mistake—you prove him. See!" and she took up a silver penholder from the table near her.—"Here is a pen,—mit ink it is used to write—zere is what you call ze Actual."

El-Râmi smiled.

"Believe me, my dear Madame, it is only a pen so long as you elect to view it in that light. Allow me!"—and he took it from her hand, fixing his eyes upon her the while. "Will you place the tips of your fingers—the fingers of the left hand—yes—so! on my wrist? Thank you!"—this, as she obeyed with a rather vague smile on her big fat face.—"Now you will let me have the satisfaction of offering you this spray of lilies—the first of the season," and he gravely extended the silver penholder.—"Is not the odour delicious!"

"Ach! it is heavenly!" and the Baroness smelt at the penholder with an inimitable expression of delight. Everybody began to laugh—El-Râmi silenced them by a look.

"Madame, you are under some delusion," he said quietly.—"You have no lilies in your hand, only a penholder."

She laughed.

"You are very funny!" she said—"but I shall not be deceived. I shall wear my lilies."

And she endeavoured to fasten the penholder in the front of her bodice,—when suddenly El-Râmi drew his hand away from hers. A startled expression passed over her face, but in a minute or two she recovered her equanimity and twirled the penholder placidly between her fingers.

"Zere is what you call ze Actual," she said, taking up the conversation where it had previously been interrupted.—"A pen—holder is always a penholder—you can make nothing more of it."

But here she was surrounded by the excited onlookers—a flood of explanations poured upon her, as to how she had taken that same penholder for a spray of lilies, and so forth, till the old lady grew quite hot and angry.

"I shall not pelieve you!" she said indignantly.—"It is impossible. You haf a joke—but I do not see it. Irene"—and she looked appealingly to Madame Vassilius, who had witnessed the whole scene—"it is not true, is it?"

"Yes, dear Baroness, it is true," said Irene soothingly.—"But it is a nothing after all. Your eyes were deceived for the moment—and Mr. El-Râmi has shown us very cleverly, by scientific exposition, how the human sight can be deluded—he conveyed an impression of lilies to your brain, and you saw lilies accordingly. I quite understand,—it is only through the brain that we receive any sense of sight. The thing is easy of comprehension, though it seems wonderful."

"It is devilry!" said the Baroness solemnly, getting up and shaking out her voluminous pink train with a wrathful gesture.

"No, Madame," said El-Râmi earnestly, with a glance at her which somehow had the effect of quieting her ruffled feelings. "It is merely science. Science was looked upon as 'devilry' in ancient times,—but we in our generation are more liberal-minded."

"But what shall it lead to, all zis science?" demanded the Baroness, still with some irritation.—"I see not any use in it. If one deceive ze eye so quickly, it is only to make peoples angry to find demselves such fools!"

"Ah, my dear lady, if we could all know to what extent exactly we could be fooled,—not only as regards our sight, but our other senses and passions, we should be wiser and more capable of self-government than we are. Every step that helps us to the attainment of such knowledge is worth the taking."

"And you have taken so many of those steps," said Irene Vassilius, "that I suppose it would be difficult to deceive you?"

"I am only human, Madame," returned El-Râmi, with a faint touch of bitterness in his tone, "and therefore I am capable of being led astray by my own emotions as others are."

"Are we not getting too analytical?" asked Lord Melthorpe cheerily. "Here is Miss Chester wanting to know where your brother Féraz is. She only caught a glimpse of him in the distance,—and she would like to make his closer acquaintance."

"He went with Mr. Ainsworth," began El-Râmi.

"Yes—I saw them together in the conservatory," said Lady Melthorpe. "They were deep in conversation—but it is time they gave us a little of their company—I'll go and fetch them here."

She went, but almost immediately returned, followed by the two individuals in question. Féraz looked a little flushed and excited,—Roy Ainsworth calm and nonchalant as usual.

"I've asked your brother to come and sit to me tomorrow," the latter said, addressing himself at once to El-Râmi. "He is quite willing to oblige me,—and I presume you have no objection?"

"Not the least in the world!" responded El-Râmi with apparent readiness, though the keen observer might have detected a slight ring of satirical coldness in his tone.

"He is a curious fellow," continued Roy, looking at Féraz where he stood, going through the formality of an introduction to Miss Chester, whose bold bright eyes rested upon him in frank and undisguised admiration. "He seems to know nothing of life."

"What do you call 'life'?" demanded El-Râmi, with harsh abruptness.

"Why, life as we men live it, of course," answered Roy, complacently.

"'Life, as we men live it!'" echoed El-Râmi. "By Heaven, there is nothing viler under the sun than life lived so! The very beasts have a more decent and self-respecting mode of behaviour,—and the everyday existence of an ordinary 'man about town' is low and contemptible as compared to that of an honest-hearted Dog!"

Ainsworth lifted his languid eyes with a stare of amazement;—Irene Vassilius smiled.

"I agree with you!" she said softly.

"Oh, of course!" murmured Roy sar—castically—"Madame Vassilius agrees with everything that points to, or suggests the utter worthlessness of Man!"

Her eyes flashed.

"Believe me," she said, with some passion, "I would give worlds to be able to honour and revere men,—and there are some whom I sincerely respect and admire,—but I frankly admit that the majority of them awaken nothing in me but the sentiment of contempt. I regret it, but I cannot help it."

"You want men to be gods," said Ainsworth, regarding her with an indulgent smile; "and when they can't succeed, poor wretches, you are hard on them. You are a born goddess, and to you it comes quite naturally to occupy a throne on Mount Olympus, and gaze with placid indifference on all below,—but to others, the process is difficult. For example, I am a groveller. I grovel round the base of the mountain and rather like it. A valley is warmer than a summit, always."

A faint sea-shell pink flush crept over Irene's cheeks, but she made no reply. She was watching Féraz, round whom a bevy of pretty women were congregated, like nineteenth-century nymphs round a new Eastern Apollo. He looked a little embarrassed, yet his very diffidence had an indefinable grace and attraction about it which was quite novel and charming to the jaded fashionable fair ones who for the moment made him their chief object of attention. They were pressing him to give them some music, and he hesitated, not out of any shyness to perform, but simply from a sense of wonder as to how such a spiritual, impersonal and divine thing as Music could be made to assert itself in the midst of so much evident frivolity. He looked appealingly at his brother,—but El-Râmi regarded him not. He understood this mute avoidance of his eyes,—he was thrown upon himself to do exactly as he chose,—and his sense of pride stimulated him to action. Breaking from the ring of his fair admirers, he advanced towards the piano.

"I will play a simple prelude," he said, "and if you like it, you shall hear more."

There was an immediate silence. Irene Vassilius moved a little apart and sat on a low divan, her hands clasped idly in her lap;—near her stood Lord Melthorpe, Roy Ainsworth, and El-Râmi;—Sir Frederick Vaughan and his fiancée, Idina Chester, occupied what is known as a "flirtation chair" together; several guests flocked in from the drawing-rooms, so that the salon was comparatively well-filled. Féraz poised his delicate and supple hands on the keyboard,—and then—why, what then? Nothing!—only music!—music divinely pure and sweet as a lark's song,—music that spoke of things as yet undeclared in mortal language,—of the mystery of an angel's tears—of the joy of a rose in bloom,—of the midsummer dreams of a lily enfolded within its green leaf-pavilion,—of the love-messages carried by silver beams from bridegroom-stars to bride-satellites,—of a hundred delicate and wordless marvels the music talked eloquently in rounded and mystic tone. And gradually, but invincibly, upon all those who listened, there fell the dreamy nameless spell of perfect harmony,—they did not understand, they could not grasp the far-off heavenly meanings which the sounds con—veyed, but they knew and felt such music was not earthly. The quest of gold, or thirst of fame, had nothing to do with such composition—it was above and beyond all that. When the delicious melody ceased, it seemed to leave an emptiness in the air,—an aching regret in the minds of the audience; it had fallen like dew on arid soil, and there were tears in many eyes, and passionate emotions stirring many hearts, as Féraz pressed his finger-tips with a velvet-like softness on the closing chord. Then came a burst of excited applause which rather startled him from his dreams. He looked round with a faint smile of wonderment, and this time chanced to meet his brother's gaze earnestly fixed upon him. Then an idea seemed to occur to him, and playing a few soft notes by way of introduction, he said aloud, almost as though he were talking to himself—

"There are in the world's history a few old legends and stories, which, whether they are related in prose or rhyme, seem to set themselves involuntarily to music. I will tell you one now, if you care to hear it,— the Story of the Priest Philemon."

There was a murmur of delight and expectation, followed by profound silence as before.

Féraz lifted his eyes,—bright stag-like eyes, now flashing with warmth and inspiration,—and pressing the piano pedals, he played a few slow solemn chords like the opening bars of a church chant; then, in a soft, rich, perfectly modulated voice, he began.

VI

Long, long ago, in a far-away province of the Eastern world, there was once a priest named Philemon. Early and late he toiled to acquire wisdom—early and late he prayed and meditated on things divine and unattainable. To the Great Unknown his aspirations turned; with all the ardour of his soul he sought to penetrate behind the mystic veil of the Supreme Centre of creation; and the joys and sorrows, hopes and labours of mortal existence seemed to him but worthless and contemptible trifles when compared with the eternal marvels of the incomprehensible Hereafter, on which, in solitude, he loved to dream and ponder."

Here Féraz paused,—and touching the keys of the piano with a caressing lightness, played a soft minor melody, which like a silver thread of sound, accompanied his next words.

"And so, by gradual and almost imperceptible degrees, the wise priest Philemon forgot the world;—forgot men, and women, and little children,—forgot the blueness of the skies, the verdure of the fields,—forgot the grace of daisies growing in the grass,—forgot the music of sweet birds singing in the boughs,—forgot indeed everything, except—himself!—and his prayers, and his wisdom, and his burning desire to approach more closely every hour to that wondrous goal of the Divine from whence all life doth come, and to which all life must, in due time, return."

Here the musical accompaniment changed to a plaintive tenderness.

"But by-and-by, news of the wise priest Philemon began to spread in the town near where he had his habitation,—and people spoke of his fastings and his watchings with awe and wonder, with hope and fear,—until at last there came a day when a great crowd of the sick and sorrowful and oppressed, surrounded his abode, and called upon him to pray for them, and give them comfort.

"'Bestow upon us some of the Divine Consolation!' they cried, kneeling in the dust and weeping as they spoke—'for we are weary and worn with labour,—we suffer with harsh wounds of the heart and spirit,—many of us have lost all that makes life dear. Pity us, O thou wise servant of the Supreme—and tell us out of thy stores of heavenly wisdom whether we shall ever regain the loves that we have lost!'

"Then the priest Philemon rose up in haste and wrath, and going out before them said—

"'Depart from me, ye accursed crew of wicked worldlings! Why have ye sought me out, and what have I to do with your petty miseries? Lo, ye have brought the evils of which ye complain upon yourselves, and justice demands that ye should suffer. Ask not from me one word of pity—seek not from me any sympathy for sin. I have severed myself from ye all, to escape pollution,—my life belongs to God, not to Humanity!'

"And the people hearing him were wroth, and went their way homewards, sore at heart, and all uncomforted. And Philemon the priest, fearing lest they might seek him out again, departed from that place for ever, and made for himself a hut in the deep thickness of the forest where never a human foot was found to wander save his own. Here in the silence and deep solitude he resolved to work and pray, keeping his heart and spirit sanctified from every soiling touch of nature that could separate his thoughts from the Divine."

Again the music changed, this time to a dulcet rippling passage of notes like the slowing of a mountain stream,—and Féraz continued,—

"One morning, as, lost in a rapture of holy meditation, he prayed his daily prayer, a small bird perched upon his window-sill, and began to sing. Not a loud song, but a sweet song—full of the utmost tenderness and playful warbling,—a song born out of the leaves and grasses and gentle winds of heaven,—as delicate a tune as ever small bird sang. The priest Philemon listened, and his mind wandered. The bird's singing was sweet; oh, so sweet, that it recalled to him many things he had imagined long ago forgotten,—almost he heard his mother's voice again,—and the blithe and gracious days of his early youth suggested themselves to his memory like the lovely fragments of a poem once familiar, but now scarce remembered. Presently the bird flew away, and the priest Philemon awoke as from a dream,—his prayer had been interrupted; his thoughts had been drawn down to earth from heaven, all through the twittering of a foolish feathered thing not worth a farthing! Angry with himself he spent the day in penitence,—and on the following morning betook himself to his devotions with more than his usual ardour. Stretched on his prayer-mat he lay entranced; when suddenly a low sweet trill of sound broke gently through the silence,— the innocent twittering voice of the little bird once more aroused him,— first to a sense of wonder, then of wrath. Starting up impatiently he looked about him, and saw the bird quite close, within his reach,—it had flown inside his hut, and now hopped lightly over the floor towards him, its bright eyes full of fearless confidence, its pretty wings still quivering with the fervour of its song. Then the priest Philemon seized a heavy oaken staff, and slew it where it stood with one remorseless blow, and flung the little heap of ruffled feathers out into the woodland, saying fiercely—

"'Thou, at least, shalt never more disturb my prayers!'

"And even as he thus spoke, a great light shone forth suddenly, more dazzling than the brightness of the day, and lo! an Angel stood within the hut, just where the dead bird's blood had stained the floor. And the priest Philemon fell upon his face and trembled greatly, for the Vision was more glorious than the grandest of his dreams. And a Voice called aloud, saying—

"Philemon, why hast thou slain My messenger?"

"And Philemon looked up in fear and wonderment, answering—"

"Dread Lord, what messenger? I have slain nothing but a bird."

"And the voice spake again, saying—"

"O thou remorseless priest!—knowest thou not that every bird in the forests is Mine,—every leaf on the trees is Mine,—every blade of grass and every flower is Mine, and is a part of Me! The song of that slain bird was sweeter than thy many prayers;—and when thou didst listen to its voice thou wert nearer Heaven than thou hast ever been! Thou hast rebelled against My law;—in rejecting Love, thou hast rejected Me,—and when thou didst turn the poor and needy from thy doors, refusing them all comfort, even so did I turn My Face from thee and refuse thy petitions. Wherefore hear now thy punishment. For the space of a thousand years thou shalt live within this forest;—no human eye shall ever find thee,— no human foot shall ever track thee—no human voice shall ever sound upon thy ears. No companions shalt thou have but birds and beasts and flowers,—from these shalt thou learn wisdom, and through thy love of these alone shalt thou make thy peace with Heaven! Pray no more,—fast no more,—for such things count but little in the eternal reckonings,— but love!—and learn to make thyself beloved, even by the least and lowest, and by this shalt thou penetrate at last the mystery of the Divine!"

"The voice ceased—the glory vanished and when the priest Philemon raised his eyes, he was alone."

Here, altering by a few delicate modulations the dreamy character of the music he had been improvising, Féraz reverted again to the quaint, simple and solemn chords with which he had opened the recitation.

"Humbled in spirit, stricken at heart, conscious of the justice of his doom, yet working as one not without hope, Philemon began his heaven-appointed task. And to this day travellers' legends tell of a vast impenetrable solitude, a forest of giant trees, where never a human step has trod, but where it is said, strange colonies of birds and beasts do congregate,—where rare and marvellous plants and flowers flourish in their fairest hues,—where golden bees and dazzling butterflies gather by thousands,—where all the songsters of the air make the woods musical,—where birds of passage, outward or homeward bound, rest on their way, sure of a pleasant haven,—and where all the beautiful, wild, and timid inhabitants of field, forest and mountain, are at peace together, mutually content in an Eden of their own. There is a guardian of the place,—so say the country people,—a Spirit, thin and white, and silver-haired, who understands the language of the birds, and knows the secrets of the flowers, and in whom all the creatures of the woods confide—a mystic being whose strange life has lasted nearly a thousand years. Generations have passed—cities and empires have crumbled to decay,—and none remember him who was once called Philemon,—the 'wise' priest, grown wise indeed at last, with the only Wisdom God ever sanctifies—the Wisdom of Love."

With a soft impressive chord the music ceased,—the story was ended,—and Féraz rose from the piano to be surrounded at once by a crowd of admirers, all vying with each other in flattering expressions of applause and delight; but though he received these compliments with unaffected and courteous grace enough, his eyes perpetually wandered to his brother's face,—that dark, absorbed beloved face,—yes, beloved!—for, rebel as he might against El-Râmi's inflexible will and despotic power, Féraz knew he could never wrench from out his heart the deep affection and reverence for him which were the natural result of years of tender and sympathetic intercourse. If his brother had commanded him, he had also loved him,—there could be no doubt of that. Was he displeased or unhappy now, that he looked so sad and absorbed in gloomy and perplexed thought? A strange pained emotion stirred Féraz's sensitive soul,—some intangible vague sense of separation seemed to have arisen between himself and El-Râmi, and he grew impatient with this brilliant assembly of well-dressed chattering folk, whose presence prevented him from giving vent to the full expression of his feelings. Lady Melthorpe talked to him in dulcet languid tones, fanning herself the while, and telling him sweetly what a "wonderful touch" he had,—what an "exquisite speaking voice"—and so forth, all which elegantly turned phrases he heard as in a dream. As soon as he could escape from her and those of her friends who were immediately round him, he made his way to El-Râmi and touched his arm.

"Let me stay beside you!" he said in a low tone in which there was a slight accent of entreaty.

El-Râmi turned, and looked at him kindly.

"Dear boy, you had better make new friends while you can, lest the old be taken from you."

"Friends!" echoed Féraz—"Friends—here?" he gave a gesture more eloquent than speech, of doubt and disdain,—then continued, "Might we not go now? Is it not time to return home and sleep?"

El-Râmi smiled.

"Nay, are we not seeing life? Here we are among pretty women, well-bred men—the rooms are elegant,—and the conversation is as delightfully vague and nearly as noisy as the chattering of monkeys— yet with all these advantages, you talk of sleep!"

Féraz laughed a little.

"Yes, I am tired," he said. "It does not seem to me real, all this—there is something shadowy and unsubstantial about it. I think sleep is better."

At that moment Irene Vassilius came up to them.

"I am just going," she said, letting her soft serious eyes dwell on Féraz with interest, "but I feel I must thank you for your story of the 'Priest Philemon.' Is it your own idea?—or does such a legend exist?"

"Nothing is really new," replied Féraz—"but such as it is, it is my own invention."

"Then you are a poet and musician at one and the same time," said Irene. "It seems a natural combination of gifts, yet the two do not always go together. I hope"—she now addressed herself to El-Râmi—"I hope very much you will come and see me, though I'm afraid I'm not a very popular person. My friends are few, so I cannot promise you much entertainment. Indeed, as a rule, people do not like me."

"I like you!" said Féraz, quickly and impulsively.

She smiled.

"Yes? That is good of you. And I believe you, for you are too unworldly to deal in flatteries. But, I assure you, that, generally speaking, literary women are never social favourites."

"Not even when they are lovely like you?" questioned Féraz, with simple frankness.

She coloured at the evident sincerity of his admiration and the boyish openness with which it was thus expressed. Then she laughed a little.

"Loveliness is not acknowledged as at all existent in literary females," she replied lightly, yet with a touch of scorn,—"even if they do possess any personal charm, it only serves as a peg for the malicious to hang a slander on. And of the two sexes, men are most cruel to a woman who dares to think for herself."

"Are you sure of that, Madame?" asked El-Râmi gently. "May not this be an error of your judgment?"

"I would that it were!" she said with intense expression—"Heaven knows how sincerely I should rejoice to be proved wrong! But I am not wrong. Men always judge women as their inferiors, not only physically (which they are) but mentally (which they are not), and always deny them an independent soul and independent emotions,—the majority of men, indeed, treat them pretty much as a sort of superior cattle;—but, nevertheless, there is a something in what the French call 'L'Eternel Feminin.' Women are distinctly the greatest sufferers in all suffering creation,—and I have often thought that for so much pain and so much misjudgment, endured often with such heroic silence and uncomplaining fortitude, the compensation will be sweeter and more glorious than we, half drowned in our own tears, can as yet hope for, or imagine!"

She paused—her eyes were dark with thought and full of a dreamy sorrow,—then, smiling gently, she held out her hand.

"I talk too much, you will say—women always do! Come and see me if you feel disposed—not otherwise; I will send you my card through Lady Melthorpe—meantime, good-night!"

El-Râmi took her hand, and as he pressed it in his own, felt again that curious thrill which had before communicated itself to his nerves through the same contact.

"Surely you must be a visionary, Madame!" he said abruptly and with a vague sense of surprise—"and you see things not at all of this world!"

Her faint roseate colour deepened, giving singular beauty to her face.

"What a tell-tale hand mine is!" she replied, withdrawing it slowly from his clasp. "Yes—you are right,—if I could not see things higher than this world, I could not endure my existence for an hour. It is because I feel the Future so close about me that I have courage for, and indifference to, the Present."

With that, she left them, and both El-Râmi and Féraz followed her graceful movements with interested eyes, as she glided through the rooms in her snowy trailing robes, with the frosty flash of diamonds in her hair, till she had altogether disappeared; then the languid voice of Lady Melthorpe addressed them.

"Isn't she an odd creature, that Irene Vassilius? So quaint and peculiar in her ideas! People detest her, you know—she is so dreadfully clever!"

"There could not be a better reason for hatred!" said El-Râmi.

"You see, she says such unpleasant things," went on Lady Melthorpe, complacently fanning herself,—"she has such decided opinions, and will not accommodate herself to people's ways. I must confess I always find her de trop, myself."

"She was your guest tonight," said Féraz suddenly, and with such a sternness in his accent as caused her ladyship to look at him in blank surprise.

"Certainly! One must always ask a celebrity."

"If one must always ask, then one is bound always to respect," said Féraz coldly. "In our code d'honneur, we never speak ill of those who have partaken of our hospitality."

So saying, he turned on his heel and walked away with so much haughtiness of demeanour that Lady Melthorpe stood as though rooted to the spot, staring speechlessly after him. Then rousing herself, she looked at El-Râmi and shrugged her shoulders.

"Really," she began,—"really, Mr. El-Râmi, your brother's manner is very strange—"

"It is," returned El-Râmi quickly—"I admit it. His behaviour is altogether unpolished—and he is quite unaccustomed to society. I told Lord Melthorpe so,—and I was against his being invited here. He says exactly what he thinks, without fear or favour, and in this regard is really a mere barbarian! Allow me to apologize for him!"

Lady Melthorpe bowed stiffly,—she saw, or fancied she saw, a faint ironical smile playing on El-Râmi's lips beneath his dark moustache. She was much annoyed,—the idea of a "boy" like Féraz, presuming to talk to her, a leader of London fashion, about a code d'honneur! The thing was monstrous,—absurd! And as for Irene Vassilius, why should not she be talked about?—she was a public person; a writer of books which Mrs. Grundy in her church-going moods had voted as "dangerous." Truly Lady Melthorpe considered she had just cause to be ruffled, and she began to regret having invited these "Eastern men," as she termed them, to her house at all. El-Râmi perceived her irritation, but he made no further remark; and as soon as he could conveniently do so, he took his formal leave of her. Quickly threading his way through the now rapidly thinning throng, he sought out Féraz, whom he found in the hall talking to Roy Ainsworth and making final arrangements for the sitting he was to give the artist next day.

"I should like to make a study of your head too," said Roy, with a keen glance at El-Râmi as he approached—"but I suppose you have no time."

"No time—and still less inclination!" responded El-Râmi laughingly; "for I have sworn that no 'counterfeit presentment' of my bodily form shall ever exist. It would always be a false picture,—it would never be Me, because it would only represent the Perishable, whilst I am the Imperishable."

"Singular man!" said Roy Ainsworth. "What do you mean?"

"What should I mean," replied El-Râmi quickly, "save what all your religions and churches mean, if in truth they have any meaning. Is there not something else besides this fleshly covering? If you can paint the imagined Soul of a man looking out of his eyes, you are a great artist,—but if you could paint the Soul itself, stripped of its mortal disguise, radiant, ethereal, brilliant as lightning, beautiful as dawn, you would be greater still. And the soul is the Me,—these features of mine, this Appearance, is mere covering,—we want a Portrait, not a Costume."

"Your argument applies to your brother as well as yourself," said Ainsworth, wondering at the eloquent wildness of this strange El-Râmi's language, and fascinated by it in spite of himself.

"Just so! Only the Earth-garment of Féraz is charming and becoming—mine is not. It is a case of 'my hair is white but not with years'—the "Prisoner of Chillon" sort of thing. Good-night!'

"Good-night!" and the artist shook hands warmly with both brothers, saying to Féraz as he parted from him—"I may expect you then tomorrow? You will not fail?"

"You may rely upon me!" and Féraz nodded lightly in adieu, and followed El-Râmi out of the house into the street, where they began to walk homeward together at a rapid rate. As they went, by some mutual involuntary instinct they lifted their eyes to the dense blue heavens, where multitudes of stars were brilliantly visible. Féraz drew a long deep breath.

"There," he said, "is the Infinite and Real,—what we have seen of life tonight is finite and unreal."

El-Râmi made no reply.

"Do you not think so?" persisted Féraz earnestly.

"I cannot say definitely what is Real and what is Unreal," said El-Râmi slowly—"both are so near akin. Féraz, are you aware you offended Lady Melthorpe tonight?"

"Why should she be offended? I only said just what I thought."

"Good heavens, my dear boy, if you always go about saying just what you think, you will find the world too hot to hold you. To say the least of it, you will never be fit for society."

"I don't want to be fit for it," said Féraz disdainfully, "if Lady Melthorpe's 'at home' is a picture of it. I want to forget it,—the most of it, I mean. I shall remember Madame Vassilius because she is sympathetic and interesting. But for the rest!—my dearest brother, I am far happier with you."

El-Râmi took his arm gently.

"Yet you leave me tomorrow to gratify an artist's whim!" he said. "Have you thought of that?"

"Oh, but that is nothing—only an hour or two's sitting. He was so very anxious that I could not refuse. Does it displease you?"

"My dear Féraz, I am displeased at nothing. You complained of my authority over you once—and I have determined you shall not complain again. Consider yourself free."

"I do not want my liberty," said Féraz, almost petulantly.

"Try it!" responded El-Râmi with a smile and half a sigh. "Liberty is sweet,—but, like other things, it brings its own responsibilities."

They walked on till they had almost reached their own door.

"Your story of the priest Philemon was very quaint and pretty," said El-Râmi then abruptly. "You meant it as a sort of allegory for me, did you not?"

Féraz looked wistfully at him, but hesitated to reply.

"It does not quite fit me," went on El-Râmi gently. "I am not impervious to love—for I love you. Perhaps the angels will take that fact into consideration, when they are settling my thousand or million years' punishment."

There was a touch of quiet pathos in his voice which moved Féraz greatly, and he could not trust himself to speak. When they entered their own abode, El-Râmi said the usual "Good-night" in his usual kindly manner,—but Feraz reverently stooped and kissed the hand extended to him,—the potent hand that had enriched his life with poesy and dowered it with dreams.

VII

All the next day El-Râmi was alone. Féraz went out early to fulfil the appointment made with Roy Ainsworth; no visitors called,—and not even old Zaroba came near the study, where, shut up with his books and papers, her master worked assiduously hour after hour, writing as rapidly as hand and pen would allow, and satisfying his appetite solely with a few biscuits dipped in wine. Just as the shadows of evening were beginning to fall, his long solitude was disturbed by the sharp knock of a telegraph-messenger, who handed him a missive which ran briefly thus—

"Your brother stays to dine with me.—AINSWORTH."

El-Râmi crushed the paper in his hand, then flinging it aside, stood for a moment, lost in meditation, with a sorrowful expression in his dark eyes.

"Ay me! the emptiness of the world!" he murmured at last—"I shall be left alone, I suppose, as my betters are left, according to the rule of this curiously designed and singularly unsatisfactory system of human life. What do the young care for the solitude of their elders who have tended and loved them? New thoughts, new scenes, new aspirations beckon them, and off they go like birds on the wing,—never to return to the old nest or the old ways. I despise the majority of women myself,—and yet I pity from my soul all those who are mothers,—the miserable dignity and pathos of maternity are, in my opinion, grotesquely painful. To think of the anguish the poor delicate wretches endure in bringing children at all into the world,—then, the tenderness and watchful devotion expended on their early years,—and then—why then, these same children grow up for the most part into indifferent (when not entirely callous) men and women, who make their own lives as it seems best to themselves, and almost forget to whom they owe their very existence. It is hard—bitterly hard. There ought to be some reason for such a wild waste of love and affliction. At present, however, I can see none."

He sighed deeply, and stared moodily into the deepening shadows.

"Loneliness is horrible!" he said aloud, as though addressing some invisible auditor. "It is the chief terror of death,—for one must always die alone. No matter how many friends and relatives stand weeping round the bed, one is absolutely alone at the hour of death, for the stunned soul wanders blindly—"

That solitary pause and shudder on the brink of the Unseen is fearful,—it unnerves us all to think of it. If Love could help us,—but even Love grows faint and feeble then."

As he mused thus, a strange vague longing came over him,—an impulse arising out of be knew not what suggestion; and acting on his thought, he went suddenly and swiftly upstairs, and straight into the chamber of Lilith. Zaroba was there, and rose from her accustomed corner silently, and moved with a somewhat feeble step into the ante-room while El-Râmi bent over the sleeping girl. Lovelier than ever she seemed that evening,—and as he stooped above her, she stretched out her fair white arms and smiled. His heart beat quickly,—he had, for the moment, ceased to analyze his own feelings,—and he permitted himself to gaze upon her beauty and absorb it, without, as usual, taking any thought of the scientific aspect of her condition.

"Tresses twisted by fairy fingers.
In which the light of the morning lingers!"

he murmured, as he touched a rippling strand of the lovely hair that lay spread like a fleece of gold floss silk on the pillow near him,—"Poor Lilith!—Sweet Lilith!"

As if responsive to his words, she turned slightly towards him, and felt the air blindly with one wandering white hand. Gently he caught it and imprisoned it within his own,—then on a strange impulse, kissed it. To his utter amazement she answered that touch as though it had been a call.

"I am here, . . . my Belovëd!"

He started, and an icy thrill ran through his veins;—that word "Belovëd" was a sort of electric shock to his system, and sent a dizzying rush of blood to his brain. What did she mean,—what could she mean? The last time she had addressed him she had declared that he was not even her friend—now she called him her "beloved"—as much to his amazement as his fear. Presently, however, he considered that here perhaps was some new development of his experiment;—the soul of Lilith might possibly be in closer communion with him than he had yet imagined. But in spite of his attempt to reason away his emotions, he was nervous, and stood by the couch silently, afraid to speak, and equally afraid to move. Lilith was silent too. A long pause ensued, in which the usually subdued tickings of the clock seemed to become painfully audible. El-Râmi's breath came and went quickly,—he was singularly excited,—some subtle warmth from the little hand he held, permeated his veins, and a sense of such utter powerlessness possessed him as he had never experienced before. What ailed him? He could not tell. Where was the iron force of his despotic will? He seemed unable to exert it,—unable even to think coherently while Lilith's hand thus rested in his. Had she grown stronger than himself? A tingling tremor ran through him, as the strange words of the monk's written warning suddenly recurred to his memory.

"Beware the end! With Lilith's love comes Lilith's freedom."

But Lilith smiled with placid sweetness, and still left her hand confidingly in his; he held that hand, so warm and soft and white, and was loth to let it go,—he studied the rapt expression of the beautiful face, the lovely curve of the sweet shut lips, the delicately veined lids of the closed eyes,—and was dimly conscious of a sense of vague happiness curiously intermingled with terror. By-and-by he began to collect his ideas which had been so suddenly scattered by that one word "Belovëd,"—and he resolved to break the mystic silence that oppressed and daunted him.

"Dreaming or waking, is she?" he queried aloud, a little tremulously, and as though he were talking to himself. "She must be dreaming!"

"Dreaming of joy!" said Lilith softly, and with quick responsiveness— "only that Joy is no dream! I hear your voice,—I am conscious of your touch,—almost I see you! The cloud hangs there between us still—but God is good,—He will remove that cloud."

El-Râmi listened, perplexed and wondering.

"Lilith," he said in a voice that strove in vain to assume its wonted firmness and authority—"What say you of clouds,—you who are in the full radiance of a light that is quenchless? Have you not told me of a glory that out-dazzles the sun, in which you move and have your being,—then what do you know of Shadow?"

"Yours is the Shadow," replied Lilith—"not mine! I would that I could lift it from your eyes, that you might see the Wonder and the Beauty. Oh, cruel Shadow, that lies between my love and me!"

"Lilith! Lilith!" exclaimed El-Râmi in strange agitation—"Why will you talk of love?"

"Do you not think of love?" said Lilith—"and must I not respond to your innermost thought?"

"Not always do you so respond, Lilith!" said El-Râmi quickly, recovering himself a little, and glad of an opportunity to bring back his mind to a more scientific level. "Often you speak of things I know not,—things that perhaps I shall never know—"

"Nay, you must know," said Lilith, with soft persistence. "Every unit of life in every planet is bound to know its Cause and Final Intention. All is clear to me, and will be so to you, hereafter. You ask me of these things—I tell you,—but you do not believe me;—you will never believe me till—the end."

"Beware the end!" The words echoed themselves so distinctly in El-Râmi's mind that he could almost have fancied they were spoken aloud in the room. "What end?" he asked eagerly.

But to this Lilith answered nothing.

He looked at the small sensitive hand he held, and stroking it gently, was about to lay it back on her bosom, when all at once she pressed her fingers closely over his palm, and sat upright, her delicate face expressive of the most intense emotion, notwithstanding her closed eyes.

"Write!" she said in a clear penetrating voice that sent silvery echoes through the room—"write these truths to the world you live in. Tell the people they all work for Evil, and therefore Evil shall be upon them. What they sow, even that shall they reap, with the measure they have used, it shall be measured to them again. O wild world!—sad world!—world wherein the pride of wealth, the joy of sin, the cruelty of avarice, the curse of selfishness, outweigh all pity, all sympathy, all love! For this God's law of Compensation makes but one return—Destruction. Wars shall prevail; plague and famine shall ravage the nations;—young children shall murder the parents who bore them; theft and rapine shall devastate the land. For your world is striving to live without God,—and a world without God is a disease that must die. Like a burnt-out star this Earth shall fall from its sphere and vanish utterly—and its sister-planets shall know it no more. For when it is born again, it will be new."

The words came from her lips with a sort of fervid eloquence which seemed to exhaust her, for she grew paler and paler, and her head began to sink backward on the pillow. El-Râmi gently put his arm round her to support her, and as he did so, a kind of supernatural light irradiated her features.

"Believe me, O my Belovëd, believe the words of Lilith!" she murmured. "There is but one Law leading to all Wisdom. Evil generates Evil, and contains within itself its own retribution. Good generates good, and holds within itself the germ of eternal reproduction. Love begets Love, and from Love is born Immortality!"

Her voice grew fainter,—she sank entirely back on her pillow; yet once again her lips moved and the word "Immortality!" floated whisperingly forth like a sigh. El-Râmi drew his arm away from her, and at the same instant disengaged his hand from her clasp. She seemed bewildered at this, and for a minute or two, felt in the air as though searching for some missing treasure,—then her arms fell passively on each side of her, seemingly inert and lifeless. El-Râmi bent over her half curiously, half anxiously,—his eyes dwelt on the ruby-like jewel that heaved gently up and down on her softly rounded bosom,—he watched the red play of light around it, and on the white satiny skin beneath,—and then,—all at once his sight grew dazzled and his brain began to swim. How lovely she was!—how much more than lovely! And how utterly she was his!—his, body and soul, and in his power! He was startled at the tenour of his own unbidden thoughts,—whence, in God's name, came these new impulses, these wild desires that fired his blood? . . . Furious with himself for what he deemed the weakness of his own emotions, he strove to regain the mastery over his nerves,— to settle his mind once more in its usual attitude of cold inflexibility and indifferent composure,—but all in vain. Some subtle chord in his mental composition had been touched mysteriously, he knew not how, and had set all the other chords a-quivering,—and he felt himself all suddenly to be as subdued and powerless as when his mysterious visitor, the monk from Cyprus, had summoned up (to daunt him, as he thought) the strange vision of an Angel in his room.

Again he looked at Lilith;—again he resisted the temptation that assailed him to clasp her in his arms, to shower a lover's kisses on her lips, and thus waken her to the full bitter-sweet consciousness of earthly life,—till in the sharp extremity of his struggle, and loathing himself for his own folly, he suddenly dropped on his knees by the side of the couch and gazed with a vague wild entreaty at the tranquil loveliness that lay there so royally enshrined.

"Have mercy, Lilith!" he prayed half aloud, and scarcely conscious of his words. "If you are stronger in your weakness than I in my strength, have mercy! Repel me,—distrust me, disobey me—but do not love me! Make me not as one of the foolish for whom a woman's smile, a woman's touch, are more than life, and more than wisdom. O let me not waste the labour of my days on a freak of passion!—let me not lose everything I have gained by long study and research, for the mere wild joy of an hour! Lilith, Lilith! Child, woman, angel!—whatever you are, have pity upon me! I dare not love you! . . . I dare not!"

So murmuring incoherently, he rose, and walking dizzily like a man abruptly startled from deep sleep, he went straight out of the room, never looking back once, else he might have seen how divinely, how victoriously Lilith smiled!

VIII

Reaching his study, he shut himself in and locked the door,—and then sitting down, buried his head in his hands and fell to thinking. Such odd thoughts too!—they came unbidden, and chased one another in and out of his brain like will-o'-the-wisps in a wilderness. It was growing late, and Féraz had not yet returned,—but he heeded not the hour, or his brother's continued absence,—he was occupied in such a mental battle with his own inward forces as made him utterly indifferent to external things. The question he chiefly asked himself was this:— Of what use was all the science he had discovered and mastered, if he was not exempt,—utterly exempt from the emotions common to the most ignorant of men? His pride had been that he was "above" human nature,—that he was able to look down upon its trivial joys and sorrows with a supreme and satiric scorn,—that he knew its ways so well as to be able to calculate its various hesitating moves in all directions, social and political, with very nearly exact accuracy. Why then was he shaken to the very centre of his being tonight, by the haunting vision of an angelic face and the echo of a sweet faint voice softly breathing the words—"My belovëd!" He could dominate others; why could he not dominate himself?

"This will never do!" he said aloud at last, starting up from his brooding attitude—"I must read—I must work,—I must, at all costs, get out of this absurd frame of mind into which I have unwittingly fallen. Besides, how often have I not assured myself that for all practical earthly considerations Lilith is dead—positively dead!"

And to reinstate himself in this idea, he unlocked his desk and took from it a small parchment volume in which he had carefully chronicled the whole account of his experiment on Lilith from the beginning. One page was written in the form of a journal-the opposite leaf being reserved for "queries," and the book bore the curious superscription "In Search of the Soul of Lilith" on its cover. The statement began at once without preamble, thus:—

August 8, 18—. 9 P.M.
Lilith, an Arab girl, aged twelve, dies in my arms. Cause of death, fever and inanition. Heart ceased to beat at ten minutes past eight this evening. While the blood is still warm in the corpse, I inject

the 'Electro-flamma' under the veins, close beneath the heart. No immediate effect visible.

11 P.M.

Arab women lay out Lilith's corpse for burial. Questioned the people as to her origin. An orphan child, of poor parentage, no education, and unquiet disposition. Not instructed in religious matters, but following the religious customs of others by instinct and imitation. Distinctive features of the girl when in health—restlessness, temper, animalism, and dislike of restraint. Troublesome to manage, and not a thinking child by any means.

August 9. 5 A.M.

The caravan has just started on its way, leaving the corpse of Lilith with me. The woman Zaroba remains behind. Féraz I sent away last night in haste. I tell Zaroba part of my intention; she is superstitious and afraid of me, but willing to serve me. Lilith remains inanimate. I again use the 'Electro-flamma,' this time close to all the chief arteries. No sign of life.

August 10. Noon

I begin rather to despair. As a last resource I have injected carefully a few drops of the 'Flamma' close to the brain; it is the mainspring of the whole machine, and if it can be set in motion—

Midnight

Victory! The brain has commenced to pulsate feebly, and the heart with it. Breathing has begun, but slowly and with difficulty. A faint colour has come into the hitherto waxen face. Success is possible now.

August 15

During these last five days Lilith has breathed, and, to a certain extent, lived. She does not open her eyes, nor move a muscle of her body, and at times still appears dead. She is kept alive (if it is life) by the vital fluid, and by that only. I must give her more time.

August 20

I have called her by name, and she has answered—but how strangely! Where does she learn the things she speaks of? She sees the Earth, she tells me, like a round ball circling redly in a cloud of vapours, and she hears music everywhere, and perceives a 'light beyond.' Where and how does she perceive anything?"

Here on the opposite side of the page was written the following "query," which in this case was headed

"PROBLEM."

"Given, a child's brain, not wholly developed in its intellectual capacity, with no impressions save those which are purely material, and place that brain in a state of perpetual trance, how does it come to imagine or comprehend things which science cannot prove? Is it the Soul which conveys these impressions, and if so, what is the Soul, and where is it?"

El-Râmi read the passage over and over again, then, sighing impatiently, closed the book and put it by.

"Since I wrote that, what has she not said—what has she not told me!" he muttered; "and the 'child's brain' is a child's brain no longer, but a woman's, while she has obtained absolutely no knowledge of any sort by external means. Yet she—she who was described by those who knew her in her former life as 'not a thinking child, troublesome and difficult to manage,' she it is who describes to me the scenery and civilization of Mars, the inhabitants of Sirius, the wonders of a myriad of worlds; she it is who talks of the ravishing beauty of things Divine and immortal, of the glory of the heavens, of the destined fate of the world. God knows it is very strange!—and the problem I wrote out six years ago is hardly nearer solving than it was then. If I could believe—but then I cannot—I must always doubt, and shall not doubt lead to discovery?"

Thus arguing with himself, and scoffing interiorly at the suggestion which just then came unbidden to his mind—"Blessed are they which have not seen and yet believed"—he turned over some more papers and sorted them, with the intention and hope of detaching his thoughts entirely from what had suddenly become the too-enthralling subject of Lilith's beauteous personality. Presently he came upon a memorandum, over which he nodded and smiled with a sort of grim satirical content, entitled, "The Passions of the Human Animal as Nature made Him;" it was only a scrap—a hint of some idea which he had intended to make use of in literary work, but he read it over now with a good deal of curious satisfaction. It ran thus:

"Man, as a purely natural creature, fairly educated, but wholly unspiritualized, is a mental composition of: Hunger, Curiosity, Self-Esteem, Avarice, Cowardice, Lust, Cruelty, Personal Ambition; and on these vile qualities alone our 'society' hangs together; the virtues have no place anywhere, and do not count at all, save as conveniently pious metaphors."

"It is true!" he said aloud—"as true as the very light of the skies! Now am I, or have I ever been, guilty of these common vices of ordinary nature? No, no; I have examined my own conscience too often and too carefully. I have been accused of personal ambition, but even that is a false accusation, for I do not seek vulgar rewards, or the noise of notoriety ringing about my name. All that I am seeking to discover is meant for the benefit of the world; that Humanity—poor, wretched, vicious Humanity—may know positively and finally that there is a Future. For till they do know it, beyond all manner of doubt, why should they strive to be better? Why should they seek to quell their animalism? Why should they need to be any better than they are? And why, above all things, should they be exhorted by their preachers and teachers to fasten their faith to a Myth, and anchor their hopes on a Dream?"

At that moment a loud and prolonged rat-tat-tatting at the street-door startled him,—he hastily thrust all his loose manuscripts into a drawer, and went to answer the summons, glancing at the clock as he passed it with an air of complete bewilderment,—for it was close upon two A.M., and he could not imagine how the time had flown. He had scarcely set foot across the hall before another furious knocking began, and he stopped abruptly to listen to the imperative clatter with a curious wondering expression on his dark handsome face. When the noise ceased again, he began slowly to undo the door.

"Patience, my dear boy," he said, as he flung it open—"is a virtue, as you must have seen it set forth in copy-books. I provided you with a latch-key—where is it?—there could not be a more timely hour for its usage."

But while he spoke, Féraz, for it was he, had sprung in swiftly like some wild animal pursued by hunters, and he now stood in the hall, nearly breathless, staring confusedly at his brother with big, feverishly-bright bewildered eyes.

"Then I have escaped!" he said in a half-whisper—"I am at home,—really at home again!"

El-Râmi looked at him steadily,—then, turning away quietly, carefully shut and bolted the door.

"Have you spent a happy day, Féraz?" he gently inquired.

"Happy!" echoed Féraz—"Happy? Yes. No! Good God!—what do you mean by happiness?"

El-Râmi looked at him again, and making no reply to this adjuration, simply turned about and went into his study. Féraz followed.

"I know what you think," he said in pained accents—"You think I've been drinking—so I have. But I'm not drunk, for all that. They gave me wine—bad Burgundy—detestable champagne—the sun never shone on the grapes that made it,—and I took very little of it. It is not that which has filled me with a terror too real to deserve your scorn,—it is not that which has driven me home here to you for help and shelter—"

"It is somewhat late to be 'driven' home," remarked El-Râmi with a slightly sarcastic smile—"Two in the morning,—and—bad champagne or good,—you are talking, my dear Féraz, to say the least of it, rather wildly."

"For God's sake do not sneer at me!" cried Féraz passionately—"I shall go mad if you do! Is it as late as you say?—I never knew it. I fled from them at midnight;—I have wandered about alone under the stars since then."

At these words, El-Râmi's expression changed from satire to compassion. His fine eyes softened, and their lustrous light grew deeper and more tender.

"Alone—and under the stars?" he repeated softly—"Are not the two things incompatible—to you? Have you not made the stars your companions—almost your friends?"

"No, no!" said Féraz, with a swift gesture of utter hopelessness. "Not now—not now! for all is changed. I see life as it is—hideous, foul, corruptible, cruel! and the once bright planets look pitiless; the heavens I thought so gloriously designed, are but an impenetrable vault arched over an ever-filling Grave. There is no light, no hope anywhere; how can there be in the face of so much sin? El-Râmi, why did you not tell me? why did you not warn me of the accursëd Evil of this pulsating movement men call Life? For it seems I have not lived, I have only dreamed!"

And with a heavy sigh that seemed wrung from his very heart, he threw himself wearily into a chair, and buried his head between his hands in an attitude of utter dejection.

El-Râmi looked at him as he sat thus, with a certain shadow of melancholy on his own fine features, then he spoke gently:

"Who told you, Féraz, that you have not lived?" he asked.

"Zaroba did, first of all," returned Féraz reluctantly; "and now he, the artist Ainsworth, says the same thing. It seems that to men of the world I look a fool. I know nothing; I am as ignorant as a barbarian—"

"Of what?" queried his brother. "Of wine, loose women, the race-course and the gaming-table? Yes, I grant you, you are ignorant of these, and you may thank God for your ignorance. And these wise 'men of the world' who are so superior to you—in what does their wisdom consist?"

Féraz sat silent, wrapt in meditation. Presently he looked up; his lashes were wet, and his lips trembled.

"I wish," he murmured, "I wish I had never gone there,—I wish I had been content to stay with you."

El-Râmi laughed a little, but it was to hide a very different emotion.

"My dear fellow," he said lightly, "I am not an old woman that I should wish you to be tied to my apron-strings. Come, make a clean breast of it; if not the champagne, what is it that has so seriously disagreed with you?"

"Everything!" replied Féraz emphatically. "The whole day has been one of discord—what wonder then that I myself am out of tune! When I first started off from the house this morning, I was full of curious anticipation—I looked upon this invitation to an artist's studio as a sort of break in what I chose to call the even monotony of my existence,—I fancied I should imbibe new ideas, and be able to understand something of the artistic world of London if I spent the day with a man truly distinguished in his profession. When I arrived at the studio, Mr. Ainsworth was already at work—he was painting—a woman."

"Well?" said El-Râmi, seeing that Feraz paused, and stammered hesitatingly.

"She was nude,—this woman," he went on in a low shamed voice, a hot flush creeping over his delicate boyish face,—"A creature without any modesty or self-respect. A model, Mr. Ainsworth called her,—and it seems that she took his money for showing herself thus. Her body was beautiful; like a statue flushed with life,—but she was a devil, El-Râmi!—the foulness of her spirit was reflected in her bold eyes—the coarseness of her mind found echo in her voice,—and I—I sickened at the sight of her; I had never believed in the existence of fiends,—but she was one!"

El-Râmi was silent, and Féraz resumed—

"As I tell you, Ainsworth was painting her, and he asked me to sit beside him and watch his work. His request surprised me,—I said to him in a whisper, 'Surely she will resent the presence of a stranger?' He stared at me. 'She? Whom do you mean?' he inquired. 'The woman there,' I answered. He burst out laughing, called me 'an innocent,' and said she was perfectly accustomed to 'pose' before twenty men at a time, so that I need have no scruples on that score. So I sat down as he bade me, and watched in silence, and thought—"

"Ah, what did you think?" asked El-Râmi.

"I thought evil things," answered Féraz deliberately. "And, while thinking them, I knew they were evil. And I put my own nature under a sort of analysis, and came to the conclusion that, when a man does wrong, he is perfectly aware that it is wrong, and that, therefore, doing wrong deliberately and consciously, he has no right to seek forgiveness, either through Christ or any other intermediary. He should be willing to bear the brunt of it, and his prayers should be for punishment, not for pardon."

"A severe doctrine," observed El-Râmi. "Strangely so, for a young man who has not 'lived,' but only 'dreamed.'"

"In my dreams I see nothing evil," said Féraz, "and I think nothing evil. All is harmonious; all works in sweet accordance with a Divine and Infinite plan, of whose ultimate perfection I am sure. I would rather dream so, than live as I have lived today."

El-Râmi forbore to press him with any questions, and, after a little pause, he went on:

"When that woman—the model—went away from the studio, I was as thankful as one might be for the removal of a plague. She dropped a curtain over her bare limbs and disappeared like some vanishing evil spirit. Then Ainsworth asked me to sit to him. I obeyed willingly. He placed me in a half-sitting, half-recumbent attitude, and began to sketch. Suddenly, after about half an hour, it occurred to me that he perhaps wanted to put me in the same picture with that fiend who had gone, and I asked him the question point-blank. 'Why, certainly!' he said. 'You will appear as the infatuated lover of that lady, in my great Academy work.' Then, El-Râmi, some suppressed rage in me broke loose. I sprang up and confronted him angrily. 'Never!' I cried. 'You shall never picture me thus! If you dared to do it, I would rip your canvas to shreds on the very walls of the Academy itself! I am no "model," to sell my personality to you for gold!' He laughed in that lazy, unmirthful way of his. 'No,' he said, 'you are certainly not a model, you are a tiger—a young tiger—quite furious and untamed. I wish you would go and rip up my picture on the Academy walls, as you say; it would make my fortune; I should have so many orders for duplicates. My dear fellow, if you won't let me put you into my canvas, you are no use to me. I want your meditative face for the face of a poet destroyed by a passion for Phryne. I really think you might oblige me.' 'Never!' I said; 'the thing would be a libel and a lie. My face is not the face you want. You want a weak face, a round foolish brow, and a receding chin. Why, as God made me, and as I am, every one of my features would falsify your picture's story! The man who voluntarily sacrifices his genius and his hopes of heaven to vulgar vice and passion, must have weakness in him somewhere, and as a true artist you are bound to show that weakness in the features you pourtray.' 'And have you no weakness, you young savage?' he asked. 'Not that weakness!' I said. 'The wretched incapacity of will that brings the whole soul down to a grovelling depth of materialism—that is not in me!' I spoke angrily, El-Râmi, perhaps violently; but I could not help myself. He stared at me curiously, and began drawing lines on his palette with his brush dipped in colour. 'You are a very singular young fellow,' he said at last. 'But I must tell you that it was the fair Irene Vassilius who suggested to me that your face would be suitable for that of the poet in my picture. I wanted to please her—' 'You will please her more by telling her what I say,' I interrupted him abruptly. 'Tell her—' 'That you are a new Parsifal,' he said mockingly. 'Ah, she will never believe it! All men in her opinion are either brutes or cowards.' Then he took up a fresh square of canvas, and added: 'Well, I promise you I will not put you in my picture, as you have such a rooted objection to figuring in public as a slave of Phryne, though, I assure you, most young fellows would be proud of such a distinction; for one is hardly considered a "man" nowadays unless one professes to be "in love"—God save the mark!—with some female beast of the stage or the music-hall. Such is life, my boy! There! now sit still with that look of supreme scorn on your countenance, and that will do excellently.' 'On your word of honour, you will not place me in your picture?' I said. 'On my word of honour,' he replied. So, of course, I could not doubt him. And he drew my features on his canvas quickly, and with much more than ordinary skill; and, when he had finished his sketch, he took me out to lunch with him at a noisy, crowded place, called the

'Criterion.' There were numbers of men and women there, eating and drinking, all of a low type, I thought, and some of them of a most vulgar and insolent bearing, more like dressed-up monkeys than human beings, I told Ainsworth; but he laughed, and said they were very fair specimens of civilized society. Then, after lunch, we went to a Club, where several men were smoking and throwing cards about. They asked me to play, and I told them I knew nothing of the game. Whereupon they explained it; and I said it seemed to me to be quite an imbecile method of losing money. Then they laughed uproariously. One said I was 'very fresh,' whatever that might mean. Another asked Ainsworth what he had brought me there for, and Ainsworth answered: 'To show you one of the greatest wonders of the century—a really young man in his youth,' and then they laughed again. Later on he took me into the Park. There I saw Madame Vassilius in her carriage. She looked fair and cold, and proud and weary all at once. Her horses came to a standstill under the trees, and Ainsworth went up and spoke to her. She looked at me very earnestly as she gave me her hand, and only said one thing: 'What a pity you are not with your brother!' I longed to ask her why, but she seemed unwilling to converse, and soon gave the signal to her coachman to drive on—in fact, she went at once out of the Park. Then Ainsworth got angry and sullen, and said: 'I hate intellectual women! That pretty scribbler has made so much money that she is perfectly independent of man's help—and, being independent, she is insolent.' I was surprised at his tone. I said I could not see where he perceived the insolence. 'Can you not?' he asked. 'She studies men instead of loving them; that is where she is insolent and—insufferable!' He was so irritated that I did not pursue the subject, and he then pressed me to stay and dine with him. I accepted—and I am sorry I did."

"Why?" asked El-Râmi in purposely indifferent tones. "At present, so far as you have told me, your day seems to have passed in a very harmless manner. A peep at a model, a lunch at the Criterion, a glance at a gaming-club, a stroll in the Park—what could be more ordinary? There is no tragedy in it, such as you seem inclined to imagine; it is all the merest bathos."

Féraz looked up indignantly, his eyes sparkling.

"Is there nothing tragic in the horrible, stifling, strangling consciousness of evil surrounding one like a plague?" he demanded passionately. "To know and to feel that God is far off, instead of near; that one is shut up in a prison of one's own making, where sweet air and pure light cannot penetrate; to be perfectly conscious that one is moving and speaking with difficulty and agitation in a thick, choking atmosphere of lies—lies—all lies! Is that not tragic? Is that all bathos?"

"My dear fellow, it is life!" said El-Râmi sedately. "It is what you wanted to see, to know, and to understand."

"It is not life!" declared Féraz hotly. "The people who accept it as such, are fools, and delude themselves. Life, as God gave it to us, is beautiful and noble—grandly suggestive of the Future beyond; but you will not tell me there is anything beautiful or noble or suggestive in the life led by such men and women as I saw today. With the exception of Madame Vassilius—and she, I am told, is considered eccentric and a 'visionary'—I have seen no one who would be worth talking to for an hour. At Ainsworth's dinner, for instance, there were some men who called themselves artists, and they talked, not of art, but of money; how much they could get, and how much they would get from certain patrons of theirs whom they called 'full-pursed fools.' Well, and that woman—that model I told you of—actually came to dine at Ainsworth's table, and other coarse women like her. Surely, El-Râmi, you can imagine what their conversation was like? And as the time went on things became worse. There was no restraint, and at last I could stand it no longer. I rose up from the table, and left the room without a word. Ainsworth followed me; he was flushed with wine, and he looked foolish. 'Where are you going?' he asked. 'Mamie Dillon,' that was the name of his model, 'wants to talk to you.' I made him no answer. 'Where are you going?' he repeated angrily. 'Home, of course,' I replied, 'I have stayed here too long as it is. Let me pass.' He was excited; he had taken too much wine, I know, and he scarcely knew what he was saying. 'Oh, I understand you!' he exclaimed. 'You and Irene Vassilius are of a piece—all purity, eh! all disgust at the manners and customs of the "lower animals." Well, I tell you we are no worse than anyone else in modern days. My lord the duke's conversation differs very little from that of his groom; and the latest imported American heiress in search of a title, rattles on to the full as volubly and ruthlessly as Mamie Dillon. Go home, if go you must; and take my advice, if you don't like what you've seen in the world today, stay home for good. Stay in your shell, and dream your dreams; I dare say they will profit you quite as much as our realities!' He laughed, and as I left him I said, 'You mistake! it is you who are "dreaming," as you call it; dreaming a bad dream, too; it is

I who live.' Then I went out of the house, as I tell you, and wandered alone, under the stars, and thought bitter things."

"Why 'bitter'?" asked El-Râmi.

"I do not know," returned Féraz moodily, "except that all the world seemed wrong. I wondered how God could endure so much degradation on the face of one of his planets, without some grand, Divine protest."

"The protest is always there," said El-Râmi quickly. "Silent, but eternal, in the existence of Good in the midst of Evil."

Féraz lifted his eyes and rested their gaze on his brother with an expression of unutterable affection.

"El-Râmi, keep me with you!" he entreated; "never let me leave you again! I think I must be crazed if the world is what it seems, and my life is so entirely opposed to it; but if so, I would rather be crazed than sane. In my wanderings tonight, on my way home hither, I met young girls and women who must have been devils in disguise, so utterly were they lost to every sense of womanhood and decency. I saw men, evil-looking and wretched, who seemed waiting but the chance to murder, or commit any other barbarous crime for gold. I saw little children, starving and in rags; old and feeble creatures, too, in the last stage of destitution, without a passer-by to wish them well; all things seemed foul and dark and hopeless, and when I entered here, I felt—ah, God knows what I felt!—that you were my Providence, that this was my home, and that surely some Angel dwelt within and hallowed it with safety and pure blessing!"

A sudden remorse softened his voice, his beautiful eyes were dim with tears.

"He remembers and thinks of Lilith!" thought El-Râmi quickly, with a singular jealous tightening emotion at his heart; but aloud he said gently:

"If one day in the 'world' has taught you to love this simple abode of ours, my dear Féraz, more than you did before, you have had a most valuable lesson. But do not be too sure of yourself. Remember, you resented my authority, and you wished to escape from my influence. Well, now—"

"Now I voluntarily place myself under both," said Féraz, rising and standing before him with bent head. "El-Râmi, my brother and my friend, do with me as you will! If from you come my dreams, in God's name let me dream! If from your potent will, exerted on my spirit, springs the fountain of the music which haunts my life, let me ever be a servant of that will! With you I have had happiness, health, peace, and mysterious joy, such as the world could never comprehend; away from you, though only for a day, I have been miserable. Take my complete obedience, El-Râmi, for what it is worth; you give me more than my life's submission can ever repay."

El-Râmi stepped up more closely to him, and laying both hands on his shoulders, looked him seriously in the eyes.

"My dear boy, consider for a moment how you involve yourself," he said earnestly, yet with great kindliness. "Remember the old Arabic volume you chanced upon, and what it said concerning the mystic powers of 'influence.' Did you quite realize it, and all that it implies?"

Féraz met his searching gaze steadily.

"Quite," he replied. "So much and so plainly do I realize it, that I can attribute everything done in the world to 'influence.' Each one of us is 'influenced' by something or someone. Even you, my dearest brother share the common lot, though I dare say you do not quite perceive where your ruling force is generated, your own powers being so extraordinary. Ainsworth, for example, is 'influenced' in very opposite directions by very opposite forces—Irene Vassilius, and—his Mamie Dillon! Now I would rather have your spell laid upon my life than that of the speculator, the gambler, the drinker, or the vile woman, for none of these can possibly give satisfaction, at least not to me; while your wizard wand invokes nothing but beauty, harmony, and peace of conscience. So I repeat it, El-Râmi, I submit to you utterly and finally— must I entreat you to accept my submission?"

He smiled, and the old happy look that he was wont to wear began to radiate over his face, which had till then seemed worn and wearied. El-Râmi's dark features appeared to reflect the smile, as he gently touched his brother's clustering curls, and said playfully:

"In spite of Zaroba?"

"In spite of Zaroba," echoed Féraz mirthfully. "Poor Zaroba! she does not seem well, or happy. I fear she has offended you?"

"No, no," said El-Râmi meditatively, "she has not offended me; she is too old to offend me. I cannot be angry with sorrowful and helpless age. And if she is not well, we will make her well, and if she is not happy, we will make her happy, . . . and be happy ourselves—shall it not be so?" His voice was very soft, and he seemed to talk at random, and to be conscious of it, for he roused himself with a slight start, and said in firmer tones: "Good-night, Féraz; good-night, dear lad. Rest, and dream!"

He smiled as Féraz impulsively caught his hand and kissed it, and after the young man had left the room he still stood, lost in a reverie, murmuring under his breath: "And be happy ourselves! Is that possible—could that be possible—in this world?"

IX

Next day towards noon, while Féraz, tired with his brief "worldly" experiences, was still sleeping, El-Râmi sought out Zaroba. She received him in the ante-room of the chamber of Lilith with more than her customary humility; her face was dark and weary, and her whole aspect one of resigned and settled melancholy. El-Râmi looked at her kindly, and with compassion.

"The sustaining of wrath is an injury to the spirit," he wrote on the slate which served for that purpose in his usual way of communication with her; "I no longer mistrust you. Once more I say, be faithful and obedient. I ask no more. The spell of silence shall be lifted from your lips today."

She read swiftly, and with apparent incre—dulity, and a tremor passed over her tall, gaunt frame. She looked at him wonderingly and wistfully, while he, standing before her, returned the look steadfastly, and seemed to be concentrating all his thoughts upon her with some fixed intention. After a minute or two he turned aside, and again wrote on the slate; this time the words ran thus:

"Speak; you are at liberty."

With a deep shuddering sigh, she extended her hands appealingly.

"Master!" she exclaimed; and before he could prevent her, she had dropped on her knees. "Forgive—forgive!" she muttered. "Terrible is thy power, O El-Râmi, ruler of spirits! terrible, mystic and wonderful! God must have given thee thy force, and I am but the meanest of slaves to rebel against thy command. Yet out of wisdom comes not happiness, but great grief and pain; and as I live, El-Râmi, in my rebellion I but dreamed of a love that should bring thee joy! Pardon the excess of my zeal, for lo, again and yet again I swear fidelity! and may all the curses of heaven fall on me if this time I break my vow!"

She bent her head—she would have kissed the floor at his feet, but that he quickly raised her up and prevented her.

"There is nothing more to pardon," he wrote. "Your wisdom is possibly greater than mine. I know there is nothing stronger than Love, nothing better perhaps; but Love is my foe whom I must vanquish,— lest he should vanquish me!"

And while Zaroba yet pored over these words, her black eyes dilating with amazement at the half confession of weakness implied in them he turned away and left the room.

That afternoon a pleasant sense of peace and restfulness seemed to settle upon the little household; delicious strains of melody filled the air; Féraz, refreshed in mind and body by a sound sleep, was seated at the piano, improvising strange melodies in his own exquisitely wild and tender fashion; while El-Râmi, seated at his writing-table, indited a long letter to Dr. Kremlin at Ilfracombe, giving in full the message left for him by the mysterious monk from Cyprus respecting the "Third Ray" or signal from Mars.

"Do not weary yourself too much with watching this phenomenon," he wrote to his friend. "From all accounts, it will be a difficult matter to track so rapid a flash on the Disc as the one indicated, and I have fears for your safety. I cannot give any satisfactory cause for my premonition of danger to you in the attempt, because if we do not admit an end to anything, then there can be no danger even in death itself, which we are accustomed to look upon as an 'end,' when it may be proved to be only a beginning. But, putting aside the idea of 'danger' or 'death,' the premonition remains in my mind as one of 'change' for you; and perhaps you are not ready or willing even to accept a different sphere of action to your present one, therefore I would say, take heed to yourself when you follow the track of the 'Third Ray.'"

Here his pen stopped abruptly; Féraz was singing in a soft mezza-voce, and he listened:

> *O Sweet, if love obtained must slay desire.*
> *And quench the light and heat of passion's fire;*
> *If you are weary of the ways of love.*
> *And fain would end the many cares thereof.*
> *I prithee tell me so that I may seek*
> *Some place to die in ere I grow too weak*
> *To look my last on your belovèd face.*
> *Yea, tell me all! The gods may yet have grace*
> *And pity enough to let me quickly die*
> *Some brief while after we have said 'Good-bye!'*
> *Nay, I have known it well for many days*
> *You have grown tired of all tender ways;*
> *Love's kisses weary you, love's eager words.*
> *Old as the hills and sweet as singing-birds.*
> *Are fetters hard to bear! O love, be free!*
> *You will lose little joy in losing me;*

Let me depart, remembering only this.
That once you loved me, and that once your kiss
Crown'd me with joy supreme enough to last
Through all my life till that brief life be past.
Forget me, Sweetest-heart, and nevermore
Turn to look back on what has gone before.
Or say, 'Such love was brief, but wondrous fair;'
The past is past forever; have no care
Or thought for me at all, no tear or sigh.
Or faint regret; for, Dearest, I shall die
And dream of you i' the dark, beneath the grass;
And o'er my head perchance your feet may pass.
Lulling me faster into sleep profound
Among the fairies of the fruitful ground.
Love wearied out by love, hath need of rest.
And when all love is ended, Death is best.

The song ceased; but though the singer's voice no longer charmed the silence, his fingers still wandered over the keys of the piano, devising intricate passages of melody as delicate and devious as the warbling of nightingales. El-Râmi, unconsciously to himself, heaved a deep sigh, and Féraz, hearing it, looked round.

"Am I disturbing you?" he asked.

"No. I love to hear you; but, like many youthful poets, you sing of what you scarcely understand—love, for instance; you know nothing of love."

"I imagine I do," replied Féraz meditatively. "I can picture my ideal woman; she is—"

"Fair, of course!" said El-Râmi, with an indulgent smile.

"Yes, fair; her hair must be golden, but not uniformly so—full of lights and shadows, suggestive of some halo woven round her brows by the sunlight, or the caressing touch of an angel. She must have deep, sweet eyes in which no actual colour is predominant; for a pronounced blue or black does away with warmth of expression. She must not be tall, for one cannot caress tall women without a sense of the ludicrous spoiling sentiment—"

"Have you tried it?" asked El-Râmi, laughing.

Féraz laughed too.

"You know I have not; I only imagine the situation. To explain more fully what I mean, I would say one could more readily draw into one's arms the Venus of Medicis than that of Milo—one could venture to caress a Psyche, but scarcely a Juno. I have never liked the idea of tall women, they are like big handsome birds—useful, no doubt, but not half so sweet as the little fluttering singing ones."

"Well, and what other attributes must this imagined lady of yours possess?" asked El-Râmi, vaguely amused at his brother's earnestness.

"Oh, many more charms than I could enumerate," replied Féraz. "And of one thing I am certain, she is not to be found on this earth. But I am quite satisfied to wait; I shall find her, even as she will find me some day. Meanwhile I 'imagine' love, and in imagination I almost feel it."

He went on playing, and El-Râmi resumed the writing of his letter to Kremlin, which he soon finished and addressed ready for post. A gentle knock at the street-door made itself heard just then through the ebb and flow of Féraz's music, and Feraz left off his improvisation abruptly and went to answer the summons. He returned, and announced with some little excitement:

"Madame Irene Vassilius."

El-Râmi rose and advanced to meet his fair visitor, bowing courteously.

"This is an unexpected pleasure, Madame," he said, the sincerity of his welcome showing itself in the expression of his face, "and an unmerited honour for which I am grateful."

She smiled, allowing her hand to rest in his for a moment; then, accepting the low chair which Féraz placed for her near his brother's writing-table, she seated herself, and lifted her eyes to El-Râmi's countenance—eyes which, like those of Féraz's ideal ladye-love, were "deep and sweet, and of no pronounced colour."

"I felt you would not resent my coming here as an intrusion," she began; "but my visit is not one of curiosity. I do not want to probe you as to your knowledge of my past, or to ask you anything as to my future. I am a lonely creature, disliked by many people, and in the literary career I have adopted I fight a desperately hard battle, and often crave for a little—just a little sympathetic comprehension. One or two questions puzzle me which you might answer if you would. They are on almost general subjects; but I should like to have your opinion."

"Madame, if you, with your exceptional gifts of insight and instinct, are baffled in these 'general' questions," said El-Râmi, "shall not I be baffled also?"

"That does not follow," replied Irene, returning his glance steadily, "for you men always claim to be wiser than women. I do not agree with this fiat, so absolutely set forth by the lords of creation; yet I am not what is termed 'strong-minded,' I simply seek justice. Pray stay with us," she added, turning to Féraz, who was about to retire, as he usually did whenever El-Râmi held an interview with any visitor; "there is no occasion for you to go away."

Féraz hesitated, glancing at his brother.

"Yes, by all means remain here, Féraz," said El-Râmi gently, "since Madame Vassilius desires it."

Delighted with the permission, Féraz ensconced himself in a corner with a book, pretending to read, but in reality listening to every word of the conversation. He liked to hear Irene's voice—it was singularly sweet and ringing, and at times had a peculiar thrill of pathos in it that went straight to the heart.

"You know," she went on, "that I am, or am supposed to be, what the world calls 'famous.' That is, I write books which the public clamour for and read, and for which I receive large sums of money. I am able to live well, dress well, and look well, and I am known as one of society's 'celebrities.' Well, now, can you tell me why, for such poor honours as these, men, supposed to be our wiser and stronger superiors, are so spitefully jealous of a woman's fame?"

"Jealous?" echoed El-Râmi dubiously, and with something of hesitation. "You mean—"

"I mean what I say," continued Madame Vassilius calmly; "neither more nor less. Spitefully jealous is the term I used. Explain to me this riddle: Why do men en—courage women to every sort of base folly and vanity that may lead them at length to become the slaves of man's lust and cruelty, and yet take every possible means to oppose and hinder them in their attempts to escape from sensuality and animalism into intellectual progress and pre-eminence? In looking back on the history of all famous women, from Sappho downwards to the present time, it is amazing to consider what men have said of them. Always a sneer at 'women's work.' And if praise is at any time given, how grudging and half-hearted it is! Men will enter no protest against women who uncover their bare limbs to the public gaze and dance lewdly in music-halls and theatres for the masculine delectation; they will defend the street-prostitute; they will pledge themselves and their family estates in order to provide jewels for the newest 'ballerina'; but for the woman of intellect they have nothing but a shrug of contempt. If she produces a great work of art in literature, it is never thoroughly acknowledged; and the hard blows delivered on Charlotte Brontë, George Eliot, Georges Sand, and others of their calibre, far out—weighed their laurels. George Eliot and Georges Sand took men's names in order to shelter themselves a little from the pitiless storm that assails literary work known to emanate from a woman's brain; but let a man write the veriest trash that ever was printed, he will still be accredited by his own sex with something better than ever the cleverest woman could compass. How is it that the 'superior' sex are cowardly enough to throw stones at those among the 'inferior,' who surpass their so-called lords and masters both in chastity and intellect?"

She spoke earnestly, her eyes shining with emotion; she looked lovely, thus inspired by the strength of her inward feelings. El-Râmi was taken aback. Like most Orientals, he had to a certain extent despised women and their work. But, then, what of Lilith? Without her aid would his discoveries in spiritual science have progressed so far? Had he or any man a right to call woman the "inferior" sex?

"Madame," he said slowly and with a vague embarrassment, "you bring an accusation against our sex which it is impossible to refute, because it is simply and undeniably true. Men do not love either chastity or intellect in women."

He paused, looking at her, then went on:

"A chaste woman is an embodied defiance and reproach to man; an intellectual woman is always a source of irritation, because she is invariably his superior. By this I mean that when a woman is thoroughly gifted, she is gifted all round; an intellectual man is generally only gifted in one direction. For example, a great poet, painter, or musician, may be admirable in his own line, but he generally lacks in something; he is stupid, perhaps, in conversation, or he blunders in some way by want of tact; but a truly brilliant woman has all the charms of mental superiority, generally combined with delicate touches of satire, humour, and wit,—points which she uses to perfection against the lumbering animal Man, with the result that she succeeds in pricking him in all his most vulnerable parts. He detests her accordingly, and flies for consolation to the empty-headed dolls of the music-hall, who flatter him to the top of his bent, in order to get as much champagne and as many diamonds as they can out of him. Man must be adored; he insists upon it, even if he pays for it."

"It is a pity he does not make himself a little more worthy of adoration," said Irene, with a slight scornful smile.

"It is," agreed El-Râmi; "but most men, even the ugliest and stupidest, consider themselves perfect."

"Do you?" she asked suddenly.

"Do I consider myself perfect?" El-Râmi smiled, and reflected on this point. "Madame, if I am frank with you, and with myself, I must answer 'Yes!' I am made of the same clay as all my sex, and consider myself worthy to be the conqueror of any woman under the sun! Ask any loathsome, crook-backed dwarf that sweeps a crossing for his livelihood, and his idea of his own personal charm will be the same."

Féraz laughed outright; Madame Vassilius looked amused and interested.

"You can never eradicate from the masculine nature," proceeded El-Râmi, "the idea that our attentions, no matter how uncouth, are, and always must be, agreeable to the feminine temperament. Here you have the whole secret of the battle carried on by men, against women who have won the prize of a world-wide fame. An intellectual woman sets a barrier between herself and the beasts; the beasts howl, but cannot leap it; hence their rage. You, Madame, are not only intellectual, but lovely to look at; you stand apart, a crowned queen, seeking no assistance from men; by your very manner you imply your scorn of their low and base desires. They must detest you in self-defence; most of your adverse critics are the poorly paid hacks of the daily journals, who envy you your house, your horses, your good fortune, and your popularity with the public; if you want them to admire you, go in for a big scandal. Run away with some blackguard; have several husbands; do something to tarnish your woman's reputation; be a vulture or a worm, not a star; men do not care for stars, they are too distant, too cold, too pure!"

"Are you speaking satirically," asked Madame Vassilius, "or in grim earnest?"

"In grim earnest, fair lady," and El-Râmi rose from his chair and confronted her with a half-smile. "In grim earnest, men are brutes! The statement is one which is frequently made by what is called the 'Shrieking Sisterhood'; but I, a man, agree to it in cold blood, without conditions. We are stupid brutes; we work well in gangs, but not so well singly. As soldiers, sailors, builders, engineers, labourers, all on the gang method, we are admirable. The finest paintings of the world were produced by bodies of men working under one head, called 'schools,' but differing from our modern 'schools' in this grand exception, that whereas now each pupil tries his hand at something of his own, then all the pupils worked at the one design of the Master. Thus were painted the frescoes of Michael Angelo, and the chief works of Raphael. Now the rule is 'every man for himself and the devil take the hindmost,' And very poorly does 'each man for himself' succeed. Men must always be helped along, either by each other—or. . . by. . . a woman! Many of them owe all their success in life to the delicate management and patient tact of woman, and yet never have the grace to own it. Herein we are thankless brutes as well as stupid. But, as far as I personally am concerned, I am willing to admit that all my best discoveries, such as they are, are due to the far-reaching intelligence and pure insight of a woman."

This remark utterly amazed Féraz; Madame Vassilius looked surprised and interested.

"Then," she said, smiling slightly, "of course you love someone?"

A shadow swept over El-Râmi's features.

"No, Madame; I am not capable of love, as this world understands loving. Love has existence no doubt, but surely not as Humanity accepts it. For example, a man loves a woman; she dies; he gradually forgets her, and loves another, and so on. That is not love, but it is what society is satisfied with, as such. You are quite right to despise such a fleeting emotion for yourself; it is not sufficient for the demands of your nature; you seek something more lasting."

"Which I shall never find," said Irene quietly.

"Which you will find, and which you must find," declared El-Râmi. "All longings, however vague, whether evil or good, are bound to be fulfilled, there being no waste in the economy of the universe. This is why it is so necessary to weigh well the results of desire before encouraging it. I quite understand your present humour, Madame—it is one of restlessness and discontent. You find your crown of fame has thorns; never mind! wear it royally, though the blood flows from the torn brows. You are solitary at times, and find the solitude irksome; Art serves her children thus—she will accept no half-love, but takes all. Were I asked to name one of the most fortunate of women, I think I should name you, for notwithstanding the progress of your intellectual capacity, you have kept your faith."

"I have kept my religion, if you mean that," said Irene, impressed by his earnestness; "but it is not the religion of the churches."

He gave an impatient gesture.

"The religion of the churches is a mere Show-Sunday," he returned. "We all know that. When I say you have kept your faith, I mean that you can believe in God without positive proofs of Him. That is a grand capability in this age. I wish I had it!"

Irene Vassilius looked at him wonderingly.

"Surely you believe in God?"

"Not till I can prove Him!" and El-Râmi's eyes flashed defiantly. "Vice triumphant, and Virtue vanquished, do not explain Him to me. Torture and death do not manifest to my spirit His much-talked-of 'love and goodness.' I must unriddle His secret; I must pierce into the heart of His plan, before I join the enforced laudations of the multitude; I must know and feel that it is the Truth I am proclaiming, before I stand up in the sight of my fellows and say, 'O God, Thou art the Fountain of Goodness, and all Thy works are wise and wonderful!'"

He spoke with remarkable power and emphasis; his attitude was full of dignity. Madame Vassilius gazed at him in involuntary admiration.

"It is a bold spirit that undertakes to catechize the Creator and examine into the value of His creation," she said.

"If there is a Creator," said El-Râmi, "and if from Him all things do come, then from Him also comes my spirit of inquiry. I have no belief in a devil, but if there were one, the Creator is answerable for him, too. And to revert again to your questions, Madame, shall we not in a way make God somewhat responsible for the universal prostitution of woman? It is a world-wide crime, and only very slight attempts as yet have been made to remedy it, because the making of the laws is in the hands of men—the criminals. The Englishman, the European generally, is as great a destroyer of woman's life and happiness as any Turk or other barbarian. The life of the average woman is purely animal; in her girlhood she is made to look attractive, and her days pass in the consideration of dress, appearance, manner, and conversation; when she has secured her mate, her next business is to bear him children. The children reared, and sent out into the world, she settles down into old age, wrinkled, fat, toothless, and frequently quarrelsome; the whole of her existence is not a grade higher than that of a leopardess or other forest creature, and sometimes not so exciting. When a woman rises above all this, she is voted by the men 'unwomanly'; she is no longer the slave or the toy of their passions; and that is why, my dear Madame, they give the music-hall dancer their diamonds, and heap upon you their sneers."

Irene sat silent for some minutes, and a sigh escaped her.

"Then it is no use trying to be a little different to the rest," she said wearily; "a little higher, a little less prone to vulgarity? If one must be hated for striving to be worthy of one's vocation—"

"My dear lady, you do not see that man will never admit that literature is your vocation! No, not even if you wrote as grand a tragedy as 'Macbeth.' Your vocation, according to them, is to adore their sex, to look fascinating, to wear pretty clothes, and purr softly like a pleased cat when they make you a compliment; not to write books that set everybody talking. They would rather see you dragged and worn to death under the burden of half a dozen children, than they would see you stepping disdainfully past them, in all the glory of fame. Yet be con—tent,—you have, like Mary in the Gospel, 'chosen the better part'; of that I feel sure, though I am unable to tell you why or how I feel it."

"If you feel sure of certain things without being able to explain how or why you feel them," put in Féraz suddenly, "is it not equally easy to feel sure of God without being able to explain how or why He exists?"

"Admirably suggested, my dear Féraz," observed El-Râmi, with a slight smile. "But please recollect that though it may be easy to you and a fair romancist like Madame Vassilius to feel sure of God, it is not at all easy to me. I am not sure of Him; I have not seen Him, and I am not conscious of Him. Moreover, if an average majority of people taken at random could be persuaded to speak the truth for once in their lives, they would all say the same thing—that they are not conscious of Him. Because if they were—if the world were—the emotion of Fear would be altogether annihilated; there would never be any 'panic' about anything; people would not shriek and wail at the terrors of an earthquake, or be seized with pallor and trembling at the crash and horror of an unexpected storm. Being sure of God would mean being sure of Good; and I'm afraid none of us are convinced in that direction. But I think and believe that if we indeed felt sure of God, Evil would be annihilated as well as fear. And the mystery is, why does He not make us sure of Him? It must be in His power to do so, and would save both Him and us an infinite deal of trouble."

Féraz grew restless and left his place, laying down the volume he had been pretending to read.

"I wish you would not be so horribly, cruelly definite in your suggestions," he said rather vexedly. "What is the good of it? It unsettles one's mind."

"Surely your mind is not unsettled by a merely reasonable idea reasonably suggested?" returned El-Râmi calmly. "Madame Vassilius here is not 'unsettled,' as you call it."

"No," said Irene slowly; "but I had thought you more of a spiritual believer—"

"Madame," said El-Râmi impressively, "I am a spiritual believer, but in this way: I believe that this world and all worlds are composed of Spirit and Matter, and not only do I believe it, but I know it! The atmosphere around us and all planets is composed of Spirit and Matter; and every living creature that breathes is made of the same dual mixture. Of the Spirit that forms part of Matter and dominates it, I, even I have some control; and others who come after me, treading in the same lines of thought, will have more than I. I can influence the spirit of man; I can influence the spirit of the air; I can draw an essence from the earth upwards that shall seem to you like the wraith of someone dead; but if you ask me whether these provable, practicable scientific tests or experiments on the spirit that is part of Nature's very existence, are manifestations of God or the Divine, I say—No. God would not permit Man to play at will with His eternal Fires; whereas, with the spirit essence that can be chemically drawn from earth and fire and water, I, a mere studious and considering biped, can do whatsoever I choose. I know how the legends of phantoms and fairies arose in the world's history, because at one time, one particular period of the pre-historic ages, the peculiar, yet natural combination of the elements and the atmosphere, formed 'fantasma' which men saw and believed in. The last trace of these now existing is the familiar 'mirage' of cities with their domes and steeples seen during certain states of the atmosphere in mid-ocean. Only give me the conditions, and I will summon up a ghostly city too. I can form numberless phantasmal figures now, and more than this, I can evoke for your ears from the very bosom of the air, music such as long ago sounded for the pleasure of men and women dead. For the air is a better phonograph than Edison's, and has the advantage of being eternal."

"But such powers are marvellous!" exclaimed Irene. "I cannot understand how you have attained to them."

"Neither can others less gifted understand how you, Madame,

have attained your literary skill," said El-Râmi. "All art, all science, all discovery, is the result of a concentrated Will, an indomitable Perseverance. My 'powers,' as you term them, are really very slight, and, as I said before, those who follow my track will obtain far greater supremacy. The secret of phantasmal splendour or 'vision,' as also the clue to what is called 'unearthly music'—anything and everything that is or appears to be of a supernatural character in this world—can be traced to natural causes, and the one key to it all is the great Fact that Nothing in the Universe is lost. Bear that statement well in mind. Light preserves all scenes; Air preserves all sounds. Therefore, it follows that if the scenes are there, and the sounds are there, they can be evoked again, and yet again, by him who has the skill to understand the fluctuations of the atmospheric waves, and the incessantly recurring vibrations of light. Do not imagine that even a Thought, which you very naturally consider your own, actually remains a fixture in your brain from whence it was germinated. It escapes while you are in the very act of thinking it; its subtle essence evaporates into the air you breathe and the light you absorb. If it presents itself to you again, it will probably be in quite a different form, and perhaps you will hardly recognise it. All Thought escapes thus; you cannot keep it to yourself any more than you can have breath without breathing."

"You mean that a Thought belongs to all, and not to one individual?" said Irene.

"Yes, I mean that," replied El-Râmi; "and Thought, I may say, is the only reflex I can admit of possible Deity, because Thought is free, absolute, all-embracing, creative, perpetual, and unwearied. Limitless too—great Heaven, how limitless! To what heights does it not soar? In what depths does it not burrow? How daring, how calm, how indifferent to the ocean-swell of approaching and receding ages! Your modern Theosophist, calmly counting his gains from the blind incredulity and stupidity of the unthinking masses, is only copying, in a very Lilliputian manner, the grand sagacity and cunning of the ancient Egyptian 'magi,' who, by scientific trickery, ruled the ignorant multitude; it is the same Thought, only dressed in modern aspect. Thought, and the proper condensation, controlling and usage of Thought, is Power,—Divinity, if you will. And it is the only existing Force that can make gods of men."

Irene Vassilius sat silent, fascinated by his words, and still more fascinated by his manner. After a few minutes she spoke—

"I am glad you admit," she said gently, "that this all-potent Thought may be a reflex of the Divine,—for we can have no reflections of light without the Light itself. I came to you in a somewhat discontented humour,—I am happier now. I suppose I ought to be satisfied with my lot,—I am certainly more fortunately situated than most women."

"You are, Madame"—said El-Râmi, smiling pensively and fixing his dark eyes upon her with a kind expression,—"And your native good sense and wit will prevent you, I hope, from marring the good which the gods have provided for you. Do not marry yet,—it would be too great a disillusion for you. The smallest touch of prose is sufficient to destroy the delicacy of love's finer sentiments; and marriage, as the married will tell you, is all prose,—very prosy prose too. Avoid it!— prosy prose is tiresome reading."

She laughed, and rose to take her leave.

"I saw your brother with Mr. Ainsworth yesterday," she observed— "And I could not understand how two such opposite natures could possibly agree."

"Oh, we did not agree,—we have not agreed," said Féraz hastily, speaking for himself—"It is not likely we shall see much of each other."

"I am glad to hear it"—and she extended her hand to him—"You are very young, and Roy Ainsworth is very old, not in years, but in heart. It would be a pity for you to catch the contagion of our modern pessimism."

"But—" Féraz hesitated and stammered, "it was you, was it not, Madame, who suggested to Mr. Ainsworth that he should take me as the model for one of the figures in his picture?"

"Yes, it was I," replied Irene with a slight smile—"But I never thought you would consent,—and I felt sure, that even if you did, he would never succeed in render—ing your expression, for he is a mere surface-painter of flesh, not Soul—still, all the same, it amused me to make the suggestion."

"Yes,—woman-like," said El-Râmi—"You took pleasure in offering him a task he could not fulfil. There you have another reason why intellectual women are frequently detested—they ask so much and give so little."

"You wrong us," answered Irene swiftly. "When we love, we give all!"

"And so you give too much!" said El-Râmi gravely—"It is the common fault of women. You should never give 'all'—you should always hold back something. To be fascinating, you should be enigmatical. When once man is allowed to understand your riddle thoroughly, the spell is broken. The placid, changeless, monotonously amiable woman has no power whatever over the masculine temperament. It is Cleopatra that makes a slave of Antony, not blameless and simple Octavia."

Irene Vassilius smiled.

"According to such a theory, the Angels must be very tame and uninteresting individuals," she said.

El-Râmi's eyes grew lustrous with the intensity of his thought.

"Ah, Madame, our conception of Angels is a very poor and false one, founded on the flabby imaginations of ignorant priests. An Angel, according to my idea, should be wild and bright and restless as lightning, speeding from star to star in search of new lives and new loves, with lips full of music and eyes full of fire, with every fibre of its immortal being palpitating with pure yet passionate desires for everything that can perfect and equalize its existence. The pallid, goose-winged object represented to us as inhabiting a country of No-Where without landscape or colour, playing on an unsatisfactory harp and singing 'Holy, holy' forever and ever, is no Angel, but rather a libel on the whole systematic creative plan of the Universe. Beauty, brilliancy, activity, glory and infinite variety of thought and disposition—if these be not in the composition of an Angel, then the Creator is but poorly served!"

"You speak as if you had seen one of these immortals?" said Irene, surprised.

A shadow darkened his features.

"Not I, Madame—except once—in a dream! You are going?—then farewell! Be happy,—and encourage the angelic qualities in yourself—for if there be a Paradise anywhere, you are on the path that leads to it."

"You think so?" and she sighed—"I hope you may be right,—but sometimes I fear, and sometimes I doubt. Thank you for all you have said,—it is the first time I have met with so much gentleness, courtesy and patience from one of your sex. Good-bye!"

She passed out, Féraz escorting her to her carriage, which waited at the door; then he returned to his brother with a slow step and meditative air.

"Do men really wrong women so much as she seems to think?" he asked.

El-Râmi paused a moment,—then answered slowly:

"Yes, Féraz, they do; and as long as this world wags, they will! Let God look to it!—for the law of feminine oppression is His—not ours!"

X

That same week was chronicled one of the worst gales that had ever been known to rage on the English coast. From all parts of the country came accounts of the havoc wrought on the budding fruit-trees by the pitiless wind and rain,—harrowing stories of floods and shipwrecks came with every fresh despatch of news,—great Atlantic steamers were reported "missing," and many a fishing-smack went down in sight of land, with all the shrieking, struggling souls on board. For four days and four nights the terrific hurricane revelled in destruction, its wrath only giving way to occasional pauses of heavy silence more awful than its uproar; and by the rocky shores of Ilfracombe, the scene of nature's riot, confusion and terror attained to a height of indescribable grandeur. The sea rose in precipitous mountain-masses, and anon wallowed in black abysmal chasms,—the clouds flew in a fierce rack overhead like the forms of huge witches astride on eagle-shaped monsters,—and with it all there was a close heat in the air, notwithstanding the tearing wind,—a heat and a sulphureous smell, suggestive of some pent-up hellish fire that but waited its opportunity to break forth and consume the land. On the third day of the gale particularly, this curious sense of suffocation was almost unbearable, and Dr. Kremlin, looking out of his high tower window in the morning at the unquiet sky and savage sea, wondered, as the wind scudded past, why it brought no freshness with it, but only an increased heat, like the "simoom" of the desert.

"It is one of those days on which it would seem that God is really angry," mused Kremlin—"angry with Himself, and still more angry with His creature."

The wind whistled and shrieked in his ears as though it strove to utter some wild response to his thought,—the sullen roaring and battling of the waves on the beach below sounded like the clashing armour of contesting foes,—and the great Disc in the tower revolved, or appeared to revolve, more rapidly than its wont, its incessant whirr-whirring being always distinctly heard above the fury of the storm. To this, his great work, the chief labour of his life, Dr. Kremlin's eyes turned wistfully, as, after a brief observation of the turbulent weather, he shut his window fast against the sheeting rain. Its shining surface, polished as steel, reflected the lights and shadows of the flying storm-clouds, in strange and beautiful groups like moving landscapes—now and then it flashed with a curious lightning glare of brilliancy as it swung round to its appointed measure, even as a planet swings in its orbit. A new feature had been added to the generally weird effect of Kremlin's strange studio or workshop,—this was a heavy black curtain made of three thicknesses of cloth sewn closely together, and weighted at the end with bullet-shaped balls of lead. It was hung on a thick iron pole, and ran easily on indiarubber rings,—when drawn forward it covered the Disc completely from the light without interfering with any portion of its mechanism. Three days since, Kremlin had received El-Râmi's letter telling him what the monk from Cyprus had said concerning the "Third Ray" or the messages from Mars, and eagerly grasping at the smallest chance of any clue to the labyrinth of the Light-vibrations, he had lost no time in making all the preparations necessary for this grand effort, this attempt to follow the track of the flashing signal whose meaning, though apparently unintelligible, might yet with patience be discovered. So, following the suggestions received, he had arranged the sable drapery, in such a manner that it could be drawn close across the Disc, or, in a second, be flung back to expose the whole surface of the crystal to the light,—all was ready for the trial, when the great storm came and interfered. Dense clouds covered the firmament,—and not for one single moment since he received the monk's message had Kremlin seen the stars. However, he was neither discouraged nor impatient,—he had not worked amid perplexities so long to be disheartened now by a mere tempest, which in the ordinary course of nature, would wear itself out, and leave the heavens all the clearer both for reflection and observation. Yet he, as a meteorologist, was bound to confess that the fury of the gale was of an exceptional character, and that the height to which the sea lifted itself before stooping savagely towards the land and breaking itself in hissing spouts of spray, was stupendous, and in a manner appalling. Karl, his servant, was entirely horrified at the scene,—he hated the noise of the wind and waves, and more than all he hated the incessant melancholy scream of the seabirds that wheeled in flocks round and round the tower.

"It is for all the world like the shrieks of drowning men"—he said, and shivered, thinking of the pleasantly devious ways of the Rhine and its placid flowing,—placid even in flood, as compared to the howling ocean, all madness and movement and terror. Twice during that turbulent day Karl had asked his master whether the tower "shook."

"Of course!" answered Dr. Kremlin with a smile in his mild eyes—"Of course it shakes,—it can hardly do otherwise in such a gale. Even a cottage shakes in a fierce wind."

"Oh yes, a cottage shakes," said Karl meditatively—"but then if a cottage blows away altogether, it doesn't so much matter. Cottages are frequently blown away in America, so they say, with all the family sitting inside. That's not a bad way of travelling. But when a tower flies through the air, it seldom carries the family with it except in bits."

Kremlin laughed, but did not pursue the conversation, and Karl went about his duties in a gloomy humour, not common to his cheerful temperament. He really had enough to put him out, all things considered. Soot fell down the kitchen chimney—a huge brick also landed itself with a crash in the fender,—there were crevices in the doors and windows through which the wind played wailing sounds like a "coronach" on the bagpipes;—and then, when he went out into the courtyard to empty the pail of soot he had taken from the grate, he came suddenly face to face with an ugly bird, whose repulsive aspect quite transfixed him for the moment and held him motionless, staring at it. It was a hooded vulture, and it stood huddled on the pavement, blinking its disagreeable eyes at Karl,—its floppy wings were drenched with the rain, and all over the yard was the wet trail of its feathers and feet.

"Shoo!" cried Karl, waving his arms and the pail of soot all together—"Shoo! Beast!"

But the vulture appeared not to mind—it merely set about preening its dirty wing.

Karl grew savage, and running back to the kitchen, brought shovel, tongs and a broom, all of which implements he flung in turn at the horrid-looking creature, which, finally startled, rose in air uttering dismal cries as it circled higher and higher, the while Karl watched its flight,—higher and higher it soared, till at last he ran out of the courtyard to see where it went. Round and round the house it flew, seeming to be literally tossed to and fro by the wind, its unpleasant shriek still echoing distinctly above the deep boom of the sea, till suddenly it made a short sweep downwards, and sat on the top of the tower like a squat black phantom of the storm.

"Nasty brute!" said Karl, shaking his clenched fist at it—"If the Herr Doctor were like any other man, which he is not, he would have a gun in the house, and I'd shoot that vile screamer. Now it will sit cackling and yelling there all day and all night perhaps. Pleasant, certainly!"

And he went indoors, grumbling more than ever. Everything seemed to go wrong that day,—the fire wouldn't burn,—the kettle wouldn't boil,—and he felt inwardly vexed that his master was not as morose and irritable as himself. But, as it happened, Dr. Kremlin was in a singularly sweet and placid frame of mind,—the noise of the gale seemed to soothe rather than agitate his nerves. For one thing, he was much better in health, and looked years younger than when El-Râmi visited him, bringing the golden flask whose contents were guaranteed to give him a new lease of life. So far indeed the Elixir had done its work,—and to all appearances, he might have been a well-preserved man of about fifty, rather than what he actually was, close upon his seventy-fourth year. As he could take no particularly interesting or useful observations from his Disc during the progress of the tempest, he amused himself with the task of perfecting one or two of his "Light-Maps" as he called them, and he kept at this work with the greatest assiduity and devotion all the morning. These maps were wonderfully interesting, if only for the extreme beauty, intricacy and regularity of the patterns,—one set of "vibrations" as copied from the reflections on the Disc, formed the exact shape of a branch of coral,—another gave the delicate outline of a frond of fern. All the lines ran in waves,—none of them were straight. Most of them were in small ripples,—others were larger—some again curved broadly, and turned round in a double twist, forming the figure 8 at long intervals of distance, but all resolved themselves into a definite pattern of some sort.

"Pictures in the sky!" he mused, as he patiently measured and re-touched the lines. "And all different!—not two of them alike! What do they all mean?—for they must mean something. Nothing—not the lowest atom that exists, is without a meaning and a purpose. Shall I ever discover the solution to the Light-mystery, or is it so much God's secret that it will never become Man's?"

So he wondered, puzzling himself, with a good deal of pleasure in the puzzle. He was happy in his work, despite its strange and difficult character,—El-Râmi's elixir had so calmed and equalized his physical temperament, that he was no longer conscious of worry or perplexity. Satisfied that he had years of life before him in which to work, he was content to let things take their course, and he laboured on in the spirit that all labour claims, "without haste, without rest." Feverish hurry in work,—eagerness to get the rewards of it before conscientiously deserving them,—this disposition is a curse of the age we live in and the ruin of true art,—and it was this delirium of haste that had seized Kremlin when he had summoned El-Râmi to his aid. Now, haste seemed unnecessary;—there was plenty of time, and—possessed of the slight clue to the "Third Ray,"—plenty of hope as well, or so he thought.

In the afternoon the gale gradually abated, and sank to a curiously sudden dead calm. The sea still lifted toppling foam-crowned peaks to the sky, and still uttered shattering roars of indignation,—but there was a break in the clouds and a pale suggestion of sunshine. As the evening closed in, the strange dull quietness of the air deepened,—the black mists on the horizon flashed into stormy red for an instant when the sun set,—and then darkened again into an ominous greenish-gray. Karl, who was busy cooking his master's dinner, stopped stirring some sauce he was making, to listen, as it were, to the silence,—the only sound to be heard was the long roll and swish of the sea on the beach,—and even the scream of the gulls was stilled. Spoon in hand he went out in the yard to observe the weather; all movement in the heavens seemed to have been suddenly checked, and masses of black cloud rested where they were, apparently motionless. And while he looked up at the sky, he could hardly avoid taking the top of the tower also into his view;—there, to his intense disgust, still sate his enemy of the morning, the hooded vulture. Something that was not quite choice in the way of language escaped his lips as he saw the hateful thing;—its presence was detestable to him and filled his mind with morbid imaginations which no amount of reasoning could chase away.

"And yet what is it but a bird!" he argued with himself angrily, as he went indoors and resumed his cooking operations—"A bird of prey, fond of carrion—nothing more. Why should I bother myself about it? If I told the Herr Doctor that it was there, squatting at ease on his tower, he would very likely open the window, invite the brute in, and offer it food and shelter for the night. For he is one of those kind-hearted people who think that all the animal creation are worthy of consideration and tenderness. Well,—it may be very good and broad philosophy,—all the same, if I caught a rat sitting in my bed, I shouldn't like it,—nor would I care to share my meals with a lively party of cockroaches. There are limits to Christian feelings. And as for that beast of a bird outside, why it's better outside than in, so I'll say nothing about it."

And he devoted himself more intently than ever to the preparation of the dinner, for his master had now an excellent appetite, and ate good things with appreciation and relish, a circumstance which greatly consoled Karl for many other drawbacks in the service he had undertaken. For he was a perfect cook, and proud of his art, and that night he was particularly conscious of the excellence of the little tasty dishes he had, to use an artterm, "created," and he watched his master enjoy their flavour, with a proud, keen sense of his own consummate skill.

"When a man relishes his food it is all right with him," he thought.— "Starving for the sake of science may be all very well, but if it kills the scientist, what becomes of the science?"

And he grew quite cheerful in the contemplation of the "Herr Doctor's" improved appetite, and by degrees almost forgot the uncanny bird that was still sitting on the topmost ledge of the tower.

Among other studious habits engendered by long solitude into which Kremlin had fallen, was the somewhat unhygienic one of reading at meals. Most frequently it was a volume of poems with which he beguiled the loneliness of his dinner, for he was one of those rare few who accept and believe in what may be called the "Prophecies" of Poesy. These are in very truth often miraculous, and it can be safely asserted that if the writers of the Bible had not been poets they would never have been prophets. A poet,—if he indeed be a poet, and not a mere manufacturer of elegant verse,—always raves,—raves madly, blindly, incoherently of things he does not really understand. Moreover, it is not himself that raves—but a Something within him,—some demoniac or angelic spirit that clamours its wants in wild music, which by throbbing measure and degree resolves itself, after some throes of pain on the poet's part, into a peculiar and occasionally vague language. The poet as man, is no more than man; but that palpitating voice in his mind gives him no rest, tears his thoughts piecemeal, rends his soul, and consumes him with feverish trouble and anxiety not his own, till he has given it some sort of speech, however mystic and strange. If it resolves itself into a statement which appals or amazes, he, the poet, cannot help it; if it enunciates a prophecy he is equally incapable of altering or refuting it. When Shakespeare wrote the three words, "Sermons in stones," he had no idea that he was briefly expounding with perfect completeness the then to him unknown science of Geology. The poet is not born of Flesh alone, but of Spirit—a Spirit which dominates him whether he will or no, from the very first hour in which his childish eyes look inquiringly on leaves and flowers and stars—a Spirit which catches him by the hands, kisses him on the lips, whispers mad nothings in his startled ears, flies restlessly round and about him, brushing his every sense with downy, warm, hurrying wings,—snatches him up altogether at times and bids him sing, write, cry out strange oracles, weep forth wild lamentations, and all this without ever condescending to explain to him the reason why. It is left to the world to discover this "Why," and the discovery is often not made till ages after the poet's mortal dust has been transformed to flowers in the grass which little children gather and wear unknowingly. The poet whose collected utterances Dr. Kremlin was now reading as he sipped the one glass of light Burgundy which concluded his meal, was Byron; the fiery singer whose exquisite music is pooh-poohed by the insipid critics of the immediate day, who, jealous of his easily-won and worldwide fame, grudge him the laurel, even though it spring from the grave of a Hero as well as Bard. The book was open at "Manfred," and the lines on which old Kremlin's eyes rested were these:—

> "How beautiful is all this visible world!
> How glorious in its action and itself!
> But we who name ourselves its sovereigns, we.
> Half dust, half deity, alike unfit
> To sink or soar, with our mix'd essence make
> A conflict of its elements, and breathe
> The breath of degradation and of pride.
> Contending with low wants and lofty will.
> Till our mortality predominates.
> And men are,—what they name not to themselves.
> And trust not to each other."

"Now that passage is every whit as fine as anything in Shakespeare," thought Kremlin—"and the whole secret of human trouble is in it;—it is not the world that is wrong, but we—we 'who make a conflict of its elements.' The question is, if we are really 'unfit to sink or soar' is it our fault?—and may we not ask without irreverence why we were made so incomplete? Ah, my clever friend El-Râmi Zarânos has set himself a superhuman task on the subject of this 'Why,' and I fancy I shall find out the riddle of Mars and many another planet besides, before he 'proves,' as he is trying to do, the conscious and individual existence of the soul."

He turned over the pages of "Manfred" thoughtfully, and then stopped, his gaze riveted on the splendid lines in which the unhappy hero of the tragedy flings his last defiance to the accusing demons—

> *"The mind which is immortal makes itself*
> *Requital for its good or evil thoughts—*
> *Is its own origin of ill and end—*
> *And its own place and time—its innate sense.*
> *When stripped of this mortality, derives*
> *No colour from the fleeting things without.*
> *But is absorbed in sufferance or in joy.*
> *Born from the knowledge of its own desert.*
> *Thou did'st not tempt me, and thou could'st not tempt;*
> *I have not been thy dupe, nor am thy prey—*
> *But was my own destroyer, and will be*
> *My own hereafter.—Back, ye baffled fiends!*
> *The hand of death is on me,—but not yours!"*

"And yet people will say that Byron was an immoral writer!" murmured Kremlin—"In spite of the tremendous lesson conveyed in those lines! There is something positively terrifying in that expression—

> *"But was my own destroyer, and will be*
> *My own hereafter.'*

What a black vista of possibilities—"

Here he broke off, suddenly startled by a snaky blue glare that flashed into the room like the swift sweep of a sword-blade. Springing up from the table, he rubbed his dazzled eyes.

"Why—what was that?" he exclaimed.

"Lightning!" replied Karl, just entering at the moment—"and a very nasty specimen of it. . . I'd better put all the knives and steel things by."

And he proceeded to do this, while Kremlin still stood in the centre of the room, his sight yet a little confused by the rapidity and brilliancy of that unexpected storm-flash. A long low ominous muttering of thunder, beginning far off and rolling up nearer and nearer till it boomed like a volley of cannon in unison with the roar of the sea, followed, then came silence. No rain fell, and the wind only blew moderately enough to sway the shrubs in front of the house lightly to and fro.

"It will be a stormy night," said Dr. Kremlin then, recovering himself and taking up his Byron—"I am sorry for the sailors! You had better see well to all the fastenings of the doors and windows."

"Trust me!" replied Karl sententiously—"You shall not be carried out to sea against your will if I can help it—nor have I any desire to make such a voyage myself. I hope, Herr Doctor"—he added with a touch of anxiety—"you are not going to spend this evening in the tower?"

"I certainly am!" answered Kremlin, smiling—"I have work up there, and I cannot afford to be idle on account of a thunderstorm. Why do you look so scared? There is no danger."

"I didn't say there was"—and Karl fidgeted uneasily—"but—though I've never been inside it, I should think the tower was lonesome, and I should fancy there might be too close a view of the lightning to be quite pleasant."

Kremlin looked amused, and walking to the window, pushed back one of the curtains.

"I believe it was a false alarm," he said, gazing at the sea—"That flash and thunder-peal were the parting notes of a storm that has taken place somewhere else. See!—the clouds are clearing."

So in truth they were; the evening, though very dark, seemed to give promise of a calm. One or two stars twinkled faintly in a blackish-blue breadth of sky, and perceiving these shining monitors and problems of his life's labour, Kremlin wasted no more time in words, but abruptly left the room and ascended to his solitary studio. Karl, listening, heard the closing of the heavy door aloft and the grating of the key as it turned in the lock,—and he also heard that strange perpetual whirring noise above, which, though he had in a manner grown accustomed to it, always remained for him a perplexing mystery. Shaking his head dolefully, and with a somewhat troubled countenance, he cleared the dining-table, set the room in order, went down to his kitchen, cleaned, rubbed, and polished everything till his surroundings were as bright as it was possible for them to be, and then, pleasantly fatigued, sat down to indite a letter to his mother in the most elaborate German phraseology he could devise. He was rather proud of his "learning," and he knew his letters home were read by nearly all the people in his native village as well as by his maternal parent, so that he was particularly careful in his efforts to impress everybody by the exceeding choiceness of his epistolary "style." Absorbed in his task, he at first scarcely noticed the gradual rising of the wind, which, having rested for a few hours, now seemed to have awakened in redoubled strength and fury. Whistling under the kitchen-door it came, with a cold and creepy chill,—it shook the windows angrily, and then, finding the door of the outside pantry open, shut it to with a tremendous bang, like an irate person worsted in an argument. Karl paused, pen in hand; and as he did so, a dismal cry echoed round the house, the sound seeming to fall from a height and then sweep over the earth with the wind, towards the sea.

"It's that brute of a bird!" said Karl half-aloud—"Nice cheerful voice he has, to be sure!"

At that moment, the kitchen was illuminated from end to end by a wide blue glare of lightning, followed, after a heavy pause, by a short loud clap of thunder. The hovering storm had at last gathered together its scattered forces, and concentrating itself blackly above the clamorous sea, now broke forth in deadly earnest.

XI

Kremlin meanwhile had reached his tower in time to secure a glimpse of the clearer portion of the sky before it clouded over again. Opening the great window, he leaned out and anxiously surveyed the heavens. There was a little glitter of star-groups above his head, and immediately opposite an almost stirless heavy fleece of blackness, which he knew by its position hid from his sight the planet Mars, the brilliant world he now sought to make the chief centre of his observations. He saw that heavy clouds were slowly rolling up from the south, and he was quite prepared for a fresh outbreak of storm and rain, but he was determined to take advantage, if possible, of even a few moments of temporary calm. And with this intention he fixed his gaze watchfully on the woolly-looking dark mass of vapour that concealed the desired Star from his view, having first carefully covered the steadily revolving Disc with its thick sable curtain. Never surely was there a more weird and solemn-looking place than the tower-room as it now appeared; no light in it at all save a fitful side-gleam from the whirling edge of the Disc,—all darkness and monotonous deep sound, with that patient solitary figure leaning at the sill of the wide-open window, gazing far upward at the pallid gleam of those few distant stars that truly did no more than make "darkness visible." The aged scientist's heart beat quickly; the weight of long years of labour and anxiety seemed to be lifted from his spirit, and it was with almost all the ardour of his young student-days that he noted the gradual slow untwisting and dividing of those threads of storm-mist, that like a dark web, woven by the Fates, veiled the "red Planet" whose flashing Signal might prove to be the key to a thousand hitherto unexplored mysteries. It was strange that just at this particular moment of vague suspense his thoughts should go wandering in a desultory wilful fashion back to this past,—and that the history of his bygone life seemed to arrange itself, as it were, in a pattern as definite as the wavy lines on his "Light-Maps" and with just as indefinite a meaning. He, who had lived that life, was as perplexed concerning its ultimate intention, as he was concerning the ultimate meanings conveyed by the light-vibrations through air. He tried to keep his ideas centred on the scientific puzzle he was attempting to unravel,—he strove to think of every small fact that bore more or less on that one central object,—he repeated to himself the A B C of his art, concerning the vibrations of light on that first natural reflector, the human eye,—how, in receiving the impression of the colour red, for instance, the nerves of the eye are set quivering four hundred and eighty-two millions of millions of times; or, of the colour violet, seven hundred and seven millions of millions of times per second. How could he hope to catch the rapid flash of the "Third Ray" under these tremendous con—ditions? Would it not vanish from the very face of the Disc before he had time to track its circuit? But though he strove to busy his brain with conjectures and calculations, he was forced, in spite of himself, to go on groping into the Past; that wonderful Past when he had been really young—young with a youth not born of El-Râmi's secret concoctions,—but youth as it is received fresh and perfect from the hand of Divinity—the talisman which makes all the world an Eden of roses without thorns. He saw himself as he used to be, a slim student, fair-haired and blue-eyed, absorbed in science, trying strange experiments, testing new chemical combinations, ferreting out the curious mysteries of atmospheric phenomena, and then being gradually led to consider the vast amount of apparently unnecessary Light per second, that pours upon us from every radiating object in the firmament, bearing in mind the fact that our Earth itself radiates through Space, even though its glimmer be no more than that of a spark amid many huge fires. He remembered how he had pored over the strange but incontestable fact that two rays of light starting from the same point and travelling in the same direction frequently combine to produce darkness, by that principle which is known in the science of Optics as the interference of the rays of light,—and how, in the midst of all this, his work had been suddenly interrupted and put a stop to by a power the stars in their courses cannot gainsay—Love. Yes—he had loved and been beloved,—this poor, gentle, dreamy man;—one winter in Russia—one winter when the snows lay deep on the wild steppes and the wolves were howling for hunger in the gloom of the forests,—he had dreamed his dream, and wakened from it—broken-hearted. She whom he loved, a beautiful girl connected with the Russian nobility, was associated, though he knew it not, with a secret society of Nihilists, and was all at once arrested with several others and accused of being party to a plot for the assassination of the Tsar. Found guilty, she was sentenced to exile in Siberia, but before the mandate could be carried out, she died by her own hand, poisoned in her prison cell. Kremlin, though not "suspect," went almost mad with grief, and fled from Russia never to set his foot on its accursëd soil again. People said that the excess of his sorrow, rage and despair had affected his brain, which was possible, as his manner and mode of living, and the peculiar grooves of study into which he fell, were undoubtedly strange and eccentric—and yet—tenderness for his dead love, self-murdered in her youth and beauty, kept him sensitively alive to human needs and human suffering,—there was no scorn or bitterness in his nature, and his faith in the unseen God was as great as El-Râmi's doubt. But left as he was all alone in the world, he plunged into the obscure depths of science with greater zest than ever, striving to forget the dire agony of that brief love-drama, the fatal end of which had nearly closed his own career in madness and death. And so the years drifted on and on in work that every day grew more abstruse and perplexing, till he had suddenly, as it were, found himself old,—too old, as he told himself with nervous trembling, ever to complete what he had begun. Then he had sent for El-Râmi; El-Râmi whom he had met and wondered at, during his travels in the East years ago. . . and El-Râmi, at his desire, by strange yet potent skill, had actually turned back time in its too rapid flight—and a new lease of life was vouchsafed to him;—he had leisure,—long, peaceful leisure in which to carry out his problems to perfection, if to carry them out were at all possible. For had not El-Râmi said—"You cannot die, except by violence"?

And thus, like the "star-patterns," all the fragments of his personal history came into his mind tonight as he waited at his tower window, watching the black pavilion under which the world of Mars swung round in its fiery orbit.

"Why do I think of all these bygone things just now?" he asked himself wonderingly—"I who so seldom waste my time in looking back, my work being all for the Future?"

As he murmured the words half aloud, a rift showed itself in the cloud he was observing,—a rift which widened gradually and broke up the dark mass by swift and ever swifter degrees. Fold after fold of mist dissolved and dispersed itself along the sky, swept by the wings of the newly-arisen wind, and Mars, angrily crimson and stormily brilliant, flashed forth a lurid fire. . . In less time than imagination can depict, Kremlin had noiselessly flung the black curtain back from his Disc, . . . and with his eyes riveted upon its gleaming pearly surface he waited. . . scarcely breathing, . . . every nerve in his body seeming to contract and grow rigid with expectation and something like dread. A pale light glistened on the huge Disc. . . it was gone! . . . another flash, . . . and this remained trembling in wavy lines and small revolving specks—now. . . now. . . the Third!—and Kremlin craned his head forward eagerly. . . it came!—like a drop of human blood it fell, and raced more rapidly than quicksilver round and round the polished surface of the Disc, paling in tint among the other innumerable silvery lines. . . flashed again redly. . . and. . . disappeared! A cry of irrepressible disappointment broke from Kremlin's lips.

"Impossible! . . . my God! . . . Impossible!"

Aye!—impossible surely to track such velocity of motion—impossible to fix the spot where first its dazzling blood-like hue fell, and where it at last vanished. And yet Kremlin waited on in feverish expectancy, his lips apart, his breath coming and going in quick uneasy gasps, his straining eyes fixed on that terrible, inscrutable creation of his own skill, that fearful Mirror of the heavens which reflected so much and betrayed so little! . . . Heedless of the muttering roar of the wind which now suddenly assailed the tower, he stood, fascinated by the dazzling play of light that illumined the Disc more brilliantly than usual. A dismal scream,—the cry of the vulture perched on the roof above him, echoed faintly in his ears, but he scarcely heard it, so absorbed was he in his monstrous Enigma; till—all at once, a blue shaft of lightning glared in at the window, its brief reflection transforming the Disc for a second to an almost overwhelming splendour of glittering colour. The strong blaze dazzled Kremlin's eyes,—and as the answer—ing thunder rattled through the sky, he reluctantly moved from his position and went towards the window to shut it against the threatening storm. But when he reached it, he saw that the planet Mars was yet distinctly visible; the lightning and thunder came from that huge bank of clouds in the south he had before noticed,—clouds which were flying rapidly up, but had not yet entirely obscured the heavens. In eager and trembling haste he hurried back to the Disc,—it seemed alive with light, and glistened from point to point like a huge jewel as it whirled and hummed its strange monotonous music,—and, shading his eyes, he remained close beside it, determined to watch it still, hoping against hope that another red flash like the one he had lately seen, might crimson the quivering mass of silvery intersecting lines which he knew were not so much the light-vibrations of stars now, as reflexes of the electricity pent up in the tempestuous atmosphere.

"Patience. . . patience!" he murmured aloud—"A moment more, and perhaps I shall see, . . . I shall know. . . I shall find what I have sought. . ."

The last words were yet trembling on his lips when a fearful forkëd tongue of red flame leaped from the clouds, descending obliquely like a colossal sword, . . . it smote the tower, splitting its arched roof and rending its walls asunder,—and with the frightful boom and bellow of thunder that followed, echoing over land and sea for miles and miles there came another sound, . . . a clanging jangle of chains and wires and ponderous metals, . . . the mighty mass of the glittering Star-Dial swirled round unsteadily once. . . twice. . . quivered. . . stopped. . . and then. . . slipping from its wondrous pendulum, hurled itself forward like a monster shield and fell! . . . fell with an appalling crash and thud, bringing the roof down upon itself in a blinding shower of stones and dust and mortar. . . And then. . . why, then nothing! Nothing but dense blackness, muttering thunder, and the roaring of the wind.

Outside, frantic with fear, Karl shook and battered at the firmly-locked and bolted door of the tower. When that forked flash of lightning had struck the house, it had stretched him senseless in his kitchen,—he had however recovered after a few minutes' unconsciousness, dazed and stunned but otherwise unhurt, and becoming gradually alive to the immediate dangers of the situation, he had, notwithstanding the fury of the gale and the deafening peals of thunder, rushed out of doors instinctively to look at the tower. One glance showed him what had happened,—it was split asunder, and showed dimly against the stormy night like a yawning ruin round which in time the ivy might twist and cling. Breathless and mad with terror, he had rushed back to the house and up the stairs, and now stood impatiently clamouring outside the impenetrable portal whose firm interior fastenings resisted all his efforts. He called, he knocked, he kicked,—and then, exhausted with the vain attempt, stopped to listen. . . Nothing! . . . not a sound! He made a hollow of his hands and put his mouth to the keyhole.

"Herr Doctor! . . . Herr Doctor!"

No answer,—except the stormy whistle of the blast.

"No help for it!" he thought desperately, tears of excitement and alarm gathering in his eyes—"I must call for assistance,—rouse the neighbours and break open the door by force."

He ran downstairs and out of the house bareheaded, to be met by a sudden sweep of rain which fell in a straight unpremeditated way from the clouds in stinging torrents. Heedless of wind and wet he sped along, making direct for some fishermen's cottages whose inhabitants he knew and whom in a manner he was friendly with, and having roused them up by shouts and cries, explained to them as briefly as possible what had happened. As soon as they understood the situation four stout fellows got ready to accompany him, and taking pickaxes, crowbars, boathooks, and any other such implements as were handy, they ran almost as quickly as Karl himself to the scene of the catastrophe. Their excitement was to the full as great as his, till they reached the top of the staircase and stood outside the mysterious door—there they hung back a moment hesitatingly.

"Call him again"—one whispered to Karl. "Mebbe he's in there safe and sound and did not hear ye at fust."

To satisfy the man's scruples Karl obeyed, and called and called, and knocked and knocked again and yet again,—with the same result,—no answer, save the derisive yell of the gale.

"He be dead an' gone for sure"—said a second man, with a slight pallor coming over his sea-tanned face—"Well. . . well! . . . if so be as we must break down th' door—"

"Here, give me one of those things"—cried Karl impatiently, and snatching a crowbar he began dealing heavy blows at the massive nail-studded oaken barrier. Seeing him so much in earnest, his companions lost the touch of superstitious dread that had made them hesitate, and also set themselves to work with a will, and in a few minutes—minutes which to the anxious Karl seemed ages,—the door was battered in, . . . and they all rushed forward, . . . but the fierce wind tearing wildly around them, caught the flame of the lamp they carried and extinguished it, so that they were left in total darkness. But over their heads the split roof yawned, showing the black sky, and about their feet there was a mass of fallen stones and dust and indistinguishable ruin. As quickly as possible they re-lit the lamp and holding it aloft, looked tremblingly and without speaking a word, at the havoc and confusion around them. At first little could be seen but heaped-up stones and bricks and mortar, but Karl's quick eyes roving eagerly about caught sight suddenly of something black under a heap of débris,—and quickly bending down over it he began with his hands to clear away the rubbish,—the other men, seeing what he was trying to do, aided him in his task, and in about twenty minutes' time they succeeded in uncovering a black mass, huge and inanimate.

"What is it?" whispered one of the men—"It's. . . it's not him?"

Karl said nothing—he felt himself turning sick with dread, . . . he touched that doubtful blackness—it was a thick cloth like a great pall—

it concealed. . . what? Recklessly he pulled and tugged at it, getting his hands lacerated by a tangled mesh of wires and metals,—till, yielding at last to a strong jerk, it came away in weighty clinging folds, disclosing what to him seemed an enormous round stone, which, as the lamp-light flashed upon it, glistened mysteriously with a thousand curious hues. Karl grasped its edge in an effort to lift it—his fingers came in contact with something moist and warm, and snatching them away in a sort of vague horror, he saw that they were stained with blood.

"Oh my God! my God!" he cried—"He is down there,—underneath this thing! . . . help me to lift it, men!—lift it for Heaven's sake!—lift it, quick—quick!"

But though they all dragged at it with a will, the work was not so easy—the great Disc had fallen flat, and lay solemnly inert—and that oozing blood,—the blood of the too daring student of the stars who had designed its mystic proportions,—trickled from under it with sickening rapidity. At last, breathless and weary, they were about to give up the task in despair, when Karl snatched from out the ruins the iron needle or pendulum on which the Disc had originally swung, and all unknowing what it was, thrust it cautiously under the body of the great stone to aid in getting a firmer hold of it, . . . to his amazement and terror the huge round mass caught and clung to it, like warm sealing wax to a piece of paper, and in an instant seemed to have magically dispensed with all its weight, for as, with his unassisted strength he lifted the pendulum, the Disc lifted itself lightly and easily with it! A cry of fear and wonder broke from all the men,—Karl himself trembled in every limb, and big drops of cold sweat broke out on his forehead at what he deemed the devilish horror of this miracle. But as he, with no more difficulty than he would have experienced in heaving up a moderate-sized log of wood, raised the Disc and flung it back and away from him shudderingly, pendulum and all, his eyes fell on what had lain beneath it, . . . a crushed pulp of human flesh and streaming blood—and reverend silver hairs. . . and with a groan that seemed to rend his very heart, Karl gave one upward sick stare at the reeling sky, and fainted, . . . as unconscious for the time being as that indistinguishable mangled mass of perished mortality that once had been his master.

Gently and with compassionate kindness, the rough fishers who stood by lifted him up and bore him out of the tower and down the stairs,—and after a whispered consultation, carried him away from the house altogether to one of their own cottages, where they put him under the care of one of their own women. None of them could sleep any more that night; they stood in a group close by their humble habitations, watching the progress of the storm, and ever and anon casting awe-stricken glances at the shattered tower.

"The devil was in it"—said one of the men at last, as he lit his pipe and endeavoured to soothe his nerves by several puffs at that smoky consoler—"or else how would it rise up like that as light as a feather at the touch of an iron pole?"

"It must a' weighed twenty stun at least"—murmured another man meditatively.

"What was it?" demanded a third—"I should a' took it for a big grindstone if it hadn't sparkled up so when the light fell on it."

"Well, it may stay where it is for all I care," said the first speaker—"I wouldn't touch it again for a hundred pound!"

"Nor I." "Nor I."

They were all agreed on that point.

"Wotever he were a' doin' on,"—said the fourth man gravely—"whether it were God's work or the devil's, it's all over now. He's done for, poor old chap—mashed into a reg'lar jelly—wiped out as it were. It's an awful end—God rest his soul!"

The others lifted their caps and murmured "Amen" with simple reverence. Then they looked out at the dark wallowing trough of the sea.

"How the wind roars!" said the last speaker.

"Ay, it do roar," replied the man who was his mate in the boat when they went fishing; "and did ye hear a vulture scream awhile ago?"

"Ay, ay! I heard it!" They were silent then, and turned in, after making inquiries concerning Karl at the cottage where they had left him. He was still unconscious.

XII

A Couple of days later, El-Râmi was engaged in what was not a very favourite occupation with him,—he was reading the morning's newspaper. He glanced over the cut-and-dry chronicle of "Storms and Floods"—he noted that a great deal of damage had been wrought by the gale at Ilfracombe and other places along the Devonshire coast,—but there was nothing of any specially dreadful import to attract his attention, and nothing either in politics or science of any pressing or vital interest. There were two or three reviews of books, one of these being pressed into a corner next to the advertisement of a patent pill; there were announcements of the movements of certain human units favoured with a little extra money and position than ordinary, as being "in" or "out" of town, and there was a loftily-patronizing paragraph on the "Theosophical Movement," or as it is more frequently termed, the "Theosophical Boom." From this, El-Râmi learned that a gentleman connected with the Press, who wrote excessively common-place verse, and thereby had got himself and his name (through the afore-said press-connection) fairly well known, had been good enough to enunciate the following amazing platitude;—"That, as a great portion of the globe is composed of elements which cannot be seen, and as the study of the invisible may be deemed as legitimate as the study of the visible, he" (the press-connected versifier) "is inclined to admit that there are great possibilities on the lines of that study."

"Inclined to admit it, is he!" and El-Râmi threw aside the paper and broke into a laugh of the sincerest enjoyment—"Heavens! what fools there are in this world, who call themselves wise men! This little poetaster, full of the conceit common to his imitative craft, is 'inclined to admit' that there are great possibilities in the study of the invisible! Excellent condescension! How the methods of life have turned topsy-turvy since the ancient days! Then the study of the Invisible was the first key to the study of the Visible,—the things which are seen being considered only as the reflexes of the things which are unseen—the Unseen being accepted as Cause, the Seen as Effect. Now we all drift the other way,—taking the Visible as Fact,—the Invisible as Fancy!"

Féraz, who was writing at a side-table, looked up at him.

"Surely you are inconsistent?" he said—"You yourself believe in nothing unless it is proved."

"But then, my dear fellow, I can prove the Invisible and follow the grades of it, and the modes by which it makes itself the Visible,—to a certain extent—but only to a certain extent. Beyond the provable limit I do not go. You, on the contrary, aided by the wings of imagination, outsoar that limit, and profess to find angels, star-kingdoms, and God Himself. I cannot go so far as this. But, unlike our blown-out frog of a versifier here, who would fain persuade mankind he is a bull, I am not only 'inclined' to admit—I do admit that there are 'great possibilities'— only I must test them all before I can accept them as facts made clear to my comprehension."

"Still, you believe in the Invisible?"

"Naturally. I believe in the millions of suns in the Milky Way, though they can scarcely be called 'visible.' I should be a fool if I did not believe in the Invisible, under the present conditions of the Universe. But I cannot be tricked by 'shams' of the Invisible. The Theosophical business is a piece of vulgar imposture, in which the professors themselves are willing to delude their own imaginations, as well as the imaginations of others—they are the most wretched imitators that ever were of the old Eastern sorcerers,—the fellows who taught Moses and Aaron how to frighten their ignorant cattle-like herds of followers. None of the modern 'mediums' as they are called, have the skill over atmospheric phenomena, metals and light-reflexes, that Apollonius of Tyana had, or Alexander the Paphlagonian. Both these scientific sorcerers were born about the same time as Christ, and Apollonius like Christ, raised a maiden from the dead. Miracles were the fashion in that period of time,—and according to the monotonous manner in which history repeats itself, they are coming into favour again in this century. All that we know now has been already known. The ancient Greeks had their 'penny-in-the-slot' machine for the purpose of scattering perfume on their clothes as they passed along the streets—they had their 'syphon' bottles and vases as we have, and they had their automatically opening and closing doors. Compare the miserable 'spiritualistic phenomena' of the Theosophists with the marvels wrought by Hakem, known as Mokanna! Mokanna could cause an orb like the moon to rise from a well at a certain hour and illumine the country for miles and miles around. How did he do it? By a knowledge of electric force applied to air and water. The 'bogies' of a modern 'séance' who talk bad grammar and pinch people's toes and fingers, are very coarse examples of necromancy, compared to the scientific skill of Mokanna and others of this tribe.

However, superstition is the same in all ages, and there will always be fools ready to believe in 'Mahatmas' or anything else,—and the old 'incantation of the Mantra,' will, if well done, influence the minds of the dupes of the nineteenth century quite as effectively as it did those of the bygone ages before Christ."

"What is the incantation of the Mantra?" asked Féraz.

"A ridiculous trick"—replied El-Râmi—"known to every Eastern conjurer and old woman who professes to see the future. You take your dupe, and fling a little water over him, fixing upon him your eyes and all the force of your will,—then, you take a certain mixture of chemical substances and perfumes, and set them on fire—the flames and fumes produce a dazzling and drowsy effect on the senses of your 'subject,' who will see whatever you choose him to see, and hear whatever you intend him to hear. But Will is the chief ingredient of the spell,—and if I, for example, choose to influence anyone, I can dispense with both water and fire—I can do it alone and without any show of preparation."

"I know you can!" said Féraz meaningly, with a slight smile, and then was silent.

"I wonder what the art of criticism is coming to now-a-days!" exclaimed El-Râmi presently, taking up the paper again—"Here is a remark worthy of Dogberry's profundity—'This is a book that must be read to be understood.'* Why, naturally! Who can understand a book without reading it?"

Féraz laughed—then his eyes darkened.

"I saw an infamous so-called critique of one of Madame Vassilius's books the other day"—he said—"I should like to have thrashed the man who wrote it. It was not criticism at all—it was a mere piece of scurrilous vulgarity."

"Ah, but that sort of thing pays!" retorted El-Râmi satirically. "The modern journalist attains his extremest height of brilliancy when he throws the refuse of his inkpot at the name and fame of a woman more gifted than himself. It's nineteenth-century chivalry you know,—above all. . . it's manly!"

Féraz shrugged his shoulders with a faint gesture of contempt.

"Then—if there is any truth in old chronicles—men are not what they were;"—he said.

---

* Copied verbatim from the current Press.

MARIE CORELLI

"No—they are not what they were, my dear boy—because all things have changed. Women were once the real slaves and drudges of men,—now, they are very nearly their equals, or can be so if they choose. And men have to get accustomed to this—at present they are in the transition state and don't like it. Besides, there will always be male tyrants and female drudges as long as the world lasts. Men are not what they were,—and, certes, they are not what they might be."

"They might be gods;"—said Féraz—"but I suppose they prefer to be devils."

"Precisely!" agreed El-Râmi—"it is easier, and more amusing."

Féraz resumed his writing in silence. He was thinking of Irene Vassilius, whom he admired;—and also of that wondrous Sleeping Beauty enshrined upstairs whose loveliness he did not dare to speak of. He had latterly noticed a great change in his brother,—an indefinable softness seemed to have imperceptibly toned down the habitual cynicism of his speech and manner,—his very expression of countenance was more gracious and benign,—he looked handsomer,—his black eyes shot forth a less fierce fire,—and yet, with all his gentleness and entire lack of impatience, he was absorbed from morning to night in such close and secret study as made Féraz sometimes fear for its ultimate result on his health.

"Do you really believe in prayer, Féraz?" was the very unexpected question he now asked, with sudden and startling abruptness; "I mean, do you think anyone in the Invisible Realms hears us when we pray?"

Féraz laid down his pen, and gazed at his brother for a moment without answering. Then he said slowly—

"Well, according to your own theories the Air is a vast Phonograph,— so it follows naturally that everything is heard and kept. But as to prayer, that depends I think, altogether on how you pray. I do not believe in it at all times. And I'm afraid my ideas on the subject are quite out of keeping with those generally accepted—"

"Never mind—let me have them, whatever they are"—interrupted El-Râmi with visible eagerness—"I want to know when and how you pray?"

"Well, the fact is I very seldom pray"—returned Féraz—"I offer up the best praise I can in mortal language devise, both night and morning—but I never ask for anything. It would seem so vile to ask for more, having already so much. And I am sure God knows best—in which case I have nothing to ask, except one thing."

"And that is—?" queried his brother.

"Punishment!" replied Féraz emphatically; "I pray for that—I crave for that—I implore that I may be punished at once when I have done wrong, that I may immediately recognise my error. I would rather be punished here, than hereafter."

El-Râmi paled a little, and his lips trembled.

"Strange boy!" he murmured—"All the churches are praying God to take away the punishments incurred for sin,—you on the contrary, ask for it as if it were a blessing."

"So it is a blessing"—declared Féraz—"It must be a blessing—and it is absurd of the churches to pray against a Law. For it is a Law. Nature punishes us, when we physically rebel against the rules of health, by physical suffering and discomfort,—God punishes us in our mental rebellions by mental wretchedness. This is as it should be. I believe we get everything in this world that we deserve—no more and no less."

"And do you never pray"—continued El-Râmi slowly, "for the accomplished perfection of some cherished aim,—the winning of some special joy—"

"Not I"—said Féraz—"because I know that if it be good for me I shall have it,—if bad, it will be withheld; all my prayers could not alter the matter."

El-Râmi sat silent for a few minutes,—then, rising, he took two or three turns up and down the room, and gradually a smile, half scornful, half sweet, illumined his dark features.

"Then, O young and serene philosopher, I will not pray!" he said, his eyes flashing a lustrous defiance—"I have a special aim in view—I mean to grasp a joy!—and whether it be good or bad for me, I will attempt it unassisted."

"If it be good you will succeed;"—said Féraz with a glance expressive of some fear as well as wonderment. "If it be bad, you will not. God arranges these things for us."

"God—God—always God!" cried El-Râmi with some impatience—"No God shall interfere with me!" At that moment there came a hesitating knock at the street-door. Féraz went to open it, and admitted a pale grief-stricken man whose eyes were red and heavy with tears and whose voice utterly failed him to reply when El-Râmi exclaimed in astonishment:

"Karl! . . . Karl! You here? Why, what has happened?"

Poor Karl made a heroic struggle to speak,—but his emotion was too strong for him—he remained silent, and two great drops rolled down his cheeks in spite of all his efforts to restrain them.

"You are ill;"—said Féraz kindly, pushing him by gentle force into a chair and fetching him a glass of wine—"Here, drink this—it will restore you."

Karl put the glass aside tremblingly, and tried to smile his gratitude,—and presently gaining a little control over himself he turned his piteous glances towards El-Râmi whose fine features had become suddenly grave and fixed in thought.

"You. . . you. . . have not heard, sir—" he stammered.

El-Râmi raised his hand gently, with a solemn and compassionate gesture.

"Peace, my good fellow!—no, I have not heard,—but I can guess;—Kremlin, your master. . . is dead."

And he was silent for many minutes. Fresh tears trickled from Karl's eyes, and he made a pretence of tasting the wine that Féraz pressed upon him—Féraz, who looked as statuesque and serene as a young Apollo.

"You must console yourself;"—he said cheerfully to Karl,—"Poor Dr. Kremlin had many troubles and few joys—now he has gone where he has no trouble and all joy."

"Ah!" sighed Karl dolefully—"I wish I could believe that, sir,—I wish I could believe it! But it was the judgment of God upon him—it was indeed!—that is what my poor mother would say,—the judgment of God!"

El-Râmi moved from his meditative attitude with a faint sense of irritation. The words he had so lately uttered—"No God shall interfere with me"—re-echoed in his mind. And now here was this man,—this servant, weeping and trembling and talking of the "judgment of God" as if it were really something divinely directed and inexorable.

"What do you mean?" he asked, endeavouring to suppress the impatience in his voice—"Of course, I know he must have had some violent end, or else he could not"—and he repeated the words impressively—"could not have died,—but was there anything more than usually strange in the manner of his death?"

Karl threw up his hands.

"More than usually strange! Ach, Gott!" and, with many interpolations of despair and expressions of horror, he related in broken accents the whole of the appalling circumstances attending his master's end. In spite of himself a faint shudder ran through El-Râmi's warm blood as he heard—he could almost see before him the horrible spectacle of the old man's mangled form lying crushed under the ponderous Disc his daring skill had designed; and under his breath he murmured—"Oh Lilith, oh my too-happy Lilith! and yet you tell me there is no death!" Féraz however, the young and sensitive Féraz, listened to the sad recital with quiet interest, unhorrified, apparently unmoved,—his eyes were bright, his expression placid.

"He could not have suffered;"—he observed at last, when Karl had finished speaking—"The flash of lightning must have severed body and spirit instantly and without pain. I think it was a good end."

Karl looked at the beautiful smiling youth in vague horror. What!— to be flattened out like a board beneath a ponderous weight of fallen stone—to be so disfigured as to be unrecognisable—to have one's mortal remains actually swept up and wiped out (as had been the case with poor Kremlin), and to be only a mangled mass of flesh difficult of decent burial,—and call that "a good end"! Karl shuddered and groaned;—he was not versed in the strange philosophies of young Féraz—he had never been out of his body on an ethereal journey to the star-kingdoms.

"It was the judgment of God,"—he repeated dully—"Neither more nor less. My poor master studied too hard, and tried to find out too much, and I think he made God angry—"

"My good fellow," interrupted El-Râmi rather irritably—"do not talk of what you do not understand. You have been faithful, hard-working and all the rest of it,—but as for your master trying to find out too much, or God getting angry with him, that is all nonsense. We were placed on this earth to find out as much as we can, about it and about ourselves, and do the best that is possible with our learning,—and the bare idea of a great God condescending to be 'angry' with one out of millions upon millions of units is absurd—"

"But even if an unit rebels against the Law the Law crushes him"— interrupted Féraz softly—"A gnat flies into flame—the flame consumes it—the Law is fulfilled,—and the Law is God's Will."

El-Râmi bit his lip vexedly.

"Well, be that as it may one must needs find out what the Law is first, before it can either be accepted, or opposed," he said.

Féraz made no answer. He was thinking of the simplicity of certain Laws of Spirit and Matter which were accepted and agreed to by the community of men of whom the monk from Cyprus was the chief master.

Karl meanwhile stared bewilderedly from Féraz to El-Râmi and from El-Râmi back to Féraz again. Their remarks were totally beyond his comprehension; he never could understand, and never wanted to understand these subtle philosophies.

"I came to ask you, sir"—he said after a pause—"whether you would not, now you know all, manage to take away that devilish thing that killed my master? I'm afraid to touch it myself, and no one else will— and there it lies up in the ruined tower shining away like a big lamp, and sticking like a burr to the iron rod I lifted it with. If it's any good to you, I'm sure you'd better have it—and by-the-bye, I found this, sir, in my master's room addressed to you."

He held out a sealed envelope, which El-Râmi opened. It contained a folded paper, on which were scratched these lines—

"To El-Râmi Zarânos. Good friend, in the event of my death, I beg you to accept all my possessions such as they are, and do me the one favour I ask, which is this—Destroy the Disc, and let my problem die with me."

This paper duly signed, bore the date of two years previously. El-Râmi read it, and handed it to Karl who read it also. They were silent for a few minutes; then El-Râmi crossed the room, and unlocking a small cupboard in the wall, took out a sealed flask full of what looked like red wine.

"See here, Karl"—he said;—"There is no devil in the great stone you are so afraid of. It is as perishable as anything else in this best of all possible worlds. It is nothing but a peculiar and rare growth of crystal, which though found in the lowest depths of the earth, has the quality of absorbing light and emitting it. It clings to the iron rod in the way you speak of because it is a magnet,—and iron not only attracts but fastens it. It is impossible for me just now to go to Ilfracombe—besides there is really no necessity for my presence there. I can fully trust you to bring me the papers and few possessions of my poor old friend,—and for the rest, you can destroy the stone yourself—the Disc, as your master called it. All you have to do is simply to pour this liquid on it,—it will pulverize—that is, it will crumble into dust while you watch it, and in ten minutes will be indistinguishable from the fallen mortar of the shattered tower. Do you understand?"

Karl's mouth opened a little in wonderment, and he nodded feebly,— he found it quite easy and natural to be afraid of the flask containing a mixture of such potent quality, and he took it from El-Râmi's hand very gingerly and reluctantly. A slight smile crossed El-Râmi's features as he said—

"No, Karl! there is no danger—no fear of pulverization for you. You can put the phial safely in your pocket,—and though its contents could pulverize a mountain if used in sufficient quantities,—the liquid has no effect on flesh and blood."

"Pulverize a mountain!" repeated Karl nervously—"Do you mean that it could turn a mountain into a dust-heap?"

"Or a city—or a fortress—or a rock-bound coast—or anything in the shape of stone that you please"—replied El-Râmi carelessly—"but it will not harm human beings."

"Will it not explode, sir?" and Karl still looked at the flask in doubt.

"Oh no—it will do its work with extraordinary silence and no less extraordinary rapidity. Do not be afraid!"

Slowly and with evident uneasiness Karl put the terrifying composition into his pocket, deeply impressed by the idea that he had about him stuff, which, if used in sufficient quantity, could "pulverize a mountain." It was awful!—worse than dynamite, he considered, his thoughts flying off wantonly to the woes of Irishmen and Russians. El—Râmi seemed not to notice his embarrassment and went on talking quietly, asking various questions concerning Kremlin's funeral, and giving advice as to the final arrangements which were necessary, till presently he inquired of Karl what he proposed doing with himself in the future.

"Oh I shall look out for another situation,"—he said—"I shall not go back to Germany. I like to think of the 'Fatherland,' and I can sing the 'Wacht am Rhein' with as much lung as anybody, but I wouldn't care to live there. I think I shall try for a place where there's a lady to serve; you know, sir, gentlemen's ways are apt to be monotonous. Whether they are clever or foolish they always stick to it, whatever it is. A gentleman that races is always racing, and always talking and thinking about racing,—a gentleman that drinks is always on the drink,—a gentleman that coaches is always coaching, and so on; now a lady does vary! One day she's all for flowers, another for pictures, another for china,— sometimes she's mad about music, sometimes about dresses,—or else she takes a fit for study, and gets heaps of books from the libraries. Now for a man-servant, all that is very agreeable and lively."

Féraz laughed at this novel view of domestic service, and Karl, growing a little more cheerful, went on with his explanation—

"You see, supposing I get into a lady's service, I shall have so much more to distract me. One afternoon I shall be waiting outside a picture-gallery with her shawls and wraps; another day I shall be running backwards and forwards to Mudie's,—and then there's always the pleasure of never quite knowing what she will do next. And it's excitement I want just now—it really is!"

The corners of his good-humoured mouth drooped again despondently, and his thoughts reverted with unpleasant suddenness to the 'pulverizing' liquid in his pocket. What a terrible thing it was to get acquainted with scientists!

El-Râmi listened to his observations patiently.

"Well, Karl," he said at last—"I think I can promise you a situation such as you would like. There is a very famous and lovely lady in London, known to the reading-world as Irene Vassilius—she writes original books; is sweetly capricious, yet nobly kind-hearted. I will write to her about you, and I have no doubt she will give you a trial."

Karl brightened up immensely at this prospect.

"Thank you, sir!" he said fervently—"You've no idea what a deal of good it will do me to take in the tea to a sweet-looking lady—a properly-served tea, you know, all silver and good china. It will be a sort of tonic to me,—it will indeed, after that terrible place at Ilfracombe. You can tell her I'm a very handy man,—I can do almost anything, from cooking a chop, up to stretching my legs all day in a porter's chair in the hall and reading the latest 'Special.' Anything she wishes whether for show or economy, she couldn't have a better hand at it than me;—will you tell her so, sir?"

"Certainly!" replied El-Râmi with a smile. "I'll tell her you are a domestic Von Moltke, and that under your management her household will be as well ordered as the German army under the great Field-Marshal."

After a little more desultory conversation, Karl took his departure, and returned by the afternoon train to Ilfracombe. He was living with one of his fisher-friends, and as it was late when he arrived, he made no attempt to go to the deserted house of his deceased master that night. But early the next morning he hurried there before breakfast, and ascended to the shattered tower,—that awful scene of desolation from whence poor Kremlin's mangled remains had been taken, and where only a dark stain of blood on the floor silently testified of the horror that had there been enacted. The Disc, lying prone, glittered as he approached it, with, as he thought, a fiendish and supernatural light—the early sunlight fell upon its surface, and a thousand prismatic tints and sparkles dazzled his eyes as he drew near and gazed dubiously at it where it still clung to the iron pendulum. What could his master have used such a strange object for?—what did it mean? And that solemn humming noise which he had used to hear when the nights were still,—had that glistening thing been the cause?—had it any sound? . . . Struck by this idea, and filled with a sudden courage, he seized a piece of thick wire, part of the many tangled coils that lay among the ruins of roof and wall, and with it, gave the Disc a smart blow on its edge. . . hush! . . . hush! . . . The wire dropped from his hand, and he stood, almost paralyzed with fear. A deep, solemn, booming sound like a great cathedral bell, rang through the air,—grand, and pure and musical, and. . . unearthly!—as might be the clarion stroke of a clock beating out, not the short pulsations of Time, but the vast throbs of Eternity. Round and round, in eddying echoes swept that sweet, sonorous note,—till—growing gradually fainter and fainter, it died entirely away from human hearing, and seemed to pass out and upwards into the gathering sunrays that poured brightly from the East, there to take its place perchance, in that immense diapason of vibrating tone-music that fills the star-strewn space for ever and ever. It was the last sound struck from the great Star-Dial:—for Karl, terrified at the solemn din, wasted no more time in speculative hesitation, but taking the flask El-Râmi had given him, he opened it tremblingly and poured all its contents on the surface of the crystal. The red liquid ran over the stone like blood, crumbling it as it ran and extinguishing its brilliancy,—eating its substance away as rapidly as vitriol eats away the human skin,—blistering it and withering it visibly before Karl's astonished eyes,—till, as El-Râmi had said, it was hardly distinguishable from the dust and mortar around it. One piece lasted just a little longer than the rest—it curled and writhed like a living thing under the absolutely noiseless and terribly destructive influence of that blood-like liquid that seemed to sink into it as water sinks into a sponge,—Karl watched it, fascinated—till all at once it broke into a sparkle like flame, gleamed, smouldered, leaped high. . . and—disappeared. The wondrous Dial with its "perpetual motion" and its measured rhythm, was as if it had never been,—it had vanished as utterly as a destroyed Planet,—and the mighty Problem reflected on its surface remained. . . and will most likely still remain. . . a mystery unsolved.

XIII

For two or three weeks after he had received the news of Kremlin's death, El-Râmi's mind was somewhat troubled and uneasy. He continued his abstruse studies ardently, yet with less interest than usual,—and he spent hour after hour in Lilith's room, sitting beside the couch on which she reposed, saying nothing, but simply watching her, himself absorbed in thought. Days went by and he never roused her,— never asked her to reply to any question concerning the deep things of time and of eternity with which her aërial spirit seemed conversant. He was more impressed by the suddenness and terror of Kremlin's end than he cared to admit to himself,—and the "Light-Maps" and other papers belonging to his deceased old friend, all of which had now come into his possession, were concise enough in many marvellous particulars, to have the effect of leading him almost imperceptibly to believe that after all there was a God,—an actual Being whose magnificent attributes baffled the highest efforts of the imagination, and who indeed, as the Bible grandly hath it—"holds the Universe in the hollow of His hand." And he began to go back to the Bible for information;—for he, like most students versed in Eastern philosophies, knew that all that was ever said or will be said on the mysteries of life and death, is to be found in that Book, which though full of much matter that does not pertain to its actual teaching, remains the one chief epitome of all the wisdom of the world. When it is once remembered that the Deity of Moses and Aaron was their own invented Hobgoblin, used for the purpose of terrifying and keeping the Jews in order, much becomes clear that is otherwise impossible to accept or comprehend. Historians, priests, lawgivers, prophets and poets have all contributed to the Bible,—and when we detach class from class and put each in its proper place, with— out confounding them all together in an inextricable jumble as "Divine inspiration," we obtain a better view of the final intention of the whole. El-Râmi considered Moses and Aaron in the light of particularly clever Eastern conjurers,—and not only conjurers, but tacticians and diplomatists, who had just the qualities necessary to rule a barbarous, ignorant, and rebellious people. The thunders of Mount Sinai,—the graving of the commandments on tablets of stone,—the serpent in the wilderness,—the bringing of water out of a rock,—the parting of the sea to let an army march through;—he, El-Râmi, knew how all these things were done, and was perfectly cognisant of the means and appliances used to compass all these seemingly miraculous events.

"What a career I could make if I chose!" he thought—"What wealth I could amass,—what position! I who know how to quell the wildest waves of the sea,—I who, by means of a few drops of liquid can corrode a name or a device so deeply on stone that centuries shall not efface it—I who can do so many things that would astonish the vulgar and make them my slaves,—why am I content to live as I do, when I could be greater than a crowned king? Why, because I scorn to trick the ignorant by scientific skill which I have neither the time nor the patience to explain to them—and again—because I want to fathom the Impossible;—I want to prove if indeed there is any Impossible. What can be done and proved, when once it is done and proved, I regard as nothing,—and because I know how to smooth the sea, call down the rain, and evoke phantoms out of the atmosphere, I think such manifestations of power trifling and inadequate. These things are all provable; and the performance of them is attained through a familiar knowledge of our own earth-elements and atmosphere; but to find out the subtle Something that is not of earth, and has not yet been made provable,—that is the aim of my ambition. The Soul! What is it? Of what ethereal composition? of what likeness? of what feeling? of what capacity? This, and this alone is the Supreme Mystery,—when once we understand it, we shall understand God. The preachers waste their time in urging men and women to save their souls, so long as we remain in total ignorance as to what the Soul Is. We cannot be expected to take any trouble to 'save' or even regard anything so vague and dubious as the Soul under its present conditions. What is visible and provable to our eyes, is that our friends die, and to all intents and purposes, disappear. We never know them as they were any more, . . . and, . . . what is still more horrible to think of, but is nevertheless true,—our natural tendency is to forget them,—indeed, after three or four years, perhaps less, we should find it difficult, without the aid of a photograph or painted picture, to recall their faces to our memories. And it is curious to think of it, but we really remember their ways, their conversation, and their notions of life better than their actual physiognomies. All this is very strange and very perplexing too,—and it is difficult to imagine the reason for such perpetual tearing down of affections, and such bitter loss and harassment, unless there is some great Intention behind it all,—an Intention of which it is arranged we shall be made duly cognisant. If we are not to be made cognisant,—if we are not to have a full and perfect Explanation,—then the very fact of Life being lived at all is a mere cruelty,—a senseless jest which lacks all point,—and the very grandeur and immensity of the Universe becomes nothing but the meanest display of gigantic Force remorselessly put forth to overwhelm creatures who have no power to offer resistance to its huge Tyranny. If I could but fathom that Ultimate Purpose of things!—if I could but seize the subtle clue—for I believe it is something very slight and delicate which by its very fineness we have missed,—something which has to do with the Eternal Infinitesimal—that marvellous power which creates animated and regularly organized beings, many thousands of whose bodies laid together would not extend one inch. It is not to the Infinitely Great one must look for the secret of creation, but to the Infinitely Little."

So he mused, as he sat by the couch of Lilith and watched her sleeping that enchanted sleep of death-in-life. Old Zaroba, though now perfectly passive and obedient, and fulfilling all his commands with scru—pulous exactitude, was not without her own ideas and hopes as she went about her various duties connected with the care of the beautiful tranced girl. She seldom spoke to Féraz now except on ordinary household matters, and he understood and silently respected her reserve. She would sit in her accustomed corner of Lilith's regal apartment, weaving her thread-work mechanically, but ever and anon lifting her burning eyes to look at El-Râmi's absorbed face and note the varied expressions she saw, or fancied she saw there.

"The feverish trouble has begun"—she muttered to herself on one occasion, as she heard her master sigh deeply—"The stir in the blood,—the restlessness—the wonder—the desire. And out of heart's pain comes heart's peace;—and out of desire, accomplishment; and shall not the old gods of the world rejoice to see love born again of flames and tears and bitter-sweet as in the ancient days? For there is no love now such as there used to be—the pale Christ has killed it,—and the red rose aglow with colour and scent is now but a dull weed on a tame shore, washed by the salt sea, but never warmed by the sun. In the days of old, in the nights when Ashtaroth was queen of the silver hours, the youths and maidens knew what it was to love in the very breath of Love!—and the magic of all Nature, the music of the woods and waters, the fire of the stars, the odours of the flowers—all these were in the dance and beat of the young blood, and in the touch of the soft red lips as they met and clung together in kisses sweeter than honey in wine. But now—now the world has grown old and cold, and dreary and joyless,—it is winter among men and the summer is past."

So she would murmur to herself in her wild half-poetical jargon of language—her voice never rising above an inarticulate whisper. El-Râmi never heard her or seemed to regard her—he had no eyes except for the drowsing Lilith.

If he had been asked, at this particular time, why he went to that room day after day, to stare silently at his beautiful "subject" and ponder on everything connected with her, he could not have answered the question. He did not himself know why. Something there was in him, as in every portion of created matter, which remained inexplicable,—something of his own nature which he neither understood nor cared to analyse. He who sought to fathom the last depth of research concerning God and the things divine, would have been compelled to own, had he been cross-examined on the matter, that he found it impossible to fathom himself. The clue to his own Ego was as desperately hard to seize, as curiously subtle and elusive as the clue to the riddle of Creation. He was wont to pride himself on his consistency—yet in his heart of hearts he knew that in many things he was inconsistent,—he justly triumphed in his herculean Will-force,—yet now he was obliged to admit to himself that there was something in the silent placid aspect of Lilith as she lay before him, subservient to his command, that quite unnerved him and scattered his thoughts. It had not used to be so—but now,—it was so. And he dated the change, whether rightly or wrongly, from the day on which the monk from Cyprus had visited him, and this thought made him restless and irritable, and full of unjust and unreasonable suspicions. For had not the "Master," as he was known in the community to which he belonged, said that he had seen the Soul of Lilith, while he, El-Râmi, had never attained to so beatific an altitude of vision? Then was it not possible that notwithstanding his rectitude and steadfastness of purpose, the "Master," great and Christ-like in self-denial though he was, might influence Lilith in some unforeseen way? Then there was Féraz—Féraz, whose supplications and protestations had won a smile from the tranced girl, and who therefore must assuredly have roused in her some faint pleasure and interest. Such thoughts as these rankled in his mind and gave him no peace—for they conveyed to him the unpleasing idea that Lilith was not all his own as he desired her to be,—others had a share in her thoughts. Could he have nothing entirely to himself? he would demand angrily of his own inner conscious—ness—not even this life which he had, as it were, robbed from death? And an idea, which had at first been the merest dim suggestion, now deepened into a passionate resolve—he would make her his own so thoroughly and indissolubly that neither gods nor devils should snatch her from him.

"Her life is mine!" he said—"And she shall live as long as I please. Her body shall sleep, . . . if I still choose, . . . or. . . it shall wake. But whether awake, or sleeping in the flesh, her spirit shall obey me always—like the satellite of a planet, that disembodied Soul shall be mine forever!"

When he spoke thus to himself, he was sitting in his usual contemplative attitude by the couch where Lilith lay;—he rose up suddenly and paced the room, drawing back the velvet portière and setting open the door of the ante-chamber as though he craved for fresh air. Music sounded through the house, . . . it was Féraz singing. His full pure tenor voice came floating up, bearing with it the words he sang:

> *"And neither the angels in heaven above.*
> *Nor the demons down under the sea.*
> *Can ever dissever my soul from the soul*
> *Of the beautiful Annabel Lee!*
> *"For the stars never rise, but I feel the bright eyes*
> *Of the beautiful Annabel Lee,—*
> *And the moon never beams without bringing me dreams*
> *Of the beautiful Annabel Lee—*
> *And so all the night-tide, I lie down by the side*
> *Of my darling, my darling, my life and my bride.*
> *In her tomb by the sounding sea!"*

With a shaking hand El-Râmi shut the door more swiftly than he had opened it, and dragged the heavy portière across it to deaden the sound of that song!—to keep it out from his ears. . . from his heart, . . . to stop its passionate vibration from throbbing along his nerves like creeping fire. . .

> *"And so all the night-tide I lie down by the side*
> *Of my darling, my darling, my life and my bride."*

"God!—my God!" he muttered incoherently—"What ails me? . . . Am I going mad that I should dream thus?"

He gazed round the room wildly, his hand still clutching the velvet portière,—and met the keenly watchful glance of Zaroba. Her hands were mechanically busy with her thread-work,—but her eyes, black, piercing and brilliant, were fixed on him steadfastly. Something in her look compelled his attention,—something in his compelled hers. They stared across the room at each other, as though a Thought had sprung between them like an armed soldier with drawn sword, demanding from each the pass-word to a mystery. In and out, across and across went the filmy glistening threads in Zaroba's wrinkled hands, but her eyes never moved from El-Râmi's face, and she looked like some weird sorceress weaving a web of destiny.

"For you were the days of Ashtaroth!" she said in a low, monotonous, yet curiously thrilling tone—"You are born too late, El-Râmi,—the youth of the world has departed and the summer seasons of the heart are known on earth no more. You are born too late—too late!—the Christ claims all,—the body, the blood, the nerve and the spirit,—every muscle of His white limbs on the cross must be atoned for by the dire penance and torture of centuries of men. So that now even love is a thorn in the flesh and its prick must be paid with a price,—these are the hours of woe preceding the end. The blood that runs in your veins, El-Râmi, has sprung from kings and strong rulers of men,—and the pale faint spirits of this dull day have naught to do with its colour and glow. And it rebels, O El-Râmi!—as God liveth, it rebels!—it burns in your heart—the proud, strong heart,—like ruddy wine in a ruby cup; it rebels, El-Râmi!—it rises to passion as rise the waves of the sea to the moon, by a force and an impulse in Nature stronger than yours! Aye, aye!—for you were the days of Ashtaroth"—and her voice sank into a wailing murmur—"but now—now—the Christ claims all."

He heard her as one may hear incoherencies in a nightmare vision;— only a few weeks ago he would have been angry with her for what he would then have termed her foolish jargon,—but he was not angry now. Why should he be angry? he wondered dully—had he time to even think of anger while thus unnerved by that keen tremor that quivered through his frame—a tremor he strove in vain to calm? His hand fell from the curtain,—the sweet distracting song of Poe's "Annabel Lee" had ceased,—and he advanced into the room again, his heart beating painfully still, his head a little drooped as though with a sense of conscious shame. He moved slowly to where the roses in the Venetian vase exhaled their odours on the air, and breaking one off its branch toyed with it aimlessly, letting its pale pink leaves flutter down one by one on the violet carpet at his feet. Suddenly, as though he had resolved a doubt and made up his mind to something, he turned towards Zaroba who watched him fixedly,—and with a mute signal bade her leave the apartment. She rose instantly, and crossing her hands upon her breast made her customary obeisance and waited,—for he looked at her with a meditative expression which implied that he had not yet completed his instruction. Presently, and with some hesitation, he made her another sign—a sign which had the effect of awakening a blaze of astonishment in her dark sunken eyes.

"No more tonight!" she repeated aloud—"It is your will that I return here no more tonight?"

He gave a slow but decided gesture of assent,—there was no mistaking it.

Zaroba paused an instant, and then with a swift noiseless step went to the couch of Lilith and bent yearningly above that exquisite sleeping form.

"Star of my heart!" she muttered—"Child whose outward fairness I have ever loved, unheedful of the soul within,—may there still be strength enough left in the old gods to bid thee wake!"

El-Râmi caught her words, and a faint smile, proud yet bitter, curved his delicate lips.

"The old gods or the new—does it matter which?" he mused vaguely—"And what is their strength compared to the Will of Man by which the very elements are conquered and made the slaves of his service? 'My Will is God's Will' should be every strong man's motto. But I—am I strong—or the weakest of the weak? . . . and. . . shall the Christ claim all?"

The soft fall of the velvet portière startled him as it dropped behind the retreating figure of Zaroba—she had left the room, and he was alone,—alone with Lilith.

END OF VOLUME II

THE SOUL OF LILITH
VOLUME 3

I

He remained quite still, standing near the tall vase that held the clustered roses,—in his hand he grasped unconsciously the stalk of the one he had pulled to pieces. He was aware of his own strange passiveness,—it was a sort of inexplicable inertia which like temporary paralysis seemed to incapacitate him from any action. It would have appeared well and natural to him that he should stay there so, dreamily, with the scented rose-stalk in his hand, for any length of time. A noise in the outer street roused him a little,—the whistling, hooting and laughing of drunken men reeling homewards,—and lifting his eyes from their studious observation of the floor, he sighed deeply.

"That is the way the great majority of men amuse themselves,"—he mused. "Drink, stupidity, brutality, sensuality—all blatant proofs of miserable unresisted weakness,—can it be possible that God can care for such? Could even the pity of Christ pardon such wilful workers of their own ruin? The pity of Christ, said I?—nay, at times even He was pitiless. Did He not curse a fig-tree because it was barren?—though truly we are not told the cause of its barrenness. Of course the lesson is that Life—the fig-tree,—has no right to be barren of results,—but why curse it, if it is? What is the use of a curse at any time? And what, may equally be asked, is the use of a blessing? Neither are heard; the curse is seldom if ever wreaked,—and the blessing, so the sorrowful say, is never granted."

The noise and the laughter outside died away,—and a deep silence ensued. He caught sight of himself in the mirror, and noted his own reflective attitude,—his brooding visage; and studied himself critically as he would have studied a picture.

"You are no Antinous, my friend"—he said aloud, addressing his own reflection with some bitterness—"A mere sun-tanned Oriental with a pair of eyes in which the light is more of hell than heaven. What should you do with yourself, frowning at Fate? You are a superb Egoist,—no more."

As he spoke, the roses in the vase beside him swayed lightly to and fro, as though a faint wind had fanned them, and their perfume stole upon the air like the delicate breath of summer wafted from some distant garden.

There was no window open—and El-Râmi had not stirred, so that no movement on his part could have shaken the vase,—and yet the roses quivered on their stalks as if brushed by a bird's wing. He watched them with a faint sense of curiosity—but with no desire to discover why they thus nodded their fair heads to an apparently causeless vibration. He was struggling with an emotion that threatened to overwhelm him,—he knew that he was not master of himself,—and instinctively he kept his face turned away from the tranced Lilith.

"I must not look upon her—I dare not;" he whispered to the silence— "Not yet—not yet."

There was a low chair close by, and he dropped into it wearily, covering his eyes with one hand. He tried to control his thoughts— but they were rebellious, and ran riot in spite of him. The words of Zaroba rang in his ears—"For you were the days of Ashtaroth." The days of Ashtaroth!—for what had they been renowned? For love and the feasts of love,—for mirth and song and dance—for crowns of flowers, for shouting of choruses and tinkling of cymbals, for exquisite luxury and voluptuous pleasures,—for men and women who were not ashamed of love and took delight in loving;—were there not better, warmer ways of life in those old times than now—now when cautious and timid souls make schemes for marriage as they scheme for wealth,—when they snigger at "love" as though it were some ludicrous defect in mortal composition, and when real passion of any kind is deemed downright improper, and not to be spoken of before cold and punctilious society?

"Aye, but the passion is there all the same;"—thought El-Râmi— "Under the ice burns the fire,—all the fiercer and the more dangerous for its repression."

And he still kept his hand over his eyes, thinking.

"The Christ claims all"—had said Zaroba. Nay, what has Christ done that He should claim all? "He died for us!" cry the preachers. Well,— others can die also. "He was Divine!" proclaim the churches. We are all Divine, if we will but let the Divinity in us have way. And moved by these ideas, El-Râmi rose up and crossed to a niche in the purple-pavilioned walls of the room, before which hung a loose breadth of velvet fringed with gold,—this he drew aside, and disclosed a picture very finely painted, of Christ standing near the sea, surrounded by his disciples—underneath it were in—scribed the words—"Whom say ye that I am?"

The dignity and beauty of the Face and Figure were truly marvellous,—the expression of the eyes had something of pride as well as sweetness, and El-Râmi confronted it as he had confronted it many times before, with a restless inquisitiveness.

"Whom say ye that I am?"

The painted Christ seemed to audibly ask the question.

"O noble Mystery of a Man, I cannot tell!" exclaimed El-Râmi suddenly and aloud—"I cannot say who you are, or who you were. A riddle for all the world to wonder at,—a white Sphinx with a smile inscrutable,—all the secrets of Egypt are as nothing to your secret, O simple, pure-souled Nazarene! You, born in miserable plight in miserable Bethlehem, changed the aspect of the world, altered and purified the modes of civilization, and thrilled all life with higher motives for work than it had ever been dowered with before. All this in three years' work, ending in a criminal's death! Truly if there was not something Divine in you, then God Himself is an Error!"

The grand Face seemed to smile upon him with a deep and solemn pity, and "Whom say ye that I am?" sounded in his ears as though it were spoken by someone in the room.

"I must be getting nervous;"—he muttered, drawing the curtain softly over the picture again, and looking uneasily round about him, "I think I cannot be much more than the weakest of men,—after all."

A faint tremor seized him as he turned slowly but resolutely round towards the couch of Lilith, and let his eyes rest on her enchanting loveliness. Step by step he drew nearer and nearer till he bent closely over her, but he did not call her by name. A loose mass of her hair lay close to his arm,—with an impetuous suddenness he gathered it in his hands and kissed it.

"A sheaf of sunbeams!"—he whispered, his lips burning as they caressed the shining wealth of silken curls—"A golden web in which kisses might be caught and killed! Ah Heaven have pity on me!" and he sank by the couch, stifling his words beneath his breath—"If I love this girl—if all this mad tumult in my soul is Love—let her never know it, O merciful Fates!—or she is lost, and so am I. Let me be bound,—let her be free,—let me fight down my weakness, but let her never know that I am weak, or I shall lose her long obedience. No, no! I will not summon her to me now—it is best she should be absent,—this body of hers, this fair fine casket of her spirit is but a dead thing when that spirit is elsewhere. She cannot hear me,—she does not see me—no, not even when I lay this hand—this 'shadow of a hand,' as she once called it, here, to quell my foolish murmurings."

And, lifting Lilith's hand as he spoke, he pressed its roseate palm against his lips,—then on his forehead. A strange sense of relief and peace came upon him with the touch of those delicate fingers—it was as though a cool wind blew, bringing freshness from some quiet mountain lake or river. Silently he knelt,—and presently, somewhat calmed, lifted his eyes again to look at Lilith,—she smiled in her deep trance—she was the very picture of some happy angel sleeping. His arm sank in the soft satin coverlid as he laid back the little hand he held upon her breast,—and with eager scrutiny he noted every tint and every line in her exquisite face;—the lovely long lashes that swept the blush-rose of her cheeks,—the rounded chin, dimpled in its curve,— the full white throat, the perfect outline of the whole fair figure as it rested like a branched lily in a bed of snow,—and as he looked, he realized that all this beauty was his—his, if he chose to take Love, and let Wisdom go. If he chose to resign the chance of increasing his knowledge of the supernatural,—if he were content to accept earth for what it is, and heaven for what it may be, Lilith, the bodily incarnation of loveliness, purity and perfect womanhood, was his—his only. He grew dizzy at the thought,—then by an effort conquered the longing of his heart. He remembered what he had sworn to do,—to discover the one great secret before he seized the joy that tempted him,—to prove the actual, individual, conscious existence of the Being that is said to occupy a temporary habitation in flesh. He knew and he saw the Body of Lilith,—he must know, and he must see her Soul. And while he leaned above her couch entranced, a sudden strain of music echoed through the stillness,—music solemn and sweet, that stirred the air into rhythmic vibrations as of slow and sacred psalmody. He listened, perplexed but not afraid,—he was not afraid of anything in earth or heaven save—himself. He knew that man has his worst enemy in his own Ego,—beyond that, there is very little in life that need give cause for alarm. He had, till now, been able to practise the stoical philosophy of an Epictetus while engaged in researches that would have puzzled the brain of a Plato,—but his philosophy was just now at fault and his self-possession gone to the four winds of heaven—and why? He knew not—but he was certain the fault lay in himself, and not in others. Of an arrogant temper and a self-reliant haughty disposition he had none of that low cowardice which people are guilty of, who finding themselves in a dilemma, cast the blame at once on others, or on "circumstances" which after all, were most probably of their own creating. And the strange music that ebbed and flowed in sonorous pulsations through the air around him, troubled him not at all,—he attributed it at once to something or other that was out of order in his own mental perceptions. He knew how in certain conditions of the brain, some infinitesimal trifle gone wrong in the aural nerves, will persuade one that trumpets are blowing, violins playing, birds singing or bells ringing in the distance,—just as a little disorder of the visual organs will help to convince one of apparitions. He knew how to cast a "glamour" better than any so-called "Theosophist" in full practice of his trickery,—and being thus perfectly aware how the human sense can be deceived, listened to the harmonious sounds he heard with speculative interest, wondering how long this "fancy" of his would last. Much more startled was he, when amid the rising and falling of the mysterious melody he heard the voice of Lilith saying softly in her usual manner—

"I am here!"

His heart beat rapidly, and he rose slowly from his kneeling position by her side. "I did not call you, Lilith!" he said tremblingly.

"No!" and her sweet lips smiled—"you did not call, . . . I came!"

"Why did you come?" he asked, still faintly.

"For my own joy and yours!" she answered in thrilling tones— "Sweeter than all the heavens is Love,—and Love is here!"

An icy cold crept through him as he heard the rapture in her accents,—such rapture!—like that of a lark singing in the sunlight on a fresh morning of May. And like the dim sound of a funeral bell came the words of the monk, tolling solemnly across his memory, in spite of his efforts to forget them, "With Lilith's love comes Lilith's freedom."

"No, no!" he muttered within himself—"It cannot be,—it shall not be!—she is mine, mine only. Her fate is in my hands; if there be justice in Heaven, who else has so much right to her body or her soul as I?"

And he stood, gazing irresolutely at the girl, who stirred restlessly and flung her white arms upward on her pillows, while the music he had heard suddenly ceased. He dared not speak,—he was afraid to express any desire or impose any command upon this "fine sprite" which had for six years obeyed him, but which might now, for all he could tell, be fluttering vagrantly on the glittering confines of realms far beyond his ken.

Her lips moved,—and presently she spoke again.

"Wonderful are the ways of Divine Law!" she murmured softly—"and infinite are the changes it works among its creatures! An old man, despised and poor, by friends rejected, perplexed in mind, but pure in soul; such Was the Spirit that now Is. Passing me flame-like on its swift way heavenward,—saved and uplifted, not by Wisdom, but by Love."

El-Râmi listened, awed and puzzled. Her words surely seemed to bear some reference to Kremlin?

"Of the knowledge of the stars and the measuring of light there is more than enough in the Universe;"—went on Lilith dreamily—"but of faithful love, such as keeps an Angel forever by one's side, there is little; therefore the Angels on earth are few."

He could no longer restrain his curiosity.

"Do you speak of one who is dead, Lilith?" he asked—"One whom I knew—"

"I speak of one who is living,"—she replied—"and one whom you know. For none are dead; and Knowledge has no Past, but is all Present."

Her voice sank into silence. El-Râmi bent above her, studying her countenance earnestly—her lashes trembled as though the eyelids were about to open,—but the tremor passed and they remained shut. How lovely she looked!—how more than lovely!

"Lilith!" he whispered, suddenly oblivious of all his former forebodings, and unconscious of the eager passion vibrating in his tone—"Sweet Lilith!"

She turned slightly towards him, and lifting her arms from their indolently graceful position on the pillows, she clasped her hands high above her head in apparent supplication.

"Love me!" she cried, with such a thrill in her accent that it rang through the room like a note of music—"Oh my Belovëd, love me!"

El-Râmi grew faint and dizzy,—his thoughts were all in a whirl, . . . was he made of marble or ice that he should not respond? Scarcely aware of what he did, he took her clasped hands in his own.

"And do I not, Lilith?" he murmured, half-anguished, half-entranced—"Do I not love you?"

"No, no!" said Lilith with passionate emphasis—"Not me,—not me, Myself! Oh my Belovëd! love Me, not my Shadow!"

He loosened her hands, and recoiled, awed and perplexed. Her appeal struck at the core of all his doubts,—and for one moment he was disposed to believe in the actual truth of the Immortal Soul without those "proofs" for which he constantly searched,—the next, he rallied himself on his folly and weakness. He dared not trust himself to answer her, so he was silent,—but she soon spoke again with such convincing earnestness of tone that almost. . . almost he believed—but not quite.

"To love the Seeming and not the Real," she said—"is the curse of all sad Humanity. It is the glamour of the air,—the barrier between Earth and Heaven. The Body is the Shadow—the Soul is the Substance. The Reflection I cast on Earth's surface for a little space, is but a Reflection only,—it is not Me:—I am beyond it!"

For a moment El-Râmi stood irresolute,—then gathering up his scattered thoughts, he began to try and resolve them into order and connection. Surely the time was ripe for his great Experiment?—and as he considered this, his nerves grew more steady,—his self-reliance returned—all his devotion to scientific research pressed back its claim upon his mind,—if he were to fail now, he thought, after all his patience and study,—fail to obtain any true insight into the spiritual side of humanity, would he not be ashamed, aye, and degraded in his own eyes? He resolved to end all his torture of pain and doubt and disquietude,—and sitting on the edge of Lilith's couch, he drew her delicate hands down from their uplifted position, and laid them one above the other cross-wise on his own breast.

"Then you must teach me, Lilith"—he said softly and with tender persuasiveness—"you must teach me to know you. If I see but your Reflection here,—let me behold your Reality. Let me love you as you are, if now I only love you as you seem. Show yourself to me in all your spiritual loveliness, Lilith!—it may be I shall die of the glory,—or—if there is no death as you say,—I shall not die, but simply pass away into the light which gives you life. Lift the veil that is between us, Lilith, and let me see you face to face. If this that seems you"—and he pressed the little hands he held—"is naught, let me realize the nothingness of so much beauty beside the greater beauty that en—genders it. Come to me as you are, Lilith!—come!"

As he spoke, his heart beat fast with a nervous thrill of expectancy; what would she answer? . . . what would she do? He could not take his eyes from her face—he half fancied he should see some change there; for the moment he even thought it possible that she might transform herself into some surpassing Being, which, like the gods of the Greek mythology, should consume by its flame-like splendour whatever of mortality dared to look upon it. But she remained unaltered, and sculpturally calm,—only her breathing seemed a little quicker, and the hands that he held trembled against his breast.

Her next words however startled him—

"I will come!" she said, and a faint sigh escaped her lips—"Be ready for me. Pray!—pray for the blessing of Christ,—for if Christ be with us, all is well."

At this, his brow clouded,—his eyes drooped gloomily.

"Christ!" he muttered more to himself than to her—"What is He to me? Who is He that He should be with us?"

"This world's Rescue and all worlds' Glory!"

The answer rang out like a silver clarion, with something full and triumphant in the sound, as though not only Lilith's voice had uttered it, but other voices had joined in a chorus. At the same moment, her hands moved, as if in an effort to escape from his hold. But he held them closely in a jealous and masterful grasp.

"When will you come to me, Lilith?" he demanded in low but eager accents—"When shall I see you and know you as Lilith? . . . my Lilith, my own forever?"

"God's Lilith—God's own forever!" murmured Lilith dreamily, and then was silent.

An angry sense of rebellion began to burn in El-Râmi's mind. Summoning up all the force of his iron will, he unclasped her hands and laid them back on each side of her, and placed his own hand on her breast, just where the ruby talisman shone and glowed.

"Answer me, Lilith!" he said, with some—thing of the old sternness which he had used to employ with her on former occasions—"When will you come to me?"

Her limbs trembled violently as though some inward cold convulsed her, and her answer came slowly, though clearly—

"When you are ready."

"I am ready now!" he cried recklessly.

"No—no!" she murmured, her voice growing fainter and fainter—"Not yet. . . not yet! Love is not strong enough, high enough, pure enough. Wait, watch and pray. When the hour has come, a sign will be given—but O my Belovëd, if you would know me, love Me!—love Me! not my Shadow!"

A pale hue fell on her face, robbing it of its delicate tint,—El-Râmi knew what that pallor indicated.

"Lilith! Lilith!" he exclaimed, "Why leave me thus if you love me? Stay with me yet a little!"

But Lilith—or rather the strange Spirit that made the body of Lilith speak,—was gone. And all that night not another sound, either of music or speech, stirred the silence of the room. Dawn came, misty and gray, and found the proud El-Râmi kneeling before the unveiled picture of the Christ,—not praying, for he could not bring himself down to the necessary humiliation for prayer,—but simply wondering vaguely as to what could be and what might be the one positive reply to that Question propounded of old—

"Whom Say Ye That I Am?"

II

Of what avail is it to propound questions that no one can answer? Of what use is it to attempt to solve the mystery of life which must for ever remain mysterious? Thus may the intelligent critic ask, and in asking, may declare that the experiments, researches, and anxieties of El-Râmi, together with El-Râmi himself, are mistaken conceptions all round. But it is necessary to remind the intelligent critic, that the eager desire of El-Râmi to prove what appears unprovable, is by no means an uncommon phase of human nature,—it is in fact, the very key-note and pulse of the present time. Every living creature who is not too stunned by misery for thought, craves to know positively whether the Soul,—the Immortal, Individual Ego, be Fable or Fact. Never more than in this, our own period, did people search with such unabated feverish yearning into the things that seem supernatural;—never were there bitterer pangs of recoil and disappointment when trickery and imposture are found to have even temporarily passed for truth. If the deepest feeling in every human heart today were suddenly given voice, the shout "Excelsior!" would rend the air in mighty chorus. For we know all the old earth-stories;—of love, of war, of adventure, of wealth, we know pretty well the beginning and the end,—we read in our histories of nations that were, but now are not, and we feel that we shall in due time go the same way with them,—that the wheel of Destiny spins on in the same round always, and that nothing—nothing can alter its relentless and monotonous course. We tread in the dust and among the fallen columns of great cities, and we vaguely wonder if the spirits of the men that built them are indeed no more,—we gaze on the glorious pile of the Duomo at Milan and think of the brain that first devised and planned its majestic proportions, and ask ourselves— Is it possible that this, the creation, should be Here, and its creator Nowhere? Would such an arrangement be reasonable or just? And so it happens that when the wielders of the pen essay to tell us of wars, of shipwrecks, of hair-breadth escapes from danger, of love and politics and society, we read their pages with merely transitory pleasure and frequent indifference, but when they touch upon subjects beyond earthly experience,—when they attempt, however feebly, to lift our inspirations to the possibilities of the Unseen, then we give them our eager attention and almost passionate interest. Critics look upon this tendency as morbid, unwholesome and pernicious; but nevertheless the tendency is there,—the demand for "Light! more light!" is in the very blood and brain of the people. It would seem as though this world has grown too narrow for the aspirations of its inhabitants;—and some of us instinctively feel that we are on the brink of strange discoveries respecting the powers unearthly, whether for good or evil we dare not presume to guess. The nonsensical tenets of "Theosophy" would not gain ground with a single individual man or woman were not this feeling very strong among many,—the tricky "mediums" and "spiritualists" would not have a chance of earning a subsistence out of the gullibility of their dupes, and the preachers of new creeds and new forms would obtain no vestige of attention if it were not for the fact that there is a very general impression all over the world that the time is ripe for a clearer revelation of God and the things of God than we have ever had before. "Give us something that will endure!" is the exclamation of weary humanity— "The things we have, pass; and by reason of their ephemeral nature, are worthless. Give us what we can keep and call our own for ever!" This is why we try and test all things that appear to give proof of the super-sensual element in man,—and when we find ourselves deceived by impostors and conjurers, our disgust and disappointment are too bitter to ever find vent in words. The happiest are those who, in the shifting up and down of faiths and formulas, ever cling stedfastly to the one pure Example of embodied Divinity in Manhood as seen in Christ. When we reject Christ, we reject the Gospel of Love and Universal Brotherhood, without which the ultimate perfection and progress of the world must ever remain impossible.

A few random thoughts such as these occurred to El-Râmi now and then as he lived his life from day to day in perpetual expectation of the "sign" promised by Lilith, which as yet was not forthcoming. He believed she would keep her word, and that the "sign" whatever it was would be unmistakable; and,—as before stated—this was the nearest approach to actual faith he had ever known. His was a nature which was originally disposed to faith, but which had persistently fought with its own inclination till that inclination had been conquered. He had been able to prove as purely natural, much that had seemed supernatural, and he now viewed everything from two points—Possi—bility and Impossibility. His various confusions and perplexities however, generally arose from the frequent discovery he made, that what he had once thought the Impossible, suddenly became through some small chance clue, the Possible. So many times had this occurred that he often caught himself wondering whether anything in very truth could be strictly declared as "impossible." And yet, . . . with the body of Lilith under his observation for six years, and an absolute ignorance as to how her intelligence had developed, or where she obtained the power to discourse with him as she did, he always had the lurking dread that her utterances might be the result of his own brain unconsciously working upon hers, and that there was no "soul" or "spirit" in the matter. This too, in spite of the fact that she had actually given him a concise description of certain planets, their laws, their government, and their inhabitants, concerning which he could know nothing,—and that she spoke with a sure conviction of the existence of a personal God, an idea that was entirely unacceptable to his nature. He was at a loss to explain her "separated consciousness" in any scientific way, and afraid of himself lest he should believe too easily, he encouraged the presence of every doubt in his mind, rather than give entrance to more than the palest glimmer of faith.

And so time went on, and May passed into June, and June deepened into its meridian-glow of bloom and sunlight, and he remained shut up within the four walls of his house, seeing no one, and displaying a total indifference to the fact that the "season" with all its bitter froth and frivolity was seething on in London in its usual monotonous manner. Unlike pretenders to "spiritualistic" powers, he had no inclination for the society of the rich and great,—"titled" people had no attraction for him save in so far as they were cultured, witty, or amiable,— "position" in the world, was a very miserable trifle in his opinion, and though many a gorgeous flunkied carriage at this time found its way into the unfashionable square where he had his domicile, no visitors were admitted to see him,—and "too busy to receive anyone" was the formula with which young Féraz dismissed any would-be intruder. Yet Féraz himself wondered all the while how it was that as a matter of fact, El-Râmi seemed to be just now less absorbed in actual study than he had ever been in his whole life. He read no books save the old Arabic vellum-bound volume which held the explanatory key to so much curious phenomena palmed off as "spiritual miracles" by the Theosophists, and he wrote a good deal,—but he answered no letters, accepted no invitations, manifested no wish to leave the house even for an hour's stroll, and seemed mentally engrossed by some great secret subject of meditation. He was uniformly kind to Féraz, exacting no duties from him save those prompted by interest and affection,—he was marvellously gentle too with Zaroba, who, agitated, restless and perplexed as to his ultimate intentions with respect to the beautiful Lilith, was vaguely uneasy and melancholy, though she deemed it wisest to perform all his commands with exactitude, and, for the present to hold her peace. She had expected something—though she knew not what—from his last interview with her beautiful charge—but all was unchanged,—Lilith slept on, and the cherished wish of Zaroba's heart, that she should wake, seemed as far off realization as ever. Day after day passed, and El-Râmi lived like a hermit amidst the roar and traffic of mighty London,—watching Lilith for long and anxious hours, but never venturing to call her down to him from wherever she might be,—waiting, waiting for her summons, and content for once to sink himself in the thought of her identity. All his ambitions were now centred on the one great object, . . . to see the Soul, as it is, if it is indeed existent, conscious and individual. For, as he argued, what is the use of a "Soul" whose capacities we are not permitted to understand?— and if it be no more to us than the Intelligent Faculty of Brain? The chief proof of a possible Something behind Man's inner consciousness, was, he considered, the quality of Discontent, and, primarily, because Discontent is so universal. No one is contented in all the world from end to end. From the powerful Emperor on his throne to the whining beggar in the street, all chafe under the goading prick of the great Necessity,—a Something Better,—a Something Lasting. Why should this resonant key-note of Discontent be perpetually resounding through space, if this life is all? No amount of philosophy or argument can argue away Discontent—it is a god-like Disquietude ever fermenting changes among us, ever propounding new suggestions for happiness, ever restless, never satisfied. And El-Râmi would ask himself—Is Discontent the voice of the Soul?—not only the Universal Soul of things, but the Soul of each individual? Then, if Individual, why should not the Individual be made manifest, if manifestation be possible? And if not possible, why should we be called upon to believe in what cannot be manifested?

Thus he argued, not altogether unwisely; he had studied profoundly all the divers conflicting theories of religion, and would at one time have become an obstinately confirmed Positivist, had it not been for the fact that the further his researches led him the more he became aware that there was nothing positive,—that is to say, nothing so apparently fixed and unalterable that it might not, under different conditions, prove capable of change. Perhaps there is no better test-example of this truth than the ordinary substance known as iron. We use in common parlance unthinkingly the phrase "as hard as iron"—while to the smith and engineer who mould and twist it in every form, it proves itself soft and malleable as wax. Again, to the surface-observer, it might and does seem an incombustible metal,—the chemist knows it will burn with the utmost fury. How then form a universal decision as to its various capabilities when it has so many variations of use all in such contrary directions? The same example, modified or enlarged, will be found to apply to all things, wherefore the word "Positivism" seems out of place in merely mortal language. God may be "positive," but we and our surroundings have no such absolute quality.

During this period of El-Râmi's self-elected seclusion and meditation, his young brother Féraz was very happy. He was in the midst of writing a poem which he fondly fancied might perhaps—only perhaps—find a publisher to take it and launch it on its own merits,—it is the privilege of youth to be over-sanguine. Then too, his brain was filled with new musical ideas,—and many an evening's hour he beguiled away by delicious improvisations on the piano, or exquisite songs to the mandoline. El-Râmi, when he was not upstairs keeping anxious vigil by the tranced Lilith's side, would sit in his chair, leaning back with half-closed eyes, listening to the entrancing melodies like another Saul to a new David, soothed by the sweetness of the sounds he heard, yet conscious that he took too deep and ardent a pleasure in hearing, when the songs Féraz chose were of love. One night Féraz elected to sing the wild and beautiful "Canticle of Love" written by the late Lord Lytton, when as "Owen Meredith" he promised to be one of the greatest poets of our century, and who would have fulfilled more than that promise if diplomacy had not claimed his brilliant intellectual gifts for the service of his country,—a country which yet deplores his untimely loss. But no fatality had as yet threatened that gallant and noble life in the days when Féraz smote the chords of his mandoline and sang:—

"I once heard an angel by night in the sky
Singing softly a song to a deep golden lute;
The pole-star, the seven little planets and I
To the song that he sang, listened mute.
For the song that he sang was so strange and so sweet.
And so tender the tones of his lute's golden strings

That the seraphs of heaven sat hush'd at his feet
And folded their heads in their wings.
And the song that he sang to the seraphs up there
Is called 'Love'! But the words. . . I had heard them elsewhere.
"For when I was last in the nethermost Hell.
On a rock 'mid the sulphurous surges I heard
A pale spirit sing to a wild hollow shell;
And his song was the same, every word.
And so sad was his singing, all Hell to the sound
Moaned, and wailing, complained like a monster in pain
While the fiends hovered near o'er the dismal profound
With their black wings weighed down by the strain;
And the song that was sung to the Lost Ones down there
Is called 'Love'! But the spirit that sang was Despair!"

The strings of the mandoline quivered mournfully in tune with the passionate beauty of the verse, and from El-Râmi's lips there came involuntarily a deep and bitter sigh.

Féraz ceased playing and looked at him.

"What is it?" he asked anxiously.

"Nothing!" replied his brother in a tranquil voice—"What should there be? Only the poem is very beautiful, and out of the common,— though to me, terribly suggestive of—a mistake somewhere in creation. Love to the Saved—Love to the Lost!—naturally it would have different aspects,—but it is an anomaly—Love, to be true to its name, should have no 'lost' ones in its chronicle."

Féraz was silent.

"Do you believe"—continued El-Râmi—"that there is a 'nethermost Hell'?—a place or a state of mind resembling that 'rock 'mid the sulphurous surges'?"

"I should imagine," replied Féraz with some diffidence, "that there must be a condition in which we are bound to look back and see where we were wrong,—a condition, too, in which we have time to be sorry—"

"Unfair and unreasonable!" exclaimed his brother hotly. "For, suppose we did not know we were wrong? We are left absolutely without guidance in this world to do as we like."

"I do not think you can quite say that"—remonstrated Féraz gently—"We do know when we are wrong—generally; some instinct tells us so—and while we have the book of Nature, we are not left without guidance. As for looking back and seeing our former mistakes, I think that is unquestionable,—for as I grow older, I begin to see where I failed in my former life, and how I deserved to lose my star-kingdom."

El-Râmi looked impatient.

"You are a dreamer"—he said decisively—"and your star-kingdom is a dream also. You cannot tell me truthfully that you remember anything of a former existence?"

"I am beginning to remember," said Féraz steadily.

"My dear boy, anybody but myself hearing you, would say you were mad—hopelessly mad!"

"They would be at perfect liberty to say so"—and Féraz smiled a little—"Everyone is free to have his own opinion—I have mine. My star exists; and I once existed in it—so did you."

"Well, I know nothing about it then," declared El-Râmi—"I have forgotten it utterly."

"Oh no! You think you have forgotten"—said Féraz mildly—"But the truth is, your very knowledge of science and other things is only—memory."

El-Râmi moved in his chair impatiently.

"Let us not argue;"—he said—"We shall never agree. Sing to me again!"

Féraz thought a moment, and then laid aside his mandoline and went to the piano, where he played a rushing rapid accompaniment like the sound of the wind among trees, and sang the following—

"Winds of the mountain, mingle with my crying.
Clouds of the tempest, flee as I am flying.
Gods of the cloudland, Christus and Apollo, Follow, O follow!"
"Through the dark valleys, up the misty mountains.
Over the black wastes, past the gleaming fountains.
Praying not, hoping not, resting nor abiding, Lo, I am riding!"
"Clangour and anger of elements are round me.
Torture has clasped me, cruelty has crown'd me.
Sorrow awaits me, Death is waiting with her, Fast speed I thither."
"Gods of the storm-cloud, drifting darkly yonder.
Point fiery hands and mock me as I wander;
Gods of the forest glimmer out upon me, Shrink back and shun me."
"Gods, let them follow!—gods, for I defy them!

> *They call me, mock me, but I gallop by them;*
> *If they would find me, touch me, whisper to me,*
> *Let them pursue me!"*

He was interrupted in the song by a smothered cry from El-Râmi, and looking round, startled, he saw his brother standing up and staring at him with something of mingled fear and horror. He came to an abrupt stop, his hands resting on the piano keys.

"Go on, go on!" cried El-Râmi irritably. "What wild chant of the gods and men have you there? Is it your own?"

"Mine!" echoed Féraz—"No indeed!—I wish it were. It is by a living poet of the day, Robert Buchanan."

"Robert Buchanan!"—and El-Râmi tried to recover his self-possession—"Ah!—Well, I wonder what devil possessed him to write it!"

"Don't you like it?" exclaimed Féraz wonderingly—"To my thinking it is one of the finest poems in the English language."

"Of course, of course I like it;"—said El-Râmi, sitting down again, angry with himself for his own emotion—"Is there more of it?"

"Yes, but I need not finish it,"—and Féraz made as though he would rise from the piano.

El-Râmi suddenly began to laugh.

"Go on, I tell you, Féraz"—he said carelessly—"There is a tempest of agitation in the words and in your music that leaves one hurried and breathless, but the sensation is not unpleasant,—especially when one is prepared, . . . go on!—I want to hear the end of this. . . this-defiance."

Féraz looked at him to see if he were in earnest, and perceiving he had settled down to give his whole attention to the rest of the ballad, he resumed his playing, and again the rush of the music filled the room—

> *"Faster, O faster! Darker and more dreary*
> *Groweth the pathway, yet I am not weary—*
> *Gods, I defy them! gods, I can unmake them, Bruise them and*
> *break them!"*
> *"White steed of wonder with thy feet of thunder.*
> *Find out their temples, tread their high-priests under—*
> *Leave them behind thee—if their gods speed after, Mock them*
> *with laughter."*
> *"Shall a god grieve me? shall a phantom win me?*

> *Nay!—by the wild wind around and o'er and in me—*
> *Be his name Vishnu, Christus or Apollo—Let the god follow!"*
> *"Clangour and anger of elements are round me.*
> *Torture has clasped me, cruelty has crown'd me.*
> *Sorrow awaits me, Death is waiting with her, Fast speed I thither!"*

The music ceased abruptly with a quick clash as of jangling bells,—and Féraz rose from the piano.

El-Râmi was sitting quite still.

"A fine outburst!" he remarked presently, seeing that his young brother waited for him to speak—"And you rendered it finely. In it the voice of the strong man speaks;—Do you believe it?"

"Believe what?" asked Féraz, a little surprised.

"This—" and El-Râmi quoted slowly—

> *"Shall a god grieve me? shall a phantom win me?*
> *Nay!—by the wild wind around and o'er and in me—*
> *Be his name Vishnu, Christus or Apollo—Let the god follow!"*

"Do you think"—he continued, "that in the matter of life's leadership, the 'god' should follow, or we the god?"

Féraz lifted his delicately marked eyebrows in amazement.

"What an odd question!" he said—"The song is only a song,—part of a poem entitled, 'The City of Dream,' which none of the press-critics have ever done justice to. If Lord Tennyson had written the 'City of Dream' what columns and columns of praise would have been poured out upon it! What I sang to you is the chant, or lyrical soliloquy of the 'Outcast Esau,' who in the poem is evidently 'outcast' from all creeds; and it is altogether a character which, if I read it rightly, represents the strong doubter, almost unbeliever, who defies Fate. But we do not receive a mere poem, no matter how beautiful, as a gospel. And if you speak of life's leadership, it is devoutly to be hoped that God not only leads, but rules us all."

"Why should you hope it?" asked El-Râmi gloomily—"Myself, I fear it!"

Féraz came to his side and rested one hand affectionately on his arm.

"You are worried and out of sorts, my brother,"—he said gently—"Why do you not seek some change from so much indoor life? You do not even get the advantages I have of going to and fro on the household business. I breathe the fresh air every day,—surely it is necessary for you also?"

"My dear boy, I am perfectly well"—and El-Râmi regarded him steadily—"Why should you doubt it? I am only—a little tired. Poor human nature cannot always escape fatigue."

Féraz said no more,—but there was a certain strangeness in his brother's manner that filled him with an indefinable uneasiness. In his own quiet fashion he strove to distract El-Râmi's mind from the persistent fixity of whatever unknown purpose seemed to so mysteriously engross him,—and whenever they were together at meals or at other hours of the day, he talked in as light and desultory a way as possible on all sorts of different topics in the hope of awakening his brother's interest more keenly in external affairs. He read much and thought more, and was a really brilliant conversationalist when he chose, in spite of his dreamy fancies—but he was obliged to admit to himself that his affectionate endeavours met with very slight success. True, El-Râmi appeared to give his attention to all that was said, but it was only an appearance,—and Féraz saw plainly enough that he was not really moved to any sort of feeling respecting the ways and doings of the outer world. And when, one morning, Féraz read aloud the account of the marriage of Sir Frederick Vaughan, Bart., with Idina, only daughter of Jabez Chester of New York, he only smiled indifferently and said nothing.

"We were invited to that wedding;"—commented Féraz.

"Were we?" El-Râmi shrugged his shoulders and seemed totally oblivious of the fact.

"Why of course we were"—went on Féraz cheerfully—"And, at your bidding I opened and read the letter Sir Frederick wrote you, which said that as you had prophesied the marriage, he would take it very kindly if you would attend in person the formal fulfilment of your prophecy. And all you did in reply was to send a curt refusal on plea of other engagements. Do you think that was quite amiable on your part?"

"Fortunately for me I am not called upon to be amiable;"—said El-Râmi, beginning to pace slowly up and down the room—"I want no favours from society, so I need not smile to order. That is one of the chief privileges of complete independence. Fancy having to grin and lie and skulk and propitiate people all one's days!—I could not endure it,—but most men can—and do!"

"Besides"—he added after a pause—"I cannot look on with patience at the marriage of fools. Vaughan is a fool, and his baronetage will scarcely pass for wisdom,—the little Chester girl is also a fool,—and I can see exactly what they will become in the course of a few years."

"Describe them, in futuro!" laughed Féraz.

"Well—the man will be 'turfy'; the woman, a blind slave to her dressmaker. That is all. There can be nothing more. They will never do any good or any harm—they are simply—nonentities. These are the sort of folk that make me doubt the immortal soul,—for Vaughan is less 'spiritual' than a well-bred dog, and little Chester less mentally gifted than a well-instructed mouse."

"Severe!"—commented Féraz smiling—"But, man or woman,—mouse or dog, I suppose they are quite happy just now?"

"Happy!" echoed El-Râmi satirically—"Well—I daresay they are,—with the only sort of happiness their intelligences can grasp. She is happy because she is now 'my lady' and because she was able to wear a wedding-gown of marvellous make and cost, to trail and rustle and sweep after her little person up to God's altar with, as though she sought to astonish the Almighty before whom she took her vows, with the exuberance of her millinery. He is happy because his debts are paid out of old Jabez Chester's millions. There the 'happiness' ends. A couple of months is sufficient to rub the bloom off such wedlock."

"And you really prophesied the marriage?" queried Féraz.

"It was easy enough"—replied his brother carelessly—"Given two uninstructed, unthinking bipeds of opposite sexes—the male with debts, the female with dollars, and an urbanely obstinate schemer to pull them together like Lord Melthorpe, and the thing is done. Half the marriages in London are made up like that,—and of the after-lives of those so wedded, 'there needs no ghost from the grave' to tell us,—the divorce-courts give every information."

"Ah!" exclaimed Féraz quickly—"That reminds me,—do you know I saw something in the evening-paper last night that might have interested you?"

"Really! You surprise me!" and El—Râmi laughed—"That is strange indeed, for papers of all sorts, whether morning or evening, are to me the dullest and worst-written literature in the world."

"Oh, for literature one does not go to them"—answered Féraz.—"But this was a paragraph about a man who came here not very long ago to see you—a clergyman. He is up as a co-respondent in some very scandalous divorce case. I did not read it all—I only saw that his Bishop had caused him to be 'unfrocked,' whatever that means—I suppose he is expelled from the ministry?"

"Yes. 'Unfrocked' means literally a stripping-off of clerical dignity," said El-Râmi. "But if it is the man who came here, he was always naked in that respect. Francis Anstruther was his name?"

"Exactly—that is the man. He is disgraced for life, and seems to be one of the most consummate scoundrels that ever lived. He has deserted his wife and eight children. . ."

"Spare me and yourself the details!" and El-Râmi gave an expressively contemptuous gesture—"I know all about him, and told him what I knew when he came here. But he'll do very well yet—he'll get on capitally in spite of his disgrace."

"How is that possible?" exclaimed Féraz.

"Easily! He can 'boom' himself as a new 'General' Booth, or he can become a 'Colonel' under Booth's orders—as long as there are fools to support Booth with money. Or he can go to America or Australia and start a new creed—he's sure to fall on his feet and make his fortune— pious hypocrites always do. One would almost fancy there must be a special Deity to protect the professors of Humbug. It is only the sincerely honest folk who get wronged in this admirably-ordered world!"

He spoke with bitterness; and Féraz glanced at him anxiously.

"I do not quite agree with you"—he said; "Surely honest folk always have their reward?—though perhaps superficial observers may not be able to perceive where it comes in. I believe in 'walking uprightly' as the Bible says—it seems to me easier to keep along a straight open road, than to take dark bye-ways and dubious short cuts."

"What do you mean by your straight open road?" demanded El-Râmi, looking at him.

"Nature,"—replied Féraz promptly—"Nature leads us up to God."

El-Râmi broke into a harsh laugh.

"O credulous beautiful lad!" he exclaimed; "You know not what you say! Nature! Consider her methods of work—her dark and cunning and cruel methods! Every living thing preys on some other living thing;— creatures wonderful, innocent, simple or complex, live apparently but to devour and be devoured;—every inch of ground we step upon is the dust of something dead. In the horrible depths of the earth, Nature,— this generous kindly Nature!—hides her dread volcanic fires,—her streams of lava, her boiling founts of sulphur and molten lead, which at any unexpected moment may destroy whole continents crowded with unsuspecting humanity. This is NATURE,—nothing but Nature! She hides her trea—sures of gold, of silver, of diamonds and rubies, in the deepest and most dangerous recesses, where human beings are lost in toiling for them,—buried in darkness and slain by thousands in the difficult search; diving for pearls, the unwary explorer is met by the remorseless monsters of the deep,—in fact, in all his efforts towards discovery and progress, Man, the most naturally defenceless creature upon earth, is met by death or blank discouragement. Suppose he were to trust to Nature alone, what would Nature do for him? He is sent into the world naked and helpless;—and all the resources of his body and brain have to be educated and brought into active requisition to enable him to live at all,—lions' whelps, bears' cubs have a better 'natural' chance than he;—and then, when he has learned how to make the best of his surroundings, he is turned out of the world again, naked and helpless as he came in, with all his knowledge of no more use to him than if he had never attained it. This is NATURE,—if Nature be thus reckless and unreasonable as the 'reflex of God'—how reckless and unreasonable must be God Himself!"

The beautiful stag-like eyes of Féraz darkened slowly, and his slim hand involuntarily clenched.

"Ay, if God were so," he said—"the veriest pigmy among men might boast of nobler qualities than He! But God is not so, El-Râmi! Of course you can argue any and every way, and I cannot confute your reasoning. Because you reason with the merely mortal intelligence; to answer you rightly I should have to reply as a Spirit,—I should need to be out of the body before I could tell you where you are wrong."

"Well!" said his brother curiously—"Then why do you not do so? Why do you not come to me out of the body, and enlighten me as to what you know?"

Féraz looked troubled.

"I cannot!" he said sadly—"When I go—away yonder—I seem to have so little remembrance of earthly things—I am separated from the world by thousands of air-spaces. I am always conscious that you exist on earth,—but it is always as of someone who will join me presently—not of one whom I am compelled to join. There is the strangeness of it. That is why I have very little belief in the notion of ghosts and spirits appearing to men—because I know positively that no detached soul willingly returns to or remains on earth. There is always the upward yearning. If it returns, it does so simply because it is for some reason, commanded, not because of its own desire."

"And who do you suppose commands it?" asked El-Râmi.

"The Highest of all Powers,"—replied Féraz reverently—"whom we all, whether spirit or mortal, obey."

"I do not obey,"—said El-Râmi composedly—"I enforce obedience."

"From whom?" cried Féraz with agitation—"O my brother, from whom? From mortals perhaps—yes,—so long as it is permitted to you— but from Heaven—no! No, not from Heaven can you win obedience. For God's sake do not boast of such power!"

He spoke passionately, and in anxious earnest.

El-Râmi smiled.

"My good fellow, why excite yourself? I do not 'boast'—I am simply— strong! If I am immortal, God Himself cannot slay me,—if I am mortal only, I can but die. I am indifferent either way. Only I will not shrink before an imaginary Divine Terror till I prove what right it has to my submission. Enough!—we have talked too much on this subject, and I have work to do."

He turned to his writing-table as he spoke and was soon busy there. Féraz took up a book and tried to read, but his heart beat quickly, and he was overwhelmed by a deep sense of fear. The daring of his brother's words smote him with a chill horror,—from time immemorial, had not the Forces Divine punished pride as the deadliest of sins? His thoughts travelled over the great plain of History, on which so many spectres of dead nations stand in our sight as pale warnings of our own possible fate, and remembered how surely it came to pass that when men became too proud and defiant and absolute,—rejecting God and serving themselves only, then they were swept away into desolation and oblivion. As with nations, so with individuals—the Law of Compensation is just, and as evenly balanced as the symmetrical motion of the Universe. And the words "Except ye become as little children ye shall not enter the Kingdom of Heaven," rang through his ears, as he sat heavily silent, and wondering, wondering where the researches of his brother would end, and how?

El-Râmi himself meanwhile was scanning the last pages of his dead friend Kremlin's private Journal. This was a strange book,—kept with exceeding care, and written in the form of letters which were all addressed "To the Beloved Maroussia in Heaven"—and amply proved that in spite of the separated seclusion and eccentricity of his life,

Kremlin had not only been faithful to the love of his early days, the girl who had died self-slain in her Russian prison,—but he had been firm in his acceptance of and belief in the immortality of the soul and the reunion of parted spirits. His last "letter" ran thus—it was unfinished and had been written the night before the fatal storm which had made an end of his life and learning together,—

"I seem to be now on the verge of the discovery for which I have yearned. Thou knowest, O heart of my heart, how I dream that these brilliant and ceaseless vibrations of light may perchance carry to the world some message which it were well and wise we should know. Oh, if this 'Light,' which is my problem and mystery, could but transmit to my earthly vision one flashing gleam of thy presence, my beloved child! But thou wilt guide me, so that I presume not too far;—I feel thou art near me, and that thou wilt not fail me at the last. If in the space of an earthly ten minutes this marvellous 'Light' can travel 111,600,000 miles, thou as a 'spirit of light' canst not be very far away. Only till my work for poor humanity is done, do I choose to be parted from thee— be the time long or short—we shall meet. . ."

Here the journal ended.

"And have they met?" thought El-Râmi, as closing the book he locked it away in his desk—"And do they remember they were ever mortal? And what are they—and where are they?"

III

In the midst of the strange "summer" weather which frequently falls to the lot of England,—weather alternating between hot and cold, wet and dry, sun and cloud with the most distracting rapidity and irregularity,—there came at last one perfect night towards the end of June,—a night which could have met with no rival even in the sunniest climes of the sunniest south. A soft tranquility hovered dove-like in the air,—a sense of perfect peace seemed to permeate all visible and created things. The sky was densely blue and thickly strewn with stars, though these glimmered but faintly, their light being put to shame by the splendid brilliancy of the full moon which swam aloft airily like a great golden bubble. El-Râmi's windows were all set open; a big bunch of heliotrope adorned the table, and the subtle fragrance of it stole out delicately to mingle with the faintly stirring evening breeze. Féraz was sitting alone,—his brother had just left the room,—and he was indulging himself in the dolce far niente as only the Southern or Eastern temperament can do. His hands were clasped lightly behind his head, and his eyes were fixed on the shabby little trees in the square which had done their best to look green among the whirling smuts of the metropolis and had failed ignominiously in the attempt, but which now, in the ethereal light of the moon, presented a soft outline of gray and silver like olive-boughs seen in the distance. He was thinking, with a certain serious satisfaction, of an odd circumstance that had occurred to himself that day. It had happened in this wise: Since the time Zaroba had taken him to look upon the beautiful creature who was the "subject" of his brother's experiments, he had always kept the memory of her in his mind without speaking of her, save that whenever he said a prayer or offered up a thanksgiving, he had invariably used the phrase—"God defend her!" He could only explain "Her" to himself by the simple pronoun, because, as El-Râmi had willed, he had utterly and hopelessly forgotten her name. But now, strange to say he remembered it!—it had flashed across his mind like a beam of light or a heaven-sent signal,—he was at work, writing at his poem, when some sudden inexplicable instinct had prompted him to lift his eyes and murmur devoutly—"God defend Lilith!" Lilith!—how soft the sound of it!—how infinitely bewitching! After having lost it for so long, it had come back to him in a moment—how or why, he could not imagine. He could only account for it in one way—namely, that El-Râmi's will-forces were so concentrated on some particularly absorbing object that his daily influence on his brother's young life was thereby materially lessened. And Féraz was by no means sorry that this should be so.

"Why should it matter that I remember her name?" he mused—"I shall never speak of her—for I have sworn I will not. But I can think of her to my heart's content,—the beautiful Lilith!"

Then he fell to considering the old legend of that Lilith who it is said was Adam's first wife,—and he smiled as he thought what a name of evil omen it was to the Jews, who had charms and talismans wherewith to exorcise the supposed evil influence connected with it,—while to him, Féraz, it was a name sweeter than honey-sweet singing. Then there came to his mind stray snatches of poesy,—delicate rhymes from the rich and varied stores of one of his favourite poets Dante Gabriel Rossetti,—rhymes that sounded in his ears just now like the strophes of a sibylline chant or spell:—

> "It was Lilith the wife of Adam:
> (Sing Eden Bower!)
> Not a drop of her blood was human.
> But she was made like a soft sweet woman."

"And that is surely true!" said Féraz to himself, a little startled,— "For—if she is dead, as El-Râmi asserts, and her seeming life is but the result of his art, then indeed in the case of this Lilith 'not a drop of her blood is human.'"

And the poem ran on in his mind—

> "Lilith stood on the skirts of Eden
> (Alas, the hour!)
> She was the first that thence was driven:
> With her was hell, and with Eve was heaven."

"Nay, I should transpose that,"—murmured the young man drowsily, staring out on the moonlit street—"I should say 'With Eve was hell, and with Lilith heaven.' How strange it is I should never have thought of this poem before!—and I have often turned over the pages of Rossetti's book,—since—since I saw her;—I must have actually seen the name of Lilith printed there, and yet it never suggested itself to me as being familiar or offering any sort of clue."

He sighed perplexedly,—the heliotrope odours floated around him, and the gleam of the lamp in the room seemed to pale in the wide splendour of the moon-rays pouring through the window,—and still the delicate sprite of Poesy continued to remind him of familiar lines and verses he loved, though all the while he thought of Lilith, and kept on wondering vaguely and vainly what would be, what could be, the end of his brother's experiment (whatever that was, for he, Féraz, did not know) on the lovely, apparently living girl who yet was dead. It was very strange—and surely, it was also very terrible!

> "*The day is dark and the night*
> *To him that would search their heart;*
> *No lips of cloud that will part.*
> *Nor morning song in the light:*
> *Only, gazing alone*
> *To him wild shadows are shown.*
> *Deep under deep unknown*
> *And height above unknown height.*
> *Still we say as we go,—*
> *'Strange to think by the way.*
> *Whatever there is to know.*
> *That shall we know one day.'*"

This passage of rhyme sang itself out with a monotonous musical gentleness in his brain,—he closed his eyes restfully,—and then—lying back thus in his chair by the open window, with the moonlight casting a wide halo round him and giving a pale spiritual beauty to his delicate classic features,—he passed away out of his body, as he would have said, and was no more on earth; or rather as we should say, he fell asleep and dreamed. And the "dream" or the "experience" was this;—

He found himself walking leisurely upon the slopes of a majestic mountain, which seemed not so much mountain as garden, for all the winding paths leading to its summit were fringed with flowers. He heard the silvery plashing of brooks and fountains, and the rustling of thickly-foliaged trees,—he knew the place well, and realized that he was in his "star" again,—the mystic Sphere he called his "home." But he was evidently an exile or an alien in it,—he had grown to realize this fact and was sorry it should be so, yet his sorrow was mingled with hope, for he felt it would not always be so. He wandered along aimlessly and alone, full of a curiously vague happiness and regret, and as he walked he was passed by crowds of beautiful youths and maidens, who were all pressing forward eagerly as to some high festival or great assembly. They sang blithe songs,—they scattered flowers,—they talked with each other in happy-toned voices,—and he stood aside gazing at them wistfully while they went on rejoicing.

"O land where life never grows old and where love is eternal!" he mused—"Why am I exiled from thy glory? Why have I lost thy joy?"

He sighed;—he longed to know what had brought together so bright a multitude of these lovely and joyous beings,—his own "dear people" as he felt they were; and yet—yet he hesitated to ask one of them the least question, feeling himself unworthy. At last he saw a girl approaching,—she was singing to herself and tying flowers in a garland as she came,—her loose gold hair streamed behind her, every glistening tress seeming to flash light as she moved. As she drew near him she glanced at him kindly and paused as though waiting to be addressed,— seeing this, he mustered up his courage and spoke.

"Whither are you all going?" he asked, with a sad gentleness—"I may not follow you, I know,—but will you tell me why, in this kingdom of joy, so much fresh joy seems added?"

She pointed upwards, and as his eyes obeyed her gesture, he saw in the opal-coloured sky that bent above them, a dazzling blaze of gold and crimson glory towards the south.

"An Angel passes!" she replied—"Below that line of light the Earth swings round in its little orbit, and from the Earth She comes! We go to watch her flight heavenward, and win the benediction that her passing presence gives. For look you!—all that splendour in the sky is not light, but wings!"

"Wings!" echoed Féraz dreamily, yet nothing doubting what she said.

"Wings or rays of glory,—which you will"—said the maiden, turning her own beautiful eyes towards the flashing brilliancy; "They are waiting there,—those who come from the furthest Divine world,—they are the friends of Lilith."

She bent her head serenely, and passed onward and upward, and Féraz stood still, his gaze fixed in the direction of that southern light which he now perceived was never still, but quivered as with a million shafts of vari-coloured fire.

"The friends of Lilith!" he repeated to himself—"Angels then,—for she is an Angel."

Angels!—angels waiting for Lilith in the glory of the South! How long—how long would they wait?—when would Lilith herself appear?—and would the very heavens open to receive her, soaring upward? He trembled,—he tried to realize the unimaginable scene,—and then,.. then he seemed to be seized and hurried away somewhere against his will. . . and all that was light grew dark. He shuddered as with icy cold, and felt that earth again encompassed him,—and presently he woke—to find his brother looking at him.

"Why in the world do you go to sleep with the window wide open?" asked El-Râmi—"Here I find you, literally bathed in the moonlight—and moonlight drives men mad they say,—so fast too in the land of Nod that I could hardly waken you. Shut the window, my dear boy, if you must sleep."

Féraz sprang up quickly,—his eyes felt dazzled still with the remembrance of that "glory of the angels in the South."

"I was not asleep,"—he said—"But certainly I was not here."

"Ah!—In your Star again of course!" murmured El-Râmi with the faintest trace of mockery in his tone. But Féraz took no offence—his one anxiety was to prevent the name of "Lilith" springing to his lips in spite of himself.

"Yes—I was there"—he answered slowly, "And do you know all the people in the land are gathering together by thousands to see an Angel pass heavenward? And there is a glory of her sister-angels, away in the Southern horizon like the splendid circle described by Dante in his 'Paradiso.' Thus—"

> "There is a light in heaven whose goodly shine
> Makes the Creator visible to all
> Created, that in seeing Him alone
> Have peace. And in a circle spreads so far
> That the circumference were too loose a zone
> To girdle in the sun!"

He quoted the lines with strange eagerness and fervour,—and El-Râmi looked at him curiously.

"What odd dreams you have!" he said, not unkindly—"Always fantastic and impossible, but beautiful in their way. You should set them down in black and white, and see how earth's critics will bespatter your heaven with the ink of their office pens! Poor boy!—how limply you would fall from 'Paradise'!—with what damp dejected wings!"

Féraz smiled.

"I do not agree with you"—he said—"If you speak of imagination,—only in this case I am not imagining,—no one can shut out that Paradise from me at any time—neither pope nor king, nor critic. Thought is free, thank God!"

"Yes—perhaps it is the only thing we have to be really thankful for,"—returned El-Râmi—"Well—I will leave you to resume your 'dreams'—only don't sleep with the windows open. Summer evenings are treacherous,—I should advise you to get to bed."

"And you?" asked Féraz, moved by a sudden anxiety which he could not explain.

"I shall not sleep tonight,"—said his brother moodily—"Something has occurred to me—a suggestion—an idea, which I am impatient to work out without loss of time. And, Féraz,—if I succeed in it—you shall know the result tomorrow."

This promise, which implied such a new departure from El-Râmi's customary reticence concerning his work, really alarmed Féraz more than gratified him.

"For Heaven's sake be careful!" he exclaimed—"You attempt so much,—you want so much,—perhaps more than can in law and justice be given. El-Râmi, my brother, leave something to God—you cannot, you dare not take all!"

"My dear visionary," replied El-Râmi gently—"You alarm yourself needlessly, I assure you. I do not want to take anything except what is my own,—and as for leaving something to God, why He is welcome to what He makes of me in the end—a pinch of dust!"

"There is more than dust in your composition—" cried Féraz impetuously—"There is divinity! And the divinity belongs to God, and to God you must render it up, pure and perfect. He claims it from you, and you are bound to give it."

A tremor passed through El-Râmi's frame, and he grew paler.

"If that be true, Féraz," he said slowly and with emphasis—"if it indeed be true that there is Divinity in me,—which I doubt!—why then let God claim and take His own particle of fire when He will, and as He will! Good-night!"

Féraz caught his hands and pressed them tenderly in his own.

"Good-night!" he murmured—"God does all things well, and to His care I commend you, my dearest brother."

And as El-Râmi turned away and left the room, he gazed after him with a chill sense of fear and desolation,—almost as if he were doomed never to see him again. He could not reason his alarm away, and yet he knew not why he should feel any alarm,—but truth to tell, his interior sense of vision seemed still to smart and ache with the radiance of the light he had seen in his "star" and that roseate sunset-flush of "glory in the south" created by the clustering angels who were "the friends of Lilith." Why were they there?—what did they wait for?—how should Lilith know them or have any intention of joining them, when she was here,—here on the earth, as he, Féraz, knew,—here under the supreme dominance of his own brother? He dared not speculate too far; and, trying to dismiss all thought from his mind, he was proceeding towards his own room there to retire for the night, when he met Zaroba coming down the stairs. Her dark withered face had a serene and almost happy expression upon it,—she smiled as she saw him.

"It is a night for dreams—" she said, sinking her harsh voice to a soft almost musical cadence—"And as the multitude of the stars in heaven, so are the countless heart-throbs that pulsate in the world at this hour to the silver sway of the moon. All over the world!—all over the world!—" and she swung her arms to and fro with a slow rhythmical movement, so that the silver bangles on them clashed softly like the subdued tinkling of bells;—then, fixing her black eyes upon Féraz with a mournful yet kindly gaze she added—"Not for you—not for you, gentlest of dreamers! not for you! It is destined that you should dream,—and for you, dreaming is best,—but for me—I would rather live one hour than dream for a century!"

Her words were vague and wild as usual,—yet somehow Féraz chafed under the hidden sense of them, and he gave a slight petulant gesture of irritation. Zaroba, seeing it, broke into a low laugh.

"As God liveth,—" she muttered—"The poor lad fights bravely! He hates the world without ever having known it,—and recoils from love without ever having tasted it! He chooses a thought, a rhyme, a song, an art, rather than a passion! Poor lad—poor lad! Dream on, child!—but pray that you may never wake. For to dream of love may be sweet, but to wake without it is bitter!"

Like a gliding wraith she passed him and disappeared. Féraz had a mind to follow her downstairs to the basement where she had the sort of rough sleeping accommodation her half-savage nature preferred, whenever she slept at all out of Lilith's room, which was but seldom,—yet on second thoughts he decided he would let her alone.

"She only worries me—" he said to himself half vexedly as he went to his own little apartment—"It was she who first disobeyed El-Râmi, and made me disobey him also, and though she did take me to see the wonderful Lilith, what was the use of it? Her matchless beauty compelled my adoration, my enthusiasm, my reverence, almost my love—but who could dare to love such a removed angelic creature? Not even El-Râmi himself,—for he must know, even as I feel, that she is beyond all love, save the Love Divine."

He cast off his loose Eastern dress, and prepared to lie down, when he was startled by a faint far sound of singing. He listened attentively;— it seemed to come from outside, and he quickly flung open his window, which only opened upon a little narrow backyard such as is common to London houses. But the moonlight transfigured its ugliness, making it look like a square white court set in walls of silver. The soft rays fell caressingly too on the bare bronze-tinted shoulders of Féraz, as half undressed, he leaned out, his eyes upturned to the halcyon heavens. Surely, surely there was singing somewhere,—why, he could distinguish words amid the sounds!

Away, away!
Where the glittering planets whirl and swim
And the glory of the sun grows dim
Away, away!
To the regions of light and fire and air
Where the spirits of life are everywhere
Come, oh come away!

Trembling in every limb, Féraz caught the song distinctly, and held his breath in fear and wonder.

Away, away!
Come, oh come! we have waited long
And we sing thee now a summoning-song
Away, away!
Thou art freed from the world of the dreaming dead.

And the splendours of Heaven are round thee spread—
Come away!—away!

The chorus grew fainter and fainter—yet still sounded like a distant musical hum on the air.

"It is my fancy"—murmured Féraz at last, as he drew in his head and noiselessly shut the window—"It is the work of my own imagination, or what is perhaps more probable, the work of El-Râmi's will. I have heard such music before,—at his bidding—no, not such music, but something very like it."

He waited a few minutes, then quietly knelt down to pray,—but no words suggested themselves, save the phrase that once before had risen to his lips that day,—"God defend Lilith!"

He uttered it aloud,—then sprang up confused and half afraid, for the name had rung out so clearly that it seemed like a call or a command.

"Well!" he said, trying to steady his nerves—"What if I did say it? There is no harm in the words 'God defend her.' If she is dead, as El-Râmi says, she needs no defence, for her soul belongs to God already."

He paused again,—the silence everywhere was now absolutely unbroken and intense, and repelling the vague presentiments that threatened to oppress his mind, he threw himself on his bed and was soon sound asleep.

IV

And what of the "sign" promised by Lilith? Had it been given? No,—but El-Râmi's impatience would brook no longer delay, and he had determined to put an end to his perplexities by violent means if necessary, and take the risk of whatever consequences might ensue. He had been passing through the strangest phases of thought and self-analysis during these latter weeks,—trying, reluctantly enough, to bend his haughty spirit down to an attitude of humility and patience which ill suited him. He was essentially masculine in his complete belief in himself,—and more than all things he resented any interference with his projects, whether such interference were human or Divine. When therefore the tranced Lilith had bidden him "wait, watch and pray," she had laid upon him the very injunctions he found most difficult to follow. He could wait and watch if he were certain of results,—but where there was the slightest glimmer of un certainty, he grew very soon tired of both waiting and watching. As for "praying"—he told himself arrogantly that to ask for what he could surely obtain by the exerted strength of his own will was not only superfluous, but implied great weakness of character. It was then, in the full-armed spirit of pride and assertive dominance that he went up that night to Lilith's chamber, and dismissing Zaroba with more than usual gentleness of demeanour towards her, sat down beside the couch on which his lovely and mysterious "subject" lay, to all appearances inanimate save for her quiet breathing. His eyes were sombre, yet glittered with a somewhat dangerous lustre under their drooping lids;—he was to be duped no longer, he said to himself,—he had kept faithful vigil night after night, hoping against hope, believing against belief, and not the smallest movement or hint that could be construed into the promised "sign" had been vouchsafed to him. And all his old doubts returned to chafe and fret his brain,—doubts as to whether he had not been deceiving himself all this while in spite of his boasted scepticism,—and whether Lilith, when she spoke, was not merely repeating like a mechanical automaton, the stray thoughts of his own mind reflected upon hers? He had "proved" the possibility of that kind of thing occurring between human beings who were scarcely connected with each other even by a tie of ordinary friendship—how much more likely then that it should happen in such a case as that of Lilith,—Lilith who had been under the sole dominance of his will for six years! Yet while he thus teased himself with misgivings, he knew it was impossible to account for the mystic tendency of her language, or the strange and super-sensual character of the information she gave or feigned to give. It was not from himself or his own information that he had obtained a description of the landscapes in Mars,—its wondrous red fields,—its rosy foliage and flowers,—its great jagged rocks ablaze with amethystine spar,—its huge conical shells, tall and light, that rose up like fairy towers, fringed with flags and garlands of marine blossom, out of oceans the colour of jasper and pearl. Certainly too, it was not from the testimony of his inner consciousness that he had evoked the faith that seemed so natural to her; her belief in a Divine Personality, and his utter rejection of any such idea, were two things wider asunder than the poles, and had no possible sort of connection. Nevertheless what he could not account for, wearied him out and irritated him by its elusiveness and unprovable character,—and finally, his long, frequent, and profitless reflections on the matter had brought him this night up to a point of determination which but a few months back would have seemed to him impossible. He had resolved to waken Lilith. What sort of a being she would seem when once awakened, he could not quite imagine. He knew she had died in his arms as a child,—and that her seeming life now, and her growth into the loveliness of womanhood was the result of artificial means evolved from the wonders of chemistry,—but he persuaded himself that though her existence was the work of science and not nature, it was better than natural, and would last as long. He determined he would break that mysterious trance of body in which the departing Intelligence had been, by his skill, detained and held in connection with its earthly habitation,—he would transform the sleeping visionary into a living woman, for—he loved her. He could no longer disguise from himself that her fair face with its heavenly smile, framed in the golden hair that circled it like a halo, haunted him in every minute of time,—he could not and would not deny that his whole being ached to clasp with a lover's embrace that exquisite beauty which had so long been passively surrendered to his experimentings,—and with the daring of a proud and unrestrained nature, he frankly avowed his feeling to himself and made no pretence of hiding it any longer. But it was a far deeper mystery than his "search for the Soul of Lilith," to find out when and how this passion had first arisen in him. He could not analyse himself so thoroughly as to discover its vague beginnings. Perhaps it was germinated by Zaroba's wild promptings,—perhaps by the fact that a certain unreasonable jealousy had chafed his spirit when he knew that his brother Féraz had won a smile of attention and response from the tranced girl,—perhaps it was owing to the irritation he had felt at the idea that his visitor, the monk from Cyprus, seemed to know more of her than he himself did,—at any rate, whatever the cause, he who had been sternly impassive once to the subtle attraction of Lilith's outward beauty, madly adored that outward beauty now. And as is usual with very self-reliant and proud dispositions, he almost began to glory in a sentiment which but a short time ago he would have repelled and scorned. What was for himself and of himself was good in his sight—his knowledge, his "proved" things, his tested discoveries, all these were excellent in his opinion, and the "Ego" of his own ability was the pivot on which all his actions turned. He had laid his plans carefully for the awakening of Lilith,—but in one little trifle they had been put out by the absence from town of Madame Irene Vassilius. She, of all women he had ever met, was the one he would have trusted with his secret, because he knew that her life, though lived in the world, was as stainless as though it were lived in heaven. He had meant to place Lilith in her care,—in order that with her fine perceptions, lofty ideals, and delicate sense of all things beautiful and artistic, she might accustom the girl to look upon the fairest and noblest side of life, so that she might not regret the "visions"—yes, he would call them "visions"—she had lost. But Irene was among the mountains of the Austrian Tyrol, enjoying a holiday in the intimate society of the fairest Queen in the world, Margherita of Italy, one of the few living Sovereigns who really strive to bestow on intellectual worth its true appreciation and reward. And her house in London was shut up, and under the sole charge of the happy Karl, former servant to Dr. Kremlin, who had now found with the fair and famous authoress a situation that suited him exactly. "Wild horses would not tear him from his lady's service" he was wont to say, and he guarded her household interests jealously, and said "Not at home" to undesired visitors like Roy Ainsworth for example, with a gruffness that would have done credit to a Russian bear. To Irene Vassilius, therefore, El-Râmi could not turn for the help he had meant to ask; and he was sorry and disappointed, for he had particularly wished to remove his "sleeper awakened" out of the companionship of both Zaroba and Féraz,—and there was no other woman like Irene,— at once so pure and proud, so brilliantly gifted, and so far removed from the touch and taint of modern social vulgarity. However, her aid was now unattainable, and he had to make up his mind to do without it. And so he resolutely put away the thought of the after-results of Lilith's awakening,—he, who was generally so careful to calculate consequences, instinct—ively avoided the consideration of them in the present instance.

The little silver timepiece ticked with an aggressive loudness as he sat now at his usual post, his black eyes fixed half-tenderly, half-fiercely on Lilith's white beauty,—beauty which was, as he told himself, all his own. Her arms were folded across her breast,—her features were pallid as marble, and her breathing was very light and low. The golden lamp burned dimly as it swung from the purple-pavilioned ceiling—the scent of the roses that were always set fresh in their vase every day, filled the room, and though the windows were closed against the night, a dainty moonbeam strayed in through a chink where the draperies were not quite drawn, and mingled its emerald glitter with the yellow lustre shed by the lamp on the darkly-carpeted floor.

"I will risk it,"—said El-Râmi in a whisper,—a whisper that sounded loud in the deep stillness—"I will risk it—why not? I have proved myself capable of arresting life, or the soul—for life is the soul—in its flight from hence into the Nowhere,—I must needs also have the power to keep it indefinitely here for myself in whatever form I please. These are the rewards of science,—rewards which I am free to claim,—and what I have done, that I have a right to do again. Now let me ask myself the question plainly;—Do I believe in the supernatural?"

He paused, thinking earnestly,—his eyes still fixed on Lilith.

"No, I do not,"—he answered himself at last—"Frankly and honestly, I do not. I have no proofs. I am, it is true, puzzled by Lilith's language,—but when I know her as she is, a woman, sentient and conscious of my presence, I may find out the seeming mystery. The dreams of Féraz are only dreams,—the vision I saw on that one occasion"—and a faint tremor came over him as he remembered the sweet yet solemn look of the shining One he had seen standing between him and his visitor the monk—"the vision was of course his work—the work of that mystic master of a no less mystic brotherhood. No—I have no proofs of the supernatural, and I must not deceive myself. Even the promise of Lilith fails. Poor child!—she sleeps like the daughter of Jairus, but when I, in my turn, pronounce the words 'Maiden I say unto thee, arise'—she will obey;—she will awake and live indeed."

"She will awake and live indeed!"

The words were repeated after him distinctly—but by whom? He started up,—looked round—there was no one in the room,—and Lilith was immovable as the dead. He began to find something chill and sad in the intense silence that followed,—everything about him was a harmony of glowing light and purple colour,—yet all seemed suddenly very dull and dim and cold. He shivered where he stood, and pressed his hands to his eyes,—his temples throbbed and ached, and he felt curiously bewildered. Presently, looking round the room again, he saw that the picture of "Christ and His Disciples" was unveiled;—he had not noticed the circumstance before. Had Zaroba inadvertently drawn aside the curtain which ordinarily hid it from view? Slowly his eyes travelled to it and dwelt upon it—slowly they followed the letters of the inscription beneath.

"Whom Say Ye That I Am?"

The question seemed to him for the moment all-paramount; he could not shake off the sense of pertinacious demand with which it impressed him.

"A good Man,"—he said aloud, staring fixedly at the divine Face and Figure, with its eloquent expression of exalted patience, grandeur and sweetness. "A good Man, misled by noble enthusiasm and unselfish desire to benefit the poor. A man with a wise knowledge of human magnetism and the methods of healing in which it can be employed,—a man too, somewhat skilled in the art of optical illusion. Yet when all is said and done, a good Man—too good and wise and pure for the peace of the rulers of the world,—too honest and clear-sighted to deserve any other reward but death. Divine?—No!—save in so far as in our highest moments we are all divine. Existing now?—a Prince of Heaven, a Pleader against Punishment? Nay, nay!—no more existing than the Soul of Lilith,—that soul for which I search, but which I feel I shall never find!"

And he drew nearer to the ivory-satin couch on which lay the lovely sleeping wonder and puzzle of his ambitious dreams. Leaning towards her he touched her hands,—they were cold, but as he laid his own upon them they grew warm and trembled. Closer still he leaned, his eyes drinking in every detail of her beauty with eager, proud and masterful eyes.

"Lilith!—my Lilith!" he murmured—"After all, why should we put off happiness for the sake of everlastingness, when happiness can be had, at any rate for a few years. One can but live and die and there an end. And Love comes but once, . . . Love!—how I have scoffed at it and made a jest of it as if it were a plaything. And even now while my whole heart craves for it, I question whether it is worth having! Poor Lilith!—only a woman after all,—a woman whose beauty will soon pass—whose days will soon be done,—only a woman—not an immortal Soul,—there is, there can be, no such thing as an immortal Soul."

Bending down over her, he resolutely unclasped the fair crossed arms, and seized the delicate small hands in a close grip.

"Lilith! Lilith!" he called imperiously.

A long and heavy pause ensued,—then the girl's limbs quivered violently as though moved by a sudden convulsion, and her lips parted in the utterance of the usual formula—

"I am here."

"Here at last, but you have been absent long"—said El-Râmi with some reproach, "Too long. And you have forgotten your promise."

"Forgotten!" she echoed—"O doubting spirit! Do such as I am, ever forget?"

Her thrilling accents awed him a little, but he pursued his own way with her, undauntedly.

"Then why have you not fulfilled it?" he demanded—"The strongest patience may tire. I have waited and watched, as you bade me—but now—now I am weary of waiting."

Oh, what a sigh broke from her lips!

"I am weary too"—she said—"The angels are weary. God is weary. All Creation is weary—of Doubt."

For a moment he was abashed,—but only for a moment; in himself he considered Doubt to be the strongest part of his nature,—a positive shield and buckler against possible error.

"You cannot wait,"—went on Lilith, speaking slowly and with evident sadness—"Neither can we. We have hoped,—in vain! We have watched—in vain! The strong man's pride will not bend, nor the stubborn spirit turn in prayer to its Creator. Therefore what is not bent must be broken,—and what voluntarily refuses Light must accept Darkness. I am bidden to come to you, my beloved,—to come to you as I am, and as I ever shall be,—I will come—but how will you receive me?"

"With ecstasy, with love, with welcome beyond all words or thoughts!" cried El—Râmi in passionate excitement. "O Lilith, Lilith!

you who read the stars, cannot you read my heart? Do you not see that I—I who have recoiled from the very thought of loving,—I, who have striven to make of myself a man of stone and iron rather than flesh and blood, am conquered by your spells, victorious Lilith!—conquered in every fibre of my being by some subtle witchcraft known to yourself alone. Am I weak?—am I false to my own beliefs? I know not,—I am only conscious of the sovereignty of beauty which has mastered many a stronger man than I. What is the fiercest fire compared to this fever in my veins? I worship you, Lilith! I love you!—more than the world, life, time and hope of heaven, I love you!"

Flushed with eagerness and trembling with his own emotion, he rained kisses on the hands he held, but Lilith strove to withdraw them from his clasp. Pale as alabaster she lay as usual with fast-closed eyes, and again a deep sigh heaved her breast.

"You love my Shadow,"—she said mournfully—"not Myself."

But El-Râmi's rapture was not to be chilled by these words. He gathered up a glittering mass of the rich hair that lay scattered on the pillow and pressed it to his lips.

"O Lilith mine, is this 'Shadow'?" he asked—"All this gold in which I net my heart like a willingly caught bird, and make an end of my boasted wisdom? Are these sweet lips, these fair features, this exquisite body, all 'shadow'? Then blessed must be the light that casts so gracious a reflection! Judge me not harshly, my Sweet,—for if indeed you are Divine, and this Beauty I behold is the mere reflex of Divinity, let me see the Divine Form of you for once, and have a guarantee for faith through love! If there is another and a fairer Lilith than the one whom I now behold, deny me not the grace of so marvellous a vision! I am ready!—I fear nothing—tonight I could face God Himself undismayed!"

He paused abruptly—he knew not why. Something in the chill and solemn look of Lilith's face checked his speech.

"Lilith—Lilith!" he began again whisper—ingly—"Do I ask too much? Surely not—not if you love me! And you do love me—I feel, I know you do!"

There was a long pause,—Lilith might have been made of marble for all the movement she gave. Her breathing was so light as to be scarcely perceptible, and when she answered him at last, her voice sounded strangely faint and far-removed. "Yes, I love you"—she said—"I love you as I have loved you for a thousand ages, and as you have never loved me. To win your love has been my task—to repel my love has been yours.

He listened, smitten by a vague sense of compunction and regret.

"But you have conquered, Lilith"—he answered—"yours is the victory. And have I not surrendered, willingly, joyfully? O my beautiful Dreamer, what would you have me do?"

"Pray!" said Lilith, with a sudden passionate thrill in her voice—"Pray! Repent!"

El-Râmi drew himself backward from her couch, impatient and angered.

"Repent!" he cried aloud—"And why should I repent? What have I done that calls for repentance? For what sin am I to blame? For doubting a God who, deaf to centuries upon centuries of human prayer and worship, will not declare Himself? and for striving to perceive Him through the cruel darkness by which we are surrounded? What crime can be discovered there? The world is most infinitely sad,—and life is most infinitely dreary,—and may I not strive to comfort those amid the struggle who fain would 'prove' and hold fast to the things beyond? Nay!—let the heavens open and cast forth upon me their fiery thunderbolts I will not repent! For, vast as my Doubt is, so vast would be my Faith, if God would speak and say to His creatures but once—'Lo! I am here!' Tortures of hell-pain would not terrify me, if in the end His Being were made clearly manifest—a cross of endless woe would I endure, to feel and see Him near me at the last, and more than all, to make the world feel and see Him,—to prove to wondering, trembling, terror-stricken, famished, heart-broken human beings that He exists,—that He is aware of their misery,—that He cares for them, that it is all well for them,—that there is Eternal Joy hiding itself somewhere amid the great star-thickets of this monstrous universe—that we are not desolate atoms whirled by a blind fierce Force into life against our will, and out of it again without a shadow of reason or a glimmer of hope. Repent for such thoughts as these? I will not! Pray to a God of such inexorable silence? I will not! No, Lilith—my Lilith whom I snatched from greedy death—even you may fail me at the last,—you may break your promise,—the promise that I should see with mortal eyes your own Immortal Self—who can blame you for the promise of a dream, poor child! You may prove yourself nothing but woman; woman, poor, frail, weak, helpless woman, to be loved and cherished and pitied and caressed in all the delicate limbs, and kissed in all the dainty golden threads of hair, and then—then—to be laid down like a broken flower in the tomb that has grudged me your beauty all this while,—all this may be, Lilith, and yet I will not pray to an unproved God, nor repent of an unproved sin!"

He uttered his words with extraordinary force and eloquence—one would have thought he was addressing a multitude of hearers instead of that one tranced girl, who, though beautiful as a sculptured saint on a sarcophagus, appeared almost as inanimate, save for the slow parting of her lips when she spoke.

"O superb Angel of the Kingdom!" she murmured—"It is no marvel that you fell!"

He heard her, dimly perplexed; but strengthened in his own convictions by what he had said, he was conscious of power,—power to defy, power to endure, power to command. Such a sense of exhilaration and high confidence had not possessed him for many a long day, and he was about to speak again, when Lilith's voice once more stole musically on the silence.

"You would reproach God for the world's misery. Your complaint is unjust. There is a Law,—a Law for the earth as for all worlds; and God cannot alter one iota of that Law without destroying Himself and His Universe. Shall all Beauty, all Order, all Creation come to an end because wilful Man is wilfully miserable? Your world trespasses against the Law in almost everything it does—hence its suffering. Other worlds accept the Law and fulfil it,—and with them, all is well."

"Who is to know this Law?" demanded El-Râmi impatiently. "And how can the world trespass against what is not explained?"

"It is explained;"—said Lilith—"The explanation is in every soul's inmost consciousness. You all know the Law and feel it—but knowing, you ignore it. Men were intended by Law—God's Law—to live in brotherhood; but your world is divided into nations all opposed to each other,—the result is Evil. There is a Law of Health, which men can scarcely be forced to follow—the majority disobey it; again, the result is Evil. There is a Law of 'Enough'—men grasp more than enough, and leave their brother with less than enough,—the result is Evil. There is a Law of Love—men make it a Law of Lust,—the result is Evil. All Sin, all Pain, all Misery, are results of the Law's transgression,—and God cannot alter the Law, He Himself being part of it and its fulfilment."

"And is Death also the Law?" asked El-Râmi—"Wise Lilith!—Death, which concludes all things, both in Law and Order?"

"There is no death."—responded Lilith—"I have told you so. What you call by that name is Life."

"Prove it!" exclaimed El-Râmi excitedly, "Prove it, Lilith! Show me Yourself! If there is another You than this beloved beauty of your visible form, let me behold it, and then—then will I repent of doubt,—then will I pray for pardon!"

"You will repent indeed,"—said Lilith sorrowfully—"And you will pray as children pray when first they learn 'Our Father.' Yes, I will come to you;—watch for me, O my erring Belovëd!—watch!—for neither my love nor my promise can fail. But O remember that you are not ready—that your will, your passion, your love, forces me hither ere the time,—that if I come, it is but to depart again—forever!"

"No, no!" cried El-Râmi desperately—"Not to depart, but to remain!—to stay with me, my Lilith, my own—body and soul,—forever!"

The last words sounded like a defiance flung at some invisible opponent. He stopped, trembling—for a sudden and mysterious wave of sound filled the room, like a great wind among the trees, or the last grand chord of an organ-symphony. A chill fear assailed him,—he kept his eyes fixed on the beautiful form of Lilith with a strained eagerness of attention that made his temples ache. She grew paler and paler,—and yet, . . . absorbed in his intent scrutiny he could not move or speak. His tongue seemed tied to the roof of his mouth,—he felt as though he could scarcely breathe All life appeared to hang on one supreme moment of time, which like a point of light wavered between earth and heaven, mortality and infinity. He,—one poor atom in the vast Universe,—stood, audaciously waiting for the declaration of God's chiefest Secret! Would it be revealed at last?—or still withheld?

V

All at once, while he thus closely watched her, Lilith with a violent effort, sat up stiffly erect and turned her head slowly towards him. Her features were rigidly statuesque, and white as snow,—the strange gaunt look of her face terrified him, but he could not cry out or utter a word—he was stricken dumb by an excess of fear. Only his black eyes blazed with an anguish of expectation,—and the tension of his nerves seemed almost greater than he could endure.

"In the great Name of God and by the Passion of Christ,"—said Lilith solemnly, in tones that sounded far-off and faint and hollow—"do not look at this Shadow of Me! Turn, turn away from this dust of Earth which belongs to the Earth alone,—and watch for the light of Heaven which comes from Heaven alone! O my love, my belovëd!—if you are wise, if you are brave, if you are strong, turn away from beholding this Image of Me, which is not Myself,—and look for me where the roses are—there will I stand and wait!"

As the last word left her lips she sank back on her pillows, inert, and deathly pale; but El-Râmi, dazed and bewildered though he was, retained sufficient consciousness to understand vaguely what she meant,—he was not to look at her as she lay there,—he was to forget that such a Lilith as he knew existed,—he was to look for another Lilith there—"where the roses are." Mechanically, and almost as if some invisible power commanded and controlled his volition, he turned sideways round from the couch, and fixed his gaze on the branching flowers, which from the crystal vase that held them, lifted their pale-pink heads daintily aloft as though they took the lamp that swung from the ceiling for some little new sun, specially invented for their pleasure. Why,—there was nothing there; . . . "Nothing there!" he half-muttered with a beating heart, rubbing his eyes and staring hard before him, . . . nothing—nothing at all, but the roses themselves, and. . . and. . . yes!—a Light behind them!—a light that wavered round them and began to stretch upward in wide circling rings!

El-Râmi gazed and gazed, . . . saying over and over again to himself that it was the reflection of the lamp, . . . the glitter of that stray moonbeam there, . . . or something wrong with his own faculty of vision, . . . and yet he gazed on, as though for the moment, all his being were made of eyes. The roses trembled and swayed to and fro delicately as the strange Light widened and brightened behind their blossoming clusters,—a light that seemed to palpitate with all the wondrous living tints of the rising sun when it shoots forth its first golden rays from the foaming green hollows of the sea. Upward, upward and ever upward the deepening glory extended, till the lamp paled and grew dimmer than the spark of a feeble match struck as a rival to a flash of lightning,—and El-Râmi's breath came and went in hard panting gasps as he stood watching it in speechless immobility.

Suddenly, two broad shafts of rainbow luminance sprang, as it seemed from the ground, and blazed against the purple hangings of the room with such a burning dazzle of prismatic colouring in every glittering line, that it was well-nigh impossible for human sight to bear it, and yet El-Râmi would rather have been stricken stone-blind than move. Had he been capable of thought, he might have remembered the beautiful old Greek myths which so truthfully and frequently taught the lesson that to look upon the purely divine, meant death to the purely human; but he could not think,—all his own mental faculties were for the time rendered numb and useless. His eyes ached and smarted as though red-hot needles were being plunged into them, but though he was conscious of, he was indifferent to the pain. His whole mind was concentrated on watching the mysterious radiance of those wing-shaped rays in the room,—and now... now while he gazed, he began to perceive an Outline between the rays, ... a Shape, becoming every second more and more distinct, as though some invisible heavenly artist were drawing the semblance of Beauty in air with a pencil dipped in morning-glory... O wonderful, ineffable Vision!—O marvellous breaking forth of the buds of life that are hid in the quiet ether!—where, where in the vast wealth and reproduction of deathless and delicate atoms, is the Beginning of things?—where the End? ...

Presently appeared soft curves, and glimmers of vapoury white flushed with rose, suggestive of fire seen through mountain-mist,— then came a glittering flash of gold that went rippling and ever rippling backward, like the flowing fall of lovely hair; and the dim Shape grew still more clearly visible, seeming to gather substance and solidity from the very light that encircled it. Had it any human likeness? Yes,—yet the resemblance it bore to humanity was so far away, so exalted and ideal, as to be no more like our material form than the actual splendour of the sun is like its painted image. The stature and majesty and brilliancy of it increased,—and now the unspeakable loveliness of a Face too fair for any mortal fairness began to suggest itself dimly; . . . El-Râmi growing faint and dizzy, thought he distinguished white outstretched arms, and hands uplifted in an ecstasy of prayer;—nay,—though he felt himself half-swooning in the struggle he made to overcome his awe and fear, he would have sworn that two star-like eyes, full-orbed and splendid with a radiant blue as of Heaven's own forget-me-nots, were turned upon him with a questioning appeal, a hope, a supplication, a love beyond all eloquence! . . . But his strength was rapidly failing him;—unsupported by faith, his mere unassisted flesh and blood could endure no more of this supernatural sight, and. . . all suddenly,..the tension o his nerves gave way, and morbid terrors shook his frame. A blind frenzied feeling that he was sinking,—sinking out of sight and sense into a drear profound, possessed him, and hardly knowing what he did, he turned desperately to the couch where Lilith, the Lilith he knew best lay, and looking,—

"Ah God!" he cried, pierced to the heart by the bitterest anguish he had ever known,—Lilith—his Lilith was withering before his very eyes! The exquisite Body he had watched and tended was shrunken and yellow as a fading leaf,—the face, no longer beautiful, was gaunt and pinched and skeleton-like—the lips were drawn in and blue,—and strange convulsions shook the wrinkling and sunken breast!

In one mad moment he forgot everything,—forgot the imperishable Soul for the perishing Body,—forgot his long studies and high ambitions,—and could think of nothing, except that this human creature he had saved from death seemed now to be passing into death's long-denied possession,—and throwing himself on the couch he clutched at his fading treasure with the desperation of frenzy.

"Lilith!—Lilith!" he cried hoarsely, the extremity of his terror choking his voice to a smothered wild moan—"Lilith! My love, my idol, my spirit, my saint! Come back!—come back!"

And clasping her in his arms he covered with burning kisses the thin peaked face—the shrinking flesh,—the tarnishing lustre of the once bright hair.

"Lilith! Lilith!" he wailed, dry-eyed and fevered with agony—"Lilith, I love you! Has love no force to keep you? Lilith, love Lilith! You shall not leave me,—you are mine—mine! I stole you from death—I kept you from God!—from all the furies of heaven and earth!—you shall come back to me—I love you!"

And lo! . . . as he spoke the body he held to his heart grew warm,—

the flesh filled up and regained its former softness and roundness—the features took back their loveliness—the fading hair brightened to its wonted rich tint and rippled upon the pillows in threads of gold—the lips reddened,—the eyelids quivered,—the little hands, trembling gently like birds' wings, nestled round his throat with a caress that thrilled his whole being and calmed the tempest of his grief as suddenly as when of old the Master walked upon the raging sea of Galilee and said to it "Peace, be still!"

Yet this very calmness oppressed him heavily,—like a cold hand laid on a fevered brow it chilled his blood even while it soothed his pain. He was conscious of a sense of irreparable loss,—and moreover he felt he had been a coward,—a coward physically and morally. For, instead of confronting the Supernatural, or what seemed the Supernatural calmly, and with the inquisitorial research of a scientist, he had allowed himself to be overcome by It, and had fled back to the consideration of the merely human, with all the delirious speed of a lover and fool. Nevertheless he had his Lilith—his own Lilith,—and holding her jealously to his heart, he presently turned his head tremblingly and in doubt to where the roses nodded drowsily in their crystal vase;—only the roses now were there! The marvellous Wingëd Brightness had fled, and the place it had illumined seemed by contrast very dark. The Soul,—the Immortal Self—had vanished;—the subtle Being he had longed to see, and whose existence and capabilities he had meant to "prove"; and he, who had consecrated his life and labour to the attainment of this one object had failed to grasp the full solution of the mystery at the very moment when it might have been his. By his own weakness he had lost the Soul,—by his own strength he had gained the Body,—or so he thought, and his mind was torn between triumph and regret. He was not yet entirely conscious of what had chanced to him—he could formulate no idea,— all he distinctly knew was that he held Lilith, warm and living, in his arms, and that he felt her light breath upon his cheek.

"Love is enough!" he murmured, kissing the hair that lay in golden clusters against his breast—"Waken, my Lilith!—waken!—and in our perfect joy we will defy all gods and angels!"

She stirred in his clasp,—he bent above her, eager, ardent, expectant,—her long eyelashes trembled,—and then,—slowly, slowly, like white leaves opening to the sun, the lids upcurled, disclosing the glorious eyes beneath,—eyes that had been closed to earthly things for six long years,—deep, starry violet-blue eyes that shone with the calm and holy lustre of unspeakable purity and peace,—eyes that in their liquid softness held all the appeal, hope, supplication and eloquent love, he had seen (or fancied he had seen) in the strange eyes of the only half-visible Soul! The Soul indeed was looking through its earthly windows for the last time, had he known it,—but he did not know it. Raised to as giddy a pinnacle of delight as suddenly as he had been lately plunged into an abyss of grief and terror, he gazed into those newly-opened wondrous worlds of mute expression with all a lover's pride, passion, tenderness and longing.

"Fear nothing, Lilith!" he said—"It is I! I whose voice you have answered and obeyed,—I, your lover and lord! It is I who claim you, my belovëd!—I who bid you waken from death to life!"

Oh, what a smile of dazzling rapture illumined her face!—it was as if the sun in all his glory had suddenly broken out of a cloud to brighten her beauty with his purest beams. Her child-like, innocent, wondering eyes remained fixed upon El-Râmi,—lifting her white arms languidly she closed them round about him with a gentle fervour that seemed touched by compassion,—and he, thrilled to the quick by that silent expression of tenderness, straightway ascended to a heaven of blind, delirious ecstasy. He wanted no word from her. . . what use of words!—her silence was the perfect eloquence of love! All her beauty was his own—his very own! . . . he had willed it so,—and his will had won its way,—the iron Will of a strong wise man without a God to help him!—and all he feared was that he might die of his own excess of triumph and joy! . . . Hush! . . . hush! . . . Music again!—that same deep sound as of the wind among trees, or the solemn organ-chord that closes the song of departing choristers. It was strange,—very strange!—but though he heard, he scarcely heeded it; unearthly terrors could not shake him now,—not now, while he held Lilith to his heart, and devoured her loveliness with his eyes, curve by curve, line by line, till with throbbing pulses, and every nerve tingling in his body, he bent his face down to hers, and pressed upon her lips a long, burning passionate kiss! . . .

But, even as he did so, she was wrenched fiercely out of his hold by a sudden and awful convulsion,—her slight frame writhed and twisted itself away from his clasp with a shuddering recoil of muscular agony—once her little hands clutched the air, . . . and then,..then, the brief struggle over, her arms dropped rigidly at her sides, and her whole body swerved and fell backward heavily upon the pillows of the couch, stark, pallid and pulseless! . . . And he,—he, gazing upon her thus with a vague and stupid stare, wondered dimly whether he were mad or dreaming? . . .

What. . . what was this sudden ailment? . . . this. . . this strange swoon? What bitter frost had stolen into her veins? . . . what insatiable hell-fire was consuming his? Those eyes, . . . those just unclosed, innocent lovely eyes of Lilith, . . . was it possible, could it be true that all the light had gone out of them?—gone, utterly gone? And what was that clammy film beginning to cover them over with a glazing veil of blankness? . . . God! . . . God! . . . he must be in a wild nightmare, he thought! . . . he should wake up presently and find all this seeming disaster unreal,—the fantastic fear of a sick brain..the "clangour and anger of elements" imaginative, not actual, . . . and here his reeling terror found voice in a hoarse, smothered cry—

"Lilith! . . . Lilith! . . ."

But stop, stop! . . . was it Lilith indeed whom he thus called? . . . That? . . . that gaunt, sunken, rigid form, growing swiftly hideous! . . . yes—hideous, with those dull marks of blue discoloration coming here and there on the no longer velvety fair skin!

"Lilith! . . . Lilith!"

The name was lost and drowned in the wave of solemn music that rolled and throbbed upon the air, and El-Râmi's distorted mind, catching at the dread suggestiveness of that unearthly harmony, accepted it as a sort of invisible challenge.

"What, good Death! brother Death, are you there?" he muttered fiercely, shaking his clenched fist at vacancy—"Are you here, and are you everywhere? Nay, we have crossed swords before now in desperate combat. . . and I have won! . . . and I will win again! Hands off, rival Death! Lilith is mine!"

And, snatching from his breast a phial of the liquid with which he had so long kept Lilith living in a trance, he swiftly injected it into her veins, and forced some drops between her lips. . . in vain. . . in vain! No breath came back to stir that silent breast—no sign whatever of returning animation evinced itself, only, . . . at the expiration of the few moments which generally sufficed the vital fluid for its working, there chanced a strange and terrible thing. Wherever the liquid had made its way, there the skin blistered, and the flesh blackened, as though the whole body were being consumed by some fierce inward fire; and El-Râmi, looking with strained wild eyes at this destructive result of his effort to save, at last realized to the full all the awfulness, all the dire agony of his fate! The Soul of Lilith had departed for ever; . . . even as the Cyprian monk had said, it had outgrown its earthly tenement, . . . its cord of communication with the body had been mysteriously and finally severed,—and the Body itself was crumbling into ashes before his very sight, helped into swifter dissolution by the electric potency of his own vaunted "life-elixir"! It was horrible. . . horrible! . . . was there no remedy?

Staring himself almost blind with despair, he dashed the phial on the ground, and stamped it under his heel in an excess of impotent fury, . . . the veins in his forehead swelled with a fulness of aching blood almost to bursting, . . . he could do nothing, . . . nothing! His science was of no avail;—his Will,—his proud inflexible Will was "as a reed shaken in the wind!" . . Ha! . . . the old stock phrase! . . . it had been said before, in old times and in new, by canting creatures who believed in Prayer. Prayer!—would it bring back beauty and vitality to that blackening corpse before him? . . . that disfigured, withering clay he had once called Lilith! . . . How ghastly It looked! . . . Shuddering violently he turned away,—turned,—to meet the grave sweet eyes of the pictured Christ on the wall, . . . to read again the words, "WHOM SAY YE THAT I AM?" The letters danced before him in characters of flame, . . . there seemed a great noise everywhere as of clashing steam-hammers and great church-bells,—the world was reeling round him as giddily as a spun wheel.

"Robber of the Soul of Lilith!" he muttered between his set teeth— "Whoever you be, whether God or Devil, I will find you out! I will pursue you to the uttermost ends of vast infinitude! I will contest her with you yet, for surely she is mine! What right have you, O Force Unknown, to steal my love from me? Answer me!—prove yourself God, as I prove myself Man! Declare something, O mute Inflexible!—Do some—thing other than mechanically grind out a reasonless, unexplained Life and Death for ever! O Lilith!—faithless Angel!—did you not say that love was sweet?—and could not love keep you here,—here, with me, your lover, Lilith?"

Involuntarily and with cowering reluctance, his eyes turned again towards the couch,—but now—now..the horror of that decaying beauty, interiorly burning itself away to nothingness was more than he could bear; . . . a mortal sickness seized him,—and he flung up his arms with a desperate gesture as though he sought to drag down some covering wherewith to hide himself and his utter misery.

"Defeated, baffled, befooled!" he exclaimed frantically—"Conquered by the Invisible and Invincible after all! Conquered! I! . . . Who would have thought it! Hear me, earth and heaven!—hear me, O rolling world of Human Wretchedness, hear me!—for I have proved a Truth! There Is a God!—a jealous God—jealous of the Soul of Lilith!—a God tyrannical, absolute, and powerful—a God of infinite and inexorable Justice! O God, I know you!—I own you—I meet you! I am part of you as the worm is!—and you can change me, but you cannot destroy me! You have done your worst,—you have fought against your own Essence in me, till light has turned to darkness and love to bitterness;—you have left me no help, no hope, no comfort; what more remains to do, O terrible God of a million Universes! . . . what more? Gone—gone is the Soul of Lilith—but Where? . . . Where in the vast Unknowable shall I find my love again? . . . Teach me that O God! . . . give me that one small clue through the million million intricate webs of star-systems, and I too will fall blindly down and adore an Imaginary Good invisible and all-paramount Evil! . . . I too will sacrifice reason, pride, wisdom and power and become as a fool for Love's sake! . . . I too will grovel before an unproved Symbol of Divinity as a savage grovels before his stone fetish, . . . I will be weak, not strong, I will babble prayers with the children, . . . only take me where Lilith is, . . . bring me to Lilith. . . angel Lilith! . . . love Lilith! . . . my Lilith! . . . ah God! God! Have mercy. . . mercy! . . ."

His voice broke suddenly in a sharp jarring shriek of delirious laughter,—blood sprang to his mouth,—and with a blind movement of his arms, as of one in thick darkness seeking light, he fell heavily face forward, insensible on the couch where the Body he had loved, deprived of its Soul, lay crumbling swiftly away into hideous disfigurement and ashes.

VI

"Awake, Féraz! Today dreams end, and Life begins."

The words sounded so distinctly in his ears that the half-roused Féraz turned drowsily on his pillows and opened his eyes, fully expecting to see the speaker of them in his room. But there was no one. It was early morning,—the birds were twittering in the outer yard, and bright sunshine poured through the window. He had had a long and refreshing sleep,—and sitting up in his bed he stretched himself with a sense of refreshment and comfort, the while he tried to think what had so mysteriously and unpleasantly oppressed him with forebodings on the previous night. By-and-by he re—membered the singing voices in the air and smiled.

"All my fancy of course!" he said lightly, springing up and beginning to dash the fresh cold water of his morning bath over his polished bronze-like skin, till all his nerves tingled with the pleasurable sensation—"I am always hearing music of some sort or other. I believe music is pent up in the air, and loosens itself at intervals like the rain. Why not? There must be such a wealth of melody aloft,—all the songs of all the birds,—all the whisperings of all the leaves;—all the dash and rush of the rivers, waterfalls and oceans,—it is all in the air, and I believe it falls in a shower sometimes and penetrates the brains of musicians like Beethoven, Schumann and Wagner."

Amused with his own fantastic imaginings he hummed a tune sotto-voce as he donned his easy and picturesque attire,—then he left his room and went to his brother's study to set it in order for the day, as was his usual custom.

He opened the door softly and with caution, because El-Râmi often slept there on the hard soldier's couch that occupied one corner,—but this morning, all was exactly as it had been left at night,—the books and papers were undisturbed,—and, curiously enough, the little sanctum presented a vacant and deserted appearance, as though it would dumbly express a fear that its master was gone from it for ever. How such a notion suggested itself to Féraz, he could not tell,—but he was certainly conscious of a strange sinking at the heart, as he paused in the act of throwing open one of the windows, and looked round the quiet room. Had anything been moved or displaced during the night that he should receive such a general impression of utter emptiness?

Nothing—so far as he could judge;—there was his brother's ebony chair wheeled slightly aside from the desk,—there were the great globes, terrestrial and celestial,—there were the various volumes lately used for reference,—and, apart from these, on the table, was the old vellum book in Arabic that Féraz had once before attempted to read. It was open,—a circum—stance that struck Féraz with some surprise, for he could not recall having seen it in that position last evening. Perhaps El-Râmi had come down in the night to refer to it and had left it there by accident? Féraz felt he must examine it more nearly, and approaching, he rested his elbows on the table and fixed his eyes on the Arabic page before him which was headed in scrolled lettering "The Mystery of Death." As he read the words, a beautiful butterfly flew in through the open window and circled joyously round his head, till presently espying the bunch of heliotrope in the glass where Féraz had set it the previous day, it fluttered off to that, and settled on the scented purple bloom, its pretty wings quivering with happiness. Mechanically Féraz watched its flight,—then his eyes returned and dwelt once more on the time-stained lettering before him; "The Mystery of Death,"—and following the close lines with his fore-finger, he soon made out the ensuing passages. "The Mystery of Death. Whereas, of this there is no mystery at all, as the ignorant suppose, but only a clearing up of many intricate matters. When the body dies,—or to express it with more pertinacious exactitude, when the body resolves itself into the living organisms of which earth is composed, it is because the Soul has outgrown its mortal habitation and can no longer endure the cramping narrowness of the same. We speak unjustly of the aged, because by their taciturnity and inaptitude for worldly business, they seem to us foolish, and of a peevish weakness; it should however be remembered that it is a folly to complain of the breaking of the husk when the corn is ripe. In old age the Soul is weary of and indifferent to earthly things, and makes of its tiresome tenement a querulous reproach,—it has exhausted earth's pleasures and surpassed earth's needs, and palpitates for larger movement. When this is gained, the husk falls, the grain sprouts forth—the Soul is freed,—and all Nature teaches this lesson. To call the process 'death' and a 'mystery' is to repeat the error of barbarian ages,—for once the Soul has no more use for the Body, you cannot detain it,—you cannot com—press its wings,—you cannot stifle its nature,—and, being Eternal, it demands Eternity."

"All that is true enough;"—murmured Féraz—"As true as any truth possible, and yet people will not accept or understand it. All the religions, all the preachers, all the teachers seem to avail them nothing,—and they go on believing in death far more than in life. What a sad and silly world it is!—always planning for itself and never for God, and only turning to God in imminent danger like a coward schoolboy who says he is sorry because he fears a whipping."

Here he lifted his eyes from the book, feeling that someone was looking at him, and true enough, there in the doorway stood Zaroba. Her withered face had an anxious expression and she held up a warning finger.

"Hush! . . ." she said whisperingly. . . "No noise! . . . where is El-Râmi?"

Féraz replied by a gesture, indicating that he was still upstairs at work on his mysterious "experiment."

Zaroba advanced slowly into the room, and seated herself on the nearest chair.

"My mind misgives me;"—she said in low awe-stricken tones,—"My mind misgives me; I have had dreams—such dreams! All night I have tossed and turned,—my head throbs here,"—and she pressed both hands upon her brow,—"and my heart—my heart aches! I have seen strange creatures clad in white,—ghostly faces of the past have stared at me,—my dead children have caressed me,—my dead husband has kissed me on the lips—a kiss of ice, freezing me to the marrow. What does it bode? No good—no good!—but ill! Like the sound of the flying feet of the whirlwind that brings death to the sons of the desert, there is a sound in my brain which says—'Sorrow! Sorrow!' again and yet again 'Sorrow!'"

Sighing, she clasped her hands about her knees and rocked herself to and fro, as though she were in pain. Féraz stood gazing at her wistfully and with a somewhat troubled air,—her words impressed him uncomfortably,—her very attitude suggested misery. The sunlight beaming across her bent figure, flashed on the silver bangles that circled her brown arms, and touched her rough gray hair to flecks of brightness,—her black eyes almost hid themselves under their tired drooping lids,—and when she ceased speaking her lips still moved as though she inwardly muttered some weird incantation. Growing impatient with her, he knew not why, the young man paced slowly up and down the room;—her deafness precluded him from speaking to her, and he just now had no inclination to communicate with her in the usual way by writing. And while he thus walked about, she continued her rocking movement, and peered at him dubiously from under her bushy gray brows.

"It is ill work meddling with the gods;"—she began again presently—"In old time they were vengeful,—and have they changed because the times are new? Nay, nay! The nature of a man may alter with the course of his passions,—but the nature of a god!—who shall make it otherwise than what it has been from the beginning? Cruel, cruel are the ways of the gods when they are thwarted;—there is no mercy in the blind eyes of Fate! To tempt Destiny is to ask the thunderbolt to fall and smite you,—to oppose the gods is as though a babe's hand should essay to lift the Universe. Have I not prayed the Master, the wise and the proud El-Râmi Zarânos, to submit and not contend? As God liveth, I say, let us submit while we can like the slaves that we are, for in submission alone is safety!"

Féraz heard her with increasing irritation,—why need she come to him with all this melancholy jabbering, he thought angrily. He leaned far out of the open window and looked at the ugly houses of the little square,—at the sooty trees, the sparrows hopping and quarrelling in the road, the tradesmen's carts that every now and again dashed to and from their various customers' doors in the aggravatingly mad fashion they affect, and tried to realize that he was actually in busy practical London, and not, as seemed at the moment more likely, in some cavern of an Eastern desert, listening to an ancient sybil croaking misfortune. Just then a neighbouring clock struck nine, and he hastily drew in his head from the outer air, and making language with his eloquent fingers, he mutely asked Zaroba if she were going upstairs now, or whether she meant to wait till El-Râmi himself came down?

She left off rocking to and fro, and half rose from her chair,—then she hesitated.

"I have never waited"—she said—"before,—and why? Because the voice of the Master has roused me from my deepest slumbers,—and like a finger of fire laid on my brain, his very thought has summoned my attendance. But this morning no such voice has called,—no such burning touch has stirred my senses,—how should I know what I must do? If I go unbidden, will he not be angered?—and his anger works like a poison in my blood! . . . yet. . . it is late, . . . and his silence is strange—"

She paused, passing her hand wearily across her eyes,—then stood up, apparently resolved.

"I will obey the voices that whisper to me,"—she said, with a certain majestic resignation and gravity—"The voices that cry to my heart 'Sorrow! Sorrow!' and yet again 'Sorrow!' If grief must come, then welcome, grief!—one cannot gainsay the Fates. I will go hence and prove the message of the air,—for the air holds invisible tongues that do not lie."

With a slow step she moved across the room,—and on a sudden impulse Féraz sprang towards her exclaiming, "Zaroba!—stay!"—then recollecting she could not hear a word, he checked himself and drew aside to let her pass, with an air of indifference which he was far from feeling. He was in truth wretched and ill at ease,—the exhilaration with which he had arisen from sleep had given way to intense depression, and he could not tell what ailed him.

"Awake, Féraz! Today dreams end, and life begins." Those were the strange words he had heard the first thing on awaking that morning,— what could they mean, he wondered rather sadly? If dreams were indeed to end, he would be sorry,—and if life, as mortals generally lived it, were to begin for him, why then, he would be sorrier still. Troubled and perplexed, he began to set the breakfast in order, hoping by occupation to divert his thoughts and combat the miserable feeling of vague dread which oppressed him, and which, though he told himself how foolish and unreasonable it was, remained increasingly persistent. All at once such a cry rang through the house as almost turned his blood to ice,—a cry wild, despairing and full of agony. It was repeated with piercing vehemence,—and Féraz, his heart beating furiously, cleared the space of the room with one breathless bound and rushed upstairs, there to confront Zaroba tossing her arms distractedly and beating her breast like a creature demented.

"Lilith!" she gasped,—"Lilith has gone. . . gone! . . . and El-Râmi is dead!"

VII

Pushing the panic-stricken woman aside, Féraz dashed back the velvet curtains, and for the second time in his life penetrated the mysterious chamber. Once in the beautiful room, rich with its purple colour and warmth, he stopped as though he were smitten with sudden paralysis,—every artery in his body pulsated with terror,—it was true! . . . true that Lilith was no longer there! This was the first astounding fact that bore itself in with awful conviction on his dazed and bewildered mind;—the next thing he saw was the figure of his brother, kneeling motionless by the vacant couch. Hushing his steps and striving to calm his excitement, Féraz approached more nearly, and throwing his arms round El-Râmi's shoulders endeavoured to raise him,—but all his efforts made no impression on that bent and rigid form. Turning his eyes once more to the ivory blankness of the satin couch on which the maiden Lilith had so long reclined, he saw with awe and wonder the distinct impression of where her figure had been, marked and hollowed out into deep curves and lines, which in their turn were outlined by a tracing of fine grayishwhite dust, like sifted ashes. Following the track of this powdery substance, he still more clearly discerned the impress of her vanished shape; and, shuddering in every limb, he asked himself—Could that—that dust—be all—all that was left of. . . of Lilith? . . . What dire tragedy had been enacted during the night?—what awful catastrophe had chanced to her,—to him, his beloved brother, whom he strove once more to lift from his kneeling position, but in vain. Zaroba stood beside him, shivering, wailing, staring, and wringing her hands, till Féraz, dry-eyed and desperate, finding his own strength not sufficient, bade her, by a passionate gesture, assist him. Trembling violently, she obeyed, and between them both they at last managed to drag El-Râmi up from the ground and get him to a chair, where Féraz chafed his hands, bathed his forehead, and used every possible means to restore animation. Did his heart still beat? Yes, feebly and irregularly;—and presently one or two faint gasping sighs came from the labouring breast.

"Thank God!" muttered Féraz—"Whatever has happened, he lives!— Thank God he lives! When he recovers, he will tell me all;—there can be no secrets now between him and me."

And he resumed his quick and careful ministrations, while Zaroba still wailed and wrung her hands, and stared miserably at the empty couch, whereon her beautiful charge had lain, slumbering away the hours and days for six long years. She too saw the little heaps and trackings of gray dust on the pillows and coverlid, and her feeble limbs shook with such terror that she could scarcely stand.

"The gods have taken her!" she whispered faintly through her pallid lips—"The gods are avenged! When did they ever have mercy! They have claimed their own with the breath and the fire of lightning, and the dust of a maiden's beauty is no more than the dust of a flower! The dreadful, terrible gods are avenged—at last. . . at last!"

And sinking down upon the floor, she huddled herself together, and drew her yellow draperies over her head, after the Eastern manner of expressing inconsolable grief, and covered her aged features from the very light of day.

Féraz heeded her not at all, his sole attention being occupied in the care of his brother, whose large black eyes now opened suddenly and regarded him with a vacant expression like the eyes of a blind man. A great shudder ran through his frame,—he looked curiously at his own hands as Féraz gently pressed and rubbed them,—and he stared all round the room in vaguely in—quiring wonderment. Presently his wandering glance came back to Féraz, and the vacancy of his expression softened into a certain pleased mildness,—his lips parted in a little smile, but he said nothing.

"You are better, El-Râmi, my brother?" murmured Féraz caressingly, trembling and almost weeping in the excess of his affectionate anxiety, the while he placed his own figure so that it might obstruct a too immediate view of Lilith's vacant couch, and the covered crouching form of old Zaroba beside it—"You have no pain? . . . you do not suffer?"

El-Râmi made no answer for the moment;—he was looking at Féraz with a gentle but puzzled inquisitiveness. Presently his dark brows contracted slightly, as though he were trying to connect some perplexing chain of ideas,—then he gave a slight gesture of fatigue and indifference.

"You will excuse me, I hope,—" he then said with plaintive courtesy—"I have forgotten your name. I believe I met you once, but I cannot remember where."

The heart of poor Féraz stood still, . . . a great sob rose in his throat. But he checked it bravely,—he would not, he could not, he dared not give way to the awful fear that began to creep like a frost through his warm young blood.

"You cannot remember Féraz?" he said gently—"Your own Féraz? . . . your little brother, to whom you have been life, hope, joy, work—everything of value in the world!" Here his voice failed him, and he nearly broke down.

El-Râmi looked at him in grave surprise.

"You are very good!" he murmured, with a feebly polite wave of his hand;—"You over-rate my poor powers. I am glad to have been useful to you—very glad!"

Here he paused;—his head sank forward on his breast, and his eyes closed.

"El-Râmi!" cried Féraz, the hot tears forcing their way between his eyelids—"Oh, my belovëd brother!—have you no thought for me?"

El-Râmi opened his eyes and stared;—then smiled.

"No thought?" he repeated—"Oh, you mistake!—I have thought very much,—very much indeed, about many things. Not about you perhaps,—but then I do not know you. You say your name is Féraz,—that is very strange; it is not at all a common name. I only knew one Féraz,—he was my brother, or seemed so for a time,—but I found out afterwards, . . . hush! . . . come closer! . . ." and he lowered his voice to a whisper,—"that he was not a mortal, but an angel,—the angel of a Star. The Star knew him better than I did."

Féraz turned away his head,—the tears were falling down his cheeks—he could not speak. He realized the bitter truth,—the delicate overstrained mechanism of his brother's mind had given way under excessive pain and pressure,—that brilliant, proud, astute, cold and defiant intellect was all unstrung and out of gear, and rendered useless, perchance for ever.

El-Râmi however seemed to have some glimmering perception of Féraz's grief, for he put out a trembling hand and turned his brother's face towards him with gentle concern.

"Tears?" he said in a surprised tone—"Why should you weep? There is nothing to weep for;—God is very good."

And with an effort, he rose from the chair in which he had sat, and standing upright, looked about him. His eye at once lighted on the vase of roses at the foot of the couch and he began to tremble violently. Féraz caught him by the arm,—and then he seemed startled and afraid.

"She promised, . . . she promised!" he began in an incoherent rambling way—"and you must not interfere,—you must let me do her bidding. 'Look for me where the roses are; there will I stand and wait!'

She said that,—and she will wait, and I will look, for she is sure to keep her word—no angel ever forgets. You must not hinder me;—I have to watch and pray,—you must help me, not hinder me. I shall die if you will not let me do what she asks;—you cannot tell how sweet her voice is;—she talks to me and tells me of such wonderful things,—things too beautiful to be believed, yet they are true. I know so well my work;—work that must be done,—you will not hinder me?"

"No, no!"—said Féraz, in anguish himself, yet willing to say anything to soothe his brother's trembling excitement—"No, no! You shall not be hindered,—I will help you,—I will watch with you,—I will pray. . ." and here again the poor fellow nearly broke down into womanish sobbing.

"Yes!" said El-Râmi, eagerly catching at the word—"Pray! You will pray—and so will I;—that is good,—that is what I need,—prayer, they say, draws all Heaven down to earth. It is strange,—but so it is. You know"—he added, with a faint gleam of intelligence lighting up for a moment his wandering eyes—"Lilith is not here! Not here, nor there, . . . she is Everywhere!"

A terrible pallor stole over his face, giving it almost the livid hue of death,—and Féraz, alarmed, threw one arm strongly and resolutely about him. But El-Râmi crouched and shuddered, and hid his eyes as though he strove to shelter himself from the fury of a whirlwind.

"Everywhere!" he moaned—"In the flowers, in the trees, in the winds, in the sound of the sea, in the silence of the night, in the slow breaking of the dawn,—in all these things is the Soul of Lilith! Beautiful, indestructible, terrible Lilith! She permeates the world, she pervades the atmosphere, she shapes and unshapes herself at pleasure,—she floats, or flies, or sleeps at will;—in substance, a cloud;—in radiance, a rainbow! She is the essence of God in the transient shape of an angel—never the same, but for ever immortal. She soars aloft—she melts like mist in the vast Unseen!—and I—I—I shall never find her, never know her, never see her—never, never again!"

The harrowing tone of voice in which he uttered these words pierced Féraz to the heart, but he would not give way to his own emotion.

"Come, El-Râmi!" he said very gently—"Do not stay here,—come with me. You are weak,—rest on my arm; you must try and recover your strength,—remember, you have work to do."

"True, true!" said El-Râmi, rousing himself—"Yes, you are right,—there is much to be done. Nothing is so difficult as patience. To be left all alone, and to be patient, is very hard,—but I will come,—I will come."

He suffered himself to be led towards the door,—then, all at once he came to an abrupt stand-still, and looking round, gazed full on the empty couch where Lilith had so long been royally enshrined. A sudden passion seemed to seize him—his eyes sparkled luridly,—a sort of inward paroxysm convulsed his features, and he clutched Féraz by the shoulder with a grip as hard as steel.

"Roses and lilies and gold!" he muttered thickly—"They were all there,—those delicate treasures, those airy nothings of which God makes woman! Roses for the features, lilies for the bosom, gold for the hair!—roses, lilies and gold! They were mine,—but I have burned them all!—I have burned the roses and lilies, and melted the gold. Dust!—dust and ashes! But the dust is not Lilith. No!—it is only the dust of the roses, the dust of lilies, the dust of gold. Roses, lilies and gold! So sweet they are and fair to the sight, one would almost take them for real substance; but they are Shadows!—shadows that pass as we touch them,—shadows that always go, when most we would have them stay!"

He finished with a deep shuddering sigh, and then, loosening his grasp of Féraz, began to stumble his way hurriedly out of the apartment, with the manner of one who is lost in a dense fog and cannot see whither he is going. Féraz hastened to assist and support him, whereupon he looked up with a pathetic and smiling gratefulness.

"You are very good to me,"—he said, with a gentle courtesy, which in his condition was peculiarly touching—"I thought I should never need any support;—but I was wrong—quite wrong,—and it is kind of you to help me. My eyes are rather dim,—there was too much light among the roses, . . . and I find this place extremely dark, . . . it makes me feel a little confused here;"—and he passed his hand across his forehead with a troubled gesture, and looked anxiously at Féraz, as though he would ask him for some explanation of his symptoms.

"Yes, yes!" murmured Féraz soothingly—"You must be tired—you will rest, and presently you will feel strong and well again. Do not hurry,—lean on me,"—and he guided his brother's trembling limbs carefully down the stairs, a step at a time, thinking within himself in deep sorrow—Could this be the proud El-Râmi, clinging to him thus like a weak old man afraid to move? Oh, what a wreck was here!—what a change had been wrought in the few hours of the past night!—and ever the fateful question returned again and again to trouble him—

What had become of Lilith? That she was gone was self-evident,—and he gathered some inkling of the awful truth from his brother's rambling words. He remembered that El-Râmi had previously declared Lilith to be dead, so far as her body was concerned, and only kept apparently alive by artificial means;—he could easily imagine it possible for those artificial means to lose their efficacy in the end, . . . and then, . . . for the girl's beautiful body to crumble into that dissolution which would have been its fate long ago, had Nature had her way. All this he could dimly surmise,—but he had been kept so much in the dark as to the real aim and intention of his brother's "experiment" that it was not likely he would ever understand everything that had occurred;—so that Lilith's mysterious evanishment seemed to him like a horrible delusion;—it could not be! he kept on repeating over and over again to himself, and yet it was!

Moving with slow and cautious tread, he got El-Râmi at last into his own study, wondering whether the sight of the familiar objects he was daily accustomed to, would bring him back to a reasonable perception of his surroundings. He waited anxiously, while his brother stood still, shivering slightly and looking about the room with listless, unrecognising eyes. Presently, in a voice that was both weary and petulant, El-Râmi spoke.

"You will not leave me alone I hope?" he said—"I am very old and feeble, and I have done you no wrong,—I do not see why you should leave me to myself. I should be glad if you would stay with me a little while, because everything is at present so strange to me;—I shall no doubt get more accustomed to it in time. You are perhaps not aware that I wished to live through a great many centuries—and my wish was granted;—I have lived longer than any man, especially since She left me,—and now I am growing old, and I am easily tired. I do not know this place at all—is it a World or a Dream?"

At this question, it seemed to Féraz that he heard again, like a silver clarion ringing through silence, the mysterious voice that had roused him that morning saying, "Awake, Féraz! Today dreams end, and life begins!" . . . He understood, and he bent his head resignedly,—he knew now what the "life" thus indicated meant;—it meant a sacrificing of all his poetic aspirations, his music, and his fantastic happy visions,—a complete immolation of himself and his own desires, for the sake of his brother. His brother, who had once ruled him absolutely, was now to be ruled by him;—helpless as a child, the once self-sufficient and haughty

El-Râmi was to be dependent for everything upon the very creature who had lately been his slave,—and Féraz, humbly reading in these reversed circumstances, the Divine Law of Compensation, answered his brother's plaintive query—"Is it a World or a Dream?" with manful tenderness.

"It is a World,"—he said—"not a Dream, beloved El-Râmi—but a Reality. It is a fair garden, belonging to God and the things of God"—he paused, seeing that El-Râmi smiled placidly and nodded his head as though he heard pleasant music,—then he went on steadily—"a garden in which immortal spirits wander for a time self-exiled, till they fully realize the worth and loveliness of the Higher Lands they have forsaken. Do you understand me, O dear and honoured one?—do you understand? None love their home so dearly as those who have left it for a time—and it is only for a time—a short, short time,"—and Féraz, deeply moved by his mingled sorrow and affection, kissed and clasped his brother's hands—"and all the beauty we see here in this beautiful small world, is made to remind us of the greater beauty yonder. We look, as it were, into a little mirror, which reflects in exquisite miniature, the face of Heaven! See!" and he pointed to the brilliant blaze of sunshine that streamed through the window and illumined the whole room—"There is the tiny copy of the larger Light above,—and in that little light the flowers grow, the harvests ripen, the trees bud, the birds sing and every living creature rejoices,—but in the other Greater Light, God lives, and angels love and have their being;"—here Féraz broke off abruptly, wondering if he might risk the utterance of the words that next rose involuntarily to his lips, while El-Râmi gazed at him with great wide-open eager eyes like those of a child listening to a fairy story.

"Yes, yes!—what next?" he demanded impatiently—"This is good news you give me;—the angels love, you say, and God lives,—yes!—tell me more, . . . more!"

"All angels love and have their being in that Greater Light,"—continued Féraz softly and steadily—"And there too is Lilith—beautiful—deathless,—faithful—"

"True!" cried El-Râmi, with a sort of sobbing cry—"True! . . . She is there,—she promised—and I shall know, . . . I shall know where to find her after all, for she told me plainly—'Look for me where the roses are,—there will I stand and wait.'"

He tottered, and seemed about to fall;—but when Féraz would have supported him, he shook his head, and pointed tremblingly to the amber ray of sunshine pouring itself upon the ground:

"Into the light!"—he murmured—"I am all in the dark;—lead me out of the darkness into the light."

And Féraz led him where he desired, and seated him in his own chair in the full glory of the morning radiance that rippled about him like molten gold, and shone caressingly on his white hair,—his dark face that in its great pallor looked as though it were carved in bronze,— and his black, piteous, wandering eyes. A butterfly danced towards him in the sparkling shower of sunbeams, the same that had flown in an hour before and alighted on the heliotrope that adorned the centre of the table. El-Râmi's attention was attracted by it—and he watched its airy flutterings with a pleased, yet vacant smile. Then he stretched out his hands in the golden light, and lifting them upward, clasped them together and closed his eyes.

"Our Father" . . . he murmured; "which art in Heaven! . . . Hallowed be Thy Name!"

Féraz, bending heedfully over him, caught the words as they were faintly whispered,—caught the hands as they dropped inert from their supplicating posture and laid them gently back;—then listened again with strained attention, the pitying tears gathering thick upon his lashes.

"Our Father!" . . . once more that familiar appeal of kinship to the Divine, stole upon the air like a far-off sigh,—then came the sound of regular and quiet breathing;—Nature had shed upon the over-taxed brain her balm of blessed unconsciousness,—and like a tired child, the proud El-Râmi slept.

VIII

Upstairs meanwhile, in the room that had been Lilith's, there reigned the silence of a deep desolation. The woman Zaroba still crouched there, huddled on the floor, a mere heap of amber draperies,—her head covered, her features hidden. Now and then a violent shuddering seized her,—but otherwise she gave no sign of life. Hours passed;—she knew nothing, she thought of nothing; she was stupefied with misery and a great inextinguishable fear. To her bewildered, darkly superstitious, more than pagan mind, it seemed as if some terrible avenging angel had descended in the night and torn away her beautiful charge out of sheer spite and jealousy lest she should awake to the joys of earth's life and love. It had always been her fixed idea that the chief and most powerful ingredient of the Divine character (and of the human also) was jealousy; and she considered therefore that all women, as soon as they were born, should be solemnly dedicated to the ancient goddess Ananitis. Ananitis was a useful and accommodating deity, who in the old days, had unlimited power to make all things pure. A woman might have fifty lovers, and yet none could dare accuse her of vileness if she were a "daughter" or "priestess" of Ananitis. She might have been guilty of any amount of moral enormity, but she was held to be the chastest of virgins if Ananitis were her protectress and mistress. And so, in the eyes of Zaroba, Ananitis was the true patroness of love,—she sanctified the joys of lovers and took away from them all imputation of sin;—and many and many a time had the poor, ignorant, heathenish old woman secretly invoked the protection of this almost forgotten pagan goddess for the holy maiden Lilith. And now—now she wondered tremblingly, if in this she had done wrong? . . . More than for anything in the world had she longed that El-Râmi, the "wise man" who scoffed at passion with a light contempt, should love with a lover's wild idolatry the beautiful creature who was so completely in his power;—in her dull, half-savage, stupid way, she had thought that such a result of the long six years "experiment" could but bring happiness to both man and maid; and she spared no pains to try and foster the spark of mere interest which El-Râmi had for his "subject" into the flame of a lover's ardour. For this cause she had brought Féraz to look upon the tranced girl, in order that El-Râmi knowing of it, might feel the subtle prick of that perpetual motor, jealousy,—for this she had said all she dared say, concerning love and its unconquerable nature;—and now, just when her long-cherished wish seemed on the point of being granted, some dreadful Invisible Power had rushed in between the two, and destroyed Lilith with the fire of wrath and revenge;—at any rate that was how she regarded it. The sleeping girl had grown dear to her,—it was impossible not to love such a picture of innocent, entrancing, ideal beauty,—and she felt as though her heart had been torn open and its very core wrenched out by a cruel and hasty hand. She knew nothing as yet of the fate that had overtaken El-Râmi himself,—for as she could not hear a sound of the human voice, she had only dimly seen that he was led from the room by his young brother, and that he looked ill, feeble and distraught. What she realized most positively and with the greatest bitterness, was the fact of Lilith's loss,—Lilith's evident destruction. This was undeniable,—this was irremediable,—and she thought of it till her aged brain burned as with some inward consuming fire, and her thin blood seemed turning to ice.

"Who has done it?" she muttered—"Who has claimed her? It must be the Christ,—the cold, quiet, pallid Christ, with His bleeding Hands and beckoning Eyes! He is a new god,—He has called, and she, Lilith has obeyed! Without love, without life, without aught in the world save the lily-garb of un—touched holiness,—it is what the pale Christ seeks, and He has found it here,—here, with the child who slept the sleep of innocent ignorance,—here where no thought of passion ever entered unless I breathed it,—or perchance he—El-Râmi—thought it, unknowingly. O what a white flower for the Christ in Heaven, is Lilith!—What a branch of bud and blossom! . . . Ah, cruel, cold new gods of the Earth!—how long shall their sorrowful reign endure! Who will bring back the wise old gods,—the gods of the ancient days,—the gods who loved and were not ashamed,—the gods of mirth and life and health,—they would have left me Lilith,—they would have said—'Lo, now this woman is old and poor,—she hath lost all that she ever had,—let us leave her the child she loves, albeit it is not her own but ours;—we are great gods, but we are merciful!' Oh, Lilith, Lilith! child of the sun and air, and daughter of sleep! would I had perished instead of thee!—Would I had passed away into darkness, and thou been spared to the light!"

Thus she wailed and moaned, her face hidden, her limbs quivering, and she knew not how long she had stayed thus, though all the morning had passed and the afternoon had begun. At last she was roused by the gentle yet firm pressure of a hand on her shoulder, and, slowly uncovering her drawn and anguished features she met the sorrowful eyes of Féraz looking into hers. With a mute earnest gesture he bade her rise. She obeyed, but so feebly and tremblingly, that he assisted her, and led her to a chair, where she sat down, still quaking all over with fear and utter wretchedness. Then he took a pencil and wrote on the slate which his brother had been wont to use,—

"A great trouble has come upon us. God has been pleased to so darken the mind of the beloved El-Râmi, that he knows us no longer, and is ignorant of where he is. The wise man has been rendered simple,—and the world seems to him as it seems to a child who has everything in its life to learn. We must accept this ordinance as the Will of the Supreme, and bring our own will in accordance with it, believing the ultimate intention to be for the Highest Good. But for his former life, El-Râmi exists no more,—the mind that guided his actions then, is gone."

Slowly, and with pained, aching eyes Zaroba read these words,— she grasped their purport and meaning thoroughly, and yet, she said not a word. She was not surprised,—she was scarcely affected;—her feelings seemed blunted or paralysed. El-Râmi was mad? To her, he had always seemed mad,—with a madness born of terrible knowledge and power. To be mad now was nothing; the loss of Lilith was amply sufficient cause for his loss of wit. Nothing could be worse in her mind than to have loved Lilith and lost her,—what was the use of uttering fresh cries and exclamations of woe! It was all over,—everything was ended,—so far as she, Zaroba, was concerned. So she sate speechless,— her grand old face rigid as bronze, with an expression upon it of stern submission, as of one who waits immovably for more onslaughts from the thunderbolts of destiny.

Féraz looked at her very compassionately, and wrote again—

"Good Zaroba, I know your grief. Rest—try to sleep. Do not see El-Râmi today. It is better I should be alone with him. He is quite peaceful and happy,—happier indeed than he has ever been. He has so much to learn, he says, and he is quite satisfied. For today we must be alone with our sorrows,—tomorrow we shall be able to see more clearly what we must do."

Still Zaroba said nothing. Presently however, she arose, and walked totteringly to the side of Lilith's couch, . . . there, with an eloquently tragic gesture of supremest despair, she pointed to the gray-white ashes that were spread in that dreadfully suggestive outline on the satin coverlet and pillows. Féraz, shuddering, shut his eyes for a moment;— then, as he opened them again, he saw, confronting him, the uncurtained picture of the "Christ and His Disciples." He remembered it well,—El-Râmi had bought it long ago from among the despoiled treasures of an old dismantled monastery,—and besides being a picture it was also a reliquary. He stepped hastily up to it and felt for the secret spring which used, he knew, to be there. He found and pressed it,—the whole of the picture flew back like a door on a hinge, and showed the interior to be a Gothic-shaped casket, lined with gold, at the back of which was inserted a small piece of wood, supposed to have been a fragment of the "True Cross." There was nothing else in the casket,—and Féraz, leaving it open, turned to Zaroba who had watched him with dull, scarcely comprehending eyes.

"Gather together these sacred ashes,"—he wrote again on the slate,— "and place them in this golden recess,—it is a holy place fit for such holy relics. El-Râmi would wish it, I know, if he could understand or wish for anything,—and wherever we go, the picture will go with us, for one day perhaps he will remember, . . . and ask, . . ."

He could trust himself to write no more,—and stood sadly enrapt, and struggling with his own emotion.

"The Christ claims all!" muttered Zaroba wearily, resorting to her old theme—"The crucified Christ, . . . He must have all;—the soul, the body, the life, the love, the very ashes of the dead,—He must have all, . . . all!"

Féraz heard her,—and taking up his pencil once more, wrote swiftly— "You are right,—Christ has claimed Lilith. She was His to claim,— for on this earth we are all His,—He gave His very life to make us so. Let us thank God that we are thus claimed,—for with Christ all things are well."

He turned away then immediately, and left her alone to her task,—a task she performed with groans and trembling, till every vestige of the delicate ashes, as fine as the dust of flowers, was safely and reverently placed in its pure golden receptacle. Strange to say, one very visible relic of the vanished Lilith's bodily beauty had somehow escaped destruction,—this was a long, bright waving tress of hair which lay trembling on the glistening satin of the pillows like a lost sunbeam. Over this lovely amber curl, old Zaroba stooped yearningly, staring at it till her tears, the slow, bitter scalding tears of age fell upon it where it lay. She longed to take it for herself,—to wear it against her own heart,—

to kiss and cherish it as though it were a living, sentient thing,—but thinking of El-Râmi, her loyalty prevailed, and she tenderly lifted the clinging, shining, soft silken curl, and laid it by with the ashes in the antique shrine. All was now done,—and she shut to the picture, which when once closed, showed no sign of any opening.

Lilith was gone indeed;—there was now no perceptible evidence to show that she had ever existed. And, to the grief-stricken Zaroba, the Face and Figure of the Christ, as painted on the reliquary at which she gazed, seemed to assume a sudden triumph and majesty which appalled while it impressed her. She read the words "Whom Say Ye That I Am?" and shuddered; this "new god" with His tranquil smile and sorrowful dignity had more terrors for her than any of the old pagan deities.

"I cannot! I cannot!" she whispered feebly; "I cannot take you to my heart, cold white Christ,—I cannot think it is good to wear the thorns of perpetual sorrow! You offer no joy to the sad and weary world,—one must sacrifice one's dearest hopes,—one must bear the cross and weep for the sins of all men, to be at all acceptable to You! I am old—but I keep the memories of joy; I would not have all happiness reft out of the poor lives of men. I would have them full of mirth,—I would have them love where they list, drink pure wine, and rejoice in the breath of Nature,—I would have them feast in the sunlight and dance in the moonbeams, and crown themselves with the flowers of the woodland and meadow, and grow ruddy and strong and manful and generous, and free—free as the air! I would have their hearts bound high for the pleasure of life;—not break in a search for things they can never win. Ah no, cold Christ! I cannot love you!—at the touch of your bleeding Hand the world freezes like a starving bird in a storm of snow;—the hearts of men grow weak and weary, and of what avail is it, O Prince of Grief, to live in sadness all one's days for the hope of a Heaven that comes not? O Lilith!—child of the sun, where art thou?—Where? Never to have known the joys of love,—never to have felt the real pulse of living,—never to have thrilled in a lover's embrace,—ah, Lilith, Lilith! Will Heaven compensate thee for such loss? . . . Never, never, never! No God, were He all the worlds' gods in One, can give aught but a desolate Eden to the loveless and lonely Soul!"

In such wise as this, she muttered and moaned all day long, never stirring from the room that was called Lilith's. Now and then she moved up and down with slow restlessness,—sometimes fixing eager eyes upon the vacant couch, with the vague idea that perhaps Lilith might come back to it as suddenly as she had fled; and sometimes pausing by the vase of roses, and touching their still fragrant, but fast-fading blossoms. Time went on, and she never thought of breaking her fast, or going to see how her master, El-Râmi, fared. His mind was gone,—she understood that well enough,—and in a strange wild way of her own, she connected this sudden darkening of his intellect with the equally sudden disappearance of Lilith; and she dreaded to look upon his face.

How the hours wore away she never knew; but by-and-by her limbs began to ache heavily, and she crouched down upon the floor to rest. She fell into a heavy stupor of unconsciousness,—and when she awoke at last, the room was quite dark. She got up, stiff and cold and terrified,—she groped about with her hands,—it seemed to her dazed mind that she was in some sepulchral cave in the desert, all alone. Her lips were dry,—her head swam,—and she tottered along, feeling her way blindly, till she touched the velvet portière that divided the room from its little antechamber, and dragging this aside in nervous haste, she stumbled through, and out on to the landing, where it was light. The staircase was before her,—the gas was lit in the hall—and the house looked quite as usual,—yet she could not in the least realize where she was. Indistinct images floated in her brain,—there were strange noises in her ears,—and she only dimly remembered El-Râmi, as though he were someone she had heard of long ago, in a dream. Pausing on the stair-head, she tried to collect her scattered senses,—but she felt sick and giddy, and her first instinct was to seek the air. Clinging to the banisters, she tottered down the stairs slowly, and reached the front-door, and fumbling cautiously with the handle a little while, succeeded in turning it, and letting herself out into the street. The door had a self-acting spring, and shut to instantly, and almost noiselessly, behind her,—but Féraz, sitting in the study with his brother, fancied he heard a slight sound, and came into the hall to see what it was. Finding everything quiet he concluded he was mistaken, and went back to his post beside El-Râmi, who had been dozing nearly all day, only waking up now and again to mildly accept the nourishment of soup and wine which Féraz prepared and gave him to keep up his strength. He was perfectly tranquil, and talked at times quite coherently of simple things, such as the flowers on the table, the lamp, the books, and other ordinary trifles. He only seemed a little troubled by his own physical weakness,—but when Féraz assured him he would soon be strong, he smiled, and with every appearance of content, dozed off again peacefully. In the evening, however, he grew a little restless,—and then Féraz tried what effect music would have upon him. Going to the piano he played soft and dreamy melodies, . . . but as he did so, a strange sense of loss stole over him,—he had the mechanism of the art, but the marvellously delicate attunement of his imagination had fled! Tears rose in his eyes,—he knew what was missing,—the guiding-prop of his brother's wondrous influence had fallen,—and with a faint terror he realized that much of his poetic faculty would perish also. He had to remember that he was not naturally born a poet or musician,—poesy and music had been El-Râmi's fairy gifts to him—the exquisitely happy poise of his mind had been due to his brother's daily influence and control. He would still retain the habit and the memory of art,—but what had been Genius, would now be simple Talent,—no more,—yet what a difference between the two! Nevertheless his touch on the familiar ivory keys was very tender and delicate, and when, distrusting his own powers of composition, he played one of the softest and quaintest of Grieg's Norwegian folk-songs, he was more than comforted by the expression of pleasure that illumined El-Râmi's features, and by the look of enraptured peace that softened the piteous dark eyes.

"It is quite beautiful,—that music!" he murmured—"It is the pretty sound the daisies make in growing."

And he leaned back in his chair and composed himself to rest,—while Féraz played on softly, thinking anxiously the while. True, most true, that for him dreams had ended, and life had begun! What was he to do? . . . how was he to meet the daily needs of living,—how was he to keep himself and his brother? His idea was to go at once to the monastery in Cyprus, where he had formerly been a visitor,—it was quiet and peaceful,—he would ask the brethren to take them in,—for he himself detested the thought of a life in the world,—it was repellant to him in every way,—and El-Râmi's affliction would necessitate solitude. And while he was thus puzzling himself as to the future, there came a sharp knock at the door,—he hastened to see who it was,—and a messenger handed him a telegram addressed to himself. It came from the very place he was thinking about, sent by the Head of the Order, and ran thus—

"We know all. It is the Will of God. Bring El-Râmi here,—our house is open to you both."

He uttered a low exclamation of thankfulness, the while he wondered amazedly how it was that they, that far-removed Brotherhood, "knew all"! It was very strange! He thought of the wondrous man whom he called the "Master," and who was understood to be "wise with the wisdom of the angels," and remembered that he was accredited with being able to acquire information when he chose, by swift and supernatural means. That he had done so in the present case seemed evident, and Féraz stood still with the telegram in his hand, stricken by a vague sense of awe as well as gratitude, thinking also of the glittering Vision he had had of that "glory of the Angels in the South";—angels who were waiting for Lilith the night she disappeared.

El-Râmi suddenly opened his weary eyes and looked at him.

"What is it?" he asked faintly—"Why has the music ceased?"

Féraz went up to his chair and knelt down beside it.

"You shall hear it again"—he said gently, "But you must sleep now, and get strong,—because we are soon going away on a journey—a far, beautiful journey—"

"To Heaven?" inquired El-Râmi—"Yes, I know—it is very far."

Féraz sighed.

"No—not to Heaven,"—he answered—"Not yet. We shall find out the way there, afterwards. But in the meantime, we are going to a place where there are fruits and flowers,—and where the sun is very bright and warm. You will come with me, will you not, El-Râmi,—there are friends there who will be glad to see you."

"I have no friends,"—said El-Râmi plaintively, "unless you are one. I do not know if you are,—I hope so, but I am not sure. You have an angel's face,—and the angels have not always been kind to me. But I will go with you wherever you wish,—is it a place in this world, or in some other star?"

"In this world,—replied Féraz—"A quiet little corner of this world."

"Ah!" and El-Râmi sighed profoundly—"I wish it had been in another. There are so many millions and millions of worlds;—it seems foolish waste of time to stay too long in this."

He closed his eyes again, and Féraz let him rest,—till, when the hour grew late, he persuaded him to lie down on his own bed, which he did with the amiable docility of a child. Féraz himself, half sitting, half reclining in a chair beside him, watched him all night long, like a faithful dog guarding its master,—and so full was he of anxious thought and tender care for his brother, that he scarcely remembered Zaroba, and when he did, he felt sure that she too was resting, and striving to forget in sleep the sorrows of the day.

IX

Z aroba had indeed forgotten her sorrows; but not in slumber, as Féraz hoped and imagined. Little did he think that she was no longer under the roof that had sheltered her for so many years; little could he guess that she was out wandering all alone in the labyrinth of the London streets,—a labyrinth of which she was almost totally ignorant, having hardly ever been out of doors since El-Râmi had brought her from the East. True, she had occasionally walked in the little square opposite the house, and in a few of the streets adjoining,—once or twice in Sloane Street itself, but no further, for the sight of the hurrying, pushing, busy throngs of men and women confused her. She had not realized what she was doing when she let herself out that night,—only when the street-door shut noiselessly upon her she was vaguely startled,—and a sudden sense of great loneliness oppressed her. Yet the fresh air blowing against her face was sweet and balmy,—it helped to relieve the sickness at her heart, the dizziness in her brain,—and she began to stroll along, neither knowing nor caring whither she was going,—chiefly impelled by the strong necessity she felt for movement,—space,—liberty. It had seemed to her that she was being suffocated and buried alive in the darkness and desolation that had fallen on the chamber of Lilith;—here, out in the open, she was free,—she could breathe more easily. And so she went on, almost unseeingly,—the people she met looked to her like the merest shadows. Her quaint garb attracted occasional attention from some of the passers-by,—but her dark fierce face and glittering eyes repelled all those who might have been inquisitive enough to stop and question her. She drifted errantly, yet safely, through the jostling crowds like a withered leaf on the edge of a storm,—her mind was dazed with grief and fear and long fasting, but now and then as she went, she smiled and seemed happy. Affliction had sunk so deep within her, that it had reached the very core and centre of imagination and touched it to vague issues of discordant joy;—wherefore, persuaded by the magic music of delusion, she believed herself to be at home again in her native Egypt. She fancied she was walking in the desert;—the pavement seemed hot to her feet and she took it for the burning sand,—and when after long and apparently interminable wanderings, she found herself opposite Nelson's column in Trafalgar Square, she stared at the four great lions with stupefied dismay.

"It is the gate of a city,"—she muttered—"and at this hour the watchmen are asleep. I will go on—on still further,—there must be water close by, else there would be no city built."

She had recovered a certain amount of physical strength in the restorative influence of the fresh air, and walked with a less feeble tread,—she became dimly conscious too of there being a number of people about, and she drew her amber-coloured draperies more closely over her head. It was a beautiful night;—the moon was full and brilliant, and hundreds of pleasure-seekers were moving hither and thither,—there was the usual rattle and roar of the vehicular traffic of the town which, it must be remembered, Zaroba did not hear. Neither did she clearly see anything that was taking place around her,—for her sight was blurred, and the dull confusion in her brain continued. She walked as in a dream,—she felt herself to be in a dream;—the images of El-Râmi, of the lost Lilith, of the beautiful young Féraz, had faded away from her recollection,—and she was living in the early memories of days long past,—days of youth and hope and love and promise. No one molested her; people in London are so accustomed to the sight of foreigners and foreign costumes, that so long as they are seen walking on their apparent way peaceably, they may do so in any garb that pleases them, provided it be decent, without attracting much attention save from a few small and irreverent street-arabs. And even the personal and pointed observations of these misguided youngsters fail to disturb the dignity of a Parsee in his fez, or to ruffle the celestial composure of a Chinaman in his slippers. Zaroba, moreover, did not present such a markedly distinctive appearance,—in her yellow wrapper and silver bangles, she only looked like one of the ayahs brought over from the East with the children of Anglo-Indian mothers,—and she passed on uninterruptedly, happily deaf to the noises around her, and almost blind to the evershifting human pageantry of the busy thoroughfares.

"The gates of the city,"—she went on murmuring—"they are shut, and the watchmen are asleep. There must be water near,—a river or a place of fountains, where the caravans pause to rest."

Now and then the glare of the lights in the streets troubled her,—and then she would come to a halt and pass her hands across her eyes,—but this hesitation only lasted a minute,—and again she continued on her aimless way. The road widened out before her,—the buildings grew taller, statelier and more imposing,—and suddenly she caught sight of what she had longed for,—the glimmering of water silvering itself in the light of the moon.

She had reached the Embankment;—and a sigh of satisfaction escaped her, as she felt the damp chillness of the wind from the river blowing against her burning forehead. The fresh coolness and silence soothed her,—there were few people about,—and she slackened her pace unconsciously, and smiled as she lifted her dark face to the clear and quiet sky. She was faint and weary,—light-headed from want of food,—but she was not conscious of this any more than a fever-patient is conscious of his own delirium. She walked quite steadily now,—in no haste, but with the grave, majestic step that belongs peculiarly to women of her type and race,—her features were perfectly composed, and her eyes very bright. And now she looked always at the river, and saw nothing else for a time but its rippling surface lit up by the moon.

"They have cut down the reeds"—she said, softly under her breath,— "and the tall palms are gone,—but the river is always the same,—they cannot change that. Nothing can dethrone the Nile-god, or disturb his sleep among the lilies, down towards the path of the sunset. Here I shall meet my beloved again,—here by the banks of the Nile;—yet, it is strange and cruel that they should have cut down the reeds. I remember how softly they rustled with the movements of the little snakes that lived in the golden sand,—yes!—and the palm-trees were high—so high that their feathery crowns seemed to touch the stars. It was Egypt then,—and is it not Egypt now? Yes—surely—surely it is Egypt!—but it is changed—changed,—all is changed except love! Love is the same for ever, and the heart beats true to the one sweet tune. Yes, we shall meet,—my belovëd and I,—and we shall tell one another how long the time has seemed since we parted yesterday. Only yesterday!—and it seems a century,—a long long century of pain and fear,—but the hours have passed, and the waiting is over,—"

She broke off abruptly, and stood suddenly still;—the Obelisk faced her. Cut sharp and dark against the brilliant sky the huge "Cleopatra's Needle" towered solemnly aloft, its apex seeming to point directly at the planet Mars which glittered with a faint redness immediately above it. Something there was in its weird and frowning aspect, that appealed strangely to Zaroba's wandering intelligence,—she gazed at it with eager, dilated eyes.

"To the memory of heroes!" she said whisperingly, with a slight proud gesture of her hand,—"To the glory of the Dead! Salutation to the great gods and crowned Kings! Salutation and witness to the world of what Hath Been! The river shall find a tongue—the shifting sands shall uphold the record, so that none shall forget the things that Were! For the things that Are, being weak, shall perish,—but the things that Were, being strong, shall endure for ever! Here, as God liveth, is the meeting-place; the palms are gone, but the Nile flows on, and the moon is the sunlight of lovers. Here will I wait for my belovëd,—he knows the appointed hour, . . . he will not be long!"

She sat down, as close to the Obelisk as she could get, her face turned towards the river and the moonlight; and the clocks of the great city around her slowly tolled eleven. Her head dropped forward on her chest,—though after a few minutes she lifted her face with an anxious look—and,—"Did the child call me?" she said, and listened. Then she relapsed into her former sunken posture, . . . once a strong shuddering shook her limbs as of intense cold in the warm June night, . . . and then she was quite still. . .

The hours passed on,—midnight came and went,—but she never stirred. She seemed to belong to the Obelisk and its attendant Sphinxes,— so rigid was her figure, so weird in its outline, so solemn in its absolute immobility. And in that same attitude she was found later on towards morning, stone dead. There was no clue to her identity,—nothing about her that gave any hint as to her possible home or friends; her statuesque old face, grander than ever in the serene pallor of death, somewhat awed the two burly policemen who lifted her stark body and turned her features to the uncertain light of early dawn, but it told them no history save that of age and sorrow. So, in the sad chronicles entitled "Found Dead," she was described as "a woman unknown, of foreign appearance and costume, seemingly of Eastern origin,"—and, after a day or two, being unrecognised and unclaimed, she was buried in the usual way common to all who perish without name and kindred in the dreary wilderness of a great city. Féraz, missing her on the morning after her disappearance, searched for her everywhere as well as he knew how,—but, as he seldom read the newspapers, and probably would not have recognised the brief account of her there if he had,—and as, moreover, he knew nothing about certain dreary buildings in London called mortuaries, where the bodies of the drowned, and murdered, and unidentified, lie for a little while awaiting recog—nition, he remained in complete and bewildered ignorance of her fate. He could not imagine what had become of her, and he almost began to believe that she must have taken ship back to her native land—and that perhaps he might hear of her again some day. And truly, she had gone back to her native land,—in fancy;—and truly, it was also possible she might be met with again some day,—in another world than this. But in the meantime she had died,—as best befitted a servant of the old gods,—alone, and in uncomplaining silence.

X

The hair's-breadth balance of a Thought,—the wrong or right control of Will;—on these things hang the world, life, time, and all Eternity. Such slight threads!—imperceptible, ungraspable,—and yet withal strong,—strong enough to weave the everlasting web of good or evil, joy or woe. On some such poise, as fine, as subtly delicate, the whole majestic Universe swings round in its appointed course,—never a pin's point awry, never halting in its work, never hesitating in the fulfilment of its laws, carrying out the Divine Command with faithful exactitude and punctuality. It is strange—mournfully strange,—that we never seem able to learn the grand lessons that are taught us by this unvarying routine of Natural Forces,—Sub—mission, Obedience, Patience, Resignation, Hope. Preachers preach the doctrine,—teachers teach it,—Nature silently and gloriously manifests it hourly; but we,— we continue to shut our ears and eyes,—we prefer to retreat within ourselves,—our little incomplete ignorant selves,—thinking we shall be able to discover some way out of what has no egress, by the cunning arguments of our own finite intellectual faculties. We fail always;—we must fail. We are bound to find out sooner or later that we must bend our stubborn knees in the presence of the Positive Eternal. But till the poor brain gives way under the prolonged pressure and strain of close inquiry and analysis, so long will it persist in attempting to probe the Impenetrable,—so long will it audaciously attempt to lift the veil that hides the Beyond instead of resting content with what Nature teaches. "Wait"—she says—"Wait till you are mentally able to understand the Explanation. Wait till the Voice which is as a silver clarion, proclaims all truth, saying 'Awake, Soul, for thy dream is past! Look now and see,—for thou art strong enough to bear the Light.'"

Alas! we will not wait,—hence our life in these latter days of analysis, is a mere querulous Complaint, instead of what it should be, a perpetual Thanksgiving.

Four seasons have passed away since the "Soul of Lilith" was caught up into its native glory,—four seasons,—summer, autumn, winter and spring—and now it is summer again,—summer in the Isle of Cyprus, that once most sacred spot, dear to historic and poetic lore. Up among the low olive-crowned hills of Baffo or Paphos, there is more shade and coolness than in other parts of the island, and the retreat believed to have been the favourite haunt of Venus, is still full of something like the mystical glamour that hallowed it of old. As the singer of "Love-Letters of a Violinist" writes:

"There is a glamour all about the bay
As if the nymphs of Greece had tarried here.
The sands are golden and the rocks appear
Crested with silver; and the breezes play
Snatches of song they humm'd when far away.
And then are hush'd as if from sudden fear."

Flowers bloom luxuriantly, as though the white, blue-veined feet of the goddess had but lately passed by,—there is a suggestive harmony in the subdued low whispering of the trees, accompanied by the gentle murmur of the waves and "Hieros Kipos" or the Sacred Grove, still bends its thick old boughs caressingly towards the greensward as though to remind the dreaming earth of the bygone glories here buried deep in its silent bosom. The poor fragment of the ruined "Temple of Venus" once gorgeous with the gold and precious stones, silks and embroideries, and other offerings brought from luxury-loving Tyre, stands in its desolation among the quiet woods, and no sound of rejoicing comes forth from its broken wall to stir the heated air. Yet there is music not far off,—the sweet and solemn music of an organ chant, accompanying a chorus of mild and mellow voices singing the "Agnus Dei." Here in this part of the country, the native inhabitants are divided in their notions of religious worship,—they talk Greek, albeit modern Greek, with impurities which were unknown to the sonorous ancient tongue, and they are heroes no more, as the heroic Byron has told us in his superb poesy, but simply slaves. They but dimly comprehend Christianity,—the joyous paganism of the past is not yet extinct, and the Virgin Mother of Christ is here adored as "Aphroditissa." Perhaps in dirty Famagousta they may be more orthodox,—but among these sea-fronting hills where the sound of the "Agnus Dei" solemnly rises and falls in soft surges of harmony, it is still the old home of the Queen of Beauty, and still the birthplace of Adonis, son of a Cyprian King. Commercial England is now the possessor of this bower of sweet fancies,—this little corner of the world haunted by a thousand poetic memories,—and in these prosy days but few pilgrimages are made to a shrine that was once the glory of a glorious age. To the native Cypriotes themselves the gods have simply changed their names and become a little sadder and less playful, that is all,—and to make up for the lost "Temple of Venus" there is, hidden deep among the foliage, a small monastic retreat with a Cross on its long low roof,—a place where a few poor monks work and pray,—good men whose virtues are chiefly known to the sick, destitute and needy. They call themselves simply "The Brotherhood," and there are only ten of them in all, including the youngest, who joined their confraternity quite recently. They are very poor,—they wear rough white garments and go barefooted, and their food is of the simplest; but they do a vast amount of good in their unassuming way, and when any of their neighbours are in trouble, such afflicted ones at once climb the little eminence where Venus was worshipped with such pomp in ancient days, and make direct for the plain unadorned habitation devoted to the service of One who was "a Man of Sorrows and acquainted with grief." There they never fail to find consolation and practical aid,—even their persistent prayers to "Aphroditissa" are condoned with a broad and tender patience by these men who honestly strive to broaden and not confine the road that leads to heaven. Thus Paphos is sacred still,—with the glamour of old creeds and the wider glory of the new,—yet though it is an interesting enough nook of the earth, it is seldom that travellers elect to go thither either to admire or explore. Therefore the sight of a travelling-carriage, a tumble-down sort of vehicle, yet one of the best to be obtained thereabouts, making its way slowly up the ascent, with people in modern fashionable dress sitting therein, was a rare and wonderful spectacle to the ragged Cypriote youth of both sexes, who either stood by the roadway, pushing their tangled locks from their dark eyes and staring at it, or else ran swiftly alongside its wheels to beg for coppers from its occupants. There were four of these,—two ladies and two gentlemen,—Sir Frederick Vaughan and Lady Vaughan (née Idina Chester); the fair and famous authoress, Irene Vassilius, and a distinguished-looking handsome man of about forty or thereabouts, the Duke of Strathlea, a friend of the Vaughans, who had entertained them royally during the previous autumn at his grand old historic house in Scotland. By a mere chance during the season, he had made the acquaintance of Madame Vassilius, with whom he had fallen suddenly, deeply and ardently in love. She, however, was the same unresponsive far-gazing dreamy sibyl as ever, and though not entirely indifferent to the gentle reverential homage paid to her by this chivalrous and honourable gentleman, she could not make up her mind to give him any decided encouragement. He appeared to make no progress with her whatever,—and of course his discouragement increased his ardour. He devised every sort of plan he could think of for obtaining as much of her society as possible,—and finally, he had entreated the Vaughans to persuade her to join them in a trip to the Mediterranean in his yacht. At first she had refused,—then, with a sudden change of humour, she had consented to go, provided the Island of Cyprus were one of the places to be visited. Strathlea eagerly caught at and agreed to this suggestion,—the journey had been undertaken, and had so far proved most enjoyable. Now they had reached the spot Irene most wished to see,—it was to please her that they were making the present excursion to the "Temple of Venus," or rather, to the small and obscure monastery among the hills which she had expressed a strong desire to visit,—and Strathlea, looking wistfully at her fair thoughtful face, wondered whether after all these pleasant days passed together between sparkling sea and radiant sky, she had any kinder thoughts of him,—whether she would always be so quiet, so impassive, so indifferent to the love of a true man's heart?

The carriage went slowly,—the view widened with every upward yard of the way,—and they were all silent, gazing at the glittering expanse of blue ocean below them.

"How very warm it is!" said Lady Vaughan at last breaking the dumb spell, and twirling her sunshade round and round to disperse a cloud of gnats and small flies—"Fred, you look absolutely broiled! You are so dreadfully sunburnt!"

"Am I?" and Sir Frederick smiled blandly,—he was as much in love with his pretty frivolous wife as it is becoming for a man to be, and all her remarks were received by him with the utmost docility—"Well, I dare say I am. Yachting doesn't improve the transparent delicacy of a man's complexion. Strathlea is too dark to show it much,—but I was always a florid sort of fellow. You've no lack of colour yourself, Idina."

"Oh, I'm sure I look a fright!" responded her ladyship vivaciously and with a slight touch of petulance—"Irene is the only one who appears to keep cool. I believe her aspect would be positively frosty with the thermometer marking 100 in the shade!"

Irene, who was gazing abstractedly out to sea, turned slowly and lifted her drooping lace parasol slightly higher from her face. She was pale,—and her deep-set gray eyes were liquid as though unshed tears filled them.

"Did you speak to me, dear?" she inquired gently. "Have I done something to vex you?"

Lady Vaughan laughed.

"No, of course you haven't. The idea of your vexing anybody! You look irritably cool in this tremendous heat,—that's all."

"I love the sun,"—said Irene dreamily—"To me it is always the visible sign of God in the world. In London we have so little sunshine,—and, one might add, so little of God also! I was just then watching that golden blaze of light upon the sea."

Strathlea looked at her interrogatively.

"And what does it suggest to you, Madame?" he asked—"The glory of a great fame, or the splendour of a great love?"

"Neither"—she replied tranquilly—"Simply the reflex of Heaven on Earth."

"Love might be designated thus," said Strathlea in a low tone.

She coloured a little, but offered no response.

"It was odd that you alone should have been told the news of poor El-Râmi's misfortune,"—said Sir Frederick, abruptly addressing her,— "None of us, not even my cousin Melthorpe, who knew him before you did, had the least idea of it."

"His brother wrote to me"—replied Irene; "Féraz, that beautiful youth who accompanied him to Lady Melthorpe's reception last year. But he gave me no details,—he simply explained that El-Râmi, through prolonged over-study had lost the balance of his mind. The letter was very short, and in it he stated he was about to enter a religious fraternity who had their abode near Baffo in Cyprus, and that the brethren had consented to receive his brother also and take charge of him in his great helplessness."

"And their place is what we are going to see now"—finished Lady Vaughan—"I dare say it will be immensely interesting. Poor El-Râmi! Who would ever have thought it possible for him to lose his wits! I shall never forget the first time I saw him at the theatre. 'Hamlet' was being played, and he entered in the very middle of the speech 'To be or not to be.' I remember how he looked, perfectly. What eyes he had!—they positively scared me!"

Her husband glanced at her admiringly.

"Do you know, Idina"—he said, "that El-Râmi told me on that very night—the night of 'Hamlet'—that I was destined to marry you?"

She lifted her eyelids in surprise.

"No! Really! And did you feel yourself compelled to carry out the prophecy?"—and she laughed.

"No, I did not feel myself compelled,—but somehow, it happened—didn't it?" he inquired with naïve persistency.

"Of course it did! How absurd you are!" and she laughed again—"Are you sorry?"

He gave her an expressive look,—he was really very much in love, and she was still a new enough bride to blush at his amorous regard. Strathlea moved impatiently in his seat;—the assured happiness of others made him envious.

"I suppose this prophet,—El-Râmi, as you call him, prophesies no longer, if his wits are lacking"—he said—"otherwise I should have asked him to prophesy something good for me."

No one answered. Lady Vaughan stole a meaning glance and smile at Irene, but there was no touch of embarrassment or flush of colour on that fair, serene, rather plaintive face.

"He always went into things with such terrible closeness, did El-Râmi,—" said Sir Frederick after a pause—"No wonder his brain gave way at last. You know you can't keep on asking the why, why, why of everything without getting shut up in the long run."

"I think we were not meant to ask 'why' at all," said Irene slowly—"We are made to accept and believe that everything is for the best."

"There is a story extant in France of a certain philosopher who was always asking why—" said Strathlea—"He was a taciturn man as a rule, and seldom opened his lips except to say 'Pourquoi?' When his wife died suddenly, he manifested no useless regrets—he merely said 'Pourquoi?' One day they told him his house in the country was burnt to the ground,—he shrugged his shoulders and said 'Pourquoi?' After a bit he lost all his fortune,—his furniture was sold up,—he stared at the bailiffs and said 'Pourquoi?' Later on he was suspected of being in a plot to assassinate the King,—men came and seized his papers and took him away to prison,—he made no resistance,—he only said 'Pourquoi?' He was tried, found guilty and condemned to death; the judge asked him if he had anything to say? He replied at once 'Pourquoi?' No answer was vouchsafed to him, and in due time he was taken to the scaffold. There the executioner bandaged his eyes,—he said 'Pourquoi?'—he was told to kneel down; he did so, but again demanded 'Pourquoi?'—the knife fell, and his head was severed from his body—yet before it rolled into the basket, it trembled on the block, its eyes opened, its lips moved and for the last time uttered that final, never-to-be-answered query 'Pourquoi?'!"

They all laughed at this story, and just then the carriage stopped. The driver got down and explained in very bad French that he could go no further,—that the road had terminated and that there was now only a footpath which led through the trees to the little monastic retreat whither they were bound. They alighted, therefore, and found themselves close to the ruin supposed to have once been the "Temple of Venus." They paused for a moment, looking at the scene in silence.

"There must have been a great joyousness in the old creeds," said Strathlea softly, with an admiring glance at Irene's slight slim, almost fairy-like figure clad in its closefitting garb of silky white—"At the shrine of Venus for example, one could declare one's love without fear or shame."

"That can be done still,"—observed Sir Frederick laughingly—"And is done, pretty often. People haven't left off making love because the faith in Venus is exploded. I expect they'll go on in the same old abandoned way to the end of the chapter."

And, throwing his arm round his wife's waist, he sauntered on with her towards the thicket of trees at the end of which their driver had told them the "refuge" was situated, leaving Strathlea and Madame Vassilius to follow. Strathlea perceived and was grateful for the opportunity thus given, and ventured to approach Irene a little more closely. She was still gazing out to the sea,—her soft eyes were dreamy and abstracted,—her small ungloved right hand hung down at her side,—after a moment's hesitation, he boldly lifted it and touched its delicate whiteness with a kiss. She started nervously—she had been away in the land of dreams,— and now she met his gaze with a certain vague reproach in the sweet expression of her face.

"I cannot help it—" said Strathlea quickly, and in a low eager tone— "I cannot, Irene! You know I love you,—you have seen it, and you have discouraged and repelled me in every possible way,—but I am not made of stone or marble—I am mere flesh and blood, and I must speak. I love you, Irene! I love you—I will not unsay it. I want you to be my wife. Will you, Irene? Do not be in a hurry to answer me—think long enough to allow some pity for me to mingle with your thoughts. Just imagine a little hand like this"—and he kissed it again—"holding the pen with such a masterful grip and inditing to the world the thoughts and words that live in the minds of thousands,—is it such a cold hand that it is impervious to love's caress? I cannot—I will not believe it. You cannot be obdurate for ever. What is there in love that it should repel you?"

She smiled gravely, and gently, very gently, withdrew her hand.

"It is not love that repels me—" she said, "It is what is called love, in this world,—a selfish sentiment that is not love at all. I assure you I am not insensible to your affection for me, my dear Duke, . . . I wish for your sake I were differently constituted."

She paused a moment, then added hastily, "See, the others are out of sight—do let us overtake them."

She moved away quickly with that soft gliding tread of hers which reminded one of a poet's sylph walking on a moonbeam, and he paced beside her, half mortified, yet not altogether without hope.

"Why are you so anxious to see this man who has lost his wits,—this El-Râmi Zarânos?" he asked, with a touch of jealousy in his accents—"Was he more to you than most people?"

She raised her eyes with an expression of grave remonstrance.

"Your thoughts wrong me—" she said simply—"I never saw El-Râmi but twice in my life,—I only pitied him greatly. I used to have a strong instinct upon me that all would not be well with him in the end."

"Why?"

"First, because he had no faith,—secondly because he had an excess of pride. He dismissed God out of his calculations altogether, and was perfectly content to rely on the onward march of his own intellect. Intellectual Egoism is always doomed to destruction,—this seems to be a Law of the Universe. Indeed, Egoism, whether sensual or intellectual, is always a defiance of God."

Strathlea walked along in silence for a minute, then he said abruptly.

"It is odd to hear you speak like this, as if you were a religious woman. You are not religious,—everyone says so,—you are a free-thinker,—and also, pardon me for repeating it, society supposes you to be full of this sin you condemn—Intellectual Egoism."

"Society may suppose what it pleases of me"—said Irene—"I was never its favourite, and never shall be, nor do I court its good opinion. Yes, I am a free-thinker, and freely think without narrow law or boundary, of the majesty, beauty and surpassing goodness of God. As for intellectual egoism,—I hope I am not in any respect guilty of it. To be proud of what one does, or what one knows, has always seemed to me the poorest sort of vanity,—and it is the stumbling-block over which a great many workers in the literary profession fall, never to rise again. But you are quite right in saying I am not a 'religious' woman; I never go to church, and I never patronize bazaars."

The sparkle of mirth in her eyes was infectious, and he laughed. But suddenly she stopped, and laid her hand on his arm.

"Listen," she said, with a slight tremor in her voice—"You love me, you say. . . and I—I am not altogether indifferent to you—I confess that much. Wait!" for in an excess of delight he had caught both her hands in his own, and she loosened them gently—"Wait—you do not know me, my dear friend. You do not understand my nature at all,—I sometimes think myself it is not what is understood as 'feminine.' I am an abnormal creature—and perhaps if you knew me better you would not like me. . ."

"I adore you!" said Strathlea impetuously, "and I shall always adore you!"

She smiled rather sadly.

"You think so now,"—she said—"but you cannot be sure,—no man can always be sure of himself. You spoke of society and its opinion of me;—now, as a rule, average people do not like me,—they are vaguely afraid of me,—and they think it is strange and almost dangerous for a 'writing woman' to be still young, and not entirely hideous. Literary women generally are so safely and harmlessly repellant in look and bearing. Then again, as you said, I am not a religious woman,—no, not at all so in the accepted sense of the term. But with all my heart and soul I believe in God, and the ultimate good of everything. I abhor those who would narrow our vision of heavenly things by dogma or rule—I resent all ideas of the Creator that seem to lessen His glory by one iota. I may truly say I live in an ecstasy of faith, accepting life as a wondrous miracle, and death as a crowning joy. I pray but seldom, as I have nothing to ask for, being given far more than I deserve,—and I complain of nothing save the blind, cruel injustice and misjudgment shown by one human unit to another. This is not God's doing, but Man's—and it will, it must, bring down full punishment in due season."

She paused a moment,—Strathlea was looking at her admiringly, and she coloured suddenly at his gaze.

"Besides"—she added with an abrupt change of tone, from enthusiasm to coldness, "you must not, my dear Duke, think that I feel myself in any way distinguished or honoured by your proposal to make me your wife. I do not. This sounds very brusque, I know, but I think as a general rule in marriage, a woman gives a great deal more than she ever receives. I am aware how very much your position and fortune might appeal to many of my sex,—but I need scarcely tell you they have no influence upon me. For, notwithstanding an entire lack of log-rollers and press 'booms'"—and she smiled—"my books bring me in large sums, sufficient and more than sufficient, for all my worldly needs. And I am not ambitious to be a duchess."

"You are cruel, Irene"—said Strathlea—"Should I ever attaint you with worldly motives? I never wanted to be a duke—I was born so,—and a horrid bore it is! If I were a poor man, could you fancy me?"

He looked at her,—and her eyes fell under his ardent gaze. He saw his advantage and profited by it.

"You do not positively hate me?" he asked.

She gave him one fleeting glance through her long lashes, and a faint smile rested on her mouth.

"How could I?" she murmured—"you are my friend."

"Well, will you try to like me a little more than a friend?"—he continued eagerly—"Will you say to yourself now and then—'He is a big, bluff, clumsy Englishman, with more faults than virtues, more money than brains, and a stupid title sticking upon him like a bow of ribbon on a boar's head, but he is very fond of me, and would give up everything in the world for me'—will you say that to yourself, and think as well as you can of me?—will you, Irene?"

She raised her head. All coldness and hauteur had left her face, and her eyes were very soft and tender.

"My dear friend, I cannot hear you do yourself wrong"—she said—"and I am not as unjust as you perhaps imagine. I know your worth. You have more virtues than faults, more brains than money,—you are generous and kindly,—and in this instance, your title sets off the grace of a true and gallant gentleman. Give me time to consider a little,—let us join the Vaughans,—I promise you I will give you your answer today."

A light flashed over his features, and stooping, he once more kissed her hand. Then, as she moved on, a gracefully gliding figure under the dark arching boughs, he followed with a firm joyous step such as might have befitted a knight of the court of King Arthur who had, after hard fighting, at last won some distinct pledge of his 'ladye's' future favour.

XI

Deeply embowered among arching boughs and covered with the luxuriant foliage of many a climbing and flowering vine, the little monastic refuge appeared at first sight more like the retreat of a poet or painter than a religious house where holy ascetics fasted and prayed and followed the difficult discipline of daily self-denial. When the little party of visitors reached its quaint low door they all paused before ringing the bell that hung visibly aloft among clustering clematis, and looked about them in admiration.

"What a delicious place!" said Lady Vaughan, bending to scent the odours of a rich musk rose that had pushed its lovely head through the leaves as though inviting attention—"How peaceful! . . . and listen! What grand music they are singing!"

She held up her finger,—the others obeyed the gesture, and hushed their steps to hear every note of the stately harmony that pealed out upon the air. The brethren were chanting part of the grand Greek "Hymn of Cleanthes," a translation of which may be roughly rendered in the following strophes:

"Many-named and most glorious of the Immortals, Almighty forever.
Ruler of Nature whose government is order and law.
Hail, all hail! for good it is that mortals should praise thee!"
"We are Thy offspring; we are the Image of Thy Voice.
And only the Image, as all mortal things are that live and
move by Thy power.
Therefore do we exalt Thy Name and sing of Thy glory forever!"
"Thee doth the splendid Universe obey
Moving whithersoever Thou leadest, And all are gladly
swayed by Thee."

"Naught is done in the earth without Thee, O God—
Nor in the divine sphere of the heavens,
nor in the deepest depths of the sea.
Save the works that evil men commit in their hours of folly."
"Yet thou knowest where to find place for superfluous things.
Thou dost order that which seems disorderly.
And things not dear to men are dear to Thee!"

"Thou dost harmonise into One both Good and Evil.
For there is One Everlasting Reason for them all."
"O thou All-Giver, Dweller in the clouds, Lord of the thunder.
Save thou men from their own self-sought unhappiness.
Do thou, Father, scatter darkness from their souls,
and give them light to discover true wisdom."
"In being honoured let them pay Thee Honour.
Hymning Thy glorious works continually as beseems mortal men.
Since there can be no greater glory for men or gods than this.
To praise for ever and ever the grand and Universal Law! Amen!—
Amen!—Amen!"

"Strange they should elect to sing that"—said Strathlea musingly—"I remember learning it off by heart in my student days. They have left out a verse of it here and there,—but it is quite a Pagan hymn."

"It seems to me very good Christianity"—said Irene Vassilius, her eyes kindling with emotion—"It is a grand and convincing act of thanksgiving, and I think we have more cause for thankfulness than supplication."

"I am not yet quite sure about that myself"—murmured Strathlea in her ear—"I shall know better when the day is ended which I need most, prayer or thanksgiving."

She coloured a little and her eyes fell,—meanwhile the solemn music ceased.

"Shall I ring?" inquired Sir Frederick as the last note died away on the air.

They all silently acquiesced,—and by means of a coarse rope hanging down among the flowers the bell was gently set in motion. Its soft clang was almost immediately answered by a venerable monk in white garments, with a long rosary twisted into his girdle and a Cross and Star blazoned in gold upon his breast.

"Benedicite!" said this personage mildly, making the sign of the cross before otherwise addressing the visitors,—then, as they instinctively bent their heads to the pious greeting, he opened the door a little wider and asked them in French what they sought.

For answer Madame Vassilius stepped forward and gave him an open letter, one which she knew would serve as a pass to obtain ready admission to the monastery, and as the monk glanced it over his pale features brightened visibly.

"Ah! Friends of our youngest brother Sebastian"—he said in fluent English—"Enter! You are most heartily welcome."

He stood aside, and they all passed under the low porch into a square hall, painted from ceiling to floor in delicate fresco. The designs were so beautiful and so admirably executed, that Strathlea could not resist stopping to look at one or two of them.

"These are very fine"—he said addressing the gray-haired recluse who escorted them—"Are they the work of some ancient or modern artist?"

The old man smiled and gave a deprecating, almost apologetic gesture.

"They are the result of a few years' pleasant labour"—he replied—"I was very happy while employed thus."

"You did them!" exclaimed Lady Vaughan, turning her eyes upon him in frank wonder and admiration—"Why then you are a genius!"

The monk shook his head.

"Oh no, Madame, not so. We none of us lay claim to 'genius'; that is for those in the outer world,—here we simply work and do our best for the mere love of doing it."

Here, preceding them a little, he threw open a door, and ushered them into a quaint low room, panelled in oak, and begged them to be seated for a few moments while he went to inform "Brother Sebastian" of their arrival.

Left alone they gazed about in silence, till Sir Frederick, after staring hard at the panelled walls said—

"You may be pretty sure these fellows have carved every bit of that oak themselves. Monks are always wonderful workmen,—'Laborare est orare' you know. By the way, I noticed that monk artist who was with us just now wore no tonsure,—I wonder why? Anyhow it's a very ugly disfigurement and quite senseless; they do well to abjure it."

"Is this man you come to see,—El-Râmi—a member of the Fraternity?" asked Strathlea of Irene in a low tone.

She shook her head compassionately.

"Oh no—poor creature,—he would not understand their rules or their discipline. He is simply in their charge, as one who must for all his life be weak and helpless."

At that moment the door opened, and a tall slim figure appeared, clad in the trailing white garments of the brotherhood; and in the dark poetic face, brilliant eyes and fine sensitive mouth there was little difficulty in recognising Féraz as the "Brother Sebastian" for whom they waited. He advanced towards them with singular grace and quiet dignity,—the former timidity and impetuosity of youth had entirely left him, and from his outward aspect and bearing he looked like a young saint whose thoughts were always set on the highest things, yet who nevertheless had known what it was to suffer in the search for peace.

"You are most welcome, Madame"—he said, inclining himself with a courteous gentleness towards Irene,—"I expected you,—I felt sure that you would one day come to see us. I know you were always interested in my brother. . ."

"I was, and am still"—replied Irene gently, "and in yourself also."

Féraz, or "Brother Sebastian" as he was now called, made another gentle salutation expressive of gratitude, and then turned his eyes questioningly on the other members of the party.

"You will not need to be reminded of Sir Frederick Vaughan and Lady Vaughan,"—went on Irene,—then as these exchanged greetings, she added—"This gentleman whom you do not know is the Duke of Strathlea,—we have made the journey from England in his yacht, and—" she hesitated a moment, the colour deepening a little in her fair cheeks—"he is a great friend of mine."

Féraz glanced at her once,—then once at Strathlea, and a grave smile softened his pensive face. He extended his hand with a frank cordiality that was charming, and Strathlea pressed it warmly, fascinated by the extreme beauty and dignity of this youthful ascetic, sworn to the solitariness of the religious life ere he had touched his manhood's prime.

"And how is El-Râmi?" asked Sir Frederick with good-natured bluffness—"My cousin Melthorpe was much distressed to hear what had happened,—and so were we all,—really—a terrible calamity—but you know over-study will upset a man,—it's no use doing too much—"

He broke off his incoherent remarks abruptly, embarrassed a little by the calmly mournful gaze of "Brother Sebastian's" deep dark eyes.

"You are very good, Sir Frederick,"—he said gently—"I am sure you sympathize truly, and I thank you all for your sympathy. But—I am not sure that I should be sorrowful for my brother's seeming affliction. God's will has been made manifest in this, as in other things,—and we must needs accept that will without complaint. For the rest, El-Râmi is well,—and not only well, but happy. Let me take you to him."

They hesitated,—all except Irene. Lady Vaughan was a nervous creature,—she had a very vivid remembrance of El-Râmi's "terrible eyes"—they looked fiery enough when he was sane,—but how would they look now when he was. . . mad? She moved uneasily,—her husband pulled his long moustache doubtfully as he studied her somewhat alarmed countenance,—and Féraz, glancing at the group, silently understood the situation.

"Will you come with me, Madame?" he said, addressing himself solely to Irene—"It is better perhaps that you should see him first alone. But he will not distress you. . . he is quite harmless. . . poor El-Râmi!"

In spite of himself his voice trembled,—and Irene's warm heart swelled for sympathy.

"I will come at once"—she said, and as she prepared to leave the room Strathlea whispered: "Let me go with you!"

She gave a mute sign of assent,—and Féraz leading the way, they quietly followed, while Sir Frederick and his wife remained behind. They passed first through a long stone corridor,—then into a beautiful quadrangular court with a fountain in its centre, and wooden benches set at equal distances under its moss-grown vine-covered colonnades. Flowers grew everywhere in the wildest, loveliest profusion,—tame doves strutted about on the pavement with peaceful and proud complacency, and palms and magnolias grew up in tall and tangled profusion wherever they could obtain root-hold, casting their long, leafy trembling shadows across the quadrangle and softening the too dazzling light reflected from the brilliant sky above. Up in a far corner of this little garden paradise, under the shade of a spreading cedar, sat the placid figure of a man,—one of the brethren at first he seemed, for he was clothed in the garb of the monastic order, and a loose cowl was flung back from his uncovered head on which the hair shone white and glistening as fine spun silver. His hands were loosely clasped together,—his large dark eyes were fixed on the rays of light that quivered prismatically in the foam of the tossing fountain, and near his feet a couple of amorous snowy doves sat brooding in the sun. He did not seem to hear the footsteps of his approaching visitors, and even when they came close up to him, it was only by slow degrees that he appeared to become conscious of their presence.

"El-Râmi!" said his brother with tender gentleness—"El-Râmi, these are friends who have journeyed hither to see you."

Then, like a man reluctantly awaking from a long and pleasant noonday dream, he rose and stood up with singularly majestic dignity, and for a moment looked so like the proud, indomitable El-Râmi of former days, that Irene Vassilius in her intense interest and compassion for him, half fancied that the surprise of seeing old acquaintances had for a brief interval brought back both reason and remembrance. But no,—his eyes rested upon her unrecognisingly, though he greeted her and Strathlea also, with the stateliest of salutations.

"Friends are always welcome"—he said, "But friends are rare in the world,—it is not in the world one must look for them. There was a time I assure you, . . . when I . . . even I, . . . could have had the most powerful of all friends for the mere asking,—but it is too late now—too late."

He sighed profoundly, and seated himself again on the bench as before.

"What does he mean?" asked Strathlea of Féraz in a low tone.

"It is not always easy to understand him" responded Féraz gently— "But in this case, when he speaks of the friend he might have had for the mere asking, he means,—God."

The warm tears rushed into Irene's eyes.

"Nay, God is his friend I am sure"—she said with fervour—"The great Creator is no man's enemy."

Féraz gave her an eloquent look.

"True, dear Madame"—he answered,—"But there are times and seasons of affliction when we feel and know ourselves to be unworthy of the Divine friendship, and when our own conscience considers God as one very far off."

Yielding to the deep impulse of pity that swayed her, she advanced softly, and sitting down beside El-Râmi, took his hand in her own. He turned and looked at her,—at the fair delicate face and soft ardent eyes,—at the slight dainty figure in its close-fitting white garb,—and a faint wondering smile brightened his features.

"What is this?" he murmured, then glancing downward at her small white ringless hand as it held his—"Is this an angel? Yes, it must be,— well then, there is hope at last. You bring me news of Lilith?"

Irene started, and her heart beat nervously,—she could not understand this, to her, new phase of his wandering mind. What was she to say in answer to so strange a question?—for who was Lilith? She gazed helplessly at Féraz,—he returned her look with one so earnest and imploring, that she answered at once as she thought most advisable—

"Yes!"

A sudden trembling shook El-Râmi's frame, and he seemed absorbed. After a long pause, he lifted his dark eyes and fixed them solemnly upon her.

"Then, she knows all now?" he de—mended—"She understands that I am patient?—that I repent?—that I believe?—and that I love her as she would have me love her,—faithfully and far beyond all life and time?"

Without hesitation, and only anxious to soothe and comfort him, Irene answered at once—

"Yes—yes—she understands. Be consoled—be patient still—you will meet her soon again."

"Soon again?" he echoed, with a pathetic glance upward at the dazzling blue sky—"Soon? In a thousand years?—or a thousand thousand?—for so do happy angels count the time. To me an hour is long—but to Lilith, cycles are moments."

His head sank on his breast,—he seemed to fall suddenly into a dreamy state of meditation,—and just then a slow bell began to toll to and fro from a wooden turret on the monastery roof.

"That is for vespers"—said Féraz—"Will you come, Madame, and hear our singing? You shall see El-Râmi again afterwards."

Silently she rose, but her movement to depart roused El-Râmi from his abstraction, and he looked at her wistfully.

"They say there is happiness in the world"—he said slowly—"but I have not found it. Little messenger of peace, are you happy?"

The pathos of his rich musical voice as he said the words "little messenger of peace," was indescribably touching. Strathlea found his eyes suddenly growing dim with tears, and Irene's voice trembled greatly as she answered—

"No, not quite happy, dear friend;—we none of us are quite happy."

"Not without love,"—said El-Râmi, speaking with sudden firmness and decision—"Without love we are powerless. With it, we can compass all things. Do not miss love; it is the clue to the great Secret,—the only key to God's mystery. But you know this already,—better than I can tell you,—for I have missed it,—not lost it, you understand, but only missed it. I shall find it again,—I hope, . . . I pray I shall find it again! God be with you, little messenger! Be happy while you can!"

He extended his hand with a gesture which might have been one of dismissal or benediction or both, and then sank into his former attitude of resigned contemplation, while Irene Vassilius, too much moved to speak, walked across the court between Strathlea and the beautiful young "Brother Sebastian," scarcely seeing the sunlight for tears. Strathlea too was deeply touched;—so splendid a figure of a man as

El-Râmi he had seldom seen, and the ruin of brilliant faculties in such a superb physique appeared to him the most disastrous of calamities.

"Is he always like that?" he inquired of Féraz, with a backward compassionate glance at the quiet figure sitting under the cedar-boughs.

"Nearly always," replied Féraz—"Sometimes he talks of birds and flowers,—sometimes he takes a childish delight in the sunlight—he is most happy, I think, when I take him alone into the chapel and play to him on the organ. He is very peaceful, and never at any time violent."

"And," pursued Strathlea hesitatingly, "who is, or who was the Lilith he speaks of?"

"A woman he loved"—answered Féraz quietly—"and whom he loves still. She lives—for him—in Heaven."

No more questions were asked, and in another minute they arrived at the open door of the little chapel, where Sir Frederick and Lady Vaughan, attracted by the sound of music, were already awaiting them. Irene briefly whispered a hurried explanation of El-Râmi's condition, and Lady Vaughan declared she would go and see him after the vesper-service was over.

"You must not expect the usual sort of vespers"—said Féraz then— "Our form is not the Roman Catholic."

"Is it not?" queried Strathlea, surprised—"Then, may one ask what is it?"

"Our own,"—was the brief response. Three or four white-cowled, white-garmented figures now began to glide into the chapel by a side-entrance, and Sir Frederick Vaughan asked with some curiosity:

"Which is the Superior?"

"We have no Superior"—replied Féraz—"There is one Master of all the Brotherhoods, but he has no fixed habitation, and he is not at present in Europe. He visits the different branches of our Fraternity at different intervals,—but he has not been here since my brother and I came. In this house we are a sort of small Republic,—each man governs himself, and we are all in perfect unity, as we all implicitly follow the same fixed rules. Will you go into the chapel now? I must leave you, as I have to sing the chorale."

They obeyed his gesture, and went softly into the little sacred place, now glowing with light, and redolent of sweet perfume, the natural incense wafted on the air from the many flowers which were clustered in every nook and corner. Seating themselves quietly on a wooden bench at the end of the building, they watched the proceedings in mingled wonder and reverence,—for such a religious service as this they had assuredly never witnessed. There was no altar,—only an arched recess, wherein stood a large, roughly carved wooden cross, the base of which was entirely surrounded with the rarest flowers. Through the stained glass window behind, the warm afternoon light streamed gloriously,—it fell upon the wooden beams of the Sign of Salvation, with a rose and purple radiance like that of newly-kindled fire,—and as the few monks gathered together and knelt before it in silent prayer, the scene was strangely impressive, though the surroundings were so simple. And when, through the deep stillness an organ-chord broke grandly like a wave from the sea, and the voice of Féraz, deep, rich, and pathetic exclaimed as it were, in song—

"Quare tristis es anima mea?
Quare conturbas me?"

Giving the reply in still sweeter accents—
"Spera in Deo!"

Then Irene Vassilius sank on her knees and hid her face in her clasped hands, her whole soul shaken by emotion and uplifted to heaven by the magic of divinest harmony. Strathlea looked at her slight kneeling figure and his heart beat passionately,—he bent his head too, close beside hers, partly out of a devotional sense, partly perhaps to have a nearer glimpse of the lovely fair hair that clustered in such tempting little ripples and curls on the back of her slim white neck. The monks, prostrating themselves before the Cross, murmured together some indistinct orisons for a few minutes,—then came a pause,—and once more the voice of Féraz rang out in soft warm vibrating notes of melody;—the words he sang were his own, and fell distinctly on the ears as roundly and perfectly as the chime of a true-toned bell—

O hear ye not the voice of the Belovëd?
Through golden seas of starry light it falls.
And like a summons in the night it calls.
Saying,—Lost children of the Father's House
Why do ye wander wilfully away?
Lo, I have sought ye sorrowing every day,—
And yet ye will not answer,—will not turn
To meet My love for which the angels yearn!
In all the causeless griefs wherewith your hearts are movëd

Have ye no time to hear the Voice of the Belovëd?
O hearken to the Voice of the Belovëd!
Sweeter it is than music,—sweeter far
Than angel-anthems in a happy star!
O wandering children of the Father's House.
Turn homeward ere the coming of the night.
Follow the pathway leading to the light!
So shall the sorrows of long exile cease
And tears be turned to smiles and pain to peace.
Lift up your hearts and let your faith be provëd;—
Answer, oh answer the Voice of the Belovëd!

Very simple stanzas these, and yet, sung by Féraz as only he could sing, they carried in their very utterance a singularly passionate and beautiful appeal. The fact of his singing the verses in English implied a gracefully intended compliment to his visitors,—and after the last line "Answer, oh answer the voice of the Belovëd!" a deep silence reigned in the little chapel. After some minutes, this silence was gently disturbed by what one might express as the gradual flowing-in of music,—a soft, persuasive ripple of sound that seemed to wind in and out as though it had crept forth from the air as a stream creeps through the grasses. And while that delicious harmony rose and fell on the otherwise absolute stillness, Strathlea was thrilled through every nerve of his being by the touch of a small soft warm hand that stole tremblingly near his own as the music stole into his heart;—a hand, that after a little hesitation placed itself on his in a wistfully submissive way that filled him with rapture and wonder. He pressed the clinging dainty fingers in his own broad palm—

"Irene!" he whispered, as he bent his head lower in apparent devotion—"Irene,—is this my answer?"

She looked up and gave him one fleeting glance through eyes that were dim with tears; a faint smile quivered on her lips,—and then, she hid her face again,—but—left her hand in his. And as the music, solemn and sweet, surged around them both like a rolling wave, Strathlea knew his cause was won, and for this favour of high Heaven, mentally uttered a brief but passionately fervent "Laus Deo." He had obtained the best blessing that God can give—Love,—and he felt devoutly certain that he had nothing more to ask for in this world or the next. Love for him was enough,—as indeed it should be enough for us all if only we will understand it in its highest sense. Shall we ever understand?—or never?

XII

The vespers over, the little party of English visitors passed out of the chapel into the corridor. There they waited in silence, the emotions of two of them at least, being sufficiently exalted to make any attempt at conversation difficult. It was not however very long before Féraz or "Brother Sebastian" joined them, and led them as though by some involuntary instinct into the flower-grown quadrangle, where two or three of the monks were now to be seen pacing up and down in the strong red sunset-light with books open in their hands, pausing ever and anon in their slow walk to speak to El-Râmi, who sat, as before, alone under the boughs of the cedar-tree. One of the tame doves that had previously been seen nestling at his feet, had now taken up its position on his knee, and was complacently huddled down there, allowing itself to be stroked, and uttering crooning sounds of satisfaction as his hand passed caressingly over its folded white wings. Féraz said very little as he escorted all his guests up to within a yard or so of El-Râmi's secluded seat,—but Lady Vaughan paused irresolutely, gazing timidly and with something of awe at the quiet reposeful figure, the drooped head, the delicate dark hand that stroked the dove's wings,—and as she looked and strove to realize that this gentle, submissive, meditative, hermit-like man was indeed the once proud and indomitable El-Râmi, a sudden trembling came over her, and a rush of tears blinded her eyes.

"I cannot speak to him"—she whispered sobbingly to her husband— "He looks so far away,—I am sure he is not here with us at all!"

Sir Frederick, distressed at his wife's tears, murmured something soothing,—but he too was rendered nervous by the situation and he could find no words in which to make his feelings intelligible. So, as before, Irene Vassilius took the initiative. Going close up to El-Râmi, she with a quick yet graceful impulsiveness threw herself in a half-kneeling attitude before him.

"El-Râmi!" she said.

He started, and stared down upon her amazedly,—yet was careful in all his movements not to disturb the drowsing white dove upon his knee.

"Who calls me?" he demanded—"Who speaks?"

"I call you"—replied Irene, regardless how her quite unconventional behaviour might affect the Vaughans as onlookers—"I ask you, dear friend, to listen to me. I want to tell you that I am happy—very happy,—and that before I go, you must give me your blessing."

A pathetic pain and wonderment crossed El-Râmi's features. He looked helplessly at Féraz,—for though he did not recognise him as his brother, he was accustomed to rely upon him for everything.

"This is very strange!" he faltered—"No one has ever asked me for a blessing. Make her understand that I have no Power at all to do any good by so much as a word or a thought. I am a very poor and ignorant man—quite at God's mercy."

Féraz bent above him with a soothing gesture.

"Dear El-Râmi," he said—"this lady honours you. You will wish her well ere she departs from us,—that is all she seeks."

El-Râmi turned again towards Irene, who remained perfectly quiet in the attitude she had assumed.

"I thought,"—he murmured slowly—"I thought you were an angel,—it seems you are a woman. Sometimes they are one and the same thing. Not often, but sometimes. Women are wronged,—much wronged,—when God endows them, they see further than we do. But you must not honour me,—I am not worthy to be honoured. A little child is much wiser than I am. Of course I must wish you well—I could not do otherwise. You see this poor bird,"—and he again stroked the dove which now dozed peacefully—"I wish it well also. It has its mate and its hole in the dove-cote, and numberless other little joys,—I would have it always happy,—and. . . so—I would have you always happy too. And,—most assuredly, if you desire it, I will say—'God bless you!'"

Here he seemed to collect his thoughts with some effort,—his dark brows contracted perplexedly,—then, after a minute, his expression brightened, and, as if he had just remembered something, he carefully and with almost trembling reverence, made the sign of the cross above Irene's drooping head. She gently caught the hovering hand and kissed it. He smiled placidly, like a child who is caressed.

"You are very good to me"—he said—"I am quite sure you are an angel. And being so, you need no blessing—God knows His own, and always claims them. . . in the end."

He closed his eyes languidly then and seemed fatigued,—his hand still mechanically stroked the dove's wings. They left him so, moving away from him with hushed and cautious steps. He had not noticed Sir Frederick or Lady Vaughan,—and they were almost glad of this, as they were themselves entirely disinclined to speak. To see so great a wreck of a once brilliant intellect was a painful spectacle to good-natured Sir Frederick,—while on Lady Vaughan it had the effect of a severe nervous shock. She thought she would have been better able to bear the sight of a distracted and howling maniac, than the solemn pitifulness of that silent submission, that grave patience of a physically strong man transformed, as it were, into a child. They walked round the court, Féraz gathering as he went bouquets of roses and jessamine and passiflora for the two ladies.

"He seems comfortable and happy"—Sir Frederick ventured to remark at last.

"He is, perfectly so"—rejoined Féraz. "It is very rarely that he is depressed or uneasy. He may live on thus till he is quite old, they tell me,—his physical health is exceptionally good."

"And you will always stay with him?" said Irene.

"Can you ask, Madame!" and Féraz smiled—"It is my one joy to serve him. I grieve sometimes that he does not know me really, who I am,—but I have a secret feeling that one day that part of the cloud will lift, and he will know. For the rest he is pleased and soothed to have me near him,—that is all I desire. He did everything for me once,—it is fitting I should do everything for him now. God is good,—and in His measure of affliction there is always a great sweetness."

"Surely you do not think it well for your brother to have lost the control of his brilliant intellectual faculties?" asked Sir Frederick, surprised.

"I think everything well that God designs"—answered Féraz gently, now giving the flowers he had gathered, to Irene and Lady Vaughan, and looking, as he stood in his white robes against a background of rosy sunset-light, like a glorified young saint in a picture,—"El-Râmi's intellectual faculties were far too brilliant, too keen, too dominant,—his great force and supremacy of will too absolute. With such powers as he had he would have ruled this world, and lost the next. That is, he would have gained the Shadow and missed the Substance. No, no—it is best as it is. 'Except ye become as little children, ye shall not enter the Kingdom of Heaven!' That is a true saying. In the Valley of Humiliation the birds of paradise sing, and in El-Râmi's earth-darkness there are gleams of the Light Divine. I am content,—and so, I firmly and devoutly believe, is he."

With this, and a few more parting words, the visitors now prepared to take their leave. Suddenly Irene Vassilius perceived an exquisite rose hanging down among the vines that clambered about the walls of the little monastery;—a rose pure white in its outer petals but tenderly tinted with a pale blush pink towards its centre. Acting on her own impulsive idea, she gathered it, and hastened back alone across the quadrangle to where El-Râmi sat absorbed and lost in his own drowsy dreams.

"Good-bye, dear friend,—good-bye!" she said softly, and held the fragrant beautiful bud towards him.

He opened his sad dark eyes and smiled,—then extended his hand and took the flower.

"I thank you, little messenger of peace!" he said—"It is a rose from Heaven,—it is The Soul of Lilith!"

FINIS

A Note About the Author

Marie Corelli (1855–1924) was an English novelist. Born Mary Mackay in London, she was sent to a Parisian convent to be educated in 1866. Returning to England in 1870, Corelli worked as a pianist and began her literary career with the novel *A Romance of Two Worlds* (1886). A favorite writer of Winston Churchill and the British Royal Family, Corelli was the most popular author of her generation. Known for her interest in mysticism and the occult, she earned a reputation through works of fantasy, Gothic, and science fiction. From 1901 to 1924, she lived in Stratford-upon-Avon, where she continued to write novels, short story collections, and works of non-fiction. Corelli, whose works have been regularly adapted for film and the theater, was largely rejected by the male-dominated literary establishment of her time. Despite this, she is remembered today as a pioneering author who wrote for the public, not for the critics who sought to deny her talent.

A Note from the Publisher

Spanning many genres, from non-fiction essays to literature classics to children's books and lyric poetry, Mint Edition books showcase the master works of our time in a modern new package. The text is freshly typeset, is clean and easy to read, and features a new note about the author in each volume. Many books also include exclusive new introductory material. Every book boasts a striking new cover, which makes it as appropriate for collecting as it is for gift giving. Mint Edition books are only printed when a reader orders them, so natural resources are not wasted. We're proud that our books are never manufactured in excess and exist only in the exact quantity they need to be read and enjoyed.

bookfinity™

Discover more of your favorite classics with Bookfinity™.

- Track your reading with custom book lists.
- Get great book recommendations for your personalized Reader Type.
- Add reviews for your favorite books.
- AND MUCH MORE!

Visit **bookfinity.com** and take the fun Reader Type quiz to get started.

Enjoy our classic and modern companion pairings!

Classic & Modern

Printed in the USA
CPSIA information can be obtained
at www.ICGtesting.com
LVHW040250070823
754491LV00002B/157

9 781513 290485